INFINITE STRANGER

Wendy Skorupski

ISBN: 978-83-957222-1-9

W. Maryla Press
Kraków, Poland

www.wendyskorupski.com

Cover design art by Jamie Harris - @jamie.ardor

First published in 2023

TABLE OF CONTENTS

MATINS

Ah Love, could Thou and I with Fate conspire
To grasp this sorry Scheme of things entire;
Would not we shatter it to bits - and then
Re-mould it nearer to the Heart's desire!

Rubaiyat of Omar Khayyam, v. 73

CHAPTER ONE

1

Lichfield, July 1983

Tomorrow is my wedding day.

Those words could be the lyrics to a song, don't you think? A joyful song; one that injects your veins with a rush of adrenaline, giddiness, the narcotic urge to dance. I can feel a strong beat there. To-*mor*-row *is* my *wed*-ding *day.* Four-four time. Could be a tango, then. I can already picture myself on the dance floor: slow, thigh-clinging strides in sync with my partner's, the occasional unexpected lurch as he tips me backwards – long hair tumbling away from my face, eyes shut in concentration as said partner holds me firmly round the waist to make sure I don't topple over completely, hitting the parquet with a thump.

I meant to say *groom*, not partner. Because come tomorrow, that's what he'll be. And I his wife. Mr and Mrs. His and hers. Happily ever after.

The zone where fairy tales fear to tread.

So tomorrow I'm getting married and you should be here with me, Mother. You should be sitting by my side, in the living room of my tumbledown cottage in Lichfield, keeping me company on my last night as a single woman. Your feet should be propped up on the coffee table; mine tucked beneath me. You always liked stretching out your feet, because you said it was good for the circulation. Our hands should be cradling mugs of hot milky coffee, our lips blowing the steam away before taking that first sip. The TV should be on, tuned into an old black and white film – Bette Davis perhaps, or better still, Vivien Leigh, your favourite, because in your youth everyone said you had a Scarlett O'Hara smile. And later at night, before making our way up the staircase to our respective bedrooms, we could have a final peek at my wedding dress. There it'll be, hanging outside the wardrobe in all its sequinned finery, catching the glow from the lightbulb as we step inside my room and flick the switch by the door, transposing drabness into magic: a shimmering satin splendour. In fact, rather like you.

You should be here on this special night, supporting me, calming my nerves, stroking my face, murmuring, *It'll be fine, darling. It'll be fine.*

But you're not here. Instead of cradling a mug of coffee in my hands, I'm clutching a letter. A crumpled letter, with fine calligraphy that's smudged with water stains. Tears, actually. A letter you never knew about, because I slipped it in my bag before you had the chance to spot it in the hall at Belle View on my last visit home. Good job I was standing there at the time, putting on my jacket and getting ready to leave at the very moment the postman pushed the envelope through the letter box. You were in the kitchen, clattering about by the sink, washing up mugs, delaying the bitter sorrow of parting. So I stole the letter - which was addressed to you but definitely from *him*, because I recognised his handwriting - and I read it on the inter-city train from Lyneham-on-Sea to Birmingham, then the local one to Lichfield. I read it multiple times, on both journeys. Every word of it. That's when I knew there was no point in calling off the wedding. That's when it finally hit home that there was no other way.

You should be here tonight, fussing me, loving me like the true mother you once were. But 'once' is a sad word, locked in that unattainable land we call *the past*. 'Once' has all the longing of a Chopin nocturne. Perhaps his E minor Opus 72, your favourite. I could have played it for you tonight. I could have given you an entire private recital, far more intimate than the concert hall.

But you refused to come, which is absolutely fine by me, because I didn't want you here anyway.

'*How could you do it? I hate you!*'

That was me two weeks ago, back home in Lyneham-on-Sea. You said nothing; just surveyed me with cold eyes. Where had all their warmth and sparkle gone? Where was the pert smile that had always won hearts?

3

'I can never go back to Greystones now! You've fucked it up well and truly this time!'

I hardly recognised my own voice. Did I really say all that? It's true that the random swear word has crept into my vocabulary these last few years, together with the odd cigarette and large glass of wine or two, but I never actually use the 'f' word. Just the occasional 'bloody' or 'sodding'.

But I don't want to think about any of that now. Not tonight, of all nights. I want to be filled with warm memories. I want us to share our longing for him one final time, before tomorrow's wedding vows put a final stop to any such stupid flights of fancy.

So let's go back. Let's exercise a little suspension of disbelief. Then you and I can time-travel to the days when you were the most important person in my life, the best mother in the world. The days when we both believed in love and its illusory dream.

Greystones Abbey. Deep in the rolling hills of North Yorkshire. That's as good a place as any to begin, because that's where I first met him, during the February half-term holiday of 1978.

2

North Yorkshire, February 1978

I'll never forget the first time I saw Greystones Abbey. If ever there was a single word to describe such an impression, I'd love to know it. To phrase it in brochure terms, I could say that *Greystones Abbey is set in over 2,000 acres of land on the edge of the North York Moors National Park, boasting an array of woodland, valleys and lakes in a tranquil and relaxed environment.*

But words aren't enough to cope with describing such a place. 'Magical' comes to mind, as does heavenly, celestial, otherworldly - yet none of these adjectives are any good, because, aside from being clichés, they only describe part of the picture. The other part was still unknown to me in that first glimpse I had of the Benedictine monastery through the snow-spattered windows of our school coach. Which is just as well. Had I known back then what awaited me over the coming years as a direct result of Greystones Abbey, things might have turned out quite differently. I might have made my way to the front of the coach and begged the dour-faced driver to take me straight back home to Lyneham-on-Sea in the neighbouring county of Lancashire.

'Oh wow, it's a real *monastery!*' Francesca cried out in her breathless little voice. She leaned forward in her seat and wiped the condensation from the window. I still think of her as *Nobbles*, the skinny girl with long, plain brown hair that she wore like a nun's veil, and wide eyes that always looked just a bit dismayed.

'Well, what did you expect it to be? A bloody casino?' Good old Jenny Swarbrick with her dry sense of humour. Best friend through thick and thin. Masses of curly black locks that I used to envy, as well as sparkly eyes, an ample bust, and a confidence-gene that the gods appeared to have missed out when forming my own DNA. She had a peculiar bent for swear words, despite her God-fearing upbringing, and a tendency to take the mickey out of religion. But she could also be a dreamer, like me, though with a cutting edge that I lacked. I was just a dreamer full stop.

The coach took a sharp turn to the right, swerving into the Abbey grounds and abandoning the steep bank of forest that had accompanied us on the last few minutes of the journey. We were all instantly silenced, as though God had raised his mighty baton upon our teenage chorus of irreverent natter and cried out: GIRLS! Our eyes widened at the sight of Greystones Abbey in its full monastic splendour, shivering in a wintry haze at the bottom of the long, snaking driveway. For a moment I thought I was in Shangri-La as I gazed out at all those turrets, towers and mullioned windows. This unearthly vision was set against a vast landscape of hills, valleys and distant forest, all coated in an undefiled layer of snow, as though reminding the monks of their vows of celibacy. How could such perfection have existed all the seventeen years of my as-yet tender life and I knew nothing about it?

Half a minute later the coach parked up outside a large villa in prime position at the top of the driveway. Mother Bernadette drew herself up from her front seat and stood in the middle of the aisle. Buttoning up her black coat to the top of her chicken-like neck, she raised her face and announced in her distinctive Irish accent, 'Right then, girls, quiet, if you please!'

As though on cue, the bus engine switched off and twenty-four restless sixth formers began to rummage for coats, scarves, bags and whatever other paraphernalia we were lumbered with. A guitar, in my case.

'I said *quiet now*, all of you!' The headmistress-nun cast her famous glare left and right, her eagle eyes catching the tail-end of my giggle. 'Leah Cavanagh, if you have something amusing to say, you will either share it with all of us or remain silent. Is that clear?'

'Yes, Mother Bernadette,' I said, eyes lowered, giggle duly purged. We all used to call her *Bernie* behind her back, and wondered if the rest of her hair was the same ginger colour as the few wisps that escaped from the front of her veil.

She clapped her hands, bringing all nattering and sniggers to a swift cadence. 'We shall be staying at the Gatehouse, which is the villa you can see over there. When you enter the hallway – in a quiet and orderly manner, if you please – you will see a list on the noticeboard with all of your names and the rooms to which you have been ascribed. Please find your room quickly and quietly, unpack your bags, and assemble in the common room on the ground floor in ten minutes' time.'

'Can't we have a wander round first?' someone from the back of the coach called out.

These Catholic girls might have been proficient in their Hail Mary's and Communion rites, but they certainly weren't shy and retiring, that's for sure. I learned this fact soon after enrolling at Lark Mount upon my piano teacher's recommendation. He was convinced that a sensitive soul like me would fare much better doing my A-levels in the calm atmosphere of a Catholic girls' school run by nuns, rather than being swallowed up by the local co-educational sixth form college. It all seemed so *different* in those first few weeks: the nuns in their flowing black habits, the well-spoken girls in their neat uniforms of brown and blue, the chapel, the lunchtime Masses where I was cajoled into playing guitar, the beautiful grounds that protected the school from the outside world. Oh, and that narrow lake at the bottom of the hill, surrounded by sycamores and low-hanging willows that provided shade on those long summer days when me and my friends would take our packed lunches down to the waterside. I can still see us there, lying on the grass, staring up at the huge sky and emptying our deepest yearnings to one another. No wonder the lot of us were always late for the first lesson after lunch on those balmy afternoons.

Mother Bernadette drew her thin ginger eyebrows together. 'All right then, girls,' she said in that broad accent, so easy to mimic behind her back. 'You can have twenty minutes to wander round the monastery grounds to find your bearings. But it'll be dark soon, so no more than that.'

'Why, will the bogeyman jump out at us from the shadows?'

This time it was Sister Miriam's turn to intervene. 'That's enough, Jenny,' she gently chided, turning round in her coach seat and raising her attractive young face just high enough to aim a reproachful look at my friend. If anyone harboured teenage fantasies about becoming a nun, Sister Miriam was their role model.

Mother Bernadette scowled at Jenny. 'The bogeyman won't get you, but Father Sebastian might.' Turning to the rest of us, she expanded, 'Father Sebastian is Warden of the Gatehouse, and I trust you will all show him due respect, girls. Is that understood?'

'*Yes, Mother Bernadette,*' we all chanted in unison.

Wetting her colourless lips, Bernie proceeded, 'We shall meet together at five o'clock in the common room for prayers and Mass practice, and at six we shall go down to Vespers in the Abbey Church. Supper is served at seven o'clock sharp in the Gatehouse refectory, and I don't expect any of you to be late. Afterwards, Father Sebastian will say Mass for us in the small chapel next to the refectory, and at nine we shall go down to the monastery for Compline, which is the last Office of the day. Now then, girls, which one of you can remember what the Offices are, hmm?'

Nobble's hand shot up. She was practically a nun herself.

'Yes, Francesca dear?'

'It's the chanting of prayers at fixed hours of the day, like Matins, Lauds, Vespers and Compline, according to the liturgy of the Church.'

Jenny rolled her eyes at me and hissed, '*Bloody hell.*'

'Yes, well done, Francesca. Good to know that at least some of you pay attention during your RE lessons. Now then, after Compline we shall re-assemble in the common room for a short talk given by Brother Matthew, who is a specialist on the power of prayer.'

'*Kuh Pow!*'

'Jenny, that's enough,' Sister Miriam said. A shower of snickers ricocheted round the coach.

'Quiet, girls!' Bernie's sharp eyes picked out random victims down the length of the aisle. 'After that final talk it'll be bed for all of you, because some of us have opted to go to Matins at five in the morning. Any questions?'

There weren't any, all of us being desperate to get off the coach after our three-hour journey across the Pennines. So we clambered out and trudged across the driveway to the Gatehouse, stamping the snow off our feet before piling up the stairs to find our rooms. I was delighted to discover that my own room was one of the singles, with a neat little desk ideal for writing my diary, and a casement window offering the most divine view imaginable. I could already see myself sitting there in the evenings, gazing out at the shimmering lights from the monastery at the bottom of the hill, with the surrounding valley and milky-white forest providing the perfect backdrop, like something out of an impressionist painting.

After unpacking my travel bag, I was ready to venture out with Jenny and Nobbles to explore the territory that I was rapidly falling in love with.

Pity I couldn't have restricted the 'falling in love' bit just to the territory.

By the end of my first day at Greystones I'd developed a grinding head-ache, so was unable to attend Compline down in the monastery. Instead, I escaped to the seclusion of my snug room at the Gatehouse. I took a pain-killer, got undressed and slipped into my pyjamas. I considered spending a few peaceful minutes writing my diary, but decided against it in view of the dull throbbing in my temples.

Switching off my bedside lamp, I opened the window and levered myself up onto the sill, where I sat huddled for some time, allowing the frosty air to tickle my face and ease the rhythmic pulsing in my head. It had stopped snowing by now and the heavy clouds from earlier in the day had dispersed, giving way to an almost garishly bright moon.

After a few minutes, my eyes focused on a distant form that was making its way up the long driveway from the monastery. The hooded figure grad-ually increased in size as it approached the Gatehouse, its snow-crunching footsteps getting louder. When it was just several feet away from my win-dow, I felt compelled to move aside, not wanting to disturb the monk's nocturnal contemplation. But before I had the chance to shift position, he suddenly looked up, perhaps drawn by the unusual sight of a wide-open window on a cold winter's night. Seeing my startled face, he smiled at me.

I caught my breath, flustered, realising that this must be the monk who was due to give us a talk after Compline on the Power of Prayer. I felt my face flushing. It was as if he'd caught me out in an act of truancy. The schoolgirl in me almost blurted out, 'Please, Sir – I'm not doing anything wrong, honest!' – or however one was supposed to address a monk. But I didn't need to. There was no chastisement in his eyes as they crinkled up at mine, only warmth and good humour, as though whispering: *Don't worry, your secret is safe with me!*

Little did I know, as I watched him disappear into the shadowed en-trance to the Gatehouse, that this day would change my life forever.

CHAPTER TWO

1

DEEPLY REGRET TO INFORM YOU

You never forgot those words, Mother, did you? The opening words of the telegram you received on the morning of 9th December 1956, when you believed that the best years of your life still lay ahead of you in the company of Peter Donald Fox. The words that your mother read aloud, immediately after you handed the piece of paper to her with shaking hand, not believing what you'd just seen. You were convinced there must have been some mistake; that the telegram couldn't possibly have been addressed to *you*, Molly Williams of 48 Talbot Road, Preston; that the Peter Donald Fox referred to couldn't possibly have been *your* Peter. Just seconds earlier you'd been dancing alone to the strains of *I'll be Loving You Always*, eyes closed, thinking of Peter, wishing he'd hurry back home from Cyprus. When your mother came into your room, looking a bit anxious as she gave you the small brown envelope and asked you to turn the gramophone player off because she couldn't hear herself think, you'd just rolled your eyes and said, 'A telegram? What the dickens has Peter been up to *now?*'

So you opened it, and you read it. And then your mother read it. There must have been a long pause, I always imagined, before she faced you with sombre eyes and slowly shook her head. How many seconds passed, I wonder, before she told you in her no-nonsense Lancashire drawl that there had been no mistake. That it was your Peter, your fiancé, your love, who would never be coming home.

You were only twenty-six at the time. An age when the world should have been your oyster. How on earth did you survive the coming years?

Or is the answer, simply, that you didn't?

A sharp knocking at the door woke me up early the following morning. It was still dark. I squinted at my watch. 4.45 am. Middle of the bloody night. But with the next rapping, it all swept back to me in a surge that washed away the murky confusion of dreams. I was on a sixth form retreat at Greystones Abbey and Jenny had promised to wake Nobbles and me up in time for Matins, which happened to be at the unearthly hour of 5.20 am.

'Leah, are you awake?' Jenny's hushed voice called out from beyond the closed door.

I heaved myself into a sitting position, rubbing my eyes. 'Yes - just give me a minute.'

'Okay, meet me downstairs in the refectory in ten. I'll put the kettle on.' Her footsteps faded into the distance.

I swung my legs over the side of the bed – my long, slender legs that were a constant source of envy amongst both my friends: Jenny, because she was on the shorter, more amply-built side, and Nobbles, because she was ashamed of her white, skinny thighs and knobbly knees that she only revealed under the coercion of Miss Slater in the PE changing rooms.

Making my way over to the sink, I splashed my face under a cold stream of water and glanced into the mirror. I needed to check if the visage that squinted back at me required touching up or if it could wait till a more human hour, when the eyes of twenty-three other, equally looks-conscious teenage girls would be upon me. How foolish we were at that age – worrying about the purity of our complexions and the length of our eyelashes and the trendiness of our clothes. Even within the strict limitations of a uniform of brown pleated skirts that had to be at least an inch below the knee, and royal-blue blouses that had to be buttoned up right to the neck, we still hoped to pass the test for sex appeal and glamour.

My reflection peered back at me with hazel, almond-shaped eyes that were rather striking, though I say so myself. I decided not to bother with mascara. Instead, I reached for my hairbrush and yanked it through the long tresses that tumbled down the left side of my face and over my shoulders. Hair duly untangled, I slipped into my skirt, buttoned up my blouse, tossed my woolly cardigan over my shoulders, and abandoned my room for the refectory on the ground floor of the Gatehouse. That's where the early-risers had agreed to assemble, before going down to the main Abbey for Matins.

The word 'Matins' still has a special ring for me, because it was the first time I ever spoke to him.

Me and my two friends were sitting on the back pew of the Abbey church. All the other sixth formers were in front of us, as well as our two supervising nuns. I was perched at the edge of the pew, right next to the central aisle. Not a hint of dawn filtered through the narrow windows carved high into cold monastic stone. Only the red candle flame below the central crucifix provided any source of light. The light of God. Except that I couldn't quite manage to get my head round His existence, which made my presence on this retreat a bit of a paradox.

A shiver of illumination rippled into the domed room, shedding just enough glow to read the words in our psalm books – or antiphonals, as I soon learned to call them. A hollow knocking sound echoed all around us. As though on cue, a procession of black-robed monks filed down the central aisle. One by one, with hoods lowered over bowed heads, they passed within inches of our pews before veering off to the choir stalls, where we'd been told that the Benedictine community chanted their devotional psalms five times a day, seven days a week, 365 days a year. Apparently they didn't get one single day off, *ever*.

The stately procession came to an end. Two of the monks left the others for a podium which sported a fearsome-looking tome. '*The Handbook of God*', Jenny sniggered. Clearing his throat, the taller of the two launched into the opening line of the first psalm, soon joined by his companion and then the rest of the community. *Lord, open my lips…*

I riffled through the pages of my own book, searching in vain for a helpful title. 'Matins', for instance, or 'First Psalm of the Day', or perhaps 'Psalms for Idiots'. But there was none.

Jenny was clearly as lost as me. '*What flipping page are we supposed to be on?*'

'You're asking *me*? The only non-Catholic in the school?'

Our muffled giggles were quashed by a swishing sound that came from the aisle behind us, along with the padding of footsteps. One of the monks was approaching our pew.

We held our breath. What was the penalty for smirking during psalms? Would we be marched off to the Abbot's office, severely reprimanded and whisked off back to Lyneham-on-Sea? Or worse – would they interrupt Matins in order to call us to the lectern and rebuke us in public? The mind boggled at the possibilities.

The anonymous monk at last stopped by our pew. As I was sitting right by the edge, it crossed my mind that I'd be the one to bear the brunt of whatever Benedictine wrath awaited us.

No such fear.

Leaning down towards me, the monk whispered, 'Here, let me show you.' There wasn't a trace of anger in his voice. He went about thumbing through the pages of the antiphonal until he found the desired psalm. I watched as his deft fingers pulled a ribbon out of the spine of the book and tucked it into the newfound page, then another psalm, and another, marking each one with a new, differently coloured ribbon. His hands were smooth, refined, with neatly trimmed nails and just the faintest smattering of hairs. He was leaning so close, I could feel his breath on my cheek. A lingering waft of coffee.

'There you are,' he said softly, his vowels oozing with class. 'That's all the psalms you'll be needing for today's Matins.'

As I looked up to thank him, I got a close-up of the bluest eyes I had ever seen – sparkling, twinkling and every other cliché that ever existed to describe such a perfect sight. I caught my breath, knowing at once that it was *him* - the monk I'd seen from my bedroom window the previous night. I was so jolted by the thudding of my heart, I didn't even remember to thank him. Instead, I found myself asking in a manic whisper: 'Sorry - but what should I call you? Is it *Father?*' I felt my cheeks burning.

His shadowed face broke into a smile. 'I'm not a priest, actually,' he whispered back. 'I'm a monk. You can call me Brother Matthew.'

'Okay.'

He glanced away, his attention diverted by something from the choir stalls. In those few moments I was able to risk a slightly better look at his profile: the chiselled nose, the strong jawline, the dark brown hair with a kink to it. And then he suddenly turned back to me, catching me out. However, I needn't have felt embarrassed, because his own gaze was filled with a matching appreciation that was unmistakable. But it was also tinged with something else. There was a hint of disquiet in his expression; a fleeting defencelessness that was only partially disguised by his faint laughter lines. Then he straightened up, turned round and strode away, his broad shoulders and tallness emphasised by his long black habit.

My head reverberated in the after-shock of the look we'd just exchanged. I knew then, with a flash of maturity beyond my seventeen years, that although he was a monk, he was a man first and foremost.

4

Thanks to you, Mother, I had the privilege of being brought up in a Victorian Bed & Breakfast house on the promenade of Lyneham-on-Sea. Whenever prospective guests phoned to make enquiries, you'd always describe our unassuming seaside resort as *a small, elegant town nestled into the wide-stretched coast of Lancashire.* You knew the place even better than me, having moved there from the neighbouring town of Preston when you returned from Cyprus, way back in 1964, together with Dad and me. I was only four at the time.

Quite apart from the beauty of my physical environment, the privileges were almost entirely thanks to you. Your devoted love for me is something I'll always be grateful for, as well as your incurably romantic spirit. Even after Peter Fox had his life cut brutally short in Kyrenia all those years ago, you nonetheless filled my entire being with the magic of true love. I was brought up on stories of Peter: the tall, haunted-eyed journalist with a sharp intellect, a wry humour, and a global conscience. You were always telling me how he used to melt your heart by quoting from the Declaration of Human Rights in that deep voice of his. In fact, you quoted those words to me so often, I eventually learned them too. *Whereas recognition of the inherent dignity and of the equal and inalienable rights of all members of the human family is the foundation of freedom, justice and peace in the world...* Sometimes I think I adored Peter almost as much as you did. You believed that Peter Fox was your man, even if in reality 'being your man' meant no more than being loyal to his ghost for the rest of your life.

Okay, to move on, there was your encouragement of my music. You were a rock for me there, steadfast through the grinding years of daily piano practice, always precipitated by an hour of scales and arpeggios. I'm sure they would have driven other, less supportive mothers beyond the bounds of endurance, especially the chromatic thirds and diminished sevenths. At least you had the common sense – not something you were naturally blessed with – to position our old Jacobean piano in the annex at the back of our B&B, so as to avoid disturbing Gran. Not that it made much difference to her constant grumbling. '*You don't happen to have any ear plugs, Molly, do you?*' she'd shout out to you above the drone of my finger drills. You always winced at this. 'Why don't you just turn the telly up, Mother?' you'd curtly suggest, and Gran would hobble away in offence, out of the annex, through the main hallway and back to her bedsit at the front of the house where you could hardly hear the piano *at all,* though she insisted it gave her a headache.

I adored my own room, way up in the gables and separated from the rest of our rambling three-story house by a spiral staircase. The room used to be nothing but a neglected storage area in the cobwebby attic, but once Dad disappeared into the mists of the Irish Sea, together with his young and glamorous secretary, you had the foresight to fill the gap that his departure left in my adolescent heart. So, out went all the junk, in came the workmen, and within a few weeks I found myself transported into a room fit for a princess. I used to love leaning out of my dormer window and gazing at the exhilarating scene: the airborne seagulls, the Victorian bandstand way down below, the long pier that stayed open till late at night in the holiday season, the endless beach that played hide and seek with the sea twice a day, every day, throughout the year. The tide went so far out, at times it got completely lost in the horizon; but a few hours later the teasing waves would once again be lapping onto the wooden posts of the pier. I must have spent thousands of hours mesmerised by the stars hanging over the distant tide, dreaming, longing … but not for the things I should have longed for, silly me. And silly you, Mother, it has to be said. Silly you for not snapping me out of at least *one* of those dreams.

Okay, so much for the privileges of my upbringing. Now I'd like to remind you of one or two disadvantages.

Well, apart from Dad walking out on us when I was thirteen (the smooth-talking *Doctor Dermot,* as you mockingly called him), there was also the claustrophobia I sometimes felt, living with a single mother and ageing grandmother. Three females of three generations all dwelling under the same roof isn't exactly the most balanced recipe for life. When the money became tight and you decided to convert our promenade home into a B&B guest house, I don't think you had any idea just how much hard work would be involved, did you? Not only in the conversion itself, but also in the on-going labour of cooking full English breakfasts, cleaning out rooms, changing bedding, and all the other chores that went hand in hand with maintaining a full guest house – only ever possible in the summer months. I always preferred the less profitable winter months. Things were quieter then; there was more time for me to practise the piano and share my dreams with you. Do you remember those long winter evenings after Gran had gone to bed and the two of us sat huddled in front of the gas fire in our snug sitting room at the back? There we'd be, watching those black and white weepies with Bette Davis and Greta Garbo and Vivien Leigh, both of us chatting away further into the night than was sensible for a schoolgirl trying to prepare for her exams.

As a matter of fact, my final year of A-levels happened to coincide with my first trip to Greystones Abbey. So let's go back, shall we?

After Matins, we all reassembled in the dimly-lit corridor outside the Abbey Church and were promptly divided into two groups of twelve. Group A was to go off with Father Sebastian for Meditation, Group B with Brother Matthew. My heart skipped a beat when I realised that I was in Group B. I made sure to position myself right at the front as he promptly led us down a set of stone steps into the crypt. We trooped single file along a narrow passage which took us to the Contemplation room.

'On the floor, ladies,' he instructed once we were inside the room. I tried to ignore Jenny's snigger. 'In a semicircle, sitting Indian style, like this.' He crouched down, scanning us with those eyes. 'Great. Now then. Hands on your legs, palms up. That's it, well done.'

Standing up again, he disappeared into an adjacent room and after a few seconds some weird panpipe music wafted over our heads. When he re-emerged, he joined us on the floor in the centre of our circle. 'Eyes closed now,' he said in a half-whisper. Jenny's twitter was immediately silenced by the look he shot at her. I wanted him to give *me* that look – *any* look – but he merely lowered his head and frowned in concentration.

'Imagine you're alone on a balloon in the night sky,' he continued, 'sailing into outer space. And no, you won't be sucked into a black hole, because God is your invisible guide. No need to fear. Just breathe deeply and empty your mind.'

For the next half-hour I tried and failed to do precisely that, but my mind stubbornly overflowed with secular thoughts. Not only was I acutely aware of Brother Matthew's physical presence, I was also beset by niggling worries that had been eating away at me in recent weeks. My upcoming audition at the Royal Northern College of Music topped the list, followed by doubts about whether Chopin's third Ballade in A-flat major was up to scratch, what I'd do if I didn't get accepted at the college, and if I did, how you, Best Mother in the World, would cope without me once I left home in September. Just Gran and the B&B business; no more of our black and white weepies to share during those long evenings we so loved. Add to this list a nagging inability to believe in the god whose existence everyone else at school took for granted, and you can see that I had a few odds and ends to clear up in my life.

When the session was over I breathed a secret sigh of relief. The cold stone was beginning to seep through my numbed bottom, and some of us were getting rumbly tummies, inspiring one or two embarrassed coughs. As everyone stood up and filed out of the room, I manoeuvred myself closer to Brother Matthew, but he walked right past without even a glance. Next thing I knew, he was gone. Back to his other world.

Freed from his magnetic presence, I realised two crucial things: I was dying for the loo, and I hadn't phoned you yet. I knew you'd be worrying, and so urgency was now of the essence. I also knew how angry you could become if I neglected to phone you when away on a school trip or visiting Dad in Ireland.

Once outside, I buttoned up my coat and ran across the compact snow to the Visitors' Lodge, where we'd been told there was a public telephone. Breakfast was the busiest time of day at Belle Vue, so I hoped to catch you just before you began serving up.

I was in luck. You picked up the receiver straight away. '*Darling*, how lovely to hear from you at last! Is everything all right?'

I basked in the warmth of your voice at the other end of the line. I could hear the tremulous violins of Nat King Cole's *Autumn Leaves* playing in the background, accompanying our conversation with that nineteen-fifties sound I so loved. I was overwhelmed by a pang of homesickness.

'Yes, everything's fine,' I said. 'It's beautiful here – like something out of a fairy tale. There's masses of snow, as well. Why can't we get this much snow in Lyneham?'

'Oh, I see. Is that why you didn't phone last night? The fairies carried you away, did they? Or was it the ghosts of dead monks?'

I couldn't tell if there was humour in your voice, or if I'd unknowingly triggered the dreaded tick-tock timer that might lead to an explosive outburst. Despite our closeness, there were times when I actually feared your alarming ability to swerve into a mood of *hell hath no fury like a mother scorned*. During such times, the texture of your face would change within seconds; your voice would rise in decibels and your vocabulary would fill with expletives of a colourful variety that's now outdated: *Hells bells!* and *Damn and blast!* and *Ye gods!* to name but a few.

'I had one of my migraines last night,' I said a tad nervously, keeping an eye on my watch. The last thing I needed was to get the third degree from old Bernie for being late, on top of your potential displeasure.

But you remained calm and loving. 'Oh, *no*, you poor thing! Did you take your aspirins with you?'

'Yes, I did. But don't worry – I'm fine now. I just missed the talk that was planned for us yesterday evening, that's all.'

'Leah, I *told* you that you'd been overdoing things, didn't I? All these nerves over your coming audition in Manchester, and then the rush to leave for Greystones yesterday morning, all because you got the timing mixed up. Thank goodness Jenny thought to give you a quick ring! Really and truly, darling, how on earth are you going to cope when you go away to music college if you can't even remember the timing of a school trip? I still can't understand how you could get eight o'clock mixed up with nine o'clock. Heavens above, Leah, you're almost eighteen! One really would think –'

'Yes, Mother, we've been through all this before. Look, I can't be long, because my money's going to run out soon and I haven't got any more change.'

'So just quickly, tell me about the monastery. Do the monks speak there, or is it one of these silent Orders?' Again there was suppressed humour in your voice. In fact, it sounded like you'd covered your mouth with your hand to prevent yourself from bursting into one of your full-blown fits of laughter. Sometimes you laughed so much, tears ran down your cheeks. Little did we know at the time how soon the laughter would be gone.

'Oh, they talk, all right,' I said, grinning. 'They're just ordinary men, except that they've taken these vows to God.' My smile softened at the thought of Brother Matthew.

'Ah yes, celibacy and all that. Well, do try not to make the poor things fantasise too much, though I know that will be extremely hard, with your beautiful face and lovely slim figure paraded right in front of their eyes.'

'Oh, *Mother* –'

'In fact, it reminds me of one of Peter's jokes. There was once a vicar … oh, heavens! Sorry, darling, must love and leave you! I can hear footsteps – that'll be Mr Tomlinson down for breakfast. He's always the first.' I could hear the *tut* in your voice. 'I wouldn't care, but he never even smiles or says good morning. Just a nod and a grunt. I know he can't help being a bit on the grumpy side by nature, but when all's said and done, you'd think he could at least retain some basic manners. After all, as your Gran says –'

'Manners maketh man.'

'Exactly. Anyway, darling, I'd better turn down the Nat King Cole, otherwise he'll be grumbling about that as well. Now you take care of yourself, promise? And don't do anything I wouldn't do - especially with those poor monks! Bye-bye, darling.'

'Bye, Mother. Love you never-stop-growing.' Ah, how many times had we exchanged that fond endearment in our long-lost world of yesterday.

After I placed the receiver back on the antiquated contraption screwed into the wall, I ran all the way back to the Gatehouse – half-smiling in the wake of your bubbly, chatty voice, and half-dreading the reception I was likely to receive from fearsome Bernie for being all of eight minutes late to breakfast.

Normally the winter months at Belle Vue were very quiet. However, this was February half-term, so all five of our guest rooms were booked up. I remember on the morning I left for Greystones Abbey, you were on the phone taking a booking for the final vacant room: the single one at the back, which was always harder to fill. You were speaking into the receiver in your usual eloquent telephone manner as I lumbered my bags and guitar across our wide reception hall, but you still made the effort to mouth the words, '*Sorry, darling – have to take this call,*' at the same time waving me a fond goodbye through your slender fingers. I was the pianist, yet you had the fingers I longed for.

If I hadn't worshipped you so much, I could have been quite jealous of many things, not just your elegant hands. There was your beautiful accent, for one, moulded by elocution lessons in the keen acting days of your youth. Then there was your perky Vivien Leigh smile which you were famous for amongst friends and family, as well as your Brigitte Bardot bust. Your generous bra size would have taken at least four of my own meagre mammary offerings. And there was your confidence and charm to which no one, not a single soul, remained impervious. Even Dad at times had bouts of nostalgia when he recalled that *femme fatal umph* of yours which had lured him out of his bachelor-status in Cyprus, where you remained for the first few years after Peter Fox's death. And when Dad decided it was time to return to England, you set about searching for the perfect property with true Scarlett O'Hara determination, right until locating our Victorian town house in Lyneham-on-Sea. But it was only when Dad did a runner on us several years later that you displayed the most admirable of all your characteristics yet. Tossing aside all thoughts of the rebound-husband with whom you'd spent fifteen years of your life, you threw your heart and soul into the mammoth task of converting our house into a Bed & Breakfast establishment. No doubt your experience as a doctor's secretary in your youth helped with the business: you knew how to charm the guests, how to maintain a warm and inviting atmosphere, how to keep the bookwork in order.

Do you remember how we used to jokingly call our establishment Belle Vue Mansions? As if! Our B&B might have once made an imposing family home, but as a guest house it definitely leaned towards the more modest class of accommodation that lined the sprawling seafront. But still, no one could deny the flare you had for interior design. I particularly loved the chic little tables in our basement dining room, draped in red and white chequered cloths that were inspired by your twenty-first birthday trip to Paris. With Peter, of course. And our back patio, with its bougainvillea and jasmine and cluttered terracotta pots that were a bitter-sweet memorial to your Cyprus days. Another reminder of Peter.

Even though I was only thirteen at the time of the conversion, I remember envying your determination, strength and romantic spirit. I only inherited the romantic bit. There were times I would have traded even the dimple by the left side of my mouth for at least one fraction of the confidence that the gods had blessed you with at the time of your conception. I was only blessed with attractive looks and a talent for playing the piano, neither of which earned me the fame you so fervently believed I was destined for. What you couldn't know, back in the February half-term holiday of 1978, was that the inner strength I so admired in you would ultimately turn itself against us.

I was ten minutes late for breakfast. As soon as I stepped inside the Gatehouse refectory, all eyes turned to me. The VIP table was positioned nearest the door, so there was no escaping a public dressing-down from Mother Bernadette. Or the fact that *he* was also there – Brother Matthew, with Bernie to his left, Father Sebastian to his right, and Sister Miriam opposite him.

True to my prediction, Mother Bernadette turned the full brunt of her glare upon me. 'Leah Cavanagh, what time do you call this?'

'Ten past eight,' I said automatically, ignoring the sniggers that rippled round the room.

'Girls, that's enough!' Bernie silenced us. 'Leah, find a seat quickly and eat your breakfast.' Her small pale eyes challenged my long hazel ones.

Looking away, I caught the tail-end of a grin on Brother Matthew's lips. Holding my breath, I walked across the room to the beckoning of Jenny and Nobbles.

'Have you noticed the handsome one?' Jenny whispered as soon as I sat down. 'Why would someone like that want to become a flippin' *monk*, for God's sake?'

'Is he still smiling at me?' I said, snatching a piece of toast from the chrome rack and buttering it in senseless panic.

Jenny glanced in his direction. 'No, he's smiling at Sister Miriam. She's gone red as a beetroot. So it looks like you're not the only one who's got the hots for him.'

Nobbles rolled her eyes. 'Honestly, you two, he's a *monk*. Or had that failed to grab your attention?'

'Ooh, who's sounding like Mother Superior now?'

Unlike Jenny, Nobbles did not import sex into every possible situation. In fact, Jenny was a bit of an expert on sin in general. She once said to me,

'You non-Catholics just don't *get* it. Sin is so exciting, don't you see? - and the guilt just heightens it! You go to confession, show due penitence, and Bob's your uncle, you're free for your next transgression.' We fantasised like crazy about boys from the nearby school in a way that only extreme youth allows. Unless you happen to have a mother who is the biggest fantasist of all.

'Pity you missed his talk last night,' Jenny said amid a mouthful of toast. 'But don't ask me what it was about, 'cause I haven't got a clue. Couldn't concentrate on a thing – and no bloody wonder! Just *look* at him.'

The clinking of a spoon upon glass silenced us. Twenty-four pairs of eyes focused on the central dining table, the See of the Holy Gatehouse.

Standing up, Mother Bernadette cast her all-encompassing stare upon her flock. 'Now then, girls. Just one or two announcements before we disperse.' She rubbed her hands together briskly. 'At ten o'clock this morning Father Sebastian has kindly offered to give us a talk on the Turin Shroud, which is his specialism. I take it you have all heard of the Turin shroud?' Tossing the briefest of glances at each table in turn, she carried straight on: 'The talk will be followed by a session of folk hymns up in the attic room. Leah, I trust you shall accompany us on the guitar for that?'

As always when put on the spot, I felt my cheeks burning. The only exception to this irritating flaw was when playing the piano. When on stage, the smooth black and white keys provided a conduit to a parallel world of sounds, textures and the deepest, most private feelings. It was a world where I alone dwelt.

I nodded, and caught a smile of conspiracy on Brother Matthew's face. But this time there was more. This time as our eyes met, he drew down a corner of his mouth in mock sympathy. He had the Unblessed Virgin Bernie well-sussed.

'Good,' she said, creasing her face at me in a rare smile before returning to the rest of her audience. 'At twelve o'clock we shall go to High Mass in the monastery, and afterwards lunch will be served back here. In the afternoon you have some free time for walking, praying, or meditating. As you know, there's a small chapel here in the Gatehouse next to the refectory, as well as the Abbey Church.' She turned to the Warden of the Gatehouse. 'Father Sebastian, have I forgotten to mention any other places where my girls can partake in silent prayer?'

'Well, let me see now ...' the older priest began, 'there's the ... er ...'

'There's the tiny chapel in the crypt,' Brother Matthew said, cocking a sardonic eyebrow at us all, 'as long as you girls don't mind sharing your prayers with the crumbling bones of our deceased brethren?'

This was met by a flurry of laughter, joined in by a somewhat reluctant Bernie. 'Yes – the crypt, of course. Thank you for that, Brother Matthew.' She coughed lightly. 'Afternoon tea will be served in the common room at four o'clock, and at six I expect to see you all at Vespers, followed by supper back here in the refectory. Then there'll be a little more free time for relaxing, and at nine o'clock we shall return to the Abbey for Compline before retiring to our rooms.'

'No time for idle hands to do the devil's work, then,' Jenny chuckled. But her words were lost in the commotion that followed, as the VIPs pushed their chairs back in unison.

Brother Matthew lingered by the doorway for a few minutes, making friendly chit-chat with the girls as they passed by him in single file. When it came to my turn, he threw me one of his melting smiles and said, 'So you play the guitar, do you?'

Ah, that voice! I nodded.

'How splendid. I've always envied people who play a musical instrument. Do you play anything else?'

'The piano.'

'The *piano*!' It was as though this was the most amazing piece of information he'd heard all year.

'It's my main instrument,' I said, tucking a loose strand of hair behind my ear. 'I'm hoping to go to music college in September.'

'Are you really? Well, that's splendid.' He clearly liked the word. 'If you need a room to practise while you're here, just let me know. I'm sure I could arrange something in the school's music department.'

'That would be great. Thank you.'

'Right, I'll see what I can do. If I forget, just give me a shout. You can usually find me in the Gatehouse at mealtimes.'

'Thank you,' I repeated.

'Well then, enjoy your prayers, and see you again at lunchtime.'

And suddenly, as though my allotted chit-chat time was up, he was off, his long black habit swishing behind him as he sailed down the corridor and disappeared out of the main door at the far end.

CHAPTER THREE

1

I was brought up on stories of you and Peter Fox. Remember how I always encouraged you to write them down, but in the end I ended up doing the job myself? As far back as I can remember, I adored the sound of your ill-fated fiancé. I was captivated by the idea of two people who were intended for each other, no matter what trials came their way. You said it was Kismet, and I loved the idea of that too. Throughout my childhood and teenage years I listened in fascination to your tales of the tall, intense-eyed journalist who entranced you with his stare whenever walking past you in the corridors of the *Lancashire Evening Post* headquarters on Fishergate in Preston, where you first met.

Peter was a young reporter and you were the junior office girl working for the secretary of the Football League, right? Yes, I'm sure I've got all the details right – I've certainly heard them enough! Your boss often sent you on errands to the *Lancashire Evening* Post, and that's where Kismet kicked in. You were twenty, Peter twenty-four. You were attractive and lively and charming, he was gaunt and serious and deep-thinking. Both of you took lead roles in a play that was yet to be written.

And then one day, after several weeks of these meaningful looks and silences, at last he spoke to you. The script came to life.

* * *

It was a gloomy October afternoon in 1950. The drizzle clung to the grim Victorian brickwork of Preston, intensifying her desire to get as far away as possible in search of distant rainbows.

She could feel his eyes on her as soon as she stepped inside the office, buzzing with the click-clacking of typewriters. His eyes were still on her when she delivered her message to the chief editor; and when she left the room to head back for the stairs, she could hear footsteps hurrying behind her. She knew it would be him.

She was right. Within seconds he was by her side. Stubbing out his cigarette in a nearby ashtray stand, he said, 'Oh, hello there.'

'Hello,' she replied, kittenish smile activated as soon as she looked up at him.

'Actually, it's rather convenient finding you here,' he continued in a dry Lancashire drawl – the very same drawl that she'd been trying hard to lose since joining the Preston Amateur Dramatic Society. 'Er – it's Molly, isn't it?'

She nodded, reluctantly. She'd been christened with the lovely name of Mary, yet had been called Molly all her life.

Not noticing her hesitation, he went straight on: 'Actually – I was wanting to ask you summat.'

'You were?' was all she managed to say, because this was the first time she found herself standing close enough to realise just how striking his face was. He had that dark, hungry look of a nineteen-thirties film star; a high forehead which she felt sure contained immense intelligence, a shock of messy brown hair, and the most intense, haunted pair of eyes she had ever seen.

It was those very eyes that were now scrutinising her. 'I was wondering if you'd like to come to a party that me and my friend are having next Saturday.'

She felt her skin flush. 'Oh. Gosh. What kind of party, exactly?'

He must have sensed her unease, because he replied a little too quickly, 'Oh, it's nothing to worry about. Just a bit of an old bash that Leo and I are throwing.'

She liked the chic twang of his voice, no doubt developed by working with a journalistic crowd. Fixing her deep brown eyes on him, she said, 'All right, then.'

'You will? I mean – you'll come?'

'I think that's what *all right* means.'

He laughed, 'Well, that's smashing. Okay. I'll – I think I've got the invitation in here somewhere .... ah, here it is.' He took the thing out of his pocket and pressed it into her hand a little too eagerly, although she didn't notice at the time. After all, she was just a silly young errand girl, albeit with high aspirations and above-average intelligence, whereas he was a serious, educated person who had an important job on a real newspaper. 'The address is inside the card. It's just off Winckley Square, in one of them old town houses. Our pad's on the second floor. Saturday at 8.00 then?'

'Pad?'

'Oh, me and Leo share a little bachelor pad. That's my flatmate - he's a cartoonist. He did the black and white etching on the invitation.'

She glanced at the artwork and felt her cheeks burning. 'Well, it's certainly very ...' how to describe the caricature of the cigar-smoking lady with large bosoms, broad hips, and a decidedly provocative wink on her full-lipped face? '... artistic,' she eventually settled for. She bit her lip, because the naughty etching, plus the mention of *Winckley Square* (far darker and leafier and creepier than the simple working class terraces of her own Talbot Road) triggered nasty mental images. Jack the Ripper vied with vulgar women in high heels and low-cut dresses. Her no-frills mother loomed in the murky background, wagging a censorious finger.

'Actually,' she said, shooing away the image, 'I just have one question, if I may.'

'Fire away.'

'Is it all right if I bring a friend along?'

His face dropped. 'A friend?'

'Yes, my best friend from school days. Is it all right if I bring her along?'

Immediately his face brightened again. 'But of course. That's fine, absolutely fine.'

'Thanks.'

He lingered a moment or two, as she did. Glancing at his watch, he eventually said, 'Right. Back to the grind. See you Saturday, then.' And off he went, without so much as a *cheerio* glance in her direction.

She quickly called after him, 'Excuse me?'

He turned to face her again with a hesitation that clearly spelt: *Oh bloody hell, she hasn't changed her mind, has she?*

'Yes?'

'I don't even know your name.'

With a return of that wide charismatic smile, he said, 'Peter. Peter Fox.'

It was the name that was to kidnap the rest of her life.

2

Lunch was served at one, and this time I made sure I wasn't late. Throughout the meal I tried not to stare at the main table where Brother Matthew was seated, with Father Sebastian now on his left, Sister Miriam on his right, and Mother Bernadette opposite. It was as though they'd been playing musical chairs in the period of time that had lapsed since breakfast. I couldn't help glance at their table, and as I did so, Brother Matthew threw me a smile that set my skin on fire. But Nobbles was convinced he paid special attention to everyone, not just me. And in a way, she was right. He was a perfectly at-ease, charming, confident young man, whereas I was just another sixth form girl to add to the dozens of Catholic school trips that no doubt took place throughout the year. So how could I possibly believe that there was something special in his smile that was reserved for me alone?

When we'd all finished eating, I stood up from our table and risked another glance at him. Mother Bernadette was yakking away ten to the dozen, but as soon as he turned his head in my direction, as though sensing my look, he cocked a questioning eyebrow at me, then raised his hands and wriggled his fingers into the air. It didn't take long for the penny to drop. He was making an imitation of piano playing, obviously referring to my need for a practice room. Smiling, I nodded at him. He gave me a thumbs-up; and all the while Mother Bernadette continued blithely chatting away, oblivious to the lightning exchange of sign language that had just taken place under her prim little nose.

Gingerly approaching the VIP table, I stood to one side while waiting for Mother Bernadette to stop jabbering. I thrilled at Brother Matthew's stolen glances at me during the next few moments, as though saying, *Don't worry, I'll be rid of her in a minute!*

It was Bernie herself who at last curtailed her incessant natter. Looking at me sharply, she interrupted her sentence mid-flow and snapped, 'Yes, Leah, what *is* it?'

Brother Matthew came to the rescue. 'Ah, Leah is waiting to be shown to the music room where I've arranged for her to practise.'

My entire being glowed at the sound of that sonorous voice uttering my name.

'Oh, I see.' For a moment poor old Bernie seemed at a loss for words. Then she pushed her chair back, rose to her full height – which wasn't much – and said, 'Well, I shall leave you to it, then. Good-day to you, Brother Matthew.'

He stood up, and Sister Miriam followed suit. It was so regimented, I almost expected them to salute at each other. Instead, Sister Miriam smiled her sweet smile at me and said, 'Enjoy your practice, Leah.' Turning back to her handsome lunch companion, she added, 'Will we be seeing you at afternoon tea, Brother Matthew?'

'Yes, of course. Four o'clock sharp.'

Another flurry of goodbyes was exchanged, after which the two sky pilots - as Jenny referred to all nuns - vanished through the refectory door.

At last we were alone.

'Well,' he said, smiling down at me and clasping his hands in that monkish way. 'I've managed to get hold of the key to the practice room, so if you like I can take you there right now. I gather you've got a free afternoon on your hands.'

'What – *right* now?'

'Unless you'd rather find a quiet chapel to meditate in?'

'Actually, I'd rather practise, if you don't mind.'

He gave a short laugh. My gormlessness had got the better of me again. 'No, I don't mind,' he said, still smiling. 'So then. Do you need to get your music notes or something?'

I nodded. 'They're in my room. Can I quickly go up?'

'Of course you can. Don't rush; I shan't be going anywhere in a hurry.'

I dashed up to my room and ransacked my travel bag for my Beethoven, Bach and Chopin. Before leaving, I glanced in the mirror and debated whether to let my hair fall naturally for the sultry look, or tuck it behind my ear for the sensible look. There was also the question of whether or not to dab a spot of *Blue Grass* eau de toilette behind my ears. I settled for the sensible, no-perfume persona, just to make sure he didn't think I'd made a special effort for him. Running back down the stairs, I stumbled to an alarmed halt on the bottom step. Brother Matthew wasn't there. In his place stood his older counterpart, Father Sebastian, whose bespectacled stare instantly put me on edge.

'Where's Brother Matthew?' I asked in ill-concealed panic.

'Ah, it's Leah, isn't it?' These monks were certainly good at remembering names, I'll say that much for them.

I nodded. 'Brother Matthew was going to show me to the practice room. I've got my audition at the Royal Northern College of Music next week and I need to practise.' The words tumbled out in a babble, as though I were guilty of a mortal sin.

'Yes, well I'm afraid Brother Matthew has been called to Castle Leeming rather urgently, so he's given me the keys to the practice room and asked me to take you there.'

'Castle Leeming?'

'It's our preparatory school just down the road. Our school administrator has been called away on a rather pressing matter, so I'm afraid Matthew has to fill in for her until she gets back.'

'But it's half-term,' I protested, unable to stop myself. I just knew, without a shadow of doubt, that this was merely a ruse to keep Brother Matthew away from me. Was it at that point when Father Sebastian became an enemy?

The cunning miscreant submerged his hands deep into the folds of his cassock – an avoidance technique they all used when feeling guilty, uncertain or irritated, as I was soon to work out on subsequent visits to the Benedictine lair.

'It may be half-term, young lady, but you don't for one moment think that we'd leave the castle empty for the entire week, do you?' His eyes glinted at me through the rimless lenses of his glasses that were perched ridiculously low on his beaked nose.

'Is it really a castle?' I asked, curiosity getting the better of me.

'Yes, it really is a castle.'

'And pupils actually go to school there? I mean – they actually *live* there?'

'They do indeed, though most of them go home at holiday times. The central part of the building is eight hundred years old.'

'And someone has to be there all on their own during school holidays? In an *eight-hundred year-old castle?*'

'I'm afraid so. Not the most tempting of jobs, is it? But yes, someone has to do it, and usually it ends up being one of the monks who knows it through and through, like Matthew. He went there himself as a boy, you see.'

'You mean Brother Matthew's been at this monastery practically all his *life?*'

'Yes, with a three-year break at Oxford in our novitiate seminary. It's what I'd call a true vocation.'

I could think of many other things to call it, like brainwashing, for a start.

'In actual fact, the castle is rather modest in size,' Father Sebastian went on, 'so it isn't really all that formidable. Hardly your average Windsor or Balmorral.' He chuckled, his cheeks filling out and pushing up the wrinkly flesh beneath his small eyes.

I wasn't sure what to say next. My inspiration had all at once dried up. Perhaps taking the cue, he extracted his hands from his cassock and peered at his watch. 'Right then. It's 1.45 now. That gives you just over two hours of practice before afternoon tea is served. Shall we go?'

The music room was in some dark and distant part of the monastery, tucked away within the boarding school section. Everything seemed dark and distant on that first trip to Greystones, though that might have been because it was winter, the school closed, electric lights in public corridors switched off, and the entire setting submerged in heavy snow clouds.

Father Sebastian left me to myself in the chilly practice room, after having delivered a long and complex set of instructions about how to get back to the Gatehouse. Alone at last, I sat myself down at the upright piano, altered the height of the stool, opened the lid and tried out a few keys. I breathed a sigh of relief. It was a decent instrument and I had the next two and a half hours all to myself. When transported into my own world of the piano, nothing mattered apart from the keys, my hands, and the music we created together. It was the only part of my life where I was truly confident about being myself.

Flexing my fingers, I launched into my greatest enemy: the scale of G-sharp melodic minor. All four octaves of it, up and down the breadth of the keyboard. Inspired by my fluent rendition – especially after two days without playing – I ventured forth into enemy No 2: B-flat minor. Next, I plunged into a succession of all the trickiest consecutive sixths and minor thirds, followed by a splattering of chromatic scales, and after that it was plain sailing. I was having a Good Piano Day. The kind of day when I felt like a trapeze artist who skipped and somersaulted across the keys, taking my invisible audience's breath away. Especially when achieving truly remarkable feats, such as the hellish C-sharp minor section of Chopin's third ballade, which I'd chosen as the closing piece for my audition. Apart from that, my repertoire was also going to include the first movement of Beethoven's Pathetique Sonata, and a fiendish Bach partita. So once I'd got the scales out of the way, those were the pieces I immersed myself in during the next two hours. I saved my beloved Chopin until the last, and ended up playing it so well I honestly wished there'd been an audience to applaud my dexterous performance.

So imagine my shock when, after releasing my hands from the final cadence in A-flat major that reverberated across the room, a solitary clapping met my ears. Spinning round, I found myself face to face with my sole audience member.

'Well done!' Brother Matthew called out from the open doorway, clapping a couple more times before tucking his hands back into the cavernous pockets of his habit.

'God, you scared me!' I gasped. 'Sorry – I meant *gosh*.'

Laughing, he stepped inside the room. 'Please don't apologise. Leah, that was incredible. I had no idea you played so well.'

There was something about the way he was looking at me - the clear blue of his eyes and their direct, unblinking expression - that was different from any look he'd given me before. At that moment I didn't know whether I was more thrilled by his praise, or simply by the fact that he was *there*.

'Anyway,' he went on, glancing at his watch, 'It's twenty past four now. If you don't get back to the Gatehouse soon, all the scones will be gobbled up.'

'Oh. Right.'

'I've got precisely thirty-five minutes before I need to be back at Castle Leeming, so if you like, I can accompany you back to the common room. I daresay you wouldn't remember how to get back there on your own.'

'Actually ...' I tucked a flyaway strand of hair behind my ear, 'I think I'd rather stay here and practise a bit more, if that's all right?'

He nodded. 'That's absolutely fine. Just as long as you don't get too dehydrated.'

'Oh, I won't. Sometimes I practise for five or six hours at weekends.'

He pulled down a corner of his mouth. 'My word, you *are* a dedicated young thing.'

I smiled uncertainly.

'Right, I'll leave you to it, then. See you anon.'

'How's Castle Leeming?' I quickly said, just before he took his leave.

He turned round again. 'Ah, sorry about that. I gather Father Sebastian told you I was needed over there rather urgently?'

I nodded.

'How's Castle Leeming?' he repeated, frowning in deep thought, which I soon realised was only mock perturbation as he raised a good-humoured eyebrow at me. 'Well … it's lonely. That's why I've taken a quick break for afternoon tea here, before whizzing back in the old monastic banger to my chateau.'

I gave a feeble laugh.

'But then again,' he went on, 'I don't suppose I'd be in this business if I minded loneliness, would I?'

'No, I guess not,' I said, after which neither of us spoke for a few seconds.

He threw me a final look, more penetrating than before, as though about to broach a tricky subject. But then he just smiled, turned round, and was gone.

Much later in the evening there was an outbreak of panic about one of the girls who had gone missing – Mandy Turner, I think it was. 'Gone missing' turned out to be a lot of fuss over nothing, as it happened. The girl in question was eventually located in a guest room in the monastery, having a nice cup of tea and chat with one of the monks who turned out to be an old family friend. No doubt the two of them felt rather baffled when Mother Bernadette barged in on them with accusing eyes. Apparently all was forgiven, profuse apologies abounded, and we were sent to bed with strict reminders to make sure we let Bernie know of our whereabouts at all times.

The only reason I'm mentioning this otherwise insignificant event is because it gave me an idea. A very crafty idea, which I'm sure Father Sebastian would have disapproved of wholeheartedly. And God. But then again, if God was so concerned about keeping my thoughts away from Brother Matthew, then He shouldn't have bloody well brought me to Greystones in the first place, should He?

Sorry, the 'bloody' just slipped in then. Back in those days I didn't swear. Or drink wine. You were never one for alcohol, were you, Mother? A nice cup of tea or milky coffee is what you preferred. How did you manage all life's stresses without at least the occasional stronger indulgence? Not only when Peter was killed, but also when your marriage broke down and you became a single parent looking after a teenage daughter and elderly mother, on top of coping with your B&B business. How did you manage it all?

Marriage. How did you cope with *that?*

My own wedding is less than twelve hours away. I need another glass of wine.

Did you feel like this on the night before your wedding to Dr Dermot Cavanagh, who, despite his Irish charm, never stood a chance against the ghost of Peter Fox?

CHAPTER FOUR

1

Brother Matthew often used to talk about the journeys we make during our lifetime. In many cases, these consist of just two main journeys: a first and second half of life journey. In the first half we're dominated by our ego and building our 'container' – for instance our career, our partner, setting up home, bringing up a family and so on. This sometimes goes wrong, so we start again with another container. The second half of life begins when we realise that the goals from our first journey are not enough and there must be more to life than this. Sometimes it takes a crisis to set us off thinking this way. If we learn from the crisis and begin going deeper, then we embark on another journey which is characterised by being more other-centred, more inclusive, more able to cope with paradox.

Actually, I have to admit those aren't my own words. I was reading them aloud just now from one of Brother Matthew's letters. I've got all his letters here on the coffee table, in the GOD IS HOPE box you gave me soon after I got back from Greystones on that first visit. *You'll want somewhere special to treasure his letters, darling,'* you said to me, when it must have dawned on you that this was very likely going to be the beginning of something special.

Your first journey with Peter lasted seven years. It commenced in love and hope, and ended in despair and the loss of innocence. Marrying Dermot Cavanagh was the beginning of your second journey. That's the one you could have rejected but chose not to. As a result, it led to an entire new set of journeys in an entirely new life that you shared with me.

Your journey with Peter started in the headquarters of the *Lancashire Evening Post* in Preston, and ended the day he was standing outside the *Katsellis* cinema in Kyrenia. The moment he stepped onto the hot sand of that small Mediterranean island, he didn't stand a chance. But you didn't know that at the time. You were young and in love. And a little irritated at times, as well.

Let's face it, Peter did have a habit of irritating you.

2

'What on earth is *that*?' she cried out from the doorstep of 48 Talbot Road. He laughed at her, placing his heavily-booted foot on the pavement to stop the moped from toppling over. 'This, my sweet, green lass, is a moped. My most recent possession, purchased upon the hard-earned savings of my slave labour at the *Lancashire Evening Post*. Fancy a spin?'

'What – on *that* thing?' She rolled her eyes. 'Ye gods, Peter! When you told me to be prepared for a surprise, I wasn't expecting a ... well, certainly not *that*.'

His smile wavered. 'Oh come on, Chubs, I thought you had an adventurous spirit, not like all them other boring, fuddy-duddy girls round here who're destined to become replicas of their mums.'

She sniffed, not yet fully accustomed to the unflattering nickname he'd seen fit to bestow upon her. After all, it was only her bust and hips that were on the ample side, so calling her *Chubs* did seem a teeny bit unfair.

'You're different from the lot of 'em,' he went on, casting her one of his desultory grins. 'That's why I love you.'

She caught her breath. 'You do?' The word 'love' acted like an instant palliative. She hadn't heard him enunciate such melting words in all of the three months they'd been courting.

His grin deepened. 'Ah. I thought that would perk you up. So come on then, fancy a spin or what?'

She hesitated, crushed by a surge of embarrassment and disappointment melted into one inglorious whole; but then the look on his handsome, journalistic face – not that she was sure what 'journalistic' comprised – brought a reluctant smile to her own.

'Oh, what the hell,' she said, giggling.

'That's my girl.' He winked at her.

'Just give me a minute while I change into something more suitable.'

'No rush,' he called after her as she stepped back inside. 'Me and my moped aren't going anywhere without you.'

But that's where he was wrong. Both he and his moped were in fact destined one day to go very far without her.

The clock was ticking.

After lunch Jenny, Nobbles and I set off on a walk to the local village, about two miles down the road. The snow squeaked beneath our boots and the raw air forced our breath out in short, conical bursts. The occasional crow cawed its winter's song as it flew past. A sea of white-washed fields sprawled into the horizon to our left, and on our right loomed an uninterrupted wall of forest, silent and watchful. We were like children of the Snow Queen, sent on a mission that was just up her street. The mission was simple: before returning to Lyneham-on-Sea I was to find an opportunity to arrange a private meeting with Brother Matthew, just as Mandy Turner had succeeded in doing with that other monk.

Greystones village consisted of no more than a handful of cottages, a post office, a church and a pub. We decided that the *King's Head* provided the most tempting reward after our toe-numbing walk. There were very few people in: just a solitary man reading a newspaper in a corner, two middle-aged guys leaning against the bar with their frothy pints of beer, and the bar tender. They all turned their heads as we tumbled inside, just like in one of these ghost stories where everyone gapes at the newcomers as they enter the room.

An open fire roared in the hearth, its red embers radiating heat and thawing out our fingertips and noses. Selecting a table by a misted-up window, we discarded our coats, scarves and gloves, left them in a cluttered dump on our chairs, and braved our way over to the bar. We placed orders for two half pints of cider and an orange juice and waited in silence while our drinks were being poured, all the while half expecting the kill-joy police to barge in through the door and shriek at us, *Why aren't you in the monastery, praying like good Catholic girls?*

Thanking the bartender, we took our glasses and returned to our table, relief etched onto our bright pink faces.

Jenny took the lead. Glancing over her shoulder then back at me, she launched into her plan. 'All you need do is think up some awful, heart-wrenching story and ask for his advice. For instance, you've been diagnosed with leukaemia.'

'Oh, come *on*,' Nobbles said, 'Leah couldn't possibly lie about something like that! It'd be mocking the suffering of real victims.'

Jenny groaned. 'Okay, so any better suggestions?'

Nobbles turned towards me. 'How about telling him …' She frowned. 'All right, how about this? You're considering becoming a nun, but as you aren't Catholic you don't know how to go about it.'

I pulled a face at her. 'For Gods' sake, Nobbles, that's no better a lie than saying I've got leukaemia!'

'No, it's *completely* different. You can't make up things about illness and death. But pretending you want to be a nun? I mean, you are attending a convent school, aren't you? So it's obvious that you could be secretly dreaming of joining a convent.'

Jenny gaped at her, then at me. 'She is kidding, right?'

'Lots of girls dream of becoming nuns,' our naïve co-conspirator persisted.

'Do they heck as like!'

'Okay, so what do you suggest then?'

Jenny placed her forefinger on her chin and faced me. 'Well – you don't have to mention the nun thing, but I suppose you could say something like you feel like a fish out of water at Lark Mount, with you being the only non-Catholic and all that, and you haven't got a flippin' clue what to do about it. Y'know, as in whether to convert to our faith or continue being a fish out of water till you get your A-levels and bugger off into the big wide world and forget all about religion.'

I stifled a laugh. 'Well, I wouldn't put it quite like that –'

'Or how about your gran? Isn't she old and ill? Why don't you say that she's dying and you're scared at the prospect of stumbling across her corpse one morning when you go into her room with a cuppa?'

'Can't we leave death out of it?' Nobbles said.

But the idea wasn't bad. 'It's true that Gran's health has been getting worse these past few months,' I said, cradling my cider glass in my hand, 'so I could say something about that. But I think I'd leave out the corpse bit.'

Suddenly Nobbles' eyes brightened. 'What about your audition next week? Why don't you ask him to pray for you?'

All three of us caught our breath at the genius of this latest suggestion. 'Fran, that's *brilliant!*' I said.

Jenny's dark eyes danced in merriment. Taking a slurp of cider, she put her glass back on the table with a decisive thud. Then she turned to me with the kind of focused concentration that our A-level teachers would have been proud of.

'Leah, this is what you do. A) You wait until Vespers. B) You sit at the end of the pew, so as to keep a look-out for Brother Matthew.'

'I always do that anyway.'

'So do it again. C) You wait for Brother Matthew to come down the aisle. D) When he reaches our pew, you stop him and ask if you can have a word.'

'Oh, he'll stop anyway,' Nobbles said. 'He always shows you the page numbers, doesn't he, Leah? You make sure of that.'

'*Brother Matthew*, you say in your sweetest, most innocent voice, making sure to gaze into his gorgeous blue eyes, *There's something that's been tormenting my soul and I was hoping I could have a word with you about it? I promise it won't take long, but I'd be most grateful if you could carve a little slot out of your busy monastic schedule to speak to me?*'

I spluttered into my glass. 'Jenny, I'm never going to say all that!'

'Okay, so shorten it. And then, when you've got him all to yourself in some cosy little room, you say, *The thing is, Brother Matthew, I'm at my wits' end. My grandmother is terminally ill and I'm like a fish out of water at this Catholic school my mum made me go to, and could you please be so kind as to pray for me on the day of my audition to music college?* How's that then, eh?'

'That is totally ludicrous!' Nobbles hooted in a piercing soprano, and we all burst out laughing.

The two gents at the bar turned their heads in our direction, and I distinctly heard one of them say to the bartender, 'Aren't they under-age, Bill?'

But whether it was ludicrous or not, and whether we were under-age or not, it did the trick.

As it turned out, the first stages of our plan worked beautifully. During Vespers I sat with lowered head, heart pounding, ears alert to the swishing sound that would signify Brother Matthew's entrance into the Abbey Church. At last he materialised. When he stopped by our pew to show me the pages, I glanced up at him and whispered, 'Brother Matthew, would it be possible to have a word with you?'

He seemed taken aback. For a moment I thought that the entire plan we'd concocted would backfire, and all the warmth that I'd sensed from him since the beginning of the retreat would cool right down. Silly me.

At last he whispered, 'Yes, of course. I'll be at the Gatehouse for supper, so how about afterwards, before Compline?'

'Okay,' I said, lowering my eyes to my antiphonal, determined not to stare at him as he walked away.

Back at the Gatehouse, supper was nothing short of an ordeal. I could barely eat a morsel. Neither could I listen to the jaunty chit-chat of Jenny, who was enthralled by the audacity of our plan, or Nobbles, who got cold feet when she realised I'd actually achieved the first part of it.

At the end of supper Mother Bernadette stood up and clapped her hands. 'Girls! she called out, casting her sharp stare across the room. 'When you have taken your dishes to the kitchen, we shall gather in the common room to sing some folk hymns. Leah will accompany us on the guitar, if that's all right with you, Leah?' Not waiting for my reply, she went straight on, 'After that, Sister Miriam has kindly offered to give us a slide show on her trip to Lourdes. Father Sebastian, I assume you would like to join us? Brother Matthew?' She glanced at her two holy companions sitting on either side of her.

I'm sure I could detect a flash of irritation in Brother Matthew's eyes. Nonetheless, he aimed his usual charming smile at Bernie and said something which made her laugh. Father Sebastian also laughed, so I gathered it was all sorted.

I sprinted up to my room to collect my guitar, my heart awash with anxiety. My plan was now under threat. Would there still be time for my talk with Brother Matthew before Compline?

As soon as I stepped inside the packed common room, humming with the buzz of girlish chatter, I could see that the only available space was on the sofa beneath the windows, where Brother Matthew was sitting. So I sat down beside him, placed my guitar on my lap and tried to ignore the tingling awareness of his close proximity. Once Bernie got us all quietened down, I spent the next hour strumming along to an endless cycle of folk hymns. *Oh Lord my God*, we sang, followed by *Go tell it on the mountain*, and *In spite of it all I'll start over again*, and I can't remember what else. Occasionally I heard Brother Matthew's voice joining in with the chorus. But other than that, he just sat back and listened.

When the sing-song session was finally over, as well as Sister Miriam's rather dull slide show about her trip to Lourdes, the bell for Compline tolled out from the monastery. I fought back tears of disappointment. That meant there'd be no time for our talk now. I could sense Brother Matthew's eyes on me, and wondered if he felt the same.

At last, clearing his throat, he said, 'Leah?'

I turned towards him.

'What time does your coach leave tomorrow?'

'Ten o'clock.'

'So maybe we could still squeeze in that chat in the morning?'

At that very instant a dazzling light filled the room. For a moment I honestly thought that God had swooped down to earth in a furious attempt to stop me pissing about with one of his monks.

But it wasn't God. It was Jenny and her wretched camera that she'd got for Christmas. 'Gotcha!' she teased, grinning at us as she wielded her Kodak in triumph.

Although my immediate reaction was to flush in embarrassment, I had no way of knowing at the time what a good deed Jenny had done. That photograph, so expertly capturing the very essence of Brother Matthew and me as we looked at each other, would end up becoming one of my prize possessions. Something I would draw out of my bag and stare at longingly over the coming years – all those moments when I yearned to be with him and knew that he felt the same way.

I was determined to make the most of my last morning at Greystones. Jenny and Nobbles had decided not to bother with Matins, so I told them I wouldn't either, but secretly went on my own. I somehow felt the need to. Quite apart from hoping to see Brother Matthew, I knew I had experienced something special during the last few days; something that touched me to the core and filled me with a longing I had never before felt. I wanted to seize every last moment of my stay here, before the coach hauled the lot of us back across the Pennines, back home to the dull normality of our lives. As I ran down the hill towards the monastery through the early morning darkness, with a ghostly layer of snow providing a sound-barrier between my footsteps and the surrounding silence, I felt I had at last found my way.

Brother Matthew wasn't at Matins. Pushing my disappointment aside, I sat down on the pew, shut my eyes, and tried to embrace this primordial sense of awe that Man has been invested with since time immemorial. But the awe didn't last long. As the twenty-minute service approached its end, my thoughts became more and more clouded, smothered in a panic as thick as any sea fog I had ever witnessed through my bedroom window back home. It was my last morning; in a few minutes it would be Lauds, then breakfast, and then I'd be gone, a prisoner in the coach back to Lyneham-on-Sea. I hadn't even established with Matthew where and when to meet for our talk. Okay, he'd probably be at breakfast, but I didn't want to risk leaving arrangements till then. What if he didn't turn up? What if he was called back to Castle Leeming? What if Father Sebastian had overheard our brief exchange in the common room last night and concocted some Machiavellian plan to keep us apart?

The closing psalm echoed across the room. One by one, the monks trooped out in solemn procession, each of them making the sign of the cross as they passed the central altar and disappeared into the shadows. I didn't make a move myself. I continued to sit there all on my own, with nothing but the lingering smell of incense and the soft light of the altar candle to keep me company. Then I heard the door open behind me, followed by the tell-tale sound of a monk making his way down the aisle. I held my breath.

Stopping by my side, the monk leaned down to me and whispered, 'Leah?'

Of course it was him. My Matthew. I could feel his warm breath.

'I'm glad I've caught you now,' he whispered. 'I'm afraid I won't be at the Gatehouse for breakfast this morning.'

'Oh?' I swallowed. So this was it. The End. He'd been called back to Castle Leeming.

'I didn't want you to leave Greystones thinking I'd forgotten all about the talk you asked for.'

'Why won't you be at breakfast?'

'I'll be having it in the monks' refectory this morning. We have a special guest from another monastery who I've been asked to look after.'

'Right.'

'So why don't you come down here after breakfast and we can go to the Visitor's Lodge? That's a nice private place to have a chat. I'll wait for you in the entrance to the monastery at 8.30. Would that give you enough time?'

My heart thudded. There WAS a God, after all! 'Erm – yes, I think so.'

'Splendid. Right, so 8.30 it is.' Then he straightened up and was on his way.

I could hardly eat a thing for breakfast. If this state of affairs went on much longer, I reckoned that I'd die of starvation. I did at least drink all my tea, and as soon as my cup was empty I stood up and excused myself from the table, hoping I didn't go bright red as Jenny gave me a knowing wink.

In my room, I put a dab of *Blue Grass* on each wrist, brushed my unruly hair and glanced in the mirror. Not bad. Then I skipped back down the stairs, out of the Gatehouse, out into the crisp morning air, all the way down the driveway to the monastery. I spotted him as soon as I pushed open the main door. He was standing inside the entrance, as promised, his shadowed form hovering in the middle of the corridor.

When he saw me, he stepped forward. 'Ah, so you made it.'

I nodded, still out of breath. But at least I managed a smile. He smiled back, his eyes lingering on mine. Then he squared his shoulders and said, 'Right. Let's go.'

The Visitor's Lodge was in a cluttered pile of outbuildings that I hadn't previously noticed. I followed Brother Matthew up a wooden staircase, across a gloomy landing, then yet more stairs. As soon as we entered the guest lounge my eyes gorged on the scene. Ancient stone fireplace, Persian rug sprawled across the floor like a giant sleeping cat, book-lined alcoves on either side of the hearth, latticed windows that allowed a soft amber glow to filter in from the lights of the monastery. It was as if we were in someone's private castle.

'Crikey, who lives here?' I asked without thinking.

Brother Matthew laughed. 'No one actually lives here. It's reserved for non-clerical VIPs. But as there isn't anyone booked in at the moment, I thought it would be a nice private place for us to have our chat. Please, sit down.' He indicated two luxurious damask armchairs.

It's hard to recall exactly what we talked about during the next half-hour. I only know that I relaxed with him in a way I wouldn't have imagined possible. I told him about Gran's ill health and my ambivalent feelings for my father, who I was duty-bound to visit every summer. I told him about my sea-view attic room and how it had become rather like my own monastic sanctuary. (I was pleased to note that this brought a smile to his lips.) I told him how I longed to have a deep-rooted faith, like all the other girls at Lark Mount. I asked him to think of me at my audition, and he promised to say a special prayer for me on the day.

When all that was done and dusted, I somehow found the courage to ask him about himself. I learned that he'd been born in India and his parents had died in a railroad accident when he was seven years old. He'd then been whisked off to England to live with his grandmother in Cumbria.

'She was my only living relative,' he explained in that suave, sophisticated voice that made me go weak at the knees. 'Although she loved me dearly, she found it hard to cope with the demands of a small child. So I was sent to Castle Leeming Preparatory School, and only visited her for school holidays.'

'So that's how the Benedictines got hold of you, then,' I said before I could stop myself. But I needn't have worried; he appeared to be amused by my bluntness.

'Yes, I suppose you could say that,' he said with a rueful smile. 'I've been in their clutches from the age of eight. First Leeming, then Greystones, then St Benet's Hall at Oxford to read theology, then back to Greystones. It took me another nine years before becoming a fully-fledged Benedictine monk.'

'Crikey!' I said, grinning, my confidence rising by the second. I worked out that he must be twenty-seven years old, which seemed quite an awe-inspiring age compared to my seventeen years. I also discovered that he taught Latin and theology at Greystones Boarding School, and helped out in the Gatehouse during retreats. But when I pushed a little further and suggested that he'd never had any choice about his life's path, for once he didn't smile.

'No, Leah,' he said in what I came to recognise as his school-masterly voice. 'We all have choices to make, and mine was to enter the religious life. I'm convinced that I'd have chosen that path, no matter where I was brought up or where I went to school. It was something deep within me that I've felt as far back as I can remember. A journey I had to take. In simple terms, you can call it a spiritual calling. A vocation.'

'So are you happy with it?'

'Yes, I'm happy,' he replied, stroking the light bristle on his chin and staring straight ahead. I hadn't noticed any bristle before, and I liked it. It made him seem more like an ordinary man. So did the way he was sitting: deeply relaxed within the folds of his armchair, his long legs fanned out, the black material of his habit stretched across his knees. I myself sat opposite him, my own legs daintily crossed. Were we born with these intuitive postures of the sexes, I wondered, or did society impose them upon us in the same way that the monastic life had been imposed upon him, whether he believed it or not?

The half-hour passed all too quickly. Next thing I knew, he was sitting forward, his face suddenly closer to mine. 'Well then, Leah, I'm afraid our time's up,' he said, sounding more like a teacher than ever. Were people really defined by their jobs? When I had only known him as a monk he seemed like the epitome of monkliness, including all the forbidden associations. Now that I knew he taught at the boarding school, I recognised all the tell-tale signs of the archetypal teacher. What did he recognise in me, I wondered? Schoolgirl, musician, dreamer?

He stood up. 'You must let me know how you get on at your audition.'

'Oh, I will,' I said, tingling all over. 'So ... should I write to you when I find out the result?'

'Yes, by all means, please do.'

'How should I address the envelope?'

'Just Greystones Abbey, York. There's a postcode as well, but you can look that up later on, because if I tell you now I daresay you'll forget it.'

'But what about your name? Should I just write "Brother Matthew"?'

'Brother Matthew Haddon, OSB,' he corrected, as though I were one of his pupils. But somehow I didn't mind. I knew that he was enjoying my company. 'The OSB stands for Order of St Benedict.'

'Matthew Haddon,' I echoed. 'That has a lovely ring to it.' And so it did. Leah Haddon would have been even nicer. Mrs Leah Haddon.

'Better make sure you get back to the Gatehouse on time. We wouldn't want the bus to go off without you, now would we?'

'Oh, I wouldn't mind that,' I said, risking my very first flirtatious smile at him.

Judging by his flustered response, and then the quieter mood that descended upon him as we walked back up the hill towards the Gatehouse, both of us blinking the snow out of our eyes, I'd say my tactics worked. I was learning fast.

The next few minutes rushed past in a flurry of activity. I hurried up to my room to strip my bed and pack my things, then trudged back down laden with travelling bag, guitar and winter's coat. In all the commotion of twenty-four disorderly sixth form girls being shepherded onto the coach, I didn't even get the chance to say goodbye to Brother Matthew. Next thing I knew, I was squeezed in between Jenny and Nobbles on the back row.

Over the next three hours the bus sped its way through the thick whiteness of the Yorkshire Dales and Pennines. The snow thinned as we got closer to Lyneham-on-Sea, with the passing towns and villages becoming greyer and wetter by the minute. I barely managed to make appropriate responses to the constant chatter of Jenny and Nobbles, my mind still swimming in the memory of Brother Matthew and me as we walked up the hill from the monastery, blinking the snow out of our eyes. And I suddenly knew, with a clairvoyant's certainty, that he would now be a part of my life forever.

CHAPTER FIVE

1

And now, Mother, it's your turn! Enter Molly Cavanagh, protagonist of all my life's journeys.

Imagine the scene. I have just stepped inside the entrance hall at Belle Vue. I've dropped my bags and guitar case on the floor, and am bombarded by a fortissimo gush of *Stranger in Paradise*. You've put it on maximum volume on our old record player, so that a wave of vibrato strings and backing chorus and Tony Benett's rich tenor voice envelopes me in the 1950s magic of your youth. You haven't yet spotted me, but I can see you in the distance, through the open door to our private quarters at the back of the house. You're wearing the floral print dress that I adore you in, with a wide belt that accentuates your curvaceous figure, and you're dancing. I can't see the person you're dancing with, because he isn't there. Your arms are stretched out round his invisible neck and your eyes are closed as you and Peter Fox sway to the music. I release a long, contented sigh. The B&B guests are evidently otherwise occupied, and I can see that you're in one of your magical-romantic moods. I'm very glad about this, because so am I.

I tiptoe across the hall, not wanting to disturb you. Leaning against the doorframe and folding my arms, a faraway smile comes to my lips as I stand there watching you, admiring you. I am so very, very glad to be home again, back with you. All the pain of leaving Greystones Abbey and Brother Matthew is washed away by the simple act of seeing you swaying to the music, dancing with the ghost of Peter Fox. Ah, Mother! You are the world to me. The whole wide world.

When the sentimental strains of the music come to an end, I step forward, beam at you and announce, 'Mother, I'm home!'

You spin round, jolted out of your reverie.

'*Darling*! I wasn't expecting you till – ' You glance at your watch. 'Heavens above, is that the time? Where has the afternoon gone?'

I laugh in pure, giddy happiness at seeing you again. We hurry over to each other, collapsing into a huge, back-squeezing embrace. The scent of *Blue Grass* upon your skin envelopes me in your evocative aura.

When the next track on the record clicks into gear, I pull away a little. 'Could you put it a bit lower, do you think, so we can talk? I've got *so* much to tell you.'

'And I want to hear all of it right this minute! Oh Leah darling, you've no idea how much I've been thinking about you these past four days. I know that something's up – I could hear it in your voice when you phoned. It's that old sixth sense of mine.'

Without waiting for a response, you skip over to the record player and turn down the volume. Then you fly back to me, take my hand in yours and lead me over to the dining table.

'Now sit yourself down while I put the kettle on and get you something to eat. I want to hear every last little detail about Greystones.'

'To spare you the tension, I can tell you the main news right now.'

'You've fallen in love!'

I gape at you. 'But - how did you know?'

You toss me an exasperated look. 'Heaven's above, Leah, I'm your mother, aren't I? Of *course* I knew. I could tell from just one glance at you that you're in love and you want the whole wide world to know it.'

Before you start launching into yet another of your favourite songs, I quickly say, 'Why don't you make that cup of tea while I nip upstairs to unpack my things? Then I'll tell you everything.'

'Oh, do try to be quiet on your way up, darling. Gran's having a nap and I wouldn't want you to wake her. She had another funny turn this morning when she was getting up. I was just on my way to the kitchen when I heard this big thump coming from her room – you can imagine my alarm, can't you? But as luck would have it, Mr Tomlinson happened to be passing by –'

'Oh no, he's not still here, is he?'

'Afraid so. It seems that wild horses wouldn't keep him away from his beloved Belle Vue Mansions, even though nothing is *ever* right for him. Ye gods! – you'd think he'd been brought up in Buckingham Palace, the way he goes on about his bedding not being soft enough, or the toast not hot enough, or the seagulls making too much of a din -'

'So is Gran all right now?'

'Well, Dr Conlon gave her some more of those tablets that she's forever grumbling about – you know, with what they do to her bowel movements and all those details we never want to hear about but she always insists on telling us about -'

'So *is* she all right?'

'It would seem so, judging by the mood she had on her this morning. She's been told to take things easy so as to keep her blood pressure down, so I think it's best you don't practise the piano today, just to be on the safe side. You know how she gets all het-up about it when you start on your scales – yes, I *know* it's a bother, darling, but she's an old woman now and we have to think of her health.'

'Mother, Gran has been an old woman all my life.'

'To you she may well have been, but not to me. And she won't be around forever, so I think we need to show her a little respect.'

I sigh. 'Okay, I suppose I'll survive. Anyway, I've got lots of catching up to do on my diary.'

'Not until you've told me absolutely *everything* about your retreat. Now hurry up and unpack. I don't want you to miss out a single detail.'

I make my way to the door, then turn round and ask, 'How long is Mr Tomlinson staying this time?'

'Just till Sunday, so don't you worry – I can manage him for another couple of days. Do you know, it's quite sad really, but I'm sure he's got a bit of a crush on me.'

'Mother, *everyone* has a bit of a crush on you. It's not fair.'

Your eyes crease in a youthful mirth that belies your forty-seven years. 'Don't be ridiculous. Now go on, up those stairs with you. And when you come back down you can tell me all about this fellow of yours. What's his name?'

'Brother Matthew.'

'*Brother* Matthew?'

'Brother Matthew Haddon.' I stare straight ahead, remembering the snow-covered driveway as we walked up to the Gatehouse together, knowing that in a few minutes we'd be saying goodbye to each other.

'Hell's bells, that's one for the books!' you say, but your laugh softens into a sigh. Not one of irritation, nor impatience, but a kind of loving exasperation. You know me too well, that's the trouble. 'I might have known. You are my daughter, after all. You wouldn't just settle for one of the dashing teachers at the boarding school, would you? Or one of the handsome sixth form boys. Oh, no, it had to be no less than one of the monks.'

The humour is making its way back to your eyes, but not mine. I feel a lump rising in my throat. Pressing the back of my hand against my mouth, I swallow and look away.

'Oh, darling – don't cry! I'm so sorry, I didn't mean to be flippant. Heaven's above, you *have* got it bad.' Next thing I know, you rush over to my side and encase me in your arms.

That does it. The floodgates are opened. The fall-out of my entire Greystones experience crashes right over me in your warm, protective arms. Even if Brother Matthew never ends up loving me, at least you always will. Yours is a love that will never fade or get bored or be fickle or die.

Backward, turn backward, oh Time in your flight, make me a child again just for tonight …

But on that February afternoon of 1978 when I'd just come home from my Greystones retreat, it wasn't your love I was crying about. It was Matthew's. Of course I'd got it bad. You were right, as always. The simple fact of the matter was that I couldn't bear the prospect of living the rest of my life and never seeing him again.

As if that was ever going to happen!

2

Do you remember placing that obituary in the *Lancashire Evening Post* after Peter died? And the New Year's Eve party, six years earlier, which was one of the happiest days of your life? At the time, how could you possibly have known what Kismet had in store for you? Kismet. Your favourite word. My most hated.

* * *

It was December 1950, just three days before New Year's Eve. They were an item now: Molly and Peter. She loved the sound of that. She was walking towards the stairs in the *Lancashire Evening Post* building when he called out to her.

'Molly, wait …' He hurried down the corridor. 'New Year's Eve?'

She stopped and turned to him. 'What about it?'

'Leo and I are throwing a bit of a bash. You've *got* to come, Chubs – please, no excuses.'

'What, not another of your wild all-nighters?' She raised her eyebrow in pretend-disdain. Of course she'd go to it, not that he need know that immediately. *Let him stew for a bit*, her younger but wiser sister would often advise.

'Well, it might not last *quite* that -'

'Oh, all right, go on then.'

'You will? You'll come? Oh Chubs, that's brilliant!'

'Heaven's above, Peter, it's only a party. What's all the fuss about?'

Three days later she found out.

The flat he shared with Leo Baxendale heaved with bodies, the air thick with cigarette fumes, booze, sweat, thrumming music. Peter kept evading her line of vision, but minutes later his eyes would find hers again and she'd shudder under the power of his Svengali gaze. In between chain-smoking his Benson & Hedges and topping up his mates' pints and dancing with whatever wasp-waisted woman happened to be at hand - the two of them swinging about to the jitterbug strains that blared from the gramophone player (she tried not to be jealous, but her efforts dwindled as the years multiplied) - he kept throwing her these perturbed glances. Her friend Marge also noticed. 'Why does he keep giving you them peculiar looks?' she loudly whispered at one point during the evening, causing Molly to snort into her gin & tonic glass, the fizzy liquid bubbling up her nostrils. She wasn't used to drinking alcohol and never developed a taste for it, unlike her future daughter.

At exactly five minutes to midnight, she discovered what the peculiarity was about.

Appearing out of nowhere, Peter pounced upon the two friends, slicing their girlish natter in two.

'Chubs, come with me, quickly!'

'Do you *mind*?' Marge snapped at him in the Lancashire drawl that her best friend Molly had managed to rid herself of, courtesy of the Preston Amateur Dramatic Society.

'Oh, sorry, but the thing is –' he peeped at his watch, then back at Marge. 'The thing is, there's summat I've got to ask Molly about before I forget.'

'What, on flippin' New Year's Eve?'

But it was too late, because he was already half-way across the smoky room, tugging his girlfriend along close behind. At last they found themselves in a quieter room where all the coats had been dumped. Peter closed the door behind him, then drew her closer to him and looked down at her with those eyes which she grew both to love and fear.

'Molly, here's the thing …'

'It's not that naughty *bras and knickers* game again, is it?' She stifled a chuckle.

'No, I just wanted to ask you summat.'

'Can't it wait till 1951? There's only a few minutes left of 1950 – heavens above, only a few seconds! Where on earth did the time ...'

But her voice was swallowed up as the entire, assembled congregation beyond the closed door chanted in boozy unison: '*Eight, seven, six, five, four, three, two, one ...* '

And there they were – 1951. The horns from Preston Docks hooted in the distance; the partying throngs cheered, the champagne corks popped, the grandfather clock chimed from the hallway, and Peter ... what was it he whispering into her ear? Why was he holding her hands so tightly, looking at her so imploringly ...

'*Will* you?' he repeated, stooping to kiss her on the lips, then standing back to examine her astounded face. 'Will you marry me, my darling, beloved Chubs?'

For a moment she thought he was being ironic, but when he kissed her again, more urgently, holding her against him in that typically manic way he had when in one of his dead-earnest moods, she knew it was no joke.

That's probably why she chose to put *Always remembered, from his beloved Chubs* in his obituary, six years later. Because she *was* his beloved Chubs, and always would be, and of course she said 'yes'.

Ever since that day, whenever the clock strikes midnight on New Year's Eve, she has to take a deep breath to hold back the tears. The bells of New Year's Eve will always ring out the memory of her beloved Peter. They will always do that, till the day she dies.

It's the day of my audition for the Royal Northern College of Music. The weather is tranquil, as though trying to calm the frenetic rush of adrenaline within me. I think you're even more nervous than I am, though you're determined not to show it.

We're on the 7.45 am train to Manchester Piccadilly, sitting opposite one another in the almost-empty compartment. My hands are clasped upon my music notes, which in turn are resting upon my lap. My eyes are glued to the window as though it were a screen, and I a spectator at the cinema. I gape at the bare fields and stripped trees that rush past. The thin morning sky is flecked with shreds of clouds, a pale winter's sun hanging over scattered farm houses that eject skeins of smoke into the air. It's as if the entire scene had been borrowed from a Constable painting entitled *Reflections on a winter's morn*.

Your face is also turned to the window. As I redirect my gaze to your profile, I'm filled with a recollection of your past which merges into my future. The relentless missing of someone who is no longer there. But at least you have me.

Your eyes flit across to mine as though sensing my gaze. We smile at each other.

'All right, darling?'

'Yes, fine.'

'I wouldn't bother looking through your notes anymore.'

'I'm not.'

'Well, don't forget to give them to me before you go in. I wouldn't want them thinking you needed the music in case you had a memory lapse. The first impression is *so* important, Leah. Always remember that.'

But I'm not in the mood for one of your lectures, however well-meaning, so I don't reply. After a few moment's silence, you ask: 'Not too nervous?'

I shrug. 'What's the worst that could happen? If I'm not accepted, I'll just have to go to a different music college. I'm sure someone will take pity on me.'

'Oh, Leah, don't even joke about it. Anyone would be a fool not to have you.'

As always, you're my number one fan. I smile at you, though at times I have to admit it's quite a burden, having a mother who is convinced that I'm the best in absolutely everything: the most beautiful, the most talented, soon destined to be the most successful in music and everything else.

I sweep such thoughts out of my mind. 'You know what I'm looking forward to most?' I ask, my eyes resting on yours.

'No, what's that, darling?'

'Walking out of the audition room when it's all over and finding a nice place for lunch.'

If only life were that simple.

* * *

I'm sitting outside the audition room, awaiting my turn. I've been given half an hour to warm up in a practice room on the third floor. The time has galloped past way too quickly. Next thing I know, a plump middle-aged lady trundles along to tell me that I should make my way down to the audition room on the first floor. I get the jitters even now, just thinking about the whole process of auditioning. It's rather like performing a striptease act. Basically, you're expected to expose your innermost musical soul, right down to the very last layer, in front of a panel of leering adjudicators who are there to watch, judge and comment, though at least they don't whistle. How do we get through it? How do we get through any of the ordeals that life throws at us? How do we survive?

The door to the audition room opens. I jump up from my chair in reflex action.

'Miss Cavanagh? Would you care to come through?'

A tall, lean man with thinning hair smiles down at me as he holds open the door. *Manners maketh man,* you always used to say. But manners are the very last thing on my mind at this moment, as I step inside the unexpectedly large room, say hello to the three anonymous faces, and walk across to the grand piano several feet away. I sit down on the stool, which is too low, so I adjust it to my height. Then I turn round to my panel of judges, and wait.

'So, Leah, what are you going to play for us first?' the tall one asks.

'The Bach partita,' I reply in a hoarse voice. But nerves are normal, so I'm not fazed. Nerves give adrenalin, and adrenalin is what makes every performance unique. Without adrenalin, a brilliant robot might as well play.

'Splendid,' the man says, which makes my heart stop. It's like déjà vu. I'm hearing Brother Matthew speak in another man's body. *Splendid.* I've been thrown completely off balance. This is not good. This is not the time to start thinking about Brother Matthew. This is *too* much adrenalin. Too much is just as bad as too little. I'd got it just right a moment ago, damn it, and here I am, thrown completely off course because of hearing the word *splendid* enunciated in a posh voice that reminds me of my faraway monk, who is now looming before my eyes.

'Everything all right?'

'Yes, fine.' *Focus.* I've set my heart and soul on this music college. It's one of the best in the country. If I don't get in, I'll be crushed.

'Well, when you're ready, then.'

I turn away from them and face the keyboard, which suddenly spreads out before me like a surreal representation of Mount Everest. Place it vertically, and it would be just as hard to climb. Especially now that Brother Matthew's crystal-blue eyes are consuming the forefront of my mind, covering up my musical soul and ambitions, as though he can't bear to see them nakedly exposed.

I have to stop this. Pushing back my hair, I flex my fingers and position my hands above the keys. I count silently to five, listening in my mind to the first few bars I'm about to play. And then I start.

* * *

Forty-five minutes later, it's all over.

You jump up from your chair as soon as you see me walking towards you in the plush foyer. I'm not quite sure whether I should be smiling, frowning or crying. I don't know what message to convey via my facial expressions, because I honestly can't tell how I've done.

Holding out your hands to me as I approach, you ask in an anxious voice, 'So? How was it?'

'Okay, I guess.'

'*Okay*? Is that all?'

'Oh, Mother, please don't push. I honestly couldn't tell what they thought. It was like all their responses were cloned.'

'But how did you play?'

'All right. Just a couple of slips, nothing too drastic.'

'Oh.' Your face drops. 'You didn't make any slips at the preliminary audition, did you?'

'No, but my programme for that wasn't as ambitious. Anyway, they were only *slips*, not whopping great mistakes.'

'What about the Chopin Ballade?'

'Okay, I guess. Just a bit mushy in the C-sharp minor section. But I think I managed to pull it off, in the main.'

You continue to look concerned for a moment or two; then you switch over to positive mode and give me one of your heartiest smiles. 'Well, not to worry, darling. It's all over now. Whatever those old fuddy-duddies decide, I'll still love you never-stop-growing.'

You draw me into your arms and hold me tight. When we eventually let go of each other, you say in a breezy voice, 'I don't know about you, but I'm famished! How about something to eat?'

Little do I realise what's in store for me a week later.

CHAPTER SIX

1

On my last day of being seventeen, you and I met at the *Beach Front Café* after school. I got there first and bought myself a milky coffee from the self-service counter before heading for our favourite window table. Placing my schoolbag on the floor, I sat down, cupped my chin in my hands and rested my eyes on our much-loved view. It was a sombre day: pewter clouds hung low over the horizon, with threadbare patches of mist folding into the distant tide of the Irish Sea.

As soon as you stepped inside the café I waved at you. Your face lit up when you spotted me and you gave me a wave back. When it came to your turn in the queue, I watched as you chatted away to the girl at the cash till, your perennial charm bringing a smile to her face. After bidding her farewell, you picked up your tray and made your way towards me. You were lumbered with bulky shopping bags that hung from the crook of your arms.

I pulled a face. 'I thought you said we could do the shopping together.'

'And so we will, darling,' you said, drawing out the chair opposite me, dumping your bags on the floor and placing your tea and scone on the Formica table top. 'I just thought it would give us more time to chat if I got the basic things out of the way first. But don't worry, there's still the birthday cake to choose - I wouldn't dream of doing that without you! And we still need some starter nibbles - nuts and crisps and things for when people arrive. And also wine, of course - or perhaps sherry?' You wafted your hand like the Queen of Sheba. 'Oh, let's have both!'

I smiled at your irrepressible enthusiasm. But the prospect of our small family gathering the following day was not at the forefront of my mind. The truth was that I'd been waiting with bated breath to show you something special. Something very special indeed.

'Anyway, darling,' you went on, moving your chair closer to the table. 'First of all, tell me how your day was.'

Barely concealing my pleasure, I extracted an envelope from my school-bag and placed it on the table in front of you.

'Ooh, what's this? A birthday card from a secret male admirer?'

'What, in an all-girls school?' I giggled. 'No, it's a photo. But when you see it, I think you'll know why I'm so happy.'

You opened the envelope and drew out the photograph. The one that Jenny had taken of me and Brother Matthew. Your face beamed when you looked at it. 'Oh, darling, you look *gorgeous*. And who is it you're smiling at –' Then you stopped. 'Is it him? Your monk?'

I nodded. 'It's Brother Matthew. What d'you think?'

You sighed. 'I think he's extremely handsome. And just look how everyone is staring at the two of you! My word, the atmosphere must have been electric. Do you know, he reminds me slightly of …' A faraway look swept across your eyes.

'Don't tell me. He reminds you of Peter Fox.'

You raised your slender fingers to your chin. 'Well, maybe just the tiniest bit. But it's not that. It's – it's just seeing young love in bloom … oh darling, it's such a *wonderful* thing.'

Immediately I felt crushed by guilt. How could I have felt irritated with you, the best mother in the world – someone who combined parent, friend and dream-conspirator all in one?

You took a sip of your tea. 'You know, darling, with it being your eighteenth birthday tomorrow, I can't help but remember my own big day. Oh, I know that eighteenths are all the rage nowadays, but in my time it was twenty-firsts. And you know how I celebrated it, don't you?'

'Peter Fox took you to Paris.'

Your eyes filled with stars as you gazed past my head, out of the window at the silvery etching of sea way out on the horizon, 'He so loved travelling. Europe, Turkey, the Middle East, always with that blasted moped of his.

He saved every penny he earned to put into his travels. Had he lived, he would have made a perfect Foreign Correspondent.'

'Well, at least he saw a lot of the world.'

'Oh, Leah, it was the most romantic trip of my life.' You were no longer listening to me, now that you'd gone to Foxland. 'Paris – can you imagine it? What a place to be young and in love! We were surrounded by the very essence of beauty – the *Eiffel Tower, Montmartre, the Sacre Coeur, Notre Dame …*' you pronounced each name with an increasingly Anglo-French accent, 'eating our baguettes and cheese on the banks of the Seine, all the time laughing and loving each other – in every sense of the word.' Suddenly you went coy. 'You know what I mean.'

I smiled indulgently, but remained silent.

'Of course I can't pretend our love was perfect. If it had been, we'd have got married, wouldn't we? But the trouble was with Peter, things kept getting in the way. His work, his travel, his moods, his depression about the state of the world, his dreams to make it a better place … oh, Leah, what fools we were! Every time Peter suggested looking for an engagement ring, I ummed and ahhed about it, and whenever *I* suggested that we set a date for the wedding, he suddenly remembered about his flaming travel plans. Your Gran always said that we wanted our heads knocking together. She really loved Peter.'

'Yes, I know.'

'He was like a son to her.'

'I *know.*'

'He always treated her like his own mother, because his real mother died before I ever met him – and as his father was in a care home because of some unfortunate mental condition, you can see how Peter was all alone in the world.'

I glanced at my watch. I couldn't help feeling a little impatient. It was supposed to be my turn now, not yours and Peter's. Much as I loved hearing your stories, this was not the time.

But you pushed straight on: 'No wonder he so loved coming over to our house and being fussed by your Gran. It could have been so perfect, if only he hadn't …'

'I know,' I filled in.

It was too late. There was no stopping you now. Your eyes misted over as you stepped back into the past, remembering your twenty-first birthday.

* * *

'So what hotel is it you've booked into, then?' Mrs Williams asked Peter the day he bought the tickets for Paris. It was early evening. The four of them were sitting round the kitchen table, with the old brown teapot plonked in its customary position in the centre.

'Oh, it's just one of them small places in the Latin Quarter,' he said, flicking the ash from his cigarette into the stained ashtray that Mr Williams had used for the past thirty years.

'And your rooms will be on the same floor, will they?'

This was met by a loud snigger from Doreen. '*Mother,* will you leave them alone!' she said with her hand over her mouth as she glanced at her older sister, Molly. Their eyes sparkled at the unspoken innuendos that hung in the air of the staid terrace home.

'Now that's no way to speak to your mam,' Mr Williams said, trying to be stern but failing miserably, as usual.

Peter remained cool as ever. 'Yep, we're both on the second floor,' he said, stubbing out his cigarette and reaching for another piece of Mrs William's Lancashire parkin. 'Two single rooms with balconies, breakfast included. Café au lait and croissants. It's going to be fab, isn't it, Chubs?'

He winked at his fiancé, and she blushed. She knew for a fact that he'd booked a double room. She was twenty-one, he was twenty-five; they'd been engaged for almost half a year, yet she could not bear to admit the secret of the double room to her parents. But whereas Peter found the whole deception amusing, she was mortified by it.

Exactly one week later they stepped into their double room at *Hotel Balzac* in the Latin Quarter. They'd both discussed sleeping arrangements many times before, but now, suddenly, she felt nervous. Peter had made her swear upon oath that he wasn't pushing her into anything she'd later regret, yet still she felt nervous. After all, it *was* her first time – and she didn't mean in Paris.

As she placed her suitcase on the small mat by the entrance, her ears tuned into the sound of Peter closing the door behind them. The *click* of the lock emphasised the imminent carnality of their situation. She shuddered.

Forcing the actress within her to take control, she raised her chin and walked across the bare floorboards to the window. It was mid-afternoon, with a sultry Parisian sun that ejected its burnished rays through the half-open slats of the continental blinds. The hotel was on a narrow side street surrounded by other tenement buildings from the turn of the century, so there wasn't much of a view, but she loved it all the same. It was all so utterly *foreign*. Wrought iron balconies faced the room from across the street, with clusters of geraniums spilling out of pretty window baskets. The lively sounds of a fruit and vegetable market two storeys below echoed upon Parisian cobblestones, and the thin chimes of a church bell – so very different from the loud clanging and clattering of English steeples – wafted towards her from a distant tower that peeked out above the red-tiled rooftops. What a perfect setting, she thought, her nervousness gradually melting away. She was young and in love and had the rest of her life in front of her. They both did. Or so they thought.

However, she didn't have the chance to think much more than that, because Peter's footsteps were approaching from behind. Next thing she knew, he rested his hands on her shoulders and buried his head into the back of her neck, kissing her hot, burning skin. Turning her round to face him, he touched her cheek with his forefinger and whispered, 'Okay?'

'Hmm,' she replied, for once lost for words.

'I do love you, you know.'

She forced a smile out of her dry lips. 'I know.'

He scowled. 'Er – sorry, but I think this is where you're supposed to respond by saying, *Oh darling, I love you too!*'

Normally she would have giggled, but somehow, she couldn't. He took a step back from her, folded his arms and peered into the deep brown eyes he so adored. He'd even written a poem about them once, although in fact it was more of a limerick. Well, it *was* a limerick. She could still remember it, whether she wanted to or not.

> *There was a young lassie from Preston*
> *Whose eyes were quite gorgeous, no question.*
> *But most won'drous of all*
> *Fore'er to enthrall –*
> *Were those whopping great bosoms to rest on.*

'C'mon, Molly, what's the matter?'

'Nothing.'

'You're not having second thoughts, are you? About the double room?'

'No, of course not.'

'I don't want to force you into doing anything you're unhappy about. You do believe that, Chubs, don't you?'

The endearing nickname she'd first hated, then accepted, then grown to love, seemed to do the trick. Facing his dark eyes full on, she said, 'Yes, I believe you, Peter. And I *do* love you. Very, very much.'

For a moment she thought she detected something wonderful in his gaze as it held her own; something deep and glorious and eternal; something that whispered a pledge never, ever to let go, never to relinquish the bond between them that had been formed in the stars. But then he grinned his usual wicked grin, unfolded his arms and said, 'Oh, well that's good to know.'

Taking her hand in his own, he led her across the room to the king-size Parisian bed.

* * *

And now, back at the *Beach Front Café* twenty-six years later, your eyes fill up as you remember the future that Kismet deprived you of.

'If only he'd never met Dermot,' you say in a shaky voice. 'If only he'd never gone to Cyprus ...'

'Which means I would never have been born,' I gently remind you.

But you aren't listening. Your tea cup is cradled between your hands, your eyes resting on the distant sea. I can see that we're going to be here all day if we're not careful. Which would be fine normally, but right at the moment I've got so much else on my mind.

'Oh Leah, I can only pray that he didn't suffer, that he died instantly when -'

'He died in the ambulance, so it must have been quick.'

'Yes, but I mean in those very first few seconds – did he realise what was going on? Did he think of me as they carried him away on a stretcher? Did he think of me as he was dying?'

'I'm sure he did.' I reach for your hand and squeeze it.

The unshed tears in your eyes are in danger of spilling over. It's time to change the subject. It's all very tragic, but it happened a long time ago. Don't get me wrong. Normally I wouldn't be feeling impatient like this. I've always loved hearing you talk about Peter, especially about your Paris trip. I've always adored the framed photograph of the two of you standing arm in arm on the steps of the *Sacre Coeur*, grinning self-consciously at the stranger who agreed to take your picture. I've also always loved the photo of you and Peter in the Beacon Fells, on one of your many day trips. You know the one I mean – with Peter looking through a telescope and you standing by his side, peering through a pair of binoculars. You both look so young, so glamorous, so *chic*. I remember in my childhood I once asked you what you what you were trying to see through those magic lenses, and you replied, 'The future, darling. The future that Peter and I should have had.'

However, I need to move on. It's *my* turn now.

2

It was my eighteenth birthday. I'd wanted to spend the day just with you: go on a day trip somewhere, have lunch in an old-worldly place with beamed ceilings, browse round cluttered second-hand shops, stop in a twee café for scones and cucumber sandwiches … all the things we so loved doing whenever you managed to get away from Belle Vue. But on this occasion you stated categorically that family is family, and so a family gathering it was to be.

You thought very carefully about the seating plan in our dining room, deciding to place Gran between you and me so that we could keep an eye on her – not so much regarding her health, but to stop her from grumbling. Opposite from us we placed Auntie Doreen and Uncle Paul, my cousin Sandra, and Great Auntie Ivy. That was it. That constituted the grand total of the 'family gathering'. They were just about the only relatives I knew, not counting Dad's sprawling mob in Southern Ireland, who I only saw once a year. But I liked it that way.

The birthday dinner turned out okay in the end. I adored my main present: a gold-plated pendant that Peter had given you for some occasion or other, and which you now presented me with, accompanied by a theatrical speech that made your eyes glisten dangerously. I loved the atmosphere you created in our dining room – the high-backed Art Nouveau chairs which bestowed a certain regality on our meagre party, the antique lace table cloth bedecked with monogrammed cutlery bought at a flea market, the huge brass candelabra that cast spectral shadows from centre-table … My own contribution to this *Victoriana* quintessence was to play Chopin waltzes before dinner was served.

But much later on, after our guests had gone, Kismet had a twist in store for us. Gran insisted on doing the washing-up – as she always did, despite sloshing soapy water all over the kitchen floor tiles – but then she suddenly collapsed mid-sentence, just like that. One moment she was grumbling away about the washing-up liquid: '*I don't know, our Molly, you will always insist on buying this cheap stuff that barely makes any foam, when everyone knows that Fairy Liquid is the –* ' and the next moment she was flat-out on the floor. Within twenty minutes she was whisked off in an ambulance to Lyneham Royal Infirmary, with you by her side.

You visited her every day for a week. And when you brought her back home, with the knowledge that her days on earth were now numbered, I was dumped with the burden of looking after our B&B guests while you remained in Gran's bedroom practically twenty-four seven, seeing to her every need. So, through no choice of my own, I became your substitute, your junior chatelaine. Not an easy task to carry out when you've only just turned eighteen and are supposed to be going to school every morning at 9.00. And then, as if all that wasn't enough, exactly one week later I received a rejection from the Royal Northern College of Music.

Things were *not* looking up.

But at least it gave me an excuse to write my very first letter to Brother Matthew.

3

February 25th 1978

Dear Brother Matthew,

Thank you for your prayers on the day of my audition, but I'm afraid they didn't work. I haven't been accepted at the Royal Northern College of Music. Or did you forget to pray for me? On top of that, my grandmother's had a stroke and is now bed-ridden. She can't speak and can barely move, so my mother is having to do everything for her. This means I now have to cope with things all by myself at Belle Vue (that's our B&B place, on the promenade of Lyneham-on-Sea), on top of trying to fit in piano practice and A-level revision, as well as write my stories – an addiction I've had since childhood. How can I possibly fit it all in?!

Anyway, thank you again for your prayers, regardless of their effectiveness. Never mind, I'm sure even monks aren't perfect. You know what they say: if you don't succeed, try, try again. I'm sure your prayers will start working one day.

Yours,

Leah Cavanagh

I've always made copies of the letters I write. Never know when they might come in handy, right, Mother? I've got the whole lot of them here on the coffee table, spread out like a pack of cards. Right from that first one I wrote him in 1978, until the last one he sent, just over a week ago. To *you*, not me. But let's not go there yet.

Anyway, just five days later joy made a grand re-entry into my life. I received Brother Matthew's reply.

Dear Leah,

I was terribly sorry to hear about your audition. I did in fact remember you and prayed for you on the day – but clearly I can't be much good at interceding, as you yourself pointed out. It's easy for me to say I suppose, but don't feel disheartened. It doesn't mean you are no good, only some other blighter is better. What will you do now? Apply elsewhere? If so, I will think of you again and hope they are more sensible next time in their selection.

I was also sorry to hear about your grandmother. I do hope she recovers soon. I often wonder why things hit one all at once – maybe to show one how dependent one is? It's happened to me these last three weeks also.

I didn't feel I did a great deal to help you at Greystones, but maybe one does more good than one knows. I'm sure you will find God – but only if you really want him, and partly that means realising that you need him. And they are often strange, the ways that one comes to see that.

I must stop and go and say some Office. I hope you do get back to Greystones, and I look forward to seeing you.

Take care and God bless,

Br. Matthew OSB

After reading and re-reading the letter at least three times over, I rushed into the kitchen to show it to you. You scrutinised it in silence, standing in the middle of the room with your apron on, a mug of tea in one hand, the letter in the other. I hovered nearby while awaiting your verdict.

When you finished, you looked at me and said, 'Oh, darling, it's happened to him as well! He said so himself.'

'But he might not be referring to me –'

'Of *course* he's referring to you!'

'Do you really think so?'

'*It's happened to me this last three weeks also,*' you quoted from the letter, before aiming your burning gaze to me. 'When did you come back from Greystones?'

'Three weeks ago.'

'Well, there you are.'

Seeing my hesitation, you plonked your tea on the table, stepped forward, and swept me into your arms. 'Oh Leah darling, you silly, doubting thing.'

I closed my eyes, enjoying the reassuring smell of *Blue Grass* on your skin. But at that very moment the front doorbell rang.

'Damn and blast, it'll be that Mr Tomlinson again!' you said, letting go of me and heading for the door – but not before I'd managed to snatch the letter back from you.

I ran upstairs to my room, hugging the sacred piece of paper to my chest. Leaping onto my bed, I opened the window and stared out at the very essence of my life – that ever-present, seagull-infested expanse of promenade, sand and sea.

Okay, so my joy abated just a little when I leaned back against the pillows and began to analyse the words as though they were a Shakespearean text. They were a mixed bag. Firstly, he'd signed himself as *Br. Matthew OSB* – so he was reminding me that he was a monk of the Order of St Benedict. Well, *duh,* as Jenny would say. Secondly, he referred to God rather more frequently than I would have liked. Thirdly, there was a certain formality in his style, for instance in his repeated use of 'one'. But on the good side, he hadn't taken offence at the sarcastic tone of my own letter; he'd expressed a hope that I come back to Greystones, and he'd implied that since meeting me three weeks ago his own life had somehow been affected. Above all, he'd *replied.* We'd broken the 'uncertainty barrier'. We were now officially in touch with each other.

Little did I know at the time just how far that first tentative exchange of letters would take Matthew and me. They became my Bible, my life's blood. If I read them aloud to you now, Mother, across the miles between us, it'll stop me going outside for another cigarette. The night is still young.

But not as young as I was back then, in the spring of 1978. Young, naïve, head over heels in love, with a tantalising future that lay in wait just round the corner. Despite my teenage hormones and angst, at the end of the day I was convinced it *would* be a wonderful future. After all, aren't we all brought up on fairy tales of true love and heroism and the fulfilment of dreams? Happy-ever-after endings? Sleeping Beauty awoken by a kiss, Cinderella saved by a glass slipper, Rapunzel redeemed by her long plait … and all those redemptions involving perfect love? So why in God's name shouldn't we believe that the bread-and-butter fairy tales of our upbringing represent fact rather than fiction, and truth rather than lies? Surely not every story-teller, chronicler, wandering minstrel, poet and raconteur throughout the ages was a total and utter bull-shitter?

So here's my fairy tale.

CHAPTER SEVEN

1

March 21ˢᵗ 1979

Dear Leah,

Thank you so much for your letter. You have no need to apologise for anything; I certainly don't consider you a hard or selfish person. On the contrary, I think you are a remarkable young woman who has been thrown into a very difficult situation and is coping splendidly. I wonder how many other eighteen-year-olds would manage as you have been doing these past few weeks? I'm sure your mother appreciates all your efforts and loves you just the same, even if she is finding it hard to show it at present. I think it's fantastic that the two of you have such a close relationship – and do believe me when I say that I'm sure it will return to its old footing once things stabilise. I suppose by that I mean once your grandmother's health improves, or once she passes away. Only God knows what the final outcome will be, but whatever it is, I have every faith that He will look after all of you every step of the way.

I didn't realise that you wrote stories as well as played the piano – how splendid! What a talented young thing you are. I'm sure you aren't 'fated to stay at Lyneham-on-Sea for ever and ever', as you put it - you're far more likely to end up in the international concert halls of Europe, and in the meantime have a book published to boot.

As for me, I plod along here with my combined duties of teaching at the boarding school and helping out at the Gatehouse. Term is in full swing now. The snow has melted, it's the first day of spring, and the shoots are already beginning to appear in Monks' Wood, where I like to escape for a few quiet minutes every day. That retreat you came on with Lark Mount seems like another lifetime now. I do hope you manage to come again sometime soon. Then you can tell me all about this Peter Fox fellow. You have quite intrigued me.

Take care, Leah, and rest assured that I do pray for you, in my own humble and meagre way.

Yours, Br. Matthew

As soon as I finished reading the letter, I kissed it, hugged it to my breast and hurried downstairs to find you. Which was hardly a difficult task, seeing as you were always in Gran's bedsit nowadays.

I burst into the room, letter in hand, but you immediately put your forefinger to your lips and whispered, 'Leah, not so loud. She's finally settled into a deep sleep, bless her.' Then you turned back to Gran and stroked her forehead.

Swallowing a lump of resentment, I tiptoed towards the bed and pulled out the spare chair that I occasionally sat on: the only time I was able to spend with you. Most of my days were now spent making full English breakfasts for our guests before school in the morning, then changing beds, cleaning and tidying up when I got back home, and trying to squeeze in what I could of my piano practice and A-level studies later in the evening.

'He's written again,' I said quietly, trying to contain my excitement as I held out the letter to you.

You turned back to me and smiled that wonderful smile of yours. 'Oh darling, that's *wonderful*. But would you mind emptying your gran's bedpan while you're here? And then could you put the kettle on? I'm parched. I'm sure this room gets stuffier by the day.'

'Then you shouldn't spend so much time in it,' I snapped.

You gave me one of your looks. 'Oh Leah, now you know you don't mean that. Go on then, take the bedpan – and do be careful not to leave trickles on the loo seat, like you did yesterday. That old codger Tomlinson complained about it no end this morning.'

Grimacing, I reached under the bed for Gran's smelly bedpan. The truth was that I was no longer Number One in your life. Gran's needs had superseded my own, and it wasn't fair. I couldn't see any point in the continued existence of someone who could only lie down, grunt, stare at the ceiling and occasionally blink in response to what you said to her. And, worst of all, cause havoc in the lives of those around her. I'd loved Gran once upon a time; but this immobile, incommunicative invalid hardly bore any resemblance to her any more. Couldn't God just let her go peacefully in her sleep? Then I could get back to my serious piano practice and be closer to you again. I challenged Brother Matthew with these very same thoughts in my last letter to him. Rather than ticking me off, he *totally* understood how I felt.

However, the Great Invisible God out there wasn't ready to take any action with Gran yet. But He did at least grant me respite from my chores in the form of Matthew's letters, which accumulated in momentum as winter melted into spring.

'Oh darling, that's *wonderful* news!' you cried, jumping up from your bedside chair to hug me. It was a drizzly morning in April and the postman had just delivered an invitation to an audition at the Birmingham College of Music. 'This definitely deserves a toast! You must write to Brother Matthew *immediately*.'

But then Gran made one of her irritating grunts, and your attention was redirected. I hurried to the dining room, poured out two generous portions of *Harveys Bristol Cream,* and took them back across the hallway at a steadier pace, hoping that you'd had sufficient time to see to Gran's needs. It was amazing how you could understand her non-verbal forms of communication. At times I couldn't help but wonder, would it be like that for us, one sad day in the future?

Glancing at me with a strained smile, you said, 'Pop the sherries on the dressing table, would you, darling? We can make a toast to your success later. Your Gran needs her chicken bouillon first - could you nip to the kitchen to put the kettle on? And remember to add some cold water when the bouillon's ready.'

'Oh, *Mother* ...'

'It'll only take a minute, Leah, please don't be selfish. Gran is a very sick woman and this is the least you can do for her.'

Fighting back tears of frustration, I went to the kitchen as commanded. I made the bouillon, poured it into Gran's special mug with a spout, carried it back to her stuffy bedsit, and before you could dish out any other chores, I hurried right back out again, up the two flights of stairs to my bedroom. If you couldn't spare any quality time for me anymore, at least Brother Matthew could. So I wrote to him with my exciting news about Birmingham.

His reply came within a week; that beautiful sleek white envelope that the postman dropped through the letter box with a gentle slapping sound I soon grew to love.

April 17th 1978

Dear Leah,

Thank you so much for sharing your wonderful news with me about your audition. Let's hope this time round the powers-that-be are more sensible in their selection.

I did indeed manage to escape my 'monastic prison', as you put it, for a few days of the Easter holiday, when the exhausting Paschal Triduum was firmly behind us. As a matter of fact I went to visit my own grandmother, who lives in Cumbria and is not putting me through any of the sort of ordeal that you are currently going through. Let me once again assure you that the resentful thoughts you are plagued by certainly don't make you a bad person. If you were, you wouldn't be putting your A-level in jeopardy by helping your mother so assiduously in what must be an extremely hard time for her. So, Leah, please don't agonise over your feelings, which to be honest I find quite refreshing.

Sorry this is so short, but I have a very busy day ahead. Please rest assured that I will remember you all, and I shall certainly say a prayer for you on the day of your audition.

Yours, Matthew

P.S. I must say that I love your letter-writing style. You have a wonderfully wry sense of humour which always brings a smile to my face. What a difference from the shy sixth form girl I met just over two months ago!

3

Gran died on May 1st 1978. Your grief was inconsolable. As for mine? To be truthful, after three months of hard slog, stress and misery, a huge wave of relief washed over my entire being. I was also relieved for Gran herself, who'd suffered badly towards the end – vomiting, shaking, breathing like a rattlesnake. But in truth it was *you*, Mother, who I could have broken my heart over. *You* were the one who suffered the most. Even reading out Brother Matthew's letters didn't bring you the joy I had hoped to see in your eyes.

But I tried, all the same.

Two days after the funeral I made us a pot of tea and sat next to you at our dining table. Opening out his latest letter, I glanced at you gingerly. 'Shall I read it aloud?'

'As you wish, darling,' you said in this latest voice you'd assumed – faint, weary, strained.

So I read it.

'*Dearest Leah,*' I began, and was pleased to note that those two simple words did at least bring a smile to your face as you stirred your teacup. '*Thank you so much for your letter – which did arrive in time for me to remember you and your mother yesterday. My very deepest sympathy and prayers for you all – by this I mean for your grandmother as well, as she now embarks on her everlasting journey. One thing that might help you take the future into perspective is thinking of life as having more than one journey. All of us take them, and most of us veer off onto various side routes along the way. Sometimes we have a choice of which route to take, and sometimes we don't. Your grandmother's final step of her journey was not of her own making – it was God's will. But the road that you and your mother now embark upon is of your own making. I hope you both find the right direction.*'

'Ah, that's lovely,' you said, still stirring your teaspoon round and round the cup. I stretched out my hand and placed it on yours.

'I think the sugar's stirred in now,' I said, trying to bring another smile to your face.

'Oh – of course.' You put the spoon back on the saucer. I could see that your hand was trembling lightly. But then, forcing yourself back to the present, you faced me with eyes that were a little more focused, though still bloodshot from all those sleepless nights and rubbed-away tears. 'How did he end it?' you asked.

I returned to the letter. '*Take care of yourself, Leah, and from time to time try to say a prayer for this wayward monk, as he does for you.*'

Your eyes sharpened. 'Wayward?'

I nodded, grinning. 'He's called himself that a couple of times now.'

'And then?'

'Then what?'

'Did he write *Love, Brother Matthew* or just *Matthew*?'

'Just Matthew. And this time there's also a PS.'

'Really?' I was glad to note the colour returning to your face. 'What did he say?'

So I read out the beautiful words: '*P.S. When will you be visiting Grey-stones again?*'

You drew in your breath. 'Oh, Leah, he's missing you!'

I nodded, trying not to laugh too loudly, bearing in mind Gran had not long since been buried. 'So I was thinking, once my A-levels are out of the way, then -'

'Then you must go back to Greystones!'

You reached out your hand to mine and squeezed it. My heart pounded in longing.

So there you are, Mother. The beginnings of my tentative relationship with Brother Matthew.

Do you remember how we used to pore over his letters every time the postman brought yet another one? Those magical interludes before Gran died, when she was rasping away, and I'd hurriedly read out yet another of Matthew's eloquent epistles, always in a whisper, so as not to wake our invalid. Do you remember how we'd push our bedside chairs closer together as we analysed every phrase, every choice of word? How we were over-the-moon every time there was a little hint of something more than friendship? For instance, when Brother Matthew dropped the 'OSB' title from his name, then the 'Brother', and then – joy upon joy! – when the concluding '*Yours, Matthew*' was replaced by '*Love, Matthew*'. And when he asked me, in that penultimate letter, when I planned on coming to Greystones again, how our hearts missed a beat! If I'd written an essay based upon the analysis of that first exchange of letters between an eighteen-year-old sixth form girl and a twenty-seven-year-old monk, I would certainly have got an A!

But after a month of agonising silence from our beloved Benedictine, a completely different kind of letter arrived.

*28*th *May 1978*

Dear Leah,

As you will have observed from the address and postmark, I'm not at Greystones at present. I hope this won't distress or surprise you, especially at this time just before A-levels, but these last three months things have got on top of me and so I was advised to take a break. I'm not too sure how long I'll be away, nor where I'll be going from this retreat in the Highlands. I've been advised to forget about everything and everyone for the time being. This might seem unreasonable – but if I decide to comply, it may mean that I won't be writing for some time. Don't worry, however, I'm fine and regaining strength each day, and the 'forgetting' will not be absolute. You and your mother will continue to be in my mind and prayers.

I must stop and get this posted. Keep trusting in God.

Yours, Matthew

P.S. I look forward to hearing the story about Peter Fox!

For days afterwards I pondered over the letter. Each time I reread it, my mood deteriorated. All the hopes I'd tried to cling onto were being hacked away one by one, and even your blind optimism couldn't bring them back.

Remember that Saturday morning at the beginning of June, about a week after the troublesome letter arrived? Mr Tomlinson had just finished his breakfast and tottered up the stairs to his room. You'd asked me to serve him his bacon & eggs, rather than take them to him yourself and run the risk of being trapped for the next half-hour. I'd finished clearing his things away, re-set his place for the following morning, and at last managed to join you in the back patio at our wrought-iron table. The sun was streaming down upon our crazy-paving flagstones, potted geraniums and bougainvillea. You'd put up the parasol to provide us with shade, hoping to steal a bit of time to ourselves. *Our* time was always the most special time of day. But on this particular morning, I have to admit that I wished you wouldn't be quite so cloying.

'If all he wanted to do was forget you and move on with his monastic life,' you said after taking a sip of tea from your gold-leaf China cup, 'then why the dickens would he add that last sentence about Peter Fox? Come on, Leah, it's *obvious* that he wants you to reply. Can you honestly not see it?'

I stretched my bare feet into the fierce sunshine that spilled out beyond the shaded diameter of our parasol.

'And another thing,' you stubbornly went on before I had the chance to formulate a reply. 'Why do you think he wrote *these last three months things have got on top of me*? Isn't it obvious that it's you he's referring to? Leah darling, just think about it. When did you go to Greystones?'

'February.' I wiggled my toes in the sun.

'And it's now May. So there you are. Three months, see?'

'Oh I don't know …' I glanced yet again at the mystifying letter, propped up against a vase of flowers in the centre of the table. 'I think you're reading way too much into it. Besides, I don't like his tone.'

You frowned. 'You don't like his *tone*? What on earth's wrong with his tone?'

'Well – for instance that bit where he says he hopes I won't be upset by his … how did he put it?' I leaned forward to snatch the letter. '*As you will have observed from the address and postmark, I'm not at Greystones at present. I hope this won't distress or surprise you.*' Slapping the accursed piece of paper on the table, I leaned back again and gave a little snort. 'Honestly! As if not writing to me will be such a mega-stress in my poor lonely life. How arrogant is that?'

'It's not arrogant at all,' you said curtly, your tanned face suddenly turning alabaster. 'It's *caring*, that's what it is, my darling. And you should show equal care to him. What if the poor man is having some sort of breakdown? Doesn't that concern you?'

I fidgeted on my chair. 'Of course it does. But if he really was having a breakdown, then he wouldn't have written at all, would he?'

You sighed. 'I can see you're too immature to think about any of this rationally.'

'Okay, so I'm too immature.'

For a few moments neither of said anything. I hated it when we exchanged cross words. Staring up at the gossamer netting of clouds miles above us, I said in a softer voice, 'Oh Mother, I honestly don't know what to think any more. I was crazy about him back at Greystones, and I was over the moon when we started writing to each other ... but now, after this latest letter ...' I chewed at my lower lip. 'Clearly he doesn't want us to continue writing.'

'Of course he does!'

I shook my head. 'No. Something's changed in him.'

'Someone's *made* something change in him. And you know who it is.'

'You mean Father Sebastian?'

'Who else? You yourself told me what bad vibes you got from the old codger.'

'Oh, I don't know ...'

'But *I* do, Leah. I have a sixth sense about it. And you know me and my sixth senses. So now it's up to you to make sure Brother Matthew changes right back again, if you don't want to let him go.'

But that was the trouble. Did I really not want to let him go?

* * *

You'd always been blessed with a sixth sense, whereas I was cursed from Day One of my existence with an intrinsic lack of self-confidence. So it was only natural that I should have questioned whether a mature, sensible Oxford graduate-cum-monk could be so smitten by an attractive but not stunning sixth form girl. No doubt he'd seen countless examples of even prettier girls over his retreat-filled years. So wasn't the notion of me being special to him all a bit far-fetched? I began to ask myself this question more and more over the next few days, while meditating upon how to reply to Matthew's recondite letter.

As for you, Mother, just why you were so taken with him right from the start, I've never quite managed to work out. Was there really something about him that reminded you of Peter Fox? Or maybe it was the setting of Greystones Abbey that set your colourful imagination on fire? Maybe you imaged yourself to be part of the scene, as though playing the lead role in one of your Amateur Dramatic Society productions? Or was it that you could read something in my face when I came home from that retreat; something that I myself wasn't aware of and only you as a mother could see? Something that told you my life would be changed forever, now that I had met my man? That I shouldn't risk wasting precious time on procrastination, as you and Peter had done?

Whatever the case, the truth of the matter is that his last letter depressed me. The days turned to weeks, my doubts to paralysis, and despite your insistence that I should reply to his letter, I honestly didn't know how to. It was now June; four months had passed since I first met him. My A-levels were looming, so was my trip to Cork to visit my father, and the picture of Brother Matthew's face was becoming blurred in my mind's eye. I even found myself re-reading my diary entries from February, to remind myself how I'd felt back then. I'd soon be leaving home for good and embarking on my student life. The future beckoned ever more enticingly, while Greystones sank deeper and deeper into the quicksand of the past.

Why didn't you let me keep it there, where it belonged?

LAUDS

Ah Moon of my Delight who knows't no Wane,
The Moon of heaven is rising once again.
How oft hereafter rising shall she look
Through this same Garden after me in vain?

Rubaiyat of Omar Khayyam, v. 89

CHAPTER EIGHT

1

I'd say that the second journey of my life began the day I was mugged at knife point.

It was a Sunday at the end of September 1978, the first day of my brand new life as a student. There I was, freshly enrolled at the Birmingham College of Music, my whole future in front of me. The previous day you'd accompanied me on the train to Birmingham. My backpack, guitar, hold-all and general clutter filled up four seats instead of two in the crowded train compartment, causing one or two grumbles from other passengers. We got a taxi straight to Cavendish Hall of Residence, then dumped all my stuff and hurried right out again to make the most of the day before you caught the 7.00 pm train back to Lyneham-on-Sea.

Our afternoon together was full of your exuberant optimism. 'Oh darling, it's *magnificent!* It makes Lyneham seem like some backwater village. Now you will make the most of your life here, promise? Never you mind pining away over Brother Matthew -' I wasn't, actually – 'Just you concentrate on enjoying yourself and making the most of this wonderful opportunity. It's up to you now, darling, so don't you waste a minute of your time here!' With you by my side, how could I help feel anything but happiness? Thank you for that, Mother. Thank you for being with me every minute of that crucial day.

The next day is when it all started.

It was about six in the evening and still very warm. I'd had a lovely afternoon exploring the Bull Ring shopping centre and felt dead chuffed with a skimpy top I'd bought at a bargain price, which I was now wearing. On the way back to Cavendish Hall I nipped into a phone booth to make a call to you.

'Mother, I've had a *fabulous* day!' I practically sang into the receiver, my head filled with the warm image of you sitting on the bottom step in our hallway, next to the telephone stand. 'I really think I'm going to love Birmingham. I found an adorable little café for lunch -'

And then the door to the cubicle swung open. A tall black youth with Rastafari hair stepped inside and rasped, '*Give me your purse!*'

I went rigid. Stared at him in disbelief. Then another Rastafari guy burst into the cubicle and repeated his mate's request. Only this one had a knife.

'*Give me your purse or I'll stick this into you!*'

I'll never forget the glint of that blade, aimed at the defenceless skin of my partially exposed stomach. I went numb, terrorised by the image of that gleaming point plunging itself into my taut, youthful flesh, blood spilling down my jeans and ankles onto the floor of the cubicle, the telephone receiver swinging to and fro on its dirty cord as I crumpled into a bloody mess, dying, crying out for you ...

'Leah? *Leah*, what's going on? Are you there? *Leah, speak to me!*'

The force of your command jolted me out of my shock.

'I – I've just been mugged,' I whispered into the receiver, trembling, unable to cry or shout or believe that any of it had actually happened. But it had. And the perpetrators had scarpered into thin air as quickly as they'd materialised, together with the paltry five pounds inside my purse.

I listened in a kind of paralysis to the frantic instructions that you barked down the phone: I must leave the booth at once, I must go straight back to Cavendish Hall, I must find the caretaker, tell him everything that happened, get him to phone the police. After a further few seconds of catatonia, I somehow managed to snap out of my stupor, abandon the phone booth and get myself back to Cavendish Hall. So that was my introduction to student life.

Oh, and it's also how I met Gus.

The two young policemen who came to interview me about half an hour later, when I was sitting on a stool in the caretaker's room cradling a ridiculously sweet mug of tea, were utterly divine specimens of the male species. The moment they introduced themselves as Gus and Jed, all the tension that had paralysed me began to trickle out of every sinew and tendon in my body.

'So you've been mugged, love, have you?' the one called Gus said. He had messy blond hair and cool-grey eyes.

I nodded.

'Leah Cavanagh, right?'

Again I nodded.

'It's a bad world out there. But no point dwelling on that, eh?'

'No,' I said, at last finding my voice.

'We'll have to take a statement,' he went on, 'and then I'll show you some mug shots, to see if you can identify the buggers who did this.' His macho demeanour reminded me of some film star I couldn't quite place.

'Jed, got a pen and paper?'

Jed was the quieter one. Not quite as macho. It was the other one - the fair-haired, Rambo one called Gus who seemed to take charge. 'Ta,' he said, taking the proffered notepad from his colleague before turning back to me. 'So could you describe the two men to us?'

I fidgeted. 'No, not really.'

'Anything will help, love. Age, height, size, colour -'

'They were Rastafarians.'

He shook his head. 'Nah, real Rastafarians don't go in for mugging. The guys we're looking for were just common thugs with dreadlocks as a fashion thing.'

'Oh.'

'Anything else you can remember?'

I drew my eyebrows together, trying to be more precise, more helpful, but I couldn't. 'Sorry. It was all over in about ten seconds.'

'Don't worry, love. It usually is. A few seconds is all it takes for a mugging. Right, I'd like you to take a look at some photos to see if you can identify either of the two lads. Think you can manage that?'

I nodded.

'You got them mug shots, Jed?'

The quieter policeman reached for his briefcase and flicked it open. Drawing out a large envelope, he gave it to the fair-haired one, who proceeded to take out a selection of photographs. He showed them to me one by one, but my mind had gone blank. I couldn't remember a single thing about the events of barely an hour ago, other than the knife blade, the voices, and the terrifying eyes that had stared at me in cold blood. I felt useless. However, apparently that was not a sentiment shared by my two men in shining armour.

Putting the photos back in the briefcase, Gus looked at me and smiled. 'Fancy a spin, then?'

I blinked at him.

'A spin round the local area to see if you can spot your assailants. They probably haven't got far.'

'Oh, right. Okay then.'

And that's how I spent the next half-hour: sitting in a flashy police car as my two escorts navigated their way round the grimy back streets of the area, every now and then slowing down if they spotted anyone young, male and black. But each time they did so, I shook my head. It was no use. Quite frankly, even if the muggers had appeared right in front of my eyes, I doubt I'd have recognised them. I was still in a state of shock and barely registered anything except the memory of that awful, gleaming knife point.

So we returned to Cavendish Hall and made our way back to the caretaker's office. He brewed us another mug of tea and then reluctantly left the room upon Gus's request. Probably my mugging was the most exciting thing that had happened to him all summer.

As soon as he was out of earshot, Gus turned to me and asked, 'Have you got anyone to take care of you tonight? Your mum? Dad? Boyfriend?'

I shook my head. 'I only arrived in Birmingham yesterday. I don't know anyone.'

'Well, you know us now, don't you?'

I felt my cheeks flush.

'Will you be all right on your own tonight, or do you want us to make a phone call to your mum? Perhaps she could come over?'

'No, I'll be fine.' And I *would* be fine. I was a student now. I was living away from home, all grown up. I didn't want to be treated like a child.

No fear of that!

'Don't suppose you'd fancy coming to a party, would you?' Gus asked quite out of the blue.

'What, *now*?' And suddenly, despite the palpitating of my heart, it dawned on me which actor he reminded me of. A younger Clint Eastwood. It must have been the clean-cut features on his lean, sexy face.

'Only if you're up for it.'

'C'mon, Gus, can't you see she's in a state? Leave her be tonight.' That was Jed.

'No I'm not in a state,' I said with unexpected force, raising my head higher. 'I'd love to go to a party.'

They both looked at me, then at each other, and then, like an incongruous sea breeze in the desert, we all laughed.

So I went to the party, and I enjoyed my first experience of flirtation, alcohol, cigarettes, loud music, dancing, and complete freedom. But later that night – or rather, in the early hours of the morning – when Gus guided me away from the dying embers of the party out onto the street, and gave me my first French kiss before helping me into the back of the taxi he'd ordered for me, I was filled with an overwhelming sensation of sorrow. I rested my spinning head against the black upholstery, closed my eyes, and imagined that the kiss had been with someone else. Someone I thought I'd forgotten. Someone dressed all in black, just like the car seat that my aching head was resting upon.

As the taxi revved into gear and sped down the alien streets of the vast metropolis, I re-opened my eyes and stared out of the window. The harsh neon lights made my head hurt. I yearned for the soft, silvery sea at Lyneham - and also for you, Mother. For your warm, lilting voice to wish me goodnight.

Over my slumber your loving watch keep, rock me to sleep, Mother, rock me to sleep.

I did not look forward to returning to my bare student room in the impersonal enclave of Cavendish Hall, with you no longer there beside me, and no letter from Greystones Abbey that the post might deliver the following morning. I'd stopped writing to Brother Matthew all of four months ago, and he didn't even have my new address.

Oh God, how I missed you both that night.

3

'I want peace of mind', says bereaved Preston girl

Do you remember that very first article that appeared in the *Lancashire Evening Post* soon after you arrived in Cyprus to visit Peter's grave? I've still got all the newspaper articles you saved from those days. You told the reporter that you wanted peace of mind. But did you ever attain it?

Sometimes I wonder why you never found yourself another man. I know you found Dad, but let's face it, that was all just tragic-rebound stuff, doomed right from the start. Why did you never allow yourself to fall in love again? I'm sure you could have done – after all, you were never short of admirers. Tony Gaston the architect, for instance - the one you got engaged to just to make Peter jealous, during one of your many break-ups with him. And the hunky Mustaffa from Yugoslavia. There were others as well, later on. Couldn't you have fallen in love – I mean *properly* in love – with at least one of them? Or by that time had you become too accustomed to your grief and your memories of Peter? Was his ghost preferable to a real, living man who could run the risk of breaking your heart again? Okay, I'd have understood that philosophy if you'd applied it to the first year or two after his death – but for the next *two decades*?

Yet the funny thing is, it's not as if you were a morose person. If you had been, I wouldn't have adored your company so much. You were full of laughter, stories, gossip, appreciation of music and films, with the occasional memory of Peter Fox that descended upon you like a bird of prey. And yet you thrived on those memories. They were your life force – those lost moments and days and years that you clung to. They became your best friends, together with all the antiques you accumulated over the years, as though to compensate for the lack of a man in your life. Your second-hand paintings and brass candlesticks and display cabinet crammed with Cloisonee vases, snuff boxes, cameos, Victorian powder compacts … weren't they all just substitutes? You always used to say that one day when you're at last reunited with Peter, the sight and touch of your ornaments will bring me closer to you. And yet don't you think that a new man in your life – someone outside the cloistered world of my upbringing – would have prevented you from living your re-invented dreams through me? Didn't you know that one day I was bound to grow up and leave home and abandon you, as children eventually do? If only you'd taken a different road, one with another man, then our own journey might have been a hell of a lot less painful.

4

Life at the Birmingham College of Music soon settled into a vague kind of routine. I say 'vague', because a lot of our timing was dependent upon the availability of practice rooms on the third and fourth floors of that concrete monstrosity of a building that was home to the college.

Apart from the three or four hours' practice I was expected to squeeze in each day, there were also several classes to attend, all of which resembled various stages of an Olympic obstacle course. Firstly, there were my two piano lessons each week with the exacting Michael Williams, who possessed the brilliant knack of simultaneously smiling and sucking in his breath whenever he was disappointed with my playing. Then there were my guitar lessons with Barry Winehouse, who was a small man with a large character and who, within the space of one lesson flat, succeeded in demonstrating to me that I did not even know how to hold a classical guitar properly, let alone play one. Then there were the excruciating sight-reading tutorials with Leonard McDowell, whose wild hair and drooping moustache uncannily resembled Albert Einstein, and whose grinding voice brought the palms of my hands out in a cold sweat each time he slapped yet another Bach Partita on the piano music stand and rasped, '*Play!*' I could elaborate further on the aural tests classes which were akin to psychological torture, and the Theory & Rudiments tutorials which were more like quadratic maths, and the conducting classes, and the History of Music, and choir … but I won't bother. Suffice it to say that most days I trudged back to Cavendish Hall feeling drained of inspiration, wondering what the hell I was doing here, and glad of Gus's regular visits to take my mind off a certain faraway monk. *He who shall not be named,* to put it in Jenny's words.

Ah, yes, Gus. My very first boyfriend. My policeman-cum-saviour. My fair-haired, slick-talking daredevil with a killer smile. But it was when he *wasn't* smiling that I found him most attractive. It was when he was ranting on about the state of the police force in the West Midlands, or the latest wanker who'd won the local elections, or whatever else got him going, that my knees went weak.

Sometimes he took me out to wine bars in the city centre, all of them plush, brand new and expensive. That's when I first developed a taste for that heady nectar of the gods. At other times we stayed in the shared kitchen at Cavendish Hall, drinking coffee and nibbling Lancashire parkin and flapjack from Lyneham-on-Sea. Eventually we'd retire to my room, which was a cue to start snogging and groping on my bed. After our second date I let Gus unbutton my blouse; on the third I allowed him to undo my bra and explore uncharted territory. I loved it when he whispered sweet nothings in my ears. '*You're the best kisser in all of Birmingham,*' he'd murmur, to which I'd whisper back, '*Only Birmingham?*' and then we'd laugh into each other's pulsing flesh. Oh yes, I was growing up fast. I sometimes couldn't help wonder what a certain faraway monk, way across the miles in North Yorkshire, would think of me if he saw me now. But mostly I curtailed such thoughts the moment they entered my head.

But getting back to Gus. Whenever it came to any attempt to undo my jeans, I'd push him away and say a determined '*No.*' I'd always had it drummed into me how special that First Time was, and how it should be saved for the man of your dreams. Hmm. Although Gus was sexy enough to send shudders all the way down my spine and back, especially when in one of his tough, eye-glinting moods, he was not the man of my dreams by any stretch of the imagination.

One October evening, after his ninth or tenth attempt to get inside my knickers, he pulled himself away from me with a great big sigh, sat on the edge of the bed and sank his head into his hands.

'What's wrong?' I asked, placing my hand on his shoulder.

He shoved me away with a jerk. 'You have to ask?'

Of course I knew what it was. 'Sorry,' I mumbled. 'I'm not ready for … for *that* yet.'

He raised his head and turned the full force of his stare upon me. 'Leah, don't piss me about, okay? I want to know the truth. Is it that you don't fancy me anymore?'

'Don't be silly. I let you do stuff to me, don't I?'

'*Do stuff*,' he mocked. 'And what stuff would that be, exactly?'

'Come on, you know what I mean.'

'Oh, *that*. Right, I get you, love. If you mean a bit of feeling up your tits, that's what twelve-year olds do.'

'But we've only been going out together a few weeks. If I let you go all the way, then you'd …'

'Lose interest? Bloody hell, Leah, that sounds like your mam talking.'

I pulled myself into an upright position. 'I'm sorry, Gus, but I don't like being pressurised into doing anything I don't feel ready for.'

'So when will you be ready?'

'I don't know. Just don't push me.'

'Fuckin' hell, Leah, I wish you'd be straight with me!'

'Please – keep your voice down.' I glanced towards the door, wondering who might be eavesdropping. Perhaps my fellow-musicians who shared my floor at Cavendish Hall? Tessa Llewellin, for instance, the Welsh prima donna soprano who looked like she'd stepped straight out of a Pre-Raphaelite painting, with her pale face and cascades of frizzy red hair? Or Emily Green, the skinny blond flautist with remnants of acne on her forehead and cheeks, but a pretty smile to compensate? I'd made friends with them both, but not deeply enough to talk about frustrated boyfriends who were desperate for sex, when in fact I only ever dreamed of making love to a man who was forbidden to me.

'Is there someone else?' Gus asked with narrowed eyes.

'No, of course not.'

'Then stop pissing me about, for fuck's sake!'

'But there really *isn't* anyone else, honest. I'm just not ready to – y'know. Go all the way. Sorry.'

'Yeah, well, you know what? I haven't got time to piss about with cock-teasers.' And with that he leapt off the bed, grabbed his jacket, and stormed out of the room.

When I heard the slamming of the main door, I slumped backwards and stared at the ceiling. Then I put my hands over my face and burst into a series of humiliated sobs. I'd been dumped.

However, youth is youth. By the following week my hurt pride had worn off, as had the novelty of my Clint Eastwood boyfriend. Policemen were passé.

Not so with clarinettists.

CHAPTER NINE

1

My next fling, if you can call it that, was with the rather odd Richard Masters, principal clarinettist in the City of Birmingham Symphony Orchestra (better known as the CBSO) and peripatetic teacher at our college. Tall, lean, thirtyish, light brown hair, with an intense expression that never abandoned his angular face for one moment. Even when he smiled – which was extremely rarely – he still looked like death warmed up, as Gran used to say.

It all started one Monday afternoon at college. I was hurrying hell for leather down the corridor towards my dreaded piano sight-reading class, piles of music tucked into the crook of my arm, and terrified of having to suffer some sarcastic comment from Malcolm McDowell for being late. Richard Masters happened to be walking down the same corridor at half my pace. As I passed by him, I bumped into his shoulder and stumbled, dropping all my notes. The whole lot of them fluttered to the floor in a great flapping of black and white wings.

'Here, let me help you,' the gawky man said, stooping to gather them up for me – my scattered Haydn, Beethoven, Szymanowski and Brahms. I also stooped, so it ended up being a race to see who could grab the most notes.

When we'd both straightened up again he threw me a probing look and said, 'So you like Szymanowski, do you?'

'Erm – yes.'

'So do I, so do I! We have good taste, it appears.'

I smiled edgily.

'I don't believe I've seen you here before?'

'No, I've just started. I'm a first year.'

'Ah, I see. Well then, welcome to the team, er … what did you say your name was?'

'Leah. Leah Cavanagh.'

'Welcome to the team, Miss Leah Cavanagh. I hope you stick it through. We're all mad musicians here.' He laughed unexpectedly loudly, displaying an expanse of crooked teeth that took ever so slightly away from his otherwise appealing looks. Then he became serious again and said, 'You must come along to the CBSO concerts. They're every Friday evening. Music students get special discounts – just 50p a go for you lot.'

'Oh. Okay.'

'So. Shall we see you this Friday, then?'

'Er – maybe. What are they playing?'

'*They* are playing Mozart, Schumann and Dvorak. And *they* happen to include me, just in case you didn't know. I'm principal clarinettist of the CBSO.'

'Oh, really? That's – er – ' But that's the problem for us unconfident, self-conscious lot. That's *what*, exactly? Interesting? Fascinating? Useful to know? A fact I already should have known?

'Well then, Lisa, I must be getting on,' he filled in. 'It was very nice talking to you and I hope to see you Friday evening. If you come, I'll treat you to a drink in the interval.'

That took me completely unawares. I didn't even manage to say 'thank you' before he turned on his heel and strode off down the corridor to whatever lesson he was headed for.

Feeling a tad wind-swept, I hurried towards the dreaded Room No 57, where the even more dreaded Leonard McDowell lay in wait, together with his Einstein moustache and Bach partitas.

2

The second time I saw Richard Masters I was rushing up the stairs two at a time, late for my piano lesson, as always. There he was, hurrying down the concrete steps, and there I was, hurrying up the same steps – both of us hurtling towards one another from opposite heights and directions, wrapped up in our own worlds, oblivious to the nuisance of gravity and velocity.

Inevitably, our courses collided.

'Oh – sorry!' I blurted out.

He threw me an irritated glance – until recognition dawned. Smiling that wide, toothy smile, he said, 'Ah, it's Lisa, isn't it?'

'Leah,' I corrected, trying not to giggle.

'Ah, yes. Leah. I knew it began with an 'L'. Well then, Leah, how is the Szymanowski coming along?'

'Okay, I guess.'

'Good, good. Mustn't hurt his feelings.'

'Sorry?'

'Szymanowski. Mustn't hurt his feelings. They're very sensitive, these Poles. Didn't you know?'

'Er – no, not really.'

'Oh, yes. It's all these revolutions and uprisings and what-nots that they're always getting their teeth into. Ask Chopin – he'll tell you all about them. You do play his Revolutionary Etude, I take it?'

'Of course.'

'Good, very good. Well then, I'd better let you get off. Where is it you're heading in such a rush?'

'Oh – I've got a piano lesson with Michael Williams. And I'm late.'

'Ah, Michael. Yes, you have to watch out for him. He's a bit brutal with the old Szymanowski. Bashes him about as though he were Bartok. Well, mustn't keep you, then, Lisa. Tiddly-ho.'

And off he went, cantering down the steps, his clarinet case bouncing up and down in the crook of his arm. And there I was, left with the uneasy feeling that he had no recollection whatsoever of asking me out for a drink.

3

On the night of the concert I sat on my red velvet seat in the auditorium of the Philharmonic hall, wedged in between my two music colleagues who I'd brought along for moral support: Tessa Llewelin the singer, and Emily Green the flautist. We shared the same college, hall of residence, floor and kitchen, but not the same taste in men, as it happened.

'Don't you find him a bit creepy?' Emily asked me with earnest brown eyes that reminded me a bit of poor old Nobbles and made me feel home-sick.

'No, not really,' I said. 'I think he's very good-looking, actually. And he's also -'

'But he's definitely a bit odd,' Tessa cut in. 'Sorry, Leah, but Emily's right.'

'Well, *I* like him,' I said, pulling at a loose thread in the clingy red dress I'd chosen to wear.

'And he obviously likes *you*,' Emily giggled. 'The principal clarinettist of the CBSO – wow!'

'So what did you do to him, Leah?' Tessa asked, grinning broadly.

The lights dimmed. A few scattered coughs ricocheted round the auditorium. The ushers closed the double doors at the back, and an expectant hush fell upon us all.

A staccato pattering of footsteps from backstage preceded the conductor's grand entry. A tall, wild-haired young man navigated his way through the tightly-packed orchestra, accompanied by a crescendo of applause. Stepping onto the podium at the front of the stage, he took a dramatic bow, his chaotic ginger hair cascading over his shoulders. Finally, he turned round to face the orchestra.

The next hour passed by in a trance of appreciation, anxiety and impatience. I tried not to single out Richard Masters too often, perched as he was on his stool near the back of the orchestra amid the woodwind section, swaying his clarinet to and fro as the sublime phrases ebbed and waned. Instead, I tried to concentrate on how superb the music was, how immaculately timed, how elegantly phrased. But in truth, all I wanted was to get through the first half of the concert, find the bar, and see if Richard Masters would actually turn up.

He did. And thankfully, Tessa and Emily had the tact to wander off as soon as I spotted him walking towards me.

'I haven't interrupted anything, have I?' he asked when he reached my side, glancing at the backs of my friends as they disappeared into the crowd.

'What? – oh, no, I just bumped into them this minute – they're with some other people.'

'Aha. So then. What can I get you, Lisa?'

Already being a lady of wine bar experience by now, I said, 'Chardonnay, please. And it's Leah, actually.'

'Ah, yes, of course.' He headed for the bar, and two minutes later returned with a glass of wine and a half pint of bitter for himself. 'Mustn't get too sozzled before the bitter end,' he said, laughing at his own pun. 'If I indulged in a full pint of this, my trills would resemble flatulence in the second half of our performance.'

His turn of phrase was as incongruous as the rest of him. So we bumbled along for the next fifteen minutes, meandering our way through a labyrinthine route of tepid jokes, questions, small talk and silences. After one particularly drawn-out pause, he peered at me and said, 'Would you care for a bite to eat after the concert, Lisa?'

I agreed, and that was that. The second half of the performance sailed past and afterwards he took me to *Zorba's,* which was my first real dinner date with a man. I liked the experienced approach he took over the menu, helping me to negotiate my way through the long list of Greek dishes, eventually choosing a Tsatziki starter and Moussaka second course for both of us, accompanied by a couple of glasses of Ouzo. At the end of the evening he gave me a lift home in his black Mazda, and when he leaned over to say goodnight before dropping me off at Cavendish Hall, he merely brushed my cheeks with his lips. I was glad of this slow approach. I'd already planned in my head that by the second or third date I'd let him enjoy a longer kiss, and maybe a bit more. Yes, this latest conquest would be *far* more long-lasting and serious than Boyfriend Number One.

At least Richard Masters didn't dump me because of enforced abstinence. He just squirmed out of my life after his wife unexpectedly turned up at the next concert. My God, how could I possibly not have known that the bastard was married? Honestly, after that excruciating encounter I could have died! When the detective-wife suddenly materialised at the bar during the interval, wedging herself with a brazen smile between the deceitful Richard and the gullible me, I could have quite readily given up on love and romance once and for all and become a nun.

Only I didn't do that, of course, thanks to the charms of Danny the Double Bassist, who I met just two days later.

4

'Er – sorry, girls, but did I hear the name *Richard Masters*, by any chance?'

I was having a gossip with Tessa in the college canteen when this tall, lanky lad suddenly intruded upon our quiet *tete a tete*. Dishy Danny, as it turned out. Or Danny and the Double Bass. Or the *dishy duo,* as I referred to them in a short story I wrote. *Bass Dreams,* it was called, which I thought rather a clever title. God, was I jealous of that bloody bass!

'Yes you did,' Tessa replied, raising an eyebrow at the sound of the newcomer's broad Scouse accent. She tossed back her long auburn hair and looked up at him with sultry eyes. 'Why d'you ask?'

The guy rested his enormous double bass against the table. Satisfied that it had been positioned at a sufficiently safe angle so as not to topple over and break all our toes, he plonked himself on a chair and grinned at us. 'So come on then, which one of you was seduced by him?'

Tessa gestured towards me in unashamed disloyalty.

My cheeks turned scarlet. 'I was not seduced by him!'

The Scouse rogue deepened his grin. 'That's what they all say.'

'But I *wasn't.*'

'So you honestly didn't know that Richard Masters has a reputation for seducing all first year girls who're gullible enough to fall for his batty charm?'

'Apparently not,' Tessa answered for me. 'But there you are. Pianists will be pianists.'

They both chuckled at my expense, quite as though I wasn't there. But the very next moment the guy's tone subtly altered. 'So you're a pianist, then?'

I nodded.

'What's your sight-reading like?'

'Pretty rubbish.'

'Then I don't suppose there's much point asking you to accompany me on my Hindemith sonata?'

'Which one's that?'

'The one for double bass and piano.'

I shrugged.

'I think that's a no,' Tessa said.

'Actually, I think it's a maybe. Isn't that right – eh, what's your name?'

'Leah.'

'Right. Mine's Danny.'

'And I'm Tessa.'

Danny acknowledged this superfluous piece of information with a brief nod, before turning his face back to me. 'Okay, Leah, I've got a lesson at five-thirty. D'you reckon you could help me out a bit beforehand? Just for half an hour, say?'

God knows why, but I agreed. After finishing our terrible college coffees he stood up, and I stood up, and he gathered his double bass into his arms, and we bade our farewells to a somewhat peeved-looking Tessa. I followed him out of the canteen and down the corridor to the lift, which took us up to the fourth floor where all the best practice rooms lurked.

When we'd finally secured a room, after some skilful bargaining with another student who was in front of us in the queue, Danny closed the door behind us and turned to the love of his life. His double bass. He then went through the complicated rigmarole of extracting the over-sized instrument from its sarcophagus, together with a bow and several sheets of music.

'Didn't you ever think of learning an instrument that was easier to carry around?' I asked, proud of my increasing confidence.

He fired a bemused grin at me. 'What, you mean like the piano?'

Confidence duly quashed, I opened the Hindemith notes that he'd placed in front of me. 'Oh my God.'

'Yeah, I know. Bit of a pig to sight-read. So let's take it nice and slow to begin with, okay?'

'Okay.'

As it happened, even taking it nice and slow was enough to bring me out in a cold sweat. Oh how I hated sight-reading!

'I'm sorry, can we start again?' I asked after the third attempt.

'Tell you what,' he said, tossing his thick dark hair out of his eyes and resting his double bass against the piano. 'How about I go back down to the canteen for twenty minutes, and in the meantime you have a look through the first three pages on your own? Okay?'

'Okay,' I said, breathing a great walloping sigh of relief.

An hour later he was back, reeking of college coffee. 'Ready?'

I nodded. 'Just the first three pages, right?'

'Right. I think that's about as much as I could stand.'

As always with Danny, I was never quite sure what he meant. The Hindemith, my sight-reading, or me?

So that was it. The beginning of our three-week fling, if you could call it that. My entire first term was a stretch of flings which couldn't *quite be called that.* This particular one consisted of drinks in the Long Boat pub after Monday evening choir practice, quick snogs and fumbles as he walked me back to Cavendish Hall, two or three coffees in the kitchen with Lancashire parkin and flapjack, followed by further snogs and fumbling in my room.

It all came to a sad end one drizzly afternoon in late November. Danny had arranged to pick me up from college and give me a lift back to Lyneham-on-Sea for the weekend, which wasn't far from his Scouse birthplace. It was my first trip home since September, and I was looking forward to it beyond belief.

I was waiting for Danny in the car park outside Cavendish Hall, bags standing by my side, coat all buttoned up, college scarf wrapped round my neck, umbrella protecting me from the insidious drizzle that appeared light at first but after half-an-hour gradually got through your outer garments and into your skin, bones and soul. That's how long I'd been waiting. Half-a-bloody-hour. I was well and truly fed up.

At last Danny's old Morris Minor emerged from round the corner, pulling into view and halt in quick succession. 'Sorry I'm late,' he called out from the wound-down window as he screeched to a halt.

The screeching effect didn't quite work, coming from such a midget lump of metal, but I didn't bother telling him that. Neither did he bother getting out of the car to put my bags in the boot and hold the door open for me to climb inside the front seat. Manners most definitely did *not* maketh this man.

'Er – there's a slight problem,' he mumbled.

'Sorry?'

'I said there's a slight problem.'

'Yes, I heard you. But what is it?'

The rain and wind suddenly increased in force, just out of spite, so we were now having to shout at each other.

'Well … the thing is, my bass takes up most of the back seat. Actually, all of the back seat – and most of the front seat as well. Sorry, completely forgot about that. I'm not sure if there'll be room for you and your bags as well.'

Silently fuming, I said, 'You could always be a gentleman and ask the bass to step out for me.'

'You what?'

'And let me sit in its place.'

After a pause in which the rain hissed maliciously all around us, echoing my own sentiments with steaming perfection, he said in a fractionally less secure voice, 'Sorry, Leah, but what're you on about?'

Stooping to pick up my bags from the pavement, I leaned towards the open car window and yelled above the din of the rain, 'Go screw your fucking bass, Danny boy!'

That was the first time I ever used the 'f' word. And I must say I felt very proud of myself as I stalked across the car park back towards Cavendish Hall.

CHAPTER TEN

1

One week later, I turned the key in the front door of Belle Vue. I'd had my fill of men and music, and needed a good dose of adoration and positivity. In other words, I needed *you*, Mother.

As soon as I stepped inside the hallway I was engulfed by the strains of Nat King Cole's *Smile*. I had hoped to hear *Stranger in Paradise*, which was my favourite, but you were evidently having one of your sad days. A day when you were in Foxland, and had to smile though your heart was aching ...

I dumped my bags on the floor and made my way towards the dining room, where I knew I'd find you. But then I stopped. Something urged me to retrace my steps to Gran's old room. I knew that you'd planned on getting rid of all her things and converting her bedsit into a ground-floor guest room; but now, as I cautiously opened the door, an intuitive wariness flooded me.

I stepped inside the room.

My suspicion was right. Everything remained just as it had been in May, when Gran died. I could understand you needing a couple of months to recover, but now it was December and still nothing had changed. I walked round the room, picking up various items of Gran's – her mother-of-pearl hairbrush on the dressing table, her hand-knitted bed jacket, her King James Bible. Then I opened her wardrobe. All her dresses, blouses and skirts were still there. Next, I moved on to her oak chest of drawers. Underwear, jumpers, knick-knacks – all there. You hadn't touched a thing. Even the bedding hadn't been changed, with Gran's favourite silk cushion lovingly placed in the centre of the pillows.

I stood in the middle of the room for a few moments, accompanied by Nat King Cole's lilting voice floating out from the dining room. *Smile though your heart is aching, smile even though it's breaking ...* But I didn't feel like smiling when viewing this shrine you had made to Gran. What I did feel was a succession of emotions that seized me within ten seconds flat: irritation, anger, sympathy, pity, fear … The irritation and anger only lasted for the first couple of seconds; after that, I was overwhelmed by an awareness of how you must have felt, losing your mother. More to the point, how would *I* one day feel when I lost you? I think at that very moment I realised that no matter how old one is, a mother will always be the most central person in anyone's life, for better or worse: a cord that even death itself will not be able to sever.

Fighting back a rogue tear, I abandoned Gran's shrine and headed for the dining room.

You were sitting at the table, a cup of tea on your place mat, your profile perfectly still, staring ahead into space; not crying, not smiling, just staring. You were with him, weren't you? I know the feeling well. I too have so often been with another *him*.

I stood silently in the open doorway, feeling overwhelmed by an even greater sadness than I'd felt in Gran's room. You had aged, Mother. In the two months since I left home, you had aged. I could see it in your profile. You were still lovely, magnificent, elegant, charismatic – it was still all there, emanating from every feature on your expressive face; but now there were additional lines from stress and hard work and, I suddenly realised, loneliness. You had missed me. My God, you had probably missed me even more than I'd missed you. That had never occurred to me till this moment. There I'd been, feeling sorry for myself with my string of bad boyfriends and my homesickness … but what about *you*? All alone on those long evenings we used to spend together, all alone at the weekends when we used to nip out to town and have a coffee in our Beach Front Café. How were *you* coping? A huge wave of guilt inundated me as I stood there, looking at your ageing profile and listening to Nat King Cole as his words crackled round and round your old record player.

You weren't dancing with Peter this time, but you were with him none-theless. I knew it. I also knew that as soon as you saw me you would immediately snap out of your reverie and I would once again become the centre of your universe, and you mine.

I waited till the song came to an end, then stepped inside the room.

Instantly you turned round, your face illuminated by joy. Leaping up from your chair, you cried, '*Darling!* I wasn't expecting you until – heavens above, is that the time?'

I laughed. 'You're always getting your times mixed up. I said I'd be back at about five, didn't I? And it's now quarter past.'

'Goodness, so it is!'

I hurried towards you for a hug. After disentangling ourselves, you held me by the shoulders and took a step back.

'My word, Leah, just *look* at you! You're a young woman now! I bet you're famished, aren't you?'

'No – well, yes – but I can wait. It's been *so* long since I've sat at this table … I've been dreaming about this all term.'

Kissing my forehead, you let go of my shoulders and said, 'Now you just sit yourself down and relax while I put the kettle on. You must be dying for a cuppa.'

You hurried into the kitchen. I waited in sheer contentment while listening to all the familiar sounds of home: the running of the tap, the opening and closing of cupboards as you took out our favourite China cups, the clattering of pottery and cutlery as you assembled the whole lot on a tray.

Less than a minute later you were back. 'I'll just give the tea another minute to brew,' you said, sitting yourself down again. Your eyes swept over me in a lightning-quick appraisal that only mothers can do. 'Leah, you look washed-out. Are you sure you're eating enough? Or is it all these late nights and gadding about that's getting to you?'

'No, I'm fine. I just …' I took a deep breath. 'I'm just sick to death of *men*. Honestly, Mother, I've had enough to last me an eternity!' I sounded like Bette Davis at the grand old age of forty-something.

You laughed. 'Oh, Leah, you've got your whole life in front of you. Your perfect man is out there waiting for you, believe me.'

'Well, so far I've found three pretty imperfect specimens.'

'Heavens above, you *are* sounding all grown-up and cynical.'

'I've had to grow up fast. First with Gus' help, then Richard's, then Danny's –'

'Darling, they're not worth it. They obviously weren't the right ones for you. Just forget the lot of them and concentrate on your music instead.'

I chewed at my lip. 'Well, actually … to be perfectly honest, even that isn't going too well. Sometimes I really wish I'd taken my English teacher's advice and studied Literature instead.'

'Oh Leah, now you know that isn't true. You've got *tremendous* talent and you've just got to be patient. Darling, I do know what you're going through with all your men-folk, believe me. How do you think I felt the first time Peter let me down? There I was, just back from our lovely weekend in Paris where we'd celebrated my twenty-first birthday and – actually, no, it was later than that. I think it was about two years after Paris …'

I glanced at my watch and wondered how the tea was doing. I was parched after that long, crowded train journey.

'Anyway, just when I thought that Peter was at last on the verge of tying the knot, next thing I know, he goes and tells me that he's given up his job at the *Lancashire Evening Post* and accepted a better position in Manchester. Of course it goes without saying that I was proud of him, being a reporter on a bigger newspaper, but at the same time it meant he had to move away – so how do you think I felt about *that*? And yet I have to say, looking back on it now, it was only natural – what with his complexes about the injustice of the world, and his desire to make a difference, perhaps write a book one day to open people's eyes -'

'What was only natural?'

'That he should have left Preston, and eventually …well, strayed.' You looked uncharacteristically flustered. Or was it just plain old hurt, even after a quarter of a century?

'Then why didn't you move to Manchester with him?'

'What, to keep an eye on him? Ye gods, as if I was going to be Peter's keeper! Besides, how could I have moved to Manchester, just like that? You think jobs grow on trees?'

'Okay, okay, sorry I asked!' But you ploughed right on:

'Good heavens, I was hardly going to give up my job at the drop of a hat! And even if I had given it up, I certainly wouldn't have moved into Peter's flat.'

'But you moved into Dad's flat when you went to Cyprus to visit Peter's grave, so what's the difference?'

'That was *completely* different.' Your voice suddenly dropped, both in volume and timbre, so I knew to leave the subject alone. The last thing I wanted was one of your huffs coming upon you and spoiling our first day together in two months.

I cast a casual look around the room, then at the door. 'Aren't there any guests?'

You shook your head. 'We've got Belle Vue Mansions all to ourselves for the whole weekend.' The ice in your voice had dissolved, thank God.

'You mean even Mr Tomlinson isn't here?'

'Thank heavens, no. Although he did ask about the possibility of coming for Christmas -'

'Oh my God, I hope you said no to him?'

'Of course I said no, silly. I wouldn't spoil our Christmas for all the tea in China!'

I closed my eyes in relief. We both adored the season of good will to all men. You made it magical every year, whether through drizzle, hail, sleet or snow. Usually drizzle. There you'd be, decorating the house with holly and tinsel from top to bottom, filling it with seasonal music – Bing Crosby, Val Doonican, King's College Choir, Tchaikovsky's *Nutcracker Suite*; stocking up on mince pies, nuts, dates, sherry, all of which you placed in permanent exhibition on our long dining table... by the time you'd finished with Belle Vue Mansions, it was transformed into a living scene from *A Christmas Carol*. Very occasionally you'd invite Auntie Ivy, who'd come up all the way from London and stay with us for a few days, and sometimes you'd ask your spinster friend Marge over for Boxing Day, as well as Auntie Doreen, Uncle Paul and cousin Sandra. But Christmas Day we always spent on our own, which was just perfect. Oh – apart from one year, when old Uncle Finbar from Dad's side in Southern Ireland came to stay. That didn't exactly turn out a barrel of laughs. He dried you out of all your whisky stock that you reserved for VIPs, and kept going on about how you and Dad should get back together seeing as you were still married in the eyes of the Catholic Church, and I kept praying that you wouldn't, which is hardly surprising, considering all the rows I remember from my childhood. After two or three days, poor old Finbar caught the ferry back to Cork with his tail between his legs, having had more than his fair dosage of rants and rages from you. '*It's a disgrace, that's what it is! I've never heard anything like it! Hell and damnation, you ought to be glad I don't write to the Pope himself, telling him exactly what kind of a husband your precious nephew was ...*' Sometimes I squirmed during those spectacular vents of yours, and sometimes I was proud of you.

Opening my eyes again, I found your dilated pupils examining me with a peculiar expression. 'What's the matter?' I asked.

'Nothing's the matter, darling. I was just thinking.'

'About what?'

Suddenly you reached for my hand. 'Oh Leah, don't you think it's time to let bygones be bygones?'

'What bygones?'

'Don't you think it would be nice if you wrote a letter to Brother Matthew? Just to wish him a happy Christmas?'

'Brother Matthew?' I swallowed. 'God, I haven't thought about him in ages.'

'Now you know that isn't true.'

'Okay, even if it isn't, what's the point? He obviously doesn't want to be bothered with me. I'm just a nuisance to him.'

'Heavens above, what the dickens gave you that idea? He was sent off to the Highlands *because* of you, don't you forget that! The only nuisance you are to him is by not being there anymore.'

Your voice was on the verge of crossing over to anger, though I wasn't quite sure why. But then your face relaxed, and you pulled your chair closer to mine. 'Look, darling, I don't mean to interfere. When all's said and done it's your life, and you must decide what's best to do. But with Christmas so near, I just thought it would be a lovely gesture for you to write to him.'

'Why? At the end of the day, he's a monk.'

'And you don't think monks need friendship as well?'

'Oh come on, we're not talking about ordinary friendship.'

'No, we're talking about a *loving* friendship, which is exactly the sort of thing you could do with now, in your state of mind. A friendship that could help you forget all about your menfolk in Birmingham and just allow you to relax in Brother Matthew's warm, mature company – even if only through letters. Think about it, darling.'

You were right, of course. The thought of Brother Matthew at that very moment was sheer heaven. Why had I considered it so impossible to write to him after his last letter, I now found myself wondering. You made everything sound so simple.

'Well – maybe just a card then,' I conceded. 'Nothing too gushing.'

Your eyes lit up. 'That's my girl! We can go to town tomorrow to choose one. It'll have to be a nice card – maybe one of those with a quote. Omar Khayyam would be ideal, with the two of you having wasted so much precious time. Something like …' You raised your head and assumed the voice of your Amateur Dramatic Society days: '*Dreaming, when Dawn's Left hand*

was in the sky, I heard a voice within the tavern cry, Awake little ones and fill
the cup, before life's liquor in its cup be dry!

I pulled a face. 'Mother, I don't think that'll be too compatible with Brother Matthew's Catholic philosophy.'

'Oh, don't be silly. It'll show him just how deep-thinking and well-read you are. Really and truly Leah, life is too short to waste – especially when you know you've made that special *click* with someone, and he also knows it, whether he admits it or not. It's Kismet, darling. You can't run away from it.'

'Oh, I don't know …'

'But you will write to him?'

I sighed, as if you were the impossible teenager and me the over-anxious mother. 'Oh, okay, then. I suppose I've got nothing to lose.'

Smiling that lovely Vivien Leigh smile of yours, you squeezed my hand. 'That's my girl. This calls for a toast!' You stood up and hurried over to the drinks cabinet at the other end of the room, completely forgetting that the tea was still brewing in the kitchen.

And so it was settled. A card it would be, which we would select together the following day.

That's how I started writing to Brother Matthew again.

December 10th 1978

Dear Leah,

I was delighted to hear from you, and am so sorry I haven't been able to keep in touch before. As you can see, I'm back at Greystones again feeling much rested and recovered. I am now firmly established in the Gatehouse, and enjoying the somewhat irregular life of never quite knowing what is going to happen next.

I was sorry to hear that your A level results were not as good as you'd hoped – but what are A levels anyway (says he who is looking back about nine years since I first did mine). I'm so glad you are enjoying your new life in Birmingham and your musical career. We must hear you play up here some time – that would certainly lighten up our monastic routine!

You sound so full of life and enthusiasm for the new experience, I'm sure you will thoroughly enjoy it. However, student life can be a disturbing time also – though being mugged at knife point is rather taking it to the extreme, I must say! How very awful for you. But no matter the circumstances, you must keep faithful to prayer and truth. I'll be thinking of you, I promise. Come and visit the Gatehouse sometime soon if you can. I'll greatly look forward to that.

Love and God bless,
Matthew

That was the first letter from Brother Matthew in six months. My joy was so enormous, I immediately ran to the phone booth nearest Cavendish Hall and read the whole thing out to you. The excitement in your voice was palpable, despite the crackly telephone line.

'Oh my darling, he's pining for you, can't you see?'

'Well, he could just be trying to be nice…'

'Oh for heaven's sake, Leah, don't be foolish! He can't wait to see you again. You must write back *immediately*.'

And so I did.

By the time his reply came, a week later, I was home for the Christmas holiday and therefore able to share his words of wisdom with you in person. We huddled together on the sofa as I read it aloud.

Dear Leah,

Your lovely letter brought a smile to my face and made me feel as though I were part of the world again. Thank you for that.

In answer to your question about Christmas, I'll be spending it with my grandmother in the Lake District. She lives alone in an old manor house, tucked away on a hill with a spectacular view over Derwent Water. Whenever I go back there, I still delight in the utter seclusion of the place – the wild vegetation that creeps up the house, the squirrels and hedgehogs and field mice that are regular visitors to the long garden … It's like something out of a Beatrix Potter tale. There's also a delightful little hamlet not too far away, with a post office, a church, and a couple of small shops – oh – and how could I forget the 'Hound and Partridge'? I've enjoyed many a pint there over the years. (So yes, to answer your other question – monks are allowed to drink alcohol!) If you've never been to the Lakes before, I would thoroughly recommend that you take a visit some time.'

'He never said that, did he?' You put your coffee mug down and leaned closer to re-read the last sentence. 'Oh darling, he's practically *inviting* you there, can't you see?' You snatched the letter from my hand and read the next bit aloud. '*You see, Leah, your charming, youthful chatter has led me to waste words reminiscing about my family home instead of giving you words of spiritual advice. So at this point I feel it my duty to remind you to try and spend some time each day in quiet reflection …* blah blah blah …'

'Mother!' I said, laughing.

Wafting your hand at me, you carried straight on: '*Amid all your fun and partying, don't forget to spare a little thought for God every now and then ...* blah blah ... Well, he *has* to say that, doesn't he? But what he really means is, don't forget to spare a little thought for *me* every now and then.'

'Oh I don't know. I think you're reading way too much into it.' But of course I secretly thrilled at every word of your analysis.

But once I returned to Birmingham after Christmas, Brother Matthew gradually faded from my mind as the swing of student life caught up with me. It wasn't until February - the anniversary of my first trip to Greystones - that my thoughts started travelling back towards those North Yorkshire hills where my heart had first been captivated. So in my next letter I dared myself to end with the words: *I miss you more than I can admit.*

He didn't reply for a while after that and I immediately regretted having gone too far, though you of course reassured me that I hadn't. In the meantime, life at music college plodded along. There was the annual piano competition I could have entered, but Michael Williams said I wasn't ready yet. The truth is, I was increasingly finding my daily piano practice a drag. Some days I gave it a miss altogether if the queue for practice rooms was too long.

And then, a whole month later, Brother Matthew's next letter arrived. Straight away I hurried to that well-used phone booth and read the whole thing out to you.

'*Dear Leah,*

May I wish you a very belated happy 19th birthday, and hope that you accept my apologies for the tardiness of this reply.'

'Tardiness?' you laughed into the receiver. 'How very quaint. Go on, then. What does he say next?'

So I carried on: '*Your letter was a sheer delight to read. I must say I can't quite equate your lively, chatty style with the shy sixth form girl I met over a year ago. Truly, Leah, your words are like a balm to the weary convalescent. I'm so glad to hear that you're living life to the full, both with the ups and downs. I myself feel about 100 at the moment – but I suppose that's the end of six drain-ing weeks and a fairly hard term, with the weather hardly helping to make life brighter. But it's Easter soon, and spring, and despite everything there seem to be green shoots appearing all over Monks' Wood in an attempt to bring life to the dead world again. So I shall try and feel young again.*

I thought of you the other week, when we had a contingent over from Lark Mount – a very pleasant and cheerful group indeed. Almost as nice as the group you came with last year. (Was it really only last year? – it seems a lot longer.)

Must dash. Say a prayer occasionally for this wayward monk, as he does for you.'

His next letter was yet again a long time in coming. You were convinced that he was making himself do penance for having unholy thoughts about me. But I wasn't sure. When he still hadn't replied in over six weeks, you urged me to send him a gentle reminder. I did more than that. I begged his forgiveness for any offence my letters might have caused him, then asked him to book me in at the Gatehouse over the summer holidays. His reply came within days. Off I hurried to that phone booth again.

'Dearest Leah,' I read aloud to you.

'I'm sure I've told you before that you don't ever need to apologise for your wonderful letters – remember, they're my balm. By all means keep sending them.

Regarding your request, I've pencilled you in at the Gatehouse from July 3rd-6th. Please let me know if these dates suit you, and then I can confirm the booking.

I hope you are still finding time in your hectic round of boyfriends and music studies to spare a few minutes for quiet prayer and contemplation each day – as well as for this wayward monk.'

'Ah, the wayward monk strikes again,' you teased from the other end of the phone line. I carried straight on:

'I do think you should enter this piano competition that you mentioned, as it will give you something to focus on and prevent you from frittering your time away on things that distract you from the reason you are at a College of Music – namely, to realise your dream of being a concert pianist.'

'Goodness knows what distracts *him*,' you said through a muffled giggle. 'You know, during all those late-night hours when he's alone in his cell.'

'Oh *Mother*,' I said, my heart missing a beat at the thought of what those thoughts might entail. I guiltily wondered if they extended as far as my own X-rated fantasies.

Trying to push such images out of my mind, I wrote to him the very next day. His reply included a timetable of buses between York and Greystones, and strict instructions on where to get off, because apparently the stop nearest to Greystones was in the wilds and easy to miss. So it was all arranged. After a whole year and a half, I was going to see him again!

I tried to keep my outrageous joy to a bare minimum in my reply.

Dear Brother Matthew,

Thank you so much for all the info about getting to Greystones. I'm sure I'll be fine.

On a different note, you'll be pleased to know that my piano teacher has finally agreed to let me enter the concerto competition in September. He's given me Mozart, which isn't exactly what I dreamed of, but it's better than not being allowed to enter at all. I had hoped to play Tchaikovsky's First, but apparently I need to wait another year for that. Anyway, this means I'm going to have to practise every day over the summer in order to get all 3 movements of the Mozart up to scratch. So could you also please make sure I have access to a practice room again, like I did last time?

Once again, thank you for everything - especially for offering to meet me in person at the Brandsby bus stop. I'm really, really look forward to seeing you again next Tuesday. I can't tell you how much.

Leah xxx

CHAPTER ELEVEN

1

It's July 2nd and I'm back home at Lyneham-on-Sea. It's the night before my second trip to Greystones. I haven't been there in almost a year and a half, and I'm a nervous wreck.

It's almost midnight. You're sitting on the edge of my bed, Ovaltine mug in one hand, stroking my forehead with the other. I myself am sitting propped up against my pillows, listening to your lovely voice and trying to steady the pace of my heartbeat at the thought of what awaits me the following day.

'Can't you see, darling,' you're saying to me cajolingly, 'he's simply calling out to you in the only way he can.'

'Oh, I don't know. What way?'

'All these coded messages in his letters, of course.'

'But what messages, exactly?'

'For instance calling himself the 'wayward monk' – I mean *wayward?* Heaven's above, Leah, I know you lean a bit on the gormless side, but surely even you have to admit that's very revealing.'

I giggle. I can't remember the last time I felt so nervous. Even more nervous than the night before my audition for the Royal Northern College of Music.

You look at me again, your eyes wrapping my entire being in your mad optimism. 'Oh, darling, the first meeting after a long break is *so* important. You have to make absolutely certain you get it right. I don't want to pressurise you, but believe me, the way you are with Brother Matthew tomorrow afternoon, when he greets you at the bus stop, could spell out the entire future of your relationship.'

'You don't want to pressurise me?' I laugh, trying to raise an ironic eyebrow. But your face has changed subtly. It has assumed that faraway look. Something has reminded you of your own lost love.

Placing your empty mug on my bedside cabinet, you fix your eyes on the wall just above my head. 'I know what it's like to be parted from someone dear to you. When Peter got that job on *The Manchester Evening News* I honestly thought my heart would break. It was three months before I managed to go over there to meet him, which seemed like an eternity at the time.' You sigh, turning your face towards the window. Then you look back at me and smile. I smile in return. I love it when you sit on my bed in the evenings and talk about your past life. As though sensing this, you stroke my forehead again.

'We'd been seeing each other almost every week from the moment we started dating, so can you imagine what a wrench it was when he left Preston? But his letters helped, just like with you and Brother Matthew. They were so lively and chatty – full of news about his social events, local gossip from work, always addressing me in that teasing way which used to drive me round the bend -'

'*Chubs,*' I fill in for you.

You roll your eyes, taking your hand away from my forehead and wafting it in the air. '*Chubs*! I ask you! Could you think of a less romantic nickname? Ye gods, anyone would think I was fat as a lump of lard! And yet I was never the *slightest* bit chubby. Just full-figured, which is what most men like, Peter included. And Tony.'

'The guy you got engaged to during one of your breaks from Peter.' I know them all.

You pull a face. 'Tony Gaston the architect. Can't imagine what the dickens I ever saw in him. Of course I liked the fact that he was an architect, but mainly I wanted to get my own back on Peter for breaking my heart with Delia, or Delilah, or whatever her pretentious name was …'

'Mother – what exactly was the original point you were going to make?'

You smile at me indulgently, as though at a six-year-old. Smoothing out the quilt by my side, you carry on, 'My point is, darling, that the very first time I went to Manchester to visit Peter, I knew within the first few moments of our reunion that the magic was still there. It was as if we'd never been apart. And I'm sure it's going to be just the same for you and Brother Matthew tomorrow, believe me. So remember my words when you're on the bus to Brandsby, feeling all jittery and worrying about how you'll be with each other after all this time. The answer is that you'll be *fine*, because it's impossible for it to be any other way. Let's face it, darling, you and Brother Matthew were meant for each other, just like Peter and I were. It's Kismet, whether you like it or not.'

You turn your eyes to the stars. The cold stars, hard and brittle, utterly detached from all this Kismet lark.

* * *

As the train wheezed to a halt at Manchester Piccadilly, she thought her heart would burst through the tightly buttoned bodice of her dress. It was a new dress, made to measure especially for the occasion of her first visit to Peter since he moved to Manchester, all of three months ago. Her mother and sister had colluded with her in the size, pattern and colour of the design. They'd been to every fitting with her over the past fortnight; and now, here at last, she stood by the open train door, gathering the folds of the voluptuous gingham material in her hands as she stepped down onto the swarming platform. She spotted him straight away.

'Hey, Molly!' he called out to her, his long legs manoeuvring the swirling eddy of disembarked passengers.

She barely managed to greet him before he swept her in his arms, which were trembling. Could it be, could it *possibly* be, that he had missed her as much as she had missed him? 'Peter, I – I can't breathe …'

He let her go with a laugh, then stepped back to view the spectacular sight of her hand placed upon the heaving bodice of that sexy frock she was wearing.

'You look bloody fantastic! Oh God, Molly, I've missed you *so* much ... I've been going crazy thinking about you each night...'

'Heavens above, you *must* be going crazy. You forgot to call me Chubs.' She also tried to laugh, amid the surge of desire and joy that coursed through her veins.

'Chubs,' he echoed in a strange kind of voice, one she hadn't heard before. 'My utterly gorgeous, darling Chubs.' He held her face in his hands and looked at her with such intensity, she had to avert her eyes. 'It's been so long – *too* long. Promise me you'll not leave it this along again before coming to see me.'

She gently freed her face from his grip. 'Well, you could also promise not to leave it so long before coming to see *me*. Or have you gone up too much in the world now to bother with the likes of crummy old Preston? Working for the *Manchester Evening News* has gone to your head, has it?'

'Nothing's gone to my head except you, you daft beggar. And I *love* the dress. C'mon then, give us a twirl.'

She readily complied, laughing as the cotton folds flapped around her thighs mid-pirouette. An elderly couple smiled at the touching scene as they hobbled past. *Ah, love in its prime...*

He pinched her cheek once she'd returned to a stationary position. 'Any road, don't know about you, but I'm famished. Fancy summat to eat? The moped's parked outside – unless someone's nicked it by now.'

'Who on earth would want to nick that ridiculous old thing?' she said snootily, mimicking her old elocution teacher.

'*Quaite*,' Peter laughed. And then, in his normal Lancastrian vowels, 'Well c'mon then, Miss Williams, are you hungry or what?'

Hungry for you, she thought, but of course didn't say it aloud. There were some things you just didn't say aloud, back then in 1953. That is, if you were a well-brought up working class girl, albeit one that was bursting at the seams, not just out of her D-cup bra, but every constriction of her neat little life.

Twenty minutes later they found themselves immersed in the greasy aromas of *Benjie's Café,* seated opposite one another at a table with a chequered cloth that complemented the green gingham of her dress.

'You're looking pale,' Peter said, nodding a friendly smile at the waitress (or was it a flirty smile?) as she placed his bacon bap in front of him. He tucked into his succulent sandwich as though it was the first meal he'd had all week. A trickle of fat glistened on his chin. 'You must be sickening for summat. Or someone.' He winked at her.

'I'm absolutely fine. Picture of health, as our family doctor always says.'

'No you're not. You're too pale. You need to get out more, you poor, forlorn, love-lost damsel. You shouldn't be going back home to your Mam every day after work.'

'Who on earth says I do that?'

'Oooh ...' He pulled down a corner of his mouth. She loved it when he did that. 'Do I detect a secret admirer lurking about somewhere?'

'I don't know about *secret.*'

'So what's his name when he's not drunk?'

She raised her right eyebrow; a skill that had taken years to perfect. 'He's never drunk, as a matter of fact. And his name is Tony Gaston, if you must know. He's just qualified as an architect, and he happens to be a very nice young man.'

'Aha. Rushing to his defence, I see.'

'But Peter –' She couldn't tell if the ironic look that shrouded his features was the result of amusement or anger. 'I don't – well, I don't like him in *that* way. Not in the least. It's just that – he's so very nice and attentive, and he keeps inviting me to concerts, but of course I've said no each time.'

'Then you shouldn't. You should say yes, if you feel that sorry for the poor bugger. Do him a good deed, for Christ's sake, and go to one of his flaming concerts.'

'Don't be silly. I don't want to.'

'Well, you should,' he said in a suddenly tight voice. 'But don't blame me for the consequences, my darling coquette.'

Just as she was about to retaliate, he lurched across the table and whispered into her ear, 'C'mon, hurry up! Can't wait to show you my flat.'

It didn't take her long to find out which room in it he was so eager to show her.

2

It's the next day, July 3ʳᵈ 1979. I'm on the bus to Brandsby, and I'm feeling every bit as jittery as you had predicted. I've been on the bus almost forty minutes now, which means we must be approaching the place where I'm supposed to get off. When I set out from York Station the bus was full, but as the smelly old vehicle chugged and wheezed its way through the dense traffic of central York, then accelerated into the silence of the countryside, all passengers one by one began to disembark. Now there's only three of us left.

The bus driver promised to give me a shout at the Brandsby stop, but to be on the safe side I'm sitting right at the front to make sure he doesn't forget. It's almost six o'clock; a fine summer evening – warm and fragrant, without a cloud in the sky. The windows in the bus are wide open. Every time we stop at yet another God-forsaken outpost in the middle of nowhere, I listen to the birds, which in turn remind me of Brother Matthew's letter when he described his grandmother's manor house in the Lakes. I can just picture Matthew and me at some amorphous point in the future – sitting on wicker chairs on the veranda as we gaze at the distant ripples of Derwent Water way down at the bottom of the hill.

Once again I look out of the bus window and drink in the breathtaking view: the undulating farmland, the wooded hills and scattered hedgerows, the occasional grey-stone cottage, the peaceful sheep quietly grazing as though accompanied by their Bach Cantata namesake ... and all of it, *all of it* – bathed in this rich amber sunlight, this unique fleeting moment I will never experience again.

We come to another stop, also in the middle of bloody nowhere. The doors judder open and yet another passenger clambers down the steps onto the sun-splashed pavement. That leaves just two of us. We should be approaching Brandsby at any moment. I lean forward and ask the driver, 'Are we almost there?'

Without turning round, he calls over his shoulder, 'Just another couple of stops, love. Don't worry, I hadn't forgotten you.'

I lean back in my seat. My breathing has quickened. Just another couple of stops, he said. Oh God, oh God, oh God, how am I going to cope? It's one thing being risqué in letters, but quite another keeping up to those standards in real life. Especially after almost a year and a half, when it's just going to be me and him all alone on this country road, in the monastery car he said he'd borrow, both of us sitting beside each other and being forced to make small talk to break the ice, as though we'd become strangers all over again. And then it occurs to me that in spite of our profuse exchange of letters these past seventeen months, at rock bottom we *are* still strangers – though not yet in paradise.

Once again I find myself trying to recall your words from the previous night.

'Remember, Leah, no matter what happens in life, I'll always love you never-stop-growing. And remember that you're a Cavanagh. Whatever can be said of that swaggering bunch of bigheads across the Irish Sea, one thing I have to give them full credit for is their good looks. Add to that the charm and charisma from my side, and you can't go wrong. Darling, he doesn't stand a chance against you.'

'But that isn't the *only* reason I'm going to Greystones ...'

'Oh, pull the other one! It's the main reason, isn't it?'

'Well –'

'Come on, Leah, be honest with yourself. Are you or are you not in love with him?'

'Well –'

'The trouble is, darling, you just don't want to face it. And I can understand that, really I can. Falling in love is terrifying – I of all people should know. But running away from the truth won't make it any easier.'

Quite honestly, way back then in 1979 I'm not sure if I was anywhere near as much in love with him as you were with the *idea* of me being in love with him. The sad thing is that at this early stage it could so easily have been stopped. With proper guidance from someone older and wiser, i.e. *you*, Mother, it could have been nipped in the bud before it was too late.

3

'*Brandsby!*' the driver calls out.

The bus wheezes to a halt.

I spring up from my seat like a jack-in-the-box. Scooping all my clutter together, I make my way over to the door that slowly hisses open.

'Thank you,' I say, clambering down the steps with difficulty as I try to balance guitar, hold-all, shoulder bag, arms and legs all in one inelegant whole.

I step onto the pavement, at last on solid ground. I'm here! I've made it!

I look to my left and right, behind, and in front. Not a single person, car, chimney or house in sight. Where exactly am I? A tremor of fear grips the hairs on my spine. Isn't the Yorkshire ripper still at large? And here I am in the depths of North Yorkshire, all on my own on a quiet country road, with evening fast approaching. Not a single car has passed by since I got off the bus. Isn't Brandsby supposed to be a village? So where are all the houses? Where's the village pub, the church, the school … where is everything and everyone? Have I got off too soon? It's like something out of a horror film. I look around again. Lots of trees, hedges, fields, birds, bees, but no sign that announces WELCOME TO BRANDSBY. It would be so easy for anyone to leap out at me from the cover of those trees and bushes and then …

Ah! At last I spot a cottage a bit further down the road. And is that another one, hidden behind that large oak tree over there? I try to rack my brains to remember exactly where Brother Matthew had told me he'd be waiting. Am I too early? I glance at my watch yet again. No, I'm not. It's now five past six, so he's late. Unless I got off at the wrong stop … come to think of it, didn't Brother Matthew mention something about there being *two* stops in Brandsby? Perhaps I should have got off at the second one?

I start walking.

After only a few steps I became aware that a car is approaching from behind. I hold my breath. It's following me very slowly along the side of the road. I quicken my pace, clutching onto my guitar and hold-all for dear life. It would be *so* unfair to have survived a mugging at knife-point in Birmingham, only to be strangled to death by the Yorkshire Ripper in Brandsby before I even have the chance to see Brother Matthew just one more time.

'*Leah!*'

I spin round, instantly recognising the sound of his voice. The voice I will never forget, as long as I live.

'You got off a stop too early,' he calls out to me from his open car window, laughing. Pulling the old clanger of a vehicle to a halt, he leans across the front passenger seat and flicks open the door. 'Come on in!'

'Oh, hello,' I say breezily, willing the insane palpitations of my heart to calm down as I approach the car.

'Here, let me help you with that. What have you got in there, a machine gun?'

I laugh, and between the two of us we somehow manage to manoeuvre the bloody great hulk of my guitar case and hold-all onto the back seat.

'Seatbelt,' he reminds me as I climb in the front and shut the door. He sounds very much like a teacher at that moment, but when I glance across at him I'm awarded one of those drop-dead gorgeous smiles that I've been treasuring in my memory box these past seventeen months. Whatever uncertainty I've been feeling up till now, it's all banished in an instant. I have the strangest feeling of coming back home.

'It's a good job I spotted you,' he says, glancing at the wing mirror as he steers the car back onto the empty road. 'And it's a good job it's still light, otherwise I might have missed you altogether. You'd have been standing by the side of the road, waiting for me all night.'

'Erm – I don't *think* so.'

'I was joking,' he laughs. 'Anyway, you're here now, that's all that matters. So then, Leah. How are you?' His sparkling blue eyes skim my face. 'You haven't changed that much. You just look ... well, a year and a half older, I suppose.'

'Thanks. You haven't changed either.'

'Ah, you're being kind. The well-brought up lass from Lancashire.' I'm not sure I like the sound of that. 'That's where you should have got off.' He gestures towards the bus stop to our left as we drive through the village of Brandsby. 'Perhaps you could remember next time, to save us both a lot of unnecessary panic?'

'Blame the bus driver,' I say, with the echo of 'next time' in my ears.

'I did tell you it was the *second* stop in Brandsby, Leah. I specifically remember stressing that to you, because the first stop often confuses new visitors who haven't done the route before. Anyway, enough of that. I want to hear all about what you've been up to since we last wrote.'

'Nothing momentous,' I say, and soon find myself filling him in with all the trivia of what's happened over the past week. I tell him about the persistent Mr Tomlinson, and I also mention how Jenny and Francesca are envious of me going back to Greystones. When I confess to him that I'd lied to them about the Gatehouse being full, he laughs.

'Leah, you bad girl! What if they'd decided to phone up and then found out there were plenty of rooms available?'

'I couldn't have cared less. I'm sorry, but I didn't want to have to share Greystones with them.' Of course what I really meant to say was that I didn't want to share *him* with them. But I think he's figured that one out, because when I glance across at his finely chiselled profile, I can detect an unmistakable hint of masculine satisfaction in it. I'm now a fully-fledged student of the world, I've had three boyfriends and I'm beginning to understand the male psyche. Yes, he knows that I want him all to myself and he's pleased as punch about it, whether or not he admits it.

4

My four days at Greystones passed by all too quickly. Thank God I'm a diary-keeper, which enables me to select whatever day of my life I want, and then action-replay it in my mind. That's what I'm doing right now. Reliving those four glorious days of my second visit to Greystones, when my infatuation for Brother Matthew was still youthful and sweet, though rapidly growing in strength.

On the first day Matthew was cheerful and chatty most of the time: asking me about my student life, my music, taking me to the practice room where I could work on my Mozart concerto, showing me the antiphonal pages during Offices, and sitting at the same table as me for meals. He even suggested that we went on a walk to the lakes – an apparently magical spot hidden deep in the Forest of Leeming, about three miles down the country road behind the monastery. But there were times when his mood grew sombre, and I would catch him looking at me with an expression that I couldn't for the life of me read. Like after breakfast on my second day, when I was helping with the washing-up.

I was standing by the sink chatting to Joelly, drying the soapy dishes that she handed to me one by one. Joelly was the Gatehouse cook and an ever-present appendage to the refectory. Early forties, maternal approach to all monastery guests and monks, and an inborn need to ensure their every culinary need was met. She also had a keen intuition. I suspect that quite early on she sensed there was something *in the air* between Brother Matthew and me.

While I was chatting away to her about the trials and tribulations of life at music college, I turned round at the sound of approaching footsteps. And there he was, hovering by the door, weighing me up with sombre eyes. He didn't even return the uncertain smile I gave him. Joelly also turned round, no doubt wondering why I'd suddenly stopped talking. As soon as she spotted Brother Matthew she glanced from him to me, then turned round again and started humming loudly as she plunged her hands back into the soapy water. Honestly, the atmosphere was so tense between Matthew and me, it was as though the air had suddenly filled with high-pitched strings from Hitchcock's *Psycho*.

We both stood there in a kind of stasis: me by the sink, tea towel in hand, Brother Matthew by the door, looking at me with those troubled eyes. I was convinced he was going to tell me that he'd have to abandon our planned walk to the lakes because of some pathetic excuse or other. But no, he didn't do that.

He just walked over to me, hesitantly, and said, 'Do you still want to go on that walk?'

I could barely contain my excitement. 'Yes, of course.'

He nodded slowly, as though we'd just agreed on the time for a funeral service. 'Okay. So that's settled then.'

I beamed at him and at last his lips twitched into some sort of response, though it could hardly be called a smile. Was it really Joelly's presence that made him so self-conscious, or was it the thought of the two of us being all on our own as we walked to those tantalising lakes in the Forest of Leeming?

Clearing his throat, he said, 'So … I'll come up to the Gatehouse just after lunch. Or do you need a little time first?'

'No, that's fine – I'll be waiting for you.' I will, oh yes, I will!

Again he nodded, attempted another smile, and left the room.

I turned back to the sink to carry on with my dish-drying task, trying to submerge the secret smile that was dying to break out. But when Joelly glanced sidewise at me, she just said, 'Be careful there, love.'

* * *

We set off soon after lunch, as arranged. It was the first time I'd ever seen Brother Matthew in ordinary clothes. He was wearing jeans, a short-sleeved T-shirt and trainers, looking like any other handsome young man I might have met in Birmingham or at Belle Vue. At first I thought he seemed a little nervous as we left the Gatehouse together and headed down the driveway. But his mood soon relaxed once we found ourselves out of the monastery grounds and strolling down the empty country road, alongside fields that were polka-dotted with sheep and cows who raised their sleepy heads at us as we walked past.

'Oh gosh, it's all so beautiful!' I said, breathing in the fragrant air. 'I envy you living here, so near to all this.' I swept my arm out to the rolling fields and huge sky and wooded horizon. It was as though we were part of a life-size painting whose artist had invited us in for a private viewing.

As he didn't reply, I stole a surreptitious glance at him. He was smiling, I was pleased to note, but it was a different sort of smile. Sadder, older – he was only about twenty-eight, but seemed so much more advanced in years than me. And then, quite out of the blue, he looked across at me and said, 'If you like all this, then you'd love Riveaux Abbey. It's even more spectacular. Perhaps I could take you there as well, if the weather holds.'

'That would be great,' I said, holding my breath, hoping he'd make the suggestion a little more definite. For instance, suggesting an exact time and day. Tomorrow? The day after? It couldn't be any later than that, because in three days I had to go back to Lyneham, worse luck.

But what happened next cast a shadow on the rest of our afternoon. Or a curse, should I say, in the form of Father Sebastian, the Grim Reaper of Greystones.

Barely ten minutes after we'd set off on our walk, a car approached us from the opposite direction. Slowing down, it drew to a halt by our side. Out of the open front window popped Father Sebastian's mean, jowly face. Despite his obsequious smile, he didn't fool me for one moment.

'Ah, Matthew, I'm glad I've caught you. Five o'clock, don't forget.'

Brother Matthew stopped dead in his tracks, forcing me to do so as well. 'Oh – yes, five o'clock,' he repeated, evidently flustered.

The older priest appeared to be happy that his message had successfully been relayed. 'Well, cheerio then,' he said, wriggling his fleshy fingers at us and driving off into the distance in a puff of smoke.

Brother Matthew's mood suffered a severe downturn after that. All my attempts to be friendly, chatty, even slightly flirty, could not bring back the contentment that had bound us just minutes before. But I was determined to make the most of those bloody lakes, if nothing else. At least we still had the next handful of hours to ourselves. And oh my God, talk about beauty! Once we veered off from the private country road, we made our way into a dense forest that was like something out of *Sleeping Beauty*. Over here we were in a different world entirely: an enchanted land where wood nymphs and leprechauns surely dwelt, dancing in a chequerboard of sunlight and shadow that filtered in through capricious gaps between the trees.

'Wow, this is *amazing*,' I said, wishing I could think of something more original. But who could blame me for not being able to? I'm sure even the greatest of Romantic poets didn't come out with ready strings of metaphors while strolling through the Alps on a summer's afternoon.

'I knew you'd like it,' he said as we approached the first lake.

He headed for a wooden bench that was positioned in a clearing just a few feet from the shore, and sat down. After the briefest hesitation, I joined him. For the next handful of moments we sat in silence.

'Does anyone ever swim here?' I presently asked, trying to break the mantle of self-consciousness that had descended upon him since Father Sebastian's intrusion.

'Occasionally. But I wouldn't fancy it myself. Even in high summer I gather the water's very cold.'

'Is it?' I stood up from the bench and walked over to the small jetty opposite us. Kneeling down on the wooden surface, I dipped my fingers into the clear water. It wasn't as cold as I'd expected. I was about to tell him this, but as I turned round to look at him I stopped myself short. It was another of those moments when I caught him completely unawares. He was watching me in a wistful kind of way, with a haunted, defenceless expression on his face. It was almost as if he was an old man trying to recapture his lost youth or lost love, or whatever it was that plagued him so visibly.

I quickly turned away and continued skimming my fingers across the water. It was no use. I just couldn't snap him out of the mood that Father Sebastian's words had imposed on him. What the hell could 'five o'clock' have meant, to have so drastically changed his former good humour? Had it been a coded warning against dangerous female-temptresses like me?

Ah, Matthew! Back then I truly didn't want to tempt you; I was just happy to be with you again, didn't you realise that? Or maybe you did realise it, and maybe you felt the same way about being with me again. Maybe *that* was what caused the sadness in your eyes, because you realised that everything we shared that summer afternoon was only for a stolen moment in our lives.

* * *

Back at the Gatehouse that evening, a new visitor appeared at suppertime: Jack Norris, as he jovially introduced himself. He was middle-aged, moustachioed and rather dashing, with a confident demeanour that instantly put everyone at their ease. Towards the end of supper he looked directly across the table at me and smiled his cavalier smile.

'So then, Leah. What are your plans for tomorrow?'

'I don't know,' I replied honestly. 'Nothing in particular.'

'Oh, that's good. Then how about a spin to Riveaulx Abbey, eh? It's a beautiful spot.'

I think my mouth must have dropped open at that point. I wanted to cry out: *But that's where Brother Matthew offered to take me!* Instead, all I could do was stare at my plate and wish to God that Brother Matthew would say something. No such luck.

In lieu of a reply, my new admirer continued, 'I'd been planning on going by myself, but such outings are always nicer in company. So what d'you say? No pressure, of course. Entirely up to you.'

Panicking, I stole an urgent glance at Brother Matthew. But he was looking at the newcomer rather than me. 'I'm sure Leah would love that,' he said before I had the chance to make any excuses.

Widening my eyes at Matthew, I spluttered without thinking, 'But I thought you said that we could –'

'It was only a *suggestion*, Leah.' He threw me an unexpectedly sharp look which silenced me in an instant. 'As it happens, I completely forgot that I'm on fire drill duty tomorrow afternoon.'

Oblivious to the cut-glass delicacy of the atmosphere, our newcomer-guest once again beamed at me and said, 'Good, so it's settled then. You're simply going to love Riveaulx.'

Oh, Matthew, why couldn't you have been my knight in shining armour and carried me off to Rievaulx Abbey on your white stallion? Why couldn't I have shared the following golden afternoon with you instead of Jack Norris? Why couldn't we have strolled amongst those clandestine archways and cloisters and courtyards, surrounded on all sides by steeply wooded hills that were relieved by splashes of sunlight upon hidden glades and clearings? And why couldn't I have sat on a blanket in one of those clearings with you instead of Jack Norris, sharing a bottle of wine and talking about life and love? Why couldn't you, instead of Jack Norris, have looked at me in an unexpectedly tender moment, and told me that I had beautiful autumn eyes?

As it happened, I managed to navigate the afternoon with Jack through a safe but guarded course, and we returned to Greystones with no hurt or embarrassed feelings. My middle-aged chaperone turned out to be a gentleman behind his Casanova façade, and so there had never really been any danger in the first place. But had it been *you* there with me, Matthew, amongst the ghosts of Cistercian monks from centuries past who glided in and out of the ancient ruins, there might have been a real danger. I might have laid myself back on the warm grass, and closed my eyes, and allowed you to lean over my waiting body and kiss me.

5

I returned to Lyneham-on-Sea older and wiser. In a nutshell, I knew I was fighting a losing battle. After all, Brother Matthew had chosen the monastic way of life long before he'd met me. Why couldn't you have accepted that, Mother? If you'd truly analysed his upbringing, you would have seen that he was pre-ordained to be a monk from the very beginning. All he had ever known was the monastery. And even if it was true that he'd looked at me with a wistful longing when he sat on that bench by the lakeside, what could it have meant other than a fugitive moment in time? A moment when he'd wondered how things might have turned out with someone like me, had he chosen the road not taken.

* * *

There was a glimmer of hope on my final morning.

After packing up and stripping my bed, I went downstairs to deposit my clutter in the hallway of the Gatehouse. Then I headed for the refectory to pour myself a glass of orange juice before preparing for the long journey home.

It was around ten o'clock, which was a no-man's time between breakfast and morning coffee. I didn't expect anyone to be there, other than possibly Joelly, though for once I hoped she wouldn't be. It wasn't that I didn't like her – on the contrary, I really enjoyed her bright Yorkshire humour and warm hospitality; it's just that I was hoping to have a final few minutes by myself. So imagine my shock when I opened the door to the refectory and found Brother Matthew there, sitting all on his own, his hands cradling a coffee mug while he stared into space. No one else was due to leave Greystones that morning, which meant, as far as I could deduce, that he'd come to the Gatehouse with the deliberate hope that he would bump into me before I left.

As I approached the table, he snapped out of his reverie and looked up at me. 'Ah, Leah. I was hoping to catch you before you left.'

'Oh?' I pulled out a chair and sat down opposite him.

'Would you like a coffee? I've just had one, but the kettle's still warm.'

'No, it's all right. I think I've had enough coffee to last me a lifetime these past few days.'

He laughed. 'Fair enough. We do try to look after our guests, as St Benedict instructed us several hundred years ago. Though I'm sure an overdose of caffeine at times is hard to avoid.'

I could see that he was back to his usual confident self, and I didn't like it. I wanted him to be morose and silent and throwing me tortured looks.

'So then,' he continued in strident cheeriness. 'How was Rievaulx?

I looked away, sighing deliberately loudly. '*Fine.*'

'Didn't I tell you you'd love it?'

And then I looked back at him. There was something about his evasive tone of voice that made me see red. I was about to catch a bus to York, then a train to Lyneham; I would very likely not be seeing him again for a year or more, and I'd had enough bullshitting.

'Yes, you did,' I said. 'And you also told me you'd take me there. So what happened, Brother Matthew? Why did you let me be taken there by some older guy I barely knew, who insisted on sharing a bottle of wine with me and looking at me with calf eyes and trying to seduce me?'

His shock was palpable. Immediately I regretted my words and quickly mumbled, 'No, he didn't try to seduce me. I was only joking.' *Though he could have done, had I given him have the chance*! I wanted to add, but didn't.

I don't think he was used to such behaviour. He obviously sensed that something was up. His convivial façade instantly faded. I was glad of that much, at least.

Frowning at his empty coffee mug, he said, 'I'm sorry if I haven't spent as much time with you as you'd hoped. I honestly did forget about the fire drill practice yesterday afternoon – it wasn't an excuse.'

'What makes you think I thought it was an excuse?'

'You know what I mean.'

'No, I'm afraid I don't.'

He raised his eyes to me and held my gaze in cross-fire with his own. That was the one glimmer of hope I had, during those few snatched moments while we looked at each other in the imminent dawning of confession. But then all he said was, 'Leah, I want you to know that I do pray for you.'

I could have crumpled up his words in a tight ball and flung them straight at him. Instead, I just folded my arms in sullen defeat. 'Well you're not very good at it then, are you?'

'No, apparently not. I'm useless at this sort of thing.'

'And what sort of thing would that be, exactly?'

'I'm sorry, I can see that I've upset you.'

'No you haven't.'

'Ah. Well, that's good then.'

'Believe me, if you'd upset me, I'd let you know.'

'Okay. So in future I won't need to worry.'

Realising we were getting nowhere fast, I pushed my chair away from the table and stood up. 'Right, better make a move. I've got a bus to catch.'

He also stood up. And moved a fraction closer to me. For a crazy moment I thought he was going to take me in his arms. But he didn't, obviously. We smiled at one another in an uneasy truce, then walked out of the room together, not saying a word.

After collecting my luggage from the hall, we headed up the driveway towards the bus stop on the country road. While waiting for the damn thing to materialise, Brother Matthew made the occasional banal comment. Fighting back rising frustration, I barely responded.

The bus arrived several minutes later. We said goodbye; I climbed up its steep steps – guitar case, bags and all – and I didn't even bother turning round to wave. I mean, what was the point? He'd made his choice in life, and it didn't include me.

* * *

I don't want to rush this night. This moment in time, trapped between the past and the future. I like it here, safely sheltered in the living room of my Lichfield cottage: letters, photos and diaries all laid out before me on the coffee table. Tonight, while I'm lost in remembering, everything is fine. I'm still in youthful, naive love with Brother Matthew; the pain of my longing for him is peripheral, not toxic. Not like *your* love, Mother. In this trapped moment between past and future, with the present on hold, I'm still your devoted daughter, and you my prized mother. The future is still my oyster, the past my coveted treasure, with our dashing Benedictine held at an enticing but safe distance. What more could I want? Isn't it the stuff of fairy tales?

My wedding day isn't until tomorrow, which might as well be next year or next century. Right now it's trapped in another dimension, another world, another time. The handful of faint stars hanging over my back yard, last time I had a peek, will be gone by the morning. Then the word 'tomorrow' will be made flesh.

So let's not rush this night, okay?

CHAPTER TWELVE

1

The summer of 1979 wasn't one that will go down in the annals of Leah Cavanagh's Happiest of Times. (Little did I know what was coming in the summer of 1980.) I was hopelessly in love with a Benedictine monk, but said monk was not hopelessly in love with me. Or if he was, he was trying as hard as damn it not to show his feelings. And it was driving me mad. Not even Jenny's sardonic humour could snap me out of the doldrums. She was studying Law at Durham University now, but come Christmas, Easter or summer holidays, we never failed to catch up with each other.

'You're still besotted with him, aren't you?' she said to me one sultry afternoon as we knelt on my bed by the open window, our eyes glued to the smartly-dressed members of a brass band three storeys below us, whose strains of *Chattanooga Choo Choo* wafted all the way up to my gables room.

I pulled a face. 'I'm not besotted with him, Jenny. I'm *in love* with him. That's completely different.'

'Oh, Leah, get a life.' She rolled her eyes, before returning them to the brass band. Leaning further out of the window, she suddenly shrieked, 'Bloody hell, will you get a look at the conductor! Can you see him? Why can't you go for someone like *him,* for Christ's sake?'

'Hey, watch it – you'll fall right into his arms if you lean out much further.'

'Ooh, I say.' She threw me a sideways grin. 'You *are* coming on.'

She had a knack of making me feel like I was still a gullible, lovelorn sixth former, whereas she herself had apparently been promoted to the far grittier world of adults. Or rather, adult *sex.* This was the summer of her first full-blown affair – which happened to be with a much older man who was fabulously unsuited to her, not least because he was married with three children. But when I tactfully pointed out this fact, she just said, 'Oh Leah, stop being so *puritanical.*' And now here she was, trying to catch the eye of the white-suited conductor three storeys below, who continued to swing his baton and hips to the beat of 1940s jazz.

* * *

On my third day back home you urged me to write Matthew a more daring letter.

We were just getting ourselves settled for the late film when you turned to look at me. Putting your coffee mug down, you said, 'Leah, you can't go on like this.'

I drew my eyebrows together. 'Can't go on like what?'

'You know what I mean. I'm talking about Brother Matthew. Why the dickens don't you finally write something *meaningful* to the poor man, for heaven's sake?'

Before I had the chance to ask what you meant by 'meaningful', you carried straight on, 'I know you think it's too soon, but believe me, life's too short to keep tiptoeing round each other's feelings. Ye gods, if Peter and I hadn't continually dilly-dallied with our wedding plans, then he'd never have gone to Cyprus and never would have been killed.'

'And I never would have existed.'

'Go and get a pen and a piece of paper, quickly!' You wafted your hand imperiously. 'Hurry up, before the film starts. Let's draft out the letter together now, while I'm feeling inspired. A good dose of romance tinged with humour is what's needed.'

So that's exactly what we did. Together. I've still got that draft now, together with all my other drafts. Hang on a minute, while I dig it out of my Pandora's box.

Okay, here it is. Are you listening, Mother, out there across the telepathic miles?

Dear Brother Matthew,

Do you think God has a sense of humour? If so, he's certainly enjoying a good laugh now. When my broken romance in Birmingham was causing me so much hurt last term, my mother said that there were other plans in store for me and that I would find another road. So, duly inspired, I set off for my place of refuge and true friend. Hmm. Miracles do happen! I left Greystones not only completely cured, but unable to believe ANYTHING could have mattered so much to me. However, this magical spot doesn't offer immunity, and so I've come back home with a far more dangerous disease; in fact, I know it's incurable. And please don't give me a sermon on how there's still another road. God isn't so complicated. He created ME with all my chemicals – and YOU with all yours. In fact, it's as simple as that: God created YOU; society made you a monk.

Oh dear, if I keep on like this, it'll be years before I hear from you again! Better stop right now.

Leah

I posted the letter the following morning, but had to wait a whole three weeks for his reply, by which time I was madly regretting having been so open.

Dear Leah,

I'm terribly sorry I haven't written before now, and you will probably have been wondering why. But really I was up to my eyes when your letter arrived, preparing for the Nuns' retreat, then giving it, and now in the middle of our own retreat. I'm just beginning to feel sane again.

Well now, to your letter. I have to confess that I had to read it a couple of times to get what was going on. But I think I have the picture roughly now. May I correct one thing, which may be a key point anyway. Society didn't make me a monk – nor did God for that matter – but I chose it, knowing pretty well what it involved. I'm realising now that far from burying you away, out of touch with people and the world, it in fact exposes you to them in a way that makes you very vulnerable. I suppose the ideal is that I be open to everyone – sharing their lives and their problems and their joys and everything else – and yet not belong to them, nor they to me. And that is the hard bit. Both from my side and from theirs. This past two years or so I have longed to belong to another and for them to belong to me – but instead I have chosen another way, which involves living a paradox of being open to everyone, yet being at the same time alone (Monachus = alone = monk).

It doesn't mean that I cannot build real friendships with other people – but it does mean that both I and the other must face the reality of what I am. I don't suppose that will help a great deal. I think what I'm trying to say is this. Don't be afraid of your feelings, of becoming involved with another – even with me. But face the reality also. I suspect there are parallels in music – there is tremendous freedom to compose or play, but within very strict limits and rules. And so it is in relationships with another.

I do hope you are enjoying the summer holidays. Stay happy, and write whenever you can. I hope something of what I've said makes sense and that I haven't interpreted your letter completely wrongly.

Love & God bless, Matthew

Uugh! That reply did not help enliven my languid mood, that's for certain. No matter how optimistically you pointed out that this 'other' person he said he wanted to belong to was obviously me, I didn't share your conviction. I was consumed by a wild regret that I'd ever written such a revealing letter to him. In the face of such emotional turmoil, I found it almost impossible to concentrate on anything else that summer, including the piano. So the Mozart concerto didn't go down too well, needless to say. I did try, of course; but whereas three or four hours was my usual daily quota, I'd be lucky to squeeze in just one or two. Then up the stairs I'd go, hurrying to my room to write my diary, and later in the evening back down the stairs to curl up on the sofa in front of the TV with you.

Yes, my main comfort that summer was from the usual source – *you*, Mother. It was always you, back then. In between seeing to the varying needs of your B&B guests, you still managed to find time for me. Either we'd nip out to the Beach Front Café, or if the weather was nice, we'd sit at the garden table in our *a la Mediterranean* patio and you'd go back into Foxland, telling me more stories from your past. Ah, so many dreams and memories shared between us, as everything in our lives was back then. Why couldn't it have stayed like that forever?

In August I went on my annual visit to Cork. It wasn't the best of trips. My heart was so over-brimming with yearning for Brother Matthew, I simply couldn't help myself mentioning him at the least available opportunity. That is, until one miserable foggy morning Dad at last lost his patience and cried out, 'For all the blessed virgins and saints, Leah, he's a *monk*! Just leave the poor fellah alone and get on with your life!'

So that's what I tried to do. I went back to Birmingham at the end of September to start my second year at the College of Music and get on with my life. A resolution which was made considerably easier by the grand entrance of a certain Adrian Midwinter.

2

It's June 1983. We're sitting next to one another at a small, neatly-laid dining table at the *King James Hotel* in Oban, on the west coast of Scotland.

Two little old ladies are seated at the same table, directly opposite us. One of them has noticed my engagement ring, and I'm dreading the inevitable question that will follow. Sure enough, follow it does, with immaculate timing.

'Ooh, you're getting married, then?' the dear old thing asks with sentimental enthusiasm. 'When's the happy day, dear?'

Inwardly squirming, I say, 'Just over two weeks.'

'I wouldn't call it a *happy* day,' is the caustic reply that you mutter in hushed undertones, making it impossible for the rest of us to ignore.

Tears are stinging my eyes. I drop my gaze to the napkin on my lap. It's an old-fashioned hotel, with pretty lace table cloths and place mats with different scenes from Scotland. Geriatric guests fill the dining room, all of them fellow holiday-makers on this week-long Scottish tour that you've booked us on. '*The last chance for us to go on holiday together*' is how you put it, with tears in your eyes. That's how you cajoled me into agreeing to this sham holiday. We are by far the youngest guests. You're like a glamorous youth compared to all the others, and I'm like a child. If everything weren't so downright horrible in my life right now, the entire set-up could be hilarious. Beauty and the Child amongst thirty-five dithery OAPs on their last legs. At this very moment I'm wishing I *was* a child again, so that everything could be as it used to be, before everything changed.

'Oh?' the bolder of the two ladies enquires, peering above her spectacles at you.

Even though my gaze is partially averted, I can see what's going on. You roll your eyes.

'Well, dear, we shall be thinking of you on the day,' the other nice old lady says to me, and I can tell that she's trying to catch my eye to give me a reassuring smile. No doubt she senses that something is amiss and I need all the smiles I can get.

'Think of *me*,' you say, after which no one says anything else. But you're not feeling the awkwardness of it any more. Oh no, you've gone beyond that now.

I feel like sticking my fork into your heart. I'm getting married in less than three weeks' time and you have made me the unhappiest woman alive.

I *hate* you.

3

Adrian Midwinter! How could any impressionable nineteen-year-old not fall in love with such a name? I didn't actually know it was his name until quite a while later, because he only materialised at the Birmingham College of Music a week after the beginning of term in my second year. No one knew much about him, though we all speculated due to his striking appearance. He wasn't that tall, but *very* dishy: slim, lithe, with dirty-blond hair that he was forever flicking aside, highlighting the sexiest green eyes I had ever seen. They were usually narrowed, creating the impression of some powerful force at work within that enigmatic character which none of us had yet been able to fathom. But most striking of all was the way he dressed, which resembled an aristocrat from the nineteenth century. Instead of the jeans and T-shirts distinctive of student-hood, he favoured dapper waistcoats, pinstriped trousers and white shirts. These would always have cufflinks and flamboyant collars that he'd leave open at the neck, revealing a tantalising hint of dark-blond chest hair as though to prove that his matching head hair was a natural colour.

Although he was a new student, he seemed older than us. This wasn't so much to do with his looks as his overall demeanour, which was a bit stand-offish. He segregated himself from the first and second years, preferring to hang out with an elite group of third years who had apparently been selected for his private entourage. Every now and then this newly-formed bunch would grace the canteen with their presence, imbuing it with glamour. Then, without warning, he would disappear from their midst for several days and the rest of the gang would revert to being ordinary, workaday students. And then, lo and behold, he would re-emerge without warning and all eyes would once again cast furtive glances in his direction. A couple of times he entered the college canteen with a *Vogue*-type girlfriend hanging onto his arm, but no one had a clue who she was. After a while she was replaced by an attractive third-year viola player, but that didn't last long, either. Most of the time Adrian Midwinter was either alone, or with his selected associates, or he wasn't there at all.

By the end of the first month of term I'd managed to glean a few enticing titbits of information about him, thanks to the detective skills of Tessa Llewelin. Apparently he was from Nottingham, he was a mature student, he already had a degree from Cambridge University in some subject not connected with music; his main study was the piano, and his passion was jazz.

And then, one unsuspecting day in late October, he spoke to me.

4

You'd have called it a *Kismet day,* Mother, because I'd woken up feeling pretty down. This might have been partially due to the weather, because after a long and gentle autumn it had turned bitterly cold. Or perhaps it was because I was feeling homesick and wondering if I'd ever be able to let go of my need for you. But most likely the main reason for my depression was because I'd been pondering over the letter I'd received from Brother Matthew three weeks earlier.

I hadn't replied to it yet, though you and I had analysed it closely on each of our Sunday phone calls since then, and I still tucked it under my pillow every night. His words were filled with an overwhelming nostalgia and poignancy, with no further reference to my previous embarrassing out-pouring.

I'm trying to get Monks' Wood into shape before the leaves fall and winter descends on us he wrote, and you suggested that I should respond by saying how I wished I could be there with him, to help clear away all those autumn leaves. But I didn't want to write that. You pushed even further by saying that I should mention how my mother loved the song *Autumn Leaves,* and from now on whenever you heard it played you would think of him way out there in the woods of Greystones. But I didn't like the sound of that, either.

Death enhances the value of life, and I want to live more fully was another comment in his letter, referring to the recent death of a former Abbot and implying, according to you, that he'd suddenly been made aware that he was wasting his life and now wanted to live it more fully. Of course you were convinced that the hidden meaning of the words 'more fully' referred to me, as in live more fully *with me.* I wanted to believe that, really I did, but at the same time I didn't want to jump to wrong conclusions and suffer heartbreak. So I erred on the cautious side and disagreed with your analysis. You thought I was either being stubborn or downright cowardly, and said that if Brother Matthew and I carried on like this, we'd both live to be a hundred without ever having grasped the love that was right there for the taking.

There was a definite 'something' in his letters – especially that last one – but at the same time there was also an underlying barrier I knew I'd never be able to break. It was as if he gave me so much, but only up to a point. Since our last meeting in July we'd exchanged a number of letters, most of which contained at least one comment that was encouraging. But whenever my adrenaline started flowing, it would be dashed again just as quickly in his very next letter. For instance when he wrote: *The other day I was walking past the music room and heard the strains of that lovely Chopin piece you played on your first visit to Greystones. It reminded me so much of you, for a moment I had to stop myself from opening the door, so convinced was I that you really were there.* Duly warmed to the heart, I responded by saying how I too wished I were at Greystones with him – but his very next communique was not only delayed, but also far more wary. More *monkly,* as you put it. Then his next letter would be warmer again – and on and on the process would go, just like a game of ping-pong. So it was hardly any wonder that by the time this latest letter arrived, I felt gripped by writer's block when contemplating how to respond.

Each time I called you from the public telephone booth outside my new digs in Washwood Heath, you asked me if I'd finally got round to replying to him. And each time I answered 'no', your tone became impatient. Especially during our last phone conversation.

'You *still* haven't written back to him?' you said in a tight voice. 'Well, my darling, all I can say is that you're never going to achieve anything in life with *that* kind of attitude.'

'And what kind of attitude would that be, exactly?' I challenged, suddenly weary of this whole, non-ending saga.

'Don't you get tetchy with me! Ye Gods, Leah, just listen to your tone of voice!'

'I'm sorry, it's just that I wish you wouldn't be quite so pushy. I actually think a break from my letters would do Brother Matthew a lot of good.'

'And *I*, my darling, think you're being very naïve, and very, very foolish.'

But not half as foolish as you, Mother. It was round about then that I began to be more careful in what I said to you about Brother Matthew. I hated it when we argued.

By the end of October I was beginning to tire of the whole letter-writing process. I just didn't know how much more pining and longing I could take. As a sixth form girl it had been fun, in a melodramatic kind of way. Now I was a young woman living away from home, trying to carve a career for myself as a concert pianist, and the 'fun' was fast losing its appeal. I missed Matthew with all my heart; I dreamed about him and kept his letters in an old wooden box that you'd given me some time before, with the words GOD IS HOPE carved on the lid in Gothic lettering. And yet I'd now reached the point where I was finding myself disinclined to do anything about it. I was, quite simply, exhausted. I was exhausted from the strain of unrequited love, unpredictable letters and the prospects of facing a terrifying future without him, should I end up losing the battle you were so keen for me to wage.

It was all these depressing thoughts that were on my mind on that *Kismet day* I was going to tell you about.

* * *

'Mind if I join you?'

I couldn't believe it! Adrian Midwinter was just about to sit down at my table in the college canteen. It was too good to be true. There were other empty places at other tables, yet he had chosen to sit with me.

I nodded, praying that Tessa and Emily would be late from their respective singing and flute lessons. The three of us had arranged to have lunch in the canteen at 1.30 and it was now 1.20. My piano lesson had ended early, so I'd gone directly to the canteen and bought myself a coffee while waiting for my two friends. My eyes were still smarting from the tears I'd shed in the bathroom just five minutes before. No, the tears were not over Brother Matthew, but rather, my meanly smiling piano teacher, Michael

Williams. He had told me that he was so disappointed with the Mozart concerto that there was no point in going any further with the lesson until I myself went further with the Mozart. And so he released me ten minutes early. And he was right, damn it! Unrequited love was not doing my piano playing any good.

But getting back to Adrian Midwinter. He sat himself down opposite me, placing his coffee mug and a plate with two slices of toast on the table surface. Reaching into his Samsonite carrier bag, he pulled out a copy of *The Times,* which he spread out before him. He took a bite of toast, chewed away for a few moments, turned a page in the newspaper, and suddenly stopped. Looking up at me with eyes that were a dark vivid green, he pushed away a thick lock of hair and said, 'Oh, I'm so sorry. It's rude to read at the table in company. My mother would go mad if she could see me now. Do please forgive me.' He aimed a slow killer-smile at me, instantly causing all the capillaries under my skin to dilate.

I laughed. 'My mother says just the same thing.'

'Really? So if you're not allowed to read at the table, then what do you do instead? Apart from eat, that is.'

'Well – we talk.'

'Exactly. And isn't that so much nicer?'

'Erm … I guess so.'

'So the moral of the story is that one should always listen to one's mother.'

I laughed again, more heartily this time round. He smiled in return, which conjured a deep groove on either side of his sexy mouth.

Within the space of three minutes flat I had found out four impressive facts about him: 1) he had a degree in Medicine, 2) he'd played the piano since the age of seven, 3) after giving up his 100-hour-a-week job as a junior doctor he'd said to himself, *sod this for a laugh* and applied to music college, and 4) his true passion was jazz. Oh, and he played in a local band that sometimes performed outside Birmingham, hence his regular absences from college.

'So what do you plan on doing when you finish music college?' he asked, finishing his toast and dabbing his mouth with a napkin.

'Well – originally I wanted to be a concert pianist, but I'm not so sure anymore.'

'Why not?'

'Because I don't know if I'm good enough to make it to the top. Or even if I want to.'

'There's a big difference between not being sure if you want something, and not being sure if you're not good enough.'

I blinked in confusion, but luckily he went straight on, 'Michael Williams is your piano teacher, I believe.'

'Right. But I don't think he rates me all that highly.'

'Maybe that's because you aren't trying hard enough.'

'How would you know that?'

'I heard you wanted to enter the piano concerto competition, but Michael's not sure if you're up to it.'

I felt my cheeks go hot. 'How on earth …? Look, I'm sorry, but I really don't think that Mr Williams should be talking about -'

'Do you like jazz?' he suddenly asked.

Stalling, I pushed a lock of fly-away hair behind my ears. 'I – to be honest, I don't really know much about it.'

'So how do you fancy finding out something about it? Like tonight at eight o'clock? I'm playing at the *Hare and Hounds* with *The Rhythm Aces*. Fancy coming along?'

'Okay,' I said without a moment's hesitation. So much for playing hard to get.

So that was that. The rocky course of my next relationship was set in motion. *Eat your heart out, Brother Matthew!* That was my mantra over the coming weeks.

Adrian rented a second-floor room in a Georgian villa in Solihull. The house belonged to a local concert pianist of some renown, I soon learned, but when I asked Adrian how in the world he'd managed to find such a great room, he explained that it had been through the College of Music. I have to admit that this made me wildly regret I hadn't got in there first, when I compared it to my own, far more basic digs.

By this time I'd moved out of Cavendish Hall and was renting a room in an old house in the less salubrious district of Washwood Heath. It was directly opposite a petrol station with florescent banners that filtered through the thin curtains of my room every night. The house was rambling and dilapidated, with a stench of dry rot that permeated the walls throughout the year. My elderly but vivacious Polish landlady had carved a kind of bedsit for herself in the downstairs sitting room, and had the habit of popping her head round the corner at the most inopportune of moments, rather like Gran.

For instance, Adrian and I would be sneaking up the stairs to my room after having returned from one of his late-night gigs, and at the very first creak of a floorboard, out would pop that old wizened head. Upon seeing us, she would beam in wrinkly mischief from her half-open door and exclaim in a heavily accented whisper, 'Ach, is *you*! I sink is bad peoples! Sorrrry, sorrrry!' and promptly toddle back to her bedsit. Her name was Mrs Zoldak and she'd emigrated to England after the Second World War. Despite living in Birmingham for thirty-five years, she spoke shockingly bad English. I never heard anyone roll her r's like she did! It's a miracle we managed to communicate at all, when I look back on it now. Both she and her house had probably been quite impressive affairs once upon a time, but by the late nineteen-seventies they'd become an anachronism in the sprawling inner-city district to which they found themselves prisoner. No wonder I was so eager to escape to the quieter, leafier avenues in Solihull where Adrian lived.

We started going out together after the gig he invited me to at *The Hare and Hounds*. As I discovered on our first date, he turned out to be quite the Victorian gentleman, albeit moody, as I was also soon to learn. When he finished playing with the band, he re-joined me at my table near the stage and asked with a twinkle in his gorgeous eyes, 'Would the fair lady care for a glass of port?'

'Erm – could I just have a red wine, please?' I said, wishing I could have thought up some equally cool, cleverly *Victoriana* response. But on the very next date he was pensive and remote – smoking his pipe, tapping his fingers to the music, giving monosyllabic replies to my nervous chatter.

'You played brilliantly,' I ventured.

'Did I,' he said, full stop. I didn't pester him any more for the rest of the evening. It was these very incongruities that I found so fascinating about him. I never fully understood what made him tick. I liked him best when he was magnanimous and breezy.

'Would the lovely lady care for a Chinese take-away later tonight?' he'd ask, before we headed for whatever club he happened to be playing at. And of course I always agreed, because the thought of going back to his otherworldly villa tucked into the mature gardens of that quiet cul-de-sac in Solihull was enough to make me forget all the advice I'd been reared on about not saying 'yes' too easily. With Adrian it became my favourite word.

I went along to his gigs whenever he invited me and sat at a table as near the stage as I could get, sometimes with other fellow students from the College of Music. We sipped our beers and wines and vodkas, and lit up our cigarettes, and listened in admiration to the strains of saxophone and double bass and piano, so utterly freed from our own strict Classical training. Every few seconds I'd find my gaze wandering back to the magnetic pull of Adrian as he sat by the piano, shoulders swaying, right foot stomping on the beer-stained floor, messy blond hair falling over half-closed eyes. And all the while I'd be waiting breathlessly for the moment it would end – when each of the band members would stand up in turn to take their bows as their names were called out amid a rush of applause and cheers, then drag themselves and their instruments off the stage and make their way over to waiting girlfriends. Like me.

I seemed to spend half my life waiting for Adrian. Waiting for us to catch the night bus back to Solihull and walk arm in arm down the lane to his Georgian abode. Waiting to creep inside the silent hallway and tip-toe up two flights of stairs to the room he rented. Waiting for him to open the bedroom window, which looked out onto a long back garden and a church where he played the organ most Sundays. Waiting to crouch on the sill together, light up a shared pipe and puff away into the night air, our jets of smoke floating across the shadowed lawn. Pipes weren't specifically to my liking, but by this stage I was so smitten with Adrian that I was willing to do whatever grabbed his fancy. Going to his gigs, smoking his pipes, playing Bach duets with him on the church organ, reading Keats sonnets aloud in bed ... ah yes, *bed* being the operative word.

By this stage I had decided it was neither prudent nor realistic to save myself for Brother Matthew, and so my much-awaited *first time* ended up being with Adrian Midwinter. I don't regret it, although the very first time wasn't quite what I'd expected, compared to all the passionate fantasies I'd indulged in. Would a 'first time' have been any better with Matthew, I used to wonder? The answer is probably not. Probably it would have been a damn sight worse, if anything – both of us fumbling around, guilt getting in the way, not sure what to do next, our arms and legs getting all tangled up in his cassock, listening out in case Father Sebastian barged in on us right in the midst of our illicit act of passion.

No such fears with Adrian! He was five years older than me and much more experienced, so I allowed him to put that experience to good use. And oh, did we have one hell of a wild time in that small room in Solihull! But was I in love with him? I honestly don't know. I certainly was crazy about him, if that can be considered the same thing. I was also awed by his talent in jazz. And I was a trifle uneasy about his changeable moods, which I never got to the bottom of. But even this dark side of his nature only served to make him sexier than ever. After all, isn't *not knowing* always far more exciting than *knowing*?

However, the truth is that there was another far greater power at work in my life. It was a power that constantly reminded me I had already pledged my heart to another man, even if that other man had already pledged *his* heart to God.

CHAPTER THIRTEEN

1

Grey-haired Mrs Williams heard yesterday that her daughter, 26-year-old Molly, had taken a flat in Kyrenia just 50 yards from the place where Molly's fiancé, Peter Fox, was killed. 'I do not want her to sacrifice her life for a memory,' said Mrs Williams.

That's what Gran told the reporter from *The Lancashire Evening Post*, way back in 1956. But you did sacrifice your life for a memory, didn't you, Mother? You sacrificed it for the memory of a passionate, handsome young man who loved you, yet could never quite commit, despite the bond that kept you both through thick and thin. Even through infidelity.

The performance you gave Peter when you found out about his first infidelity was a hundred times better than any Shakespearean play you ever acted in. That's what you always told me. Peter was so alarmed by the tone of your recriminatory letter that he hurried all the way from Manchester back home to Preston as soon as he could, and persuaded you to meet him at *Bruccianis*, remember? The cafe owned by an Italian family with two dashing sons, both of whom had a crush on you? You loved the continental *chic* of the place, so alien to 1950s-Preston. You loved the whirring fans suspended from the ceiling, the blown-up photographs of film stars, the small round tables cluttered upon bare wooden floorboards, and the huge gilt-framed mirror on the wall by the entrance, where ladies in stilettos could cast subtle glances at themselves while stepping inside upon the arms of smartly-dressed chaperones. Unfortunately, you never had the chance to step inside upon Peter's smartly-dressed arm, because Peter had an infuriating habit of always being late. So this time, you made damn sure that you were even later.

* * *

At first she almost didn't notice him, so far away did he seem in the bustling cafe. For the briefest of moments she felt herself weaken at the sight of his forlorn profile as he sat hunched over his coffee, totally oblivious to the chatter and laughter that echoed all round him. She manoeuvred her way in and out of the closely packed tables, her steps click-clacking in rhythm with the smooth Italianesque love song that was playing in the background – Dean Martin's *That's Amore* – until at last she reached his solitary corner. No doubt he'd chosen it deliberately, just in case she decided to make a scene. He was well accustomed to her temper by now.

'Sorry I'm late,' she said in a casual voice as she approached his hunched form.

It was then she realised that he hadn't been sitting despondently, as she'd thought. He'd just been doing the *Times* crossword. Nonetheless, there was unmistakable anxiety in his demeanour as he jumped up from the table and faced her with eyes that had the look of a guilty schoolboy. 'Ah, Molly! You're here, thank God!'

She took off her coat and hung it round the back of the chair that he pulled out for her. It was her lunch break and she was dressed in simple but smart clothes: a pleated knee-length skirt which showed off her shapely calves, a tight polo neck jumper which emphasised her generous bust. She knew she looked good. Her boss's appreciative eyes confirmed as much when she'd piled into his office that morning, apologetic and out of breath, but oozing femininity.

He pulled his own chair closer to her. 'Molly, I honestly thought that you'd –'

'Well, you know what thought did, don't you?'

His eyes twitched nervously. 'Er – what?'

'Ran off with a mud cart and thought it was a wedding.' She stifled a giggle. That was one of her mother's bizarre sayings that no one could ever work out.

'Chubs, give it a break. I meant to say that I thought you'd chucked me or summat.'

'Who's to say I haven't?'

'Oh come on, you haven't, have you? Chucked me?' His eyes widened into saucers. '*Have* you?'

'Can't a girl get a drink round here?' she craned her head, raising that carefully trained eyebrow.

'Oh, sorry – of course.' He jumped up from his chair once again. She almost felt sorry for him. He was beginning to resemble a Jack in the Box. 'What would you like?'

'The usual.'

He headed off for the self-service counter in the adjoining room. Waiting until he was out of sight, she shovelled around in her bag for her compact mirror amid the hidden chaos of lipsticks, scented hankies, *Blue Grass* perfume, bus tickets, concert tickets, nail file, comb and loose change. At last she found it, flicked it open and hastily applied a fresh coating of powder to her face. Just as she snapped the compact shut and slipped it back into her bag, her errant fiancé re-appeared round the corner. He placed her cup and saucer on the table with great care before resuming his seat.

'So,' he said.

'Yes indeed. So.'

'Aw, come on, Chubs, don't be like that.'

'Like what?'

'You know what I mean. All prim and proper. It's because you're the exact opposite of all those nauseating characteristics that I fell for you in the first place.'

'You mean until she came on the scene.'

He sighed. '*She* is called Delia Hungerford – an ex-girlfriend, as I already told you, and an unfortunate mistake as far as last Saturday was concerned. It meant absolutely *nothing*. How was I to know that she'd be at that party in Manchester? Dermot was also there, by the way. You know the Irish doctor I told you about, who's got a place in Cyprus? Well -'

'I'll thank you not to change the subject, if you please. So, if this Hungering trollop meant nothing to you, then why did you -' she could hardly bear to say the words, 'why did you sleep with her?'

'*Hungerford,* not Hungering,' he corrected. 'And she's not a trollop. Look, Chubs, the thing, is -'

'*Don't* call me that!'

He winced. 'Hey, now don't get like that. I was only trying to explain -'

'How your divine Delilah just couldn't keep her hands off you as soon as she saw you walk in the room?'

'*Delia,* not Delilah. And it wasn't like that at all. I could tell that she still – well, y'know, fancied me a bit. I was just trying to find the appropriate moment to -'

'To hold her hand while you told her you were already committed to someone else?'

'Oh, for crying out loud, Molly! Will you stop interrupting and just let me say what I'm trying to say?'

'Certainly.' She was almost beginning to enjoy herself, despite the smarting she still felt after his recent confession about his one-night stand. The fact that he had at least confessed, in a semi-drunken outburst of guilt, didn't hold much weight.

So he struggled on, 'The thing is, I thought I'd already made it clear to her that I wasn't in the least interested in any of her flirty games when she walked over to me and said *hello* in that sultry way of hers that always -'

'Lurid details are not necessary, thank you.'

'But *you're* the one who's been pressing me for details ever since I flippin' told you!'

For once, she remained silent.

'Any road, obviously I hadn't made my message clear enough, because when I mentioned to her that I was going to see *Hamlet* the next evening, the very last thing on earth I expected was for her to turn up on my doorstep, dressed to the nines, just before I left my flat. Molly? Are you listening?'

'I'm utterly riveted,' she said, resting her chin upon her hands and allowing him the first smile of their meeting.

He lit up another cigarette. Since being promoted to *The Manchester Evening News* he had practically become a chain smoker. 'Well, what with her being all dressed up and reeking of expensive perfume, and then me having to leave the flat at any minute to get to the theatre on time ... it would've been too bloody awkward to tell her there and then that she'd got it all wrong. So I thought I might as well let her come along and – y'know, somehow try to find the right time to tell her during the interval. But then when I met up with Dermot Cavanagh and all the others, it didn't seem ... appropriate, somehow. It were only much later, when we all went for a drink and got more than a bit tight, that she asked to come back to my digs for a coffee to sober up before catching the night bus home. And then ... well, y'know. The next day I could hardly remember a thing, I was that drunk. But it meant nothing. You've *got* to believe me, Chubs.'

'Peter,' she said, taking a long sip of tea, 'I couldn't care less what you managed or didn't manage to tell your drunken Delilah, and I certainly don't want to sit around here listening to your bumbling excuses. You either want me or you don't. When you've made up your mind about it, I might *just* still be available, if I decide not to take the job I've been offered in Edinburgh. So if I were you, I wouldn't take too long in letting me know.'

He opened his mouth to say something, but then closed it again. Taking another sip of tea, she glanced at the clock on the wall opposite and, placing her cup back on its saucer, pushed her chair back and stood up.

'Hey, now hang on a minute, Molly –'

'Heavens above, will you *look* at the time!' she cried out, leaving it to her clever-clogs fiancé to work out whether she was in a genuine hurry or just being flippant, and whether, for that matter, she really had been offered a job in Edinburgh. 'Must dash – bye, darling!' It was the first and last time she used the arty-farty endearment with him. Many years later she transferred it on to her only child, but she never again used it with Peter.

Slipping her coat over her shoulders, she clip-clopped a little unsteadily in her brand new high-heeled shoes all the way towards the exit. As she stepped out into the chilly air she felt proud of herself. She had given the performance of a lifetime, without even needing the assistance of Mr Shakespeare!

But later that night, as she lay in bed next to her sleeping sister, she just couldn't hold back the tears. They certainly wouldn't be the last she was destined to shed over the man Kismet had chosen for her.

2

It's December 6th, St Nicholas Day, and I'm at Pebble Mill TV Studios. The organisers have invited dozens of musical groups from different cultures that have sprouted round the environs of Birmingham these last couple of decades. There are Hindus and Sikhs and Buddhists and Moslems and Jews and Greek Orthodox and Russian Orthodox and Polish Catholics ... and it's the Polish Catholics, in the form of the *Polish Youth Choir and Dancing Troupe*, that are the reason I'm here. I'm their accompanist.

As soon as I arrive at Pebble Mill, I wander around the cavernous television complex for a good ten minutes before finally locating the rehearsal room. That is, the room where the Polish youth choir and dance troupe are supposed to be practising their Slavonic Christmas carols. I'm gripped by a horrible feeling that I've made a big mistake. Why in the world did I agree to accompany all these loud, chaotic Polish youths? Many of them are the same age as me, but they're making a damn sight more noise and commotion than any music rehearsal I've ever been to, that's for sure!

It's utter chaos. There must be twenty-five or thirty of them altogether – a whole gaggle of feisty, dolled-up young things, male and female, yakking away ten to the dozen in a mishmash of Polish and Brummy English, shouting flirty jokes across the room at each other, laughing, constantly nipping in and out of the room for the loo, for the vending machine, for a ciggie and God knows what else. However, the entire troupe does look very fetching, I'll say that much for them, all decked out in their Polish national costume. The girls are sporting floral calf-length skirts, laced-up ankle boots, white frilly blouses, velvet waistcoats sequined in brilliant colours, triple layers of beads round their pretty necks, and elaborate garlands of flowers in their plaited hair. As for the guys – they're wearing thick highlander trousers buckled just below the knees, brown leather boots, wide leather belts, white shirts, embroidered waistcoats, broad black caps with decorated rims, and wooden staffs to twirl around and jump over in their energetic dance numbers. If I wasn't so exasperated by all the confusion and noise, it would have been a wonderful introduction to the Birmingham Polish Club, which ended up becoming a big part of my life.

When I first saw the advertisement that had been posted in the Birmingham College of Music foyer just three days earlier, I thought it might be an interesting experience.

PIANO ACCOMPANIST URGENTLY REQUIRED FOR PEBBLE MILL LIVE RECORDING SESSION OF POLISH CAROLS, DECEMBER 6TH 10.00 – 18.00, PAY NEGOTIATED AT INTERVIEW.

I also thought that the 'pay negotiated at interview' might come in handy for a poor struggling student such as myself. For instance, it could pay for an unplanned trip back home to Lyneham-on-Sea. Or it could supply me with another set of corset, camisole and suspenders, for which Adrian had a particularly strong penchant. It was all part of his Victoriana passion. Apparently it was the Victorians who started all this sexy lingerie lark: doe-eyed damsels strutting around with wasp-waists kept in line by dozens of tiny hooks that had to be unfastened, one by one, in the hotly brocaded luxury of the boudoir, each discarded layer coyly revealing yet another inch of fetching feminine flesh ... But that's beside the point. Apart from the handy cash the advert promised, it was the experience of accompanying a Polish choir on live TV that I found most intriguing.

A telephone number was given, so I noted it down and a couple of hours later nipped out to the nearest phone booth and dialled the number.

'Hello, I'm calling about the advert – ' I began, but was immediately interrupted by a sharp, trenchant voice that made me wince.

'Are you a pianist?'

'Yes, I'm a student at the Birmingham College of Music. That's where I saw the advert.'

'Yeah, obviously. Right. So the interview's at five this afternoon at the Polish Club. The address is -' and he proceeded to garble out a long string of directions. Not being possessed of a photographic memory, I had to interrupt him and ask him to hang on while I got a piece of paper and pen out of my bag, during which the receiver crackled with a string of fiery foreign syllables, presumably aimed at a third party. By the time I returned my mouth to the receiver I was beginning to feel a bit doubtful about the whole thing. But the pendulum had been set in motion. Kismet had struck again.

I finally managed to jot down the street name and number, and even succeeded in persuading the irate man to agree to a compromise of five-thirty for the interview. My piano lesson ended at five and I didn't dare cancel it if I wanted to avoid the smiling wrath of Michael Williams, especially considering I had only just withdrawn my application from the piano concerto competition.

So I made it to the Polish Club by five-thirty, and hovered in the foyer until an elderly porter approached me. After blinking at his unintelligible questions, I at last succeeded in making myself understood by repeating the words *Pebble Mill*. He nodded, led me upstairs to a large concert hall, and promptly buggered off.

For a moment or two I just stood there, not yet noticed by the two men on the stage at the far end of the enormous room. The older one was tall and elegantly suited, sporting a headful of white hair and a long, drooping moustache like some aristocrat out of *War & Peace*. The other guy was young and medium-built, with scruffy brown hair and glasses, wearing jeans and a sweatshirt with the word *POLSKA* sprawled across the front. His sleeves were partially rolled up, revealing a muscly pair of forearms. Both of them were jabbering away at lightning speed in Polish. The younger one seemed to have the most to say, judging by the way he kept waving his arms about and pouring forth a continual stream of explosive syllables that the white-haired gentleman occasionally managed to interrupt.

'Excuse me?' I called out as I tip-toed across the parquet floor.

They both stopped talking and turned to face me. I felt rather like Alice in Wonderland at the mad hatter's tea party. As I approached, the older one smiled warmly and was just about to say something when the younger one loudly shouted, 'Come on up, come on up!'

When I reached the other side of the hall I climbed up three or four steps onto the stage and made my way over to the grand piano. 'Hello, I'm Leah Cavanagh,' I said, offering a wary smile of greeting. 'I've come about the interview for the Pebble Mill recording session on Sunday.'

The older one stepped forward. Clasping my hand, he raised my fingers to his lips and said, 'You like angel from the heaven!'

'Well – thank you.'

'My name Krzysztof Oginski, and this, he Marek Topolski.'

'Yeah, yeah, pleased to meet you, Leah. Right, well I suppose we'd better hear you play, then.' That was the one called Marek, who I'd spoken to on the phone. His physiognomy totally matched the gruff voice from our last conversation. He had a hard-set mouth, a strong chin shadowed by bristle, and a pair of narrow eyes that caught flecks from his glasses and gleamed in an indeterminate mix between brown and grey. He could *almost* have bordered on good-looking, had he not been so irritating. 'So what're you going to play for us, darling? Some Chopin, I reckon, yeah?' He asked this in a broad Birmingham accent, unlike his less linguistically talented companion.

'If you like.'

'We like very much,' the older one said, intensifying his cavalier smile.

'Perhaps a waltz, or a mazurka?' I suggested. 'Or maybe something more powerful – for instance the polonaise in F-sharp mi-'

'Yeah, yeah, whatever, we haven't got all day. Just play something nice and we'll have a listen, all right?'

I sat myself down at the piano, adjusted the height of the stool, and launched into the Heroic Polonaise. About a quarter of the way through my performance, Marek Topolski stopped me.

'Hey, that's great, darling. Okay, so you can play. So you'll accompany us at Pebble Mill on Sunday, right?'

'Well, I suppose so, if – '

'Okay, terrific, let me go and get the music notes for you. I'll be back in a tick.'

And so it was settled.

* * *

So here I am at Pebble Mill Studios, breaking out in a panicky sweat. I've hardly had any time to practise all the carols lent me by Marek Topolski, who is trying to organise everyone but in the meantime causing more chaos than ever - and in just over two hours' time we're going to be filmed live for a Christmas edition on local Birmingham TV! What's more, I feel like a dowdy Plain Jane compared to all these glamorous Polish coquettes, with their doll-like faces and long plaits and swirling skirts and their bilingual chatter and sing-song.

After what seems like a small eternity, order is restored. The Polish Youth Choir is sorted out into rows of male and female, all according to height. I sit down by the upright piano, and at last we begin our rehearsal. Despite the short time I've had to familiarise myself with the music, everything goes remarkably well. The carols are beautiful – lyrical, joyous, vibrant, poignant – every emotion under the sun is exposed through their Slavonic charm. By the end of our two-hour rehearsal everyone is ready to troop along to the recording room and pour their hearts and souls into the live TV performance. Everything goes extremely well. The Polish youths sing and dance with a vitality and coordination that totally belies the chaos that had reigned less than an hour earlier. And I accompany them pretty well, I have to say. When it's all over with, several members of the troupe come over to congratulate me on my playing. They tell me that if they hadn't managed to find an accompanist in time, the whole thing would have been called off. So I am now the heroine of the day.

The last one to congratulate me is none other than the irate group leader, Marek Topolski. Except that he is no longer irate. He has miraculously transformed into the beaming young man who is standing before me right now, his eyes glinting in the reflected light of his spectacles.

'Hey, that was *brilliant!*' he says, taking hold of my hands and squeezing them. They are very physical, these Poles, I soon realise. 'You deserve a medal, Leah!'

I'm surprised he's even remembered my name. 'Oh, God, no – *you* lot are the ones who did all the hard work. You were brilliant, I mean it. I've now officially become a fan of Polish Christmas carols.'

'Yeah, they make all the English ones seem like dirges, right?'

I laugh. 'That lovely gentle one – what was it called – Lula something or other …?'

'*Lulajże Jezuniu,*' he fills in for me. He still hasn't let go of my hands, and I'm beginning to feel just a tad uncomfortable.

'Yes, that's the one. It was absolutely divine. I'd love to get a recording of it.'

'No probs, darling. I can organise that for you easily. If you give me your address, I could drop one off for you tomorrow.'

Warning bells toll in my ears. 'Oh no, it's okay, you don't need to do that. I'm sure I'll be able to find one myself. Anyway, I really must be getting off.'

'Rubbish! After eight hours of putting up with us rowdy lot, you deserve a good nosh-up. I'm taking you out to dinner. No arguments.'

'Oh –' I finally manage to free my hands from his grasp, 'that's really nice of you, but I'm afraid I can't. I'm meeting someone at nine, so I really must be off. It was a wonderful day and I shall always remember it. If you ever need an accompanist again, please feel free to contact me.'

'You'll still be at music college next year, will you?' Although he looks a tiny bit disappointed, he's doing a good job of covering it up.

'Yes, I graduate next June.'

'Right. Well I might hold you to your word on that one, love. So make sure you don't leave Birmingham without letting me know first, okay? It's not often we stumble across an accompanist who's both talented and gorgeous.'

He's flirting with me. Which seems quite out of character with his former brusque self. But now that all the stress is over with, I'm beginning to see a much nicer side to him. And he has a very charming smile which I never noticed before, probably because I never saw him smile until now. But I really am in a hurry to meet Adrian at nine o'clock and it's already well past eight. I risk a peek at my watch.

'Yeah, all right, I won't keep you,' he says, too observant to be fooled. 'Thanks a million, Leah, and I hope to see you again.' He takes my hand in his once more, raises it to his lips, and grins at me with decidedly inviting eyes.

By the end of term I was desperate to go back home for the Christmas holiday. It had been a long three months: pining for Brother Matthew, being told my Mozart wasn't good enough to be entered for the piano concerto competition, and by mid-term, being swept off my feet by the enigmatic Adrian Midwinter. And now, mid-December, my mind and heart were awash with confusion: not knowing who I loved, who I really wanted ... It was all too much. All I knew right now, as I boarded the train at New Street Station headed for Lyneham-on-Sea, was that I only wanted *you*, Mother.

So imagine my surprise when Adrian appeared on the platform just five minutes before the train was due to leave! Armed with a bright cluster of roses in his hand, he tapped on the window next to my seat. I stared at him, realised it wasn't a dream, then jumped up and hurried down the aisle towards the door, which was still open.

'Thought I'd surprise you,' he said as I stepped down onto the platform, his green eyes narrowing in that slow, seductive smile that never failed to make my knees buckle.

I laughed. 'Well, you certainly managed that all right. Oh – thank you.' I took the bouquet of roses that he handed to me. 'Wow, they're beautiful! How sweet of you.'

He pulled a face. 'Sweet? I can assure you that was not my intention.'

'No, I didn't mean -'

'They're a *bon voyage* gift. Something to remember me by, just in case an IRA bomb goes off at the *Hare and Hounds* during one of our gigs over Christmas.'

'Oh, Adrian, don't tempt fate.'

'Don't worry, I won't. Seeing as there isn't any fate in the first place. We're the makers of our own destiny.'

I smiled at him and he smiled back, and for the first time ever I realised that for all his good looks and debonair assurance, he was actually quite unsure of himself right at this moment. Probably because the previous night he'd suggested that we meet each other over the Christmas holiday, and I'd been all evasive about it, saying how I'd be pretty tied up helping my mother out at our B&B – which was all bullshit, of course. We barely had any guests booked in at Belle Vue. The truth of the matter was that the closer I got to Adrian, the more I felt something holding me back. Or rather, some*one*. I needed an urgent break from all matters of romance, sex and commitment.

* * *

The three weeks I spent at Lyneham-on-Sea over the Christmas holiday of 1979 passed by just as I had hoped – uneventfully, peacefully, and shared only by you and me. And the occasional drink out with Jenny. Oh – and one weekend our togetherness was interrupted by Mr Tomlinson, who demanded at least a small fraction of your time, if only for you to serve him his full English breakfast and bestow upon him your graceful charm. That was evidently enough to keep the poor old codger going till his next visit.

You weren't too enamoured with news of my latest boyfriend, to say the least. And so, after my initial gush of enthusiasm when gabbling on about the wondrous Adrian Midwinter, I kept any further mention of him to a minimum. Could you tell that this one was more serious than all the others? In truth, though, I was beginning to struggle with the intensity of my feelings for Adrian. Was he really the one who would at last exorcise the ghost of my love for Matthew?

As though sensing this, late one evening you unexpectedly asked me, 'Leah, how long is it since you last wrote to Brother Matthew?'

I didn't hesitate in my reply. 'Five and a half weeks,' I said, and you looked at me sadly, knowing all about the waiting game, the counting of days and weeks, the pride in holding back.

'Well then, darling, don't you think it's about time you let him know that you're still on the same planet as the rest of us?'

So I wrote to him. And once again I found myself propped up in bed late at night, reading his old letters and gazing at the faint network of stars hanging over the distant sea as I dreamed my dreams of *what if.* All his letters were still kept in my GOD IS HOPE box. I'd recently brought it back home from Birmingham and stashed it under my bed in the futile hope that out of sight would be out of mind.

Three days before Christmas, I received a bouquet of flowers from Adrian and a Season's Greetings card from Brother Matthew. Both delivered on the same day. Was Kismet asking me to choose?

Dearest Leah,

As Christmas approaches, I couldn't let this opportunity go past without a wave from my island to yours.

Love, Matthew

As I hugged the card to my chest, I knew there was no choice.

4

I celebrated my twentieth birthday on a glorious Sunday towards the end of February 1980. Adrian treated me to dinner at a quaint French restaurant in Henley-in-Arden called *La Vie en Rose*. About half-way through the meal, he turned to the carrier bag by his chair and drew out a large parcel.

'Happy birthday,' he said, handing it over to me with a mischievous smile. Then he leaned across the table and whispered into my ear, 'You can open it when we're at your place later tonight.'

So I opened it at about midnight, when we were back in my digs.

'Oh, *Adrian* …!' I laughed, sitting on the edge of my bed as I extracted item after item of the silkiest, flimsiest, most gossamer assortment of lingerie you could imagine. By the time he'd helped me get all hooked and strapped up in my new Victorian brothel attire, we didn't even make it as far as the bed. We caused such a din that night, it was a miracle Mrs Zoldak didn't come banging on the door!

* * *

During the entire spring term of 1980 I was in a constant state of seventh heaven. I had at last found myself a steady boyfriend. A *proper* one. Brother Matthew had once again faded from my mind's eye, thanks to my decision to leave his box of letters back in Lyneham and not mention him at all during my weekly phone calls to you. Adrian was now the one who consumed my thoughts. Adrian, with his falling-in-the-eyes hair, his down-turned mouth with those deep grooves on either side, his tightly-compact chest with matching dark-golden curls, his … actually, I'd better stop here. The thing is, by this stage I was also beginning to discover that he was actually quite a nice guy. Do you know, Mother, I think we might have been happy together.

We spent two or three nights a week at his plush room in Solihull, and the occasional night at my dump in Washwood Heath. Mrs Zoldak had developed a soft spot for Adrian, no doubt helped by discovering that he had beautiful manners underneath his cool-dude jazz façade.

'Madam, I must say you have the most beautiful home I have ever seen,' he crooned to her one evening as she popped her head round her bedroom door to make sure he wasn't a burglar.

'Ach, you real English chentleman!' she grinned, waddling forward to grab his face in her hands and kiss both cheeks in turn. Later that night, as Adrian heaved himself upon me, he murmured into my ear, *'Madam, I must say you have the most beautiful tits I have ever seen.'*

One Sunday afternoon we found ourselves sitting on a bench on top of a steep bank in the Malvern Hills, admiring the panorama of rolling horizon against porcelain sky. It was a chilly day, so I cuddled myself up against Adrian's warm body, his arm tightly wrapped around my shoulders.

'Isn't this divine,' he murmured to me, not as a question, but rather a statement which we both knew to be an unalterable truth, just like a maths equation. One plus one equals two; Malvern Hills plus azure sky equals beauty; Adrian plus Leah equals happiness.

When did it all happen? He'd even mentioned taking me to his home in Nottingham, which would mean *meeting the parents.* Now that, by any-one's book, is serious stuff. But I stalled at his offer, because I suspected that you'd have been a little bit peeved if I went to his family home before he came to mine. Any anyway, I still wasn't sure if I was ready to bring a boyfriend home to meet you just yet; an invader of our mother-daughter space.

Was I in love? According to you, no, it was just infatuation. But wasn't that the same case with Brother Matthew? Was I serious about Adrian? Yes! Was I attracted to him? Oh, yes! Was I happy with him? Yes! So why should you have worried about anything else? I was happy, couldn't you see it? I was *happy,* damn it!

* * *

'I think I might be falling in love with Adrian,' I said to you one Sunday afternoon in March during our weekly phone call. And held my breath.

There was a slight pause from the other end of the line. And then: 'Oh, Leah, that's – why, that's wonderful.'

I sighed. 'Okay, Mother, out with it.'

You laughed. 'You know me too well, darling. I was just going to say, what about Brother Matthew?'

'He doesn't want me. Adrian does.'

'Oh, don't be absurd, Leah. Do you really think Brother Matthew would bother writing to you if he didn't want you?'

'His letters are nothing special. He probably writes similar things to at least twenty other correspondents.'

But you weren't listening. 'The fact that he writes to you *at all* speaks volumes. He must sense you've been drifting away recently, and yet still he remembers you. He needs reassurance, darling, otherwise you're not going to get anywhere with this.'

'With what?' Suddenly I felt angry. 'What exactly is it that Matthew and I have? Not a great deal, if you look at it head-on.' I swallowed hard. 'With Adrian at least there's a chance that there could be something in the future. I mean something *real*.'

'With a man who can't decide what direction to take in life? First a degree in medicine, now one in music, supposedly studying classical piano but spending most of his time flitting around playing at jazz clubs?'

'I thought you said you liked him.'

'I *do* like him, darling. He sounds like a very nice young man, from everything you've said about him. I just feel sorry for Brother Matthew, that's all. I'm so worried that you're throwing away the chance of something special, something that was meant to be. Just like Peter Fox and I were meant to be, even though we were too foolish and headstrong to see it at the time. I don't want you to make the same terrible mistake, darling.'

In this war of romances, Mother, you were a cunning strategist. You filled me with doubt and needless guilt. I just couldn't win.

March 1ˢᵗ 1980

Dear Leah,

The Benedictines are celebrating their 1500ᵗʰ anniversary this year, which gives us all a lot of food for thought here at Greystones. 1500 hundred years of the way of life that I am now leading – with some modifications for the modern world - but basically, not all that different. It's probably hard for you to understand the significance of this anniversary for us, with you leading your full student life in Birmingham. I suppose what I'm trying to say is this: don't forget about the spiritual side of things, Leah. It's so easy to get caught up with the mad pace and pressures of modern life when you're young, but don't forget about what really counts.

That's the kind of thing I didn't particularly want to hear from Brother Matthew. What I *did* want to hear – although I'd reached the stage of not admitting it you – was when he wrote things like this:

Lark Mount have just been over on their annual retreat. Is it really two years since you came that first time? I must be getting old. It seems like yesterday. When are we likely to see you again up here?

Or this:

I want you to know that I often pray for you and remember you, Leah. If you can come up here some time, please do. I'd look forward to that greatly.

That's the sort of letter that warmed my heart to the core, and also made me feel a little distant with Adrian. That is, until he seduced me yet again with his sultry looks and brilliant jazz improvisations at the *Hare & Hounds* in King's Heath, followed by a Chinese takeaway and sizzling sex back home. Then I'd collapse into the oblivion of sleep and wake up the following morning feeling refreshed and glowing, ready to face another day of piano practice, sight reading, aural tests, Theory & Rudiments and all the rest.

My piano playing was coming on in leaps and bounds. I was once again considering entering the piano concerto in the autumn, which would be my final year and therefore my last chance to go for it. I was full of ambition and hopes; I was aware of being young and desirable, I revelled in being in a steady relationship that I knew aroused envy amongst my friends, and I … what else can I say? I was happy in a way that Brother Matthew never, ever made me feel. How could he have done? He was a *monk,* for Christ's sake, as Dad kept taking pains to point out.

And then this letter arrived in the post.

Dear Leah,

I received a gorgeous calendar from your mother the other day, with a photograph of you sitting between Father Sebastian and myself – the two pillars of the Gatehouse. Please do thank your mother for her thoughtfulness. I shall keep the calendar long after 1980 has ceased to exist.

'What on earth got *into* you, Mother?' I demanded of you the next time I phoned. 'Honestly, I was so embarrassed!'

You merely laughed down the receiver, 'Heavens above, darling, don't be so *petit bourgeois.* I just thought it would be something to lighten up his long dreary days. And let's face it, you do look gorgeous in that photo.'

'But you should have asked me first!'

'If I had asked you, what would you have said? *No*, obviously, so thank goodness I didn't. And now just look at the pleasure my little surprise has given him. How often do you think he receives presents? Especially when they happen to be the souvenir of a lovely young woman he's sitting just inches away from, close enough to put his arm around her – though of course we all know he can only do that in his dreams, poor man. So let him have his dreams. What wrong is there in that? After all, *we are such stuff as dreams are* made on.'

Sometimes I felt like saying a loud *Amen!* after one of your mini-lectures. Instead, I just closed my eyes and counted silently to ten.

The photo we're speaking of is the one that Frank Norris took and sent me a print of. The one you stole out of my desk at Lyneham and made into a calendar centrepiece. I must admit, it was rather a fetching photograph of Matthew and me – but to make a *calendar* of it? And then to *post it to him?* What were you even thinking?

As it happened, a damn sight less than you ended up thinking just a couple of weeks ago.

But I'm not ready to go there yet.

6

Bereaved Preston Girl Tells Her Secret

Mary Williams, attractive 26-year-old secretary, told of her close-ly-kept secret yesterday. This month she should have married Peter Fox, 30-year-old British journalist whose life came to a tragic end on the Mediterranean island of Cyprus.

You've always had a melodramatic streak in you, haven't you, Mother? Come on, be honest with yourself. You obviously told that reporter on *The Lancashire Evening Post* that you and Peter had secret wedding plans, and that the date was set for the very month in which he was killed. What poignant irony, and what a clever ploy to generate maximum dramatic effect. I'm sorry, I don't mean to be hard, but that was you to a tee, wasn't it? Drama – the passion of your life. What you obviously didn't tell the reporter was that there was never in fact any date set for the wedding, because you and Peter could never quite get your act together. Either Peter was too busy and distracted, or you were too offended by his flippancy on the rare occasion he vowed to make haste for the nearest jeweller's. Let's face it, you secretly hoped that one of these days he would just turn up with an eighteen-carat thing of beauty, wrapped up in a beautiful little box which he would promptly flick open as he announced in tremulous words, *Let's finally do it, Chubs! Let's get married!* Of course he did say words to this effect many times before, but never tremulously. And never with a ring.

I can understand your hurt, but what I can't even begin to comprehend is why you got engaged to Tony Gaston when you were still head over heels in love with Peter. It's as if you were determined to play the lead dramatic role, at whatever cost, in the grand theatre of your life.

* * *

196

They were walking side by side along a conker-strewn avenue in Avenham Park. Not arm in arm, nor even hand in hand. Just side by side, with the accidental brushing of shoulders every now and then, like a silent statement that hung suspended in the air between them. It was as though the intermittent contact between their bodies claimed the rights to physical attraction at least, if nothing else.

Another bumping of shoulders precipitated his next remark. 'So why don't you just bloody get on with it, and marry the bugger?'

She sighed with great emphasis. 'Because I'm not sure if it's what I really want. And I'd appreciate it if you refrained from using that kind of language when talking about Tony.'

'Then what *do* you want, for Christ's sake?'

Oh God, she thought, aiming her frown at the autumn sky, as though the answer to her dilemma lay scrawled in gold-leaf script across its sombre face. *Who am I trying to kid? I know what I want! I want to marry YOU!* But all she said was, 'I honestly don't know anymore.'

He made a snorting sound. 'Well, I'll tell you this much for nothing. You'll be miserable as sin if you marry Tony, no matter how much they pay architects. And what about your married name, eh? Mrs Molly Gastric? I get ulcers thinking of it. I mean, come *on.*'

'*Gaston,* if you please. And I wouldn't be miserable. At least he'd love me properly.'

'But *I* love you properly!' He stopped walking, forcing her to come to a halt. 'I do love you, Chubs, honest to God I do ... why can't you believe it?'

She thought long and hard. Actually, not all that hard. Then she faced him with her deep brown eyes; the ones he was forever praising, together with her Brigit Bardot bust and swinging hips. He loved all the things she did *not* love about herself, including the famous eyes, which she thought were too round.

'Because, Peter,' she began carefully, 'sometimes it occurs to me that you just don't know *how* to love. Whenever you say anything romantic to me, you always say it for a reason. Either you're in one of your magnanimous moods, or you want to prepare me for something horrid you're about to confess, or you immediately follow your words with one of your wretched limericks.'

'My limericks are not wretched, I'll have you know. I'm actually considering finding a publisher for them.'

'There you again with your flippancy.'

'I'm not being flippant. I reckon they stand a bloody good chance of getting into print.'

'Peter, your limericks epitomise the most frustrating element of your entire character.'

'Oooh … so when did we start getting so grandiloquent? First *magnanimous,* now *epitomise* … is this the works of your Amateur Dramatics?'

'Oh, for heaven's sake, will you just *shut up* with your idiotic banter for once?'

He looked taken aback for the flakiest of moments, but in a jiffy managed to reverse into ironic gear. 'Dear heart, my lips are veritably sealed.'

'You know, Peter, sometimes I think you're only able to show true depth of feeling for *situations* rather than people. Books and films, current affairs … all those famines and civil wars and fights for independence you're always going on about. You aren't quite so flippant when talking about *those* sorts of things. It's as if they matter to you more than -'

'More than you?' He frowned. 'Without meaning to hurt you, my love, in a way you're right. If more people cared as much as I do about *those sorts of things,* then the world would be a damn sight better place.'

'So why don't you get out there and do something about it?'

'That's precisely what I intend to do, once I've saved up enough money to chuck my job and mount the old moped and whizz off into the global sunset. As a freelance reporter I'd be able to make people back home sit up and listen. I'd be able to make a *difference.* And if I get blown up by a bomb in the meantime – well, at least you'd be free of me once and for all. Then you could go running into the surrogate arms of your besotted architect.'

'There you go again, making fun of all this.'

'How can I possibly be making fun of it, when the girl I was engaged not so long ago is now about to get engaged to someone else? Bloody hell, Molly, where's your head gone?'

'I never said I was going to get engaged to Tony. He's asked me to marry him, but I haven't given him my answer yet.'

'Why not? Get a kick out of dangling your men on strings, do you?'

'Of course not!' she practically shouted, making him wince. 'I don't love Tony, and that's why I haven't given him my answer yet. But I do happen to like him very much. He's thoughtful and well-mannered, and – and cultured and intelligent, without being in the least showy about it, and … well, sometimes it just seems to me that I could have a very nice life with him. Certainly not the kind of life where I'd constantly be wondering who my husband had slept with. Tony would be faithful to me, I know he would.'

'So you're prepared to dump the man you love, so as to marry a bloke you *like,* just because you think he'd be faithful to you?'

'He *would* be faithful to me. And you wouldn't.'

'Aha. So you're finally admitting that I'm not the right man for you.'

You're the ONLY man for me! she silently screamed within the clogged-up whirring of her mind. But the words that came out were quite different. 'Well, you don't exactly help yourself. And by the way, just for your information, Tony and I haven't ever – I mean, all he's ever tried to do is kiss me. That's the truth. You see, I don't make a habit of sleeping with every Tom, Dick and Harry who happens to ask me out. I wish the same thing could be said for you.'

'Molly.' He took her hands in his and looked at her with an expression that was unlike any she'd seen on him before. 'This isn't working out.'

She gulped. 'I know. That's why I – that's why I found myself getting involved with Tony without ever meaning to.'

'But if you'd felt differently about me, you wouldn't have needed to get involved with him in the first place. So there's obviously more to it than you're letting on.'

'No there isn't …'

'Look, Chubs,' he said, drawing his eyebrows together and at the same time attempting a smile, the resulting expression being rather tortuous. 'Just marry him, okay? I can't take any more of this bloody farce.'

And with that he dropped her hands and turned round, kicking at a fallen conker as he abruptly walked away.

CHAPTER FOURTEEN

1

It's the penultimate day of the spring term of 1980, just before the Easter holiday. The following day I'm going home to Lyneham, and Adrian is returning to his hometown of Nottingham. So it's our last evening together. We're both feeling sad, despite having had a magical evening – first at the *Hare & Hounds,* then at a cosy little restaurant for a late dinner, and finally, back at my digs in Washwood Heath. It's three in the morning and Adrian has just dragged himself out of my bed, got dressed and gone down the creaking staircase, with me following close behind. We're tiptoeing and whispering, fumbling about in the dark hallway, trying not to wake up Mrs Zoldak. At last we reach the front door.

Before releasing the catch, Adrian looks at me with a melting expression I have never before seen on him. Touching my cheek with his fingertips, he whispers, 'Leah, I think I'm beginning to fall in love with you.'

I catch my breath. Neither of us has ever mentioned the 'love' word before. Part of me feels giddy. But I'm also engulfed by a deep foreboding and, above all, a sense of betrayal. I can't love Adrian. I just can't. I know it sounds ridiculous, but I honestly don't feel *free* to love him.

So I mumble without thinking, 'Erm – the thing is, I'm not sure if – I mean – well, I don't really like getting too close to anyone, sort of.'

He drops his hand from my cheek as though a high-voltage current had suddenly charged my skin. 'Right.'

'I'm sorry, that didn't come out very well.'

'No, it didn't.'

I wet my lips. 'What I meant to say is that – I guess these things take time, sort of.'

'It would help if you stopped saying *sort of.*'

'Sorry.'

'And apologising.'

'Sor – ' Once again I wet my lips, which have gone horribly dry. I look at his gorgeous eyes – and they really *are* gorgeous, as all of him is, so what the hell am I playing at? 'Adrian, I really am happy with you. I mean *really* happy - and I'm so grateful for that - and I like you an awful lot, but -'

'But you don't love me.'

'No, it's not that, either; it's just –' oh God, what exactly am I trying to say?

Whatever it is, I can see it's too late. I'm instantly regretting my words. I'm a total and utter idiot. I probably *do* love Adrian. And I'm so happy with him, so very, very happy. He's almost succeeded in making me forget Brother Matthew … Ah, but there's the rub. *Almost.* And anyway, what does it matter now? I've screwed up, and it's too late to undo my words. I've hurt him. I've hurt him badly.

Through the fog of awkwardness and hurt, he tries to smile at me, very inadequately, and even kisses me a fleeting goodbye – but on the cheek, not the lips. Then he opens the door and walks out into the dark night.

Nothing will ever again be the same between us. And whose fault is that?

* * *

Over the Easter holiday I met Jenny for a long-overdue chat. We met at the *Nag's Head* in the town centre rather than Belle Vue, because just for once I didn't want you to be anywhere nearby when discussing my love life.

Jenny was home for the holidays, like me. She had a steady boyfriend at Durham who she'd met in her first year at uni. They were very serious about each other and I must confess that I felt a tiny bit envious. No unobtainable Benedictine monks in her life, that's for sure. Her contentment reflected itself in her overall demeanour, which had become decidedly more mature, though still speckled with her bubbly charm and sense of fun. Her hair had grown longer, her curls wilder, and she'd lost a little weight. She was a very attractive woman now, and a woman with a mission: she had found the love of her life. Or so she thought, back in the summer of 1980.

We spent the first half hour catching up on local gossip and exchanging titbits of news that we'd managed to glean about Nobbles, who was in danger of disappearing from our lives. All we knew was that she had abandoned her nunly aspirations and was now engaged to a nice Protestant chap.

Then we got on to my affairs.

'But surely you know if you're in love with someone or not?' Jenny asked me in her usual direct manner.

I shook my head. 'I keep changing my mind about Adrian. One day all he has to do is look at me in a certain way and I go all shuddery and am absolutely convinced it's love. Then the next day I get a letter from you-know-who, and I'm convinced that Adrian is just a passionate fling. Albeit *very* passionate.'

'Do you ever wonder how passionate it might have been with Brother Matthew?'

'Of *course* I do! God, Jenny, that's all I've been fantasising about these past two and a half years. I'll probably be fantasising about it all my life.'

'Well in that case, don't you think it would be rather a *wasted* life? Just wondering how it might have been, instead of falling in love with someone you have a proper chance with?'

'I know, that's why I just can't understand myself. I have a real, proper chance with Adrian, but at the same time I'm terrified of screwing things up. My mother's convinced he's only a passing fancy, like the others were, whereas Brother Matthew is the real one for me. Just like Peter Fox was for her.'

'Yeah right, and look what happened to *him*.'

'But if he hadn't died, then -'

'Then they probably wouldn't have had a happy marriage anyway. Why else did they keep on splitting up and going out with other people during the seven years they were together?' She knew all the Peter Fox stories. 'Honestly, Leah, your mum's an even worse dreamer than you! She's clung onto this demented notion all her life that things would've been perfect if Peter hadn't died.'

I nodded. 'And that's exactly what she thinks about Brother Matthew and me. She's convinced that I'll never find as great a love as him, which means he's worth waiting for.'

'Oh, for God's sake. Hasn't it ever occurred to you that your mum's a bit of a fruitcake? I mean an adorable fruitcake, of course – I really do love her to bits, and she's always made me so welcome in her home, but … well come on, if she honestly thinks you should wait for Brother Matthew to leave the monastery because it's *true love*, then don't you think you might risk waiting just a teeny weeny bit too long?'

'You sound like my dad.'

'Then he's bloody right! Why can't you just stick with Adrian? I mean, come on, that photo of him – bloody hell, he's drop-dead gorgeous! He's even better-looking than your monk. If you don't want him, then *I'll* have him.'

We both collapsed into funny-bone hysterics. Several heads from neighbouring tables turned to us. But in the very next moment Jenny straightened her face.

'Oh, Leah. Promise me that you'll think carefully about all this. If you're pushing Adrian away because of Brother Matthew, then you might end up having neither of them. So just watch out, okay? Mummy does *not* always know best.'

2

Unfortunately, Jenny's advice came too late.

During my month apart from Adrian, he only sent me a couple of short letters. I sensed there was a change in him. And sure enough, when he finally appeared at college after the Easter holiday, over a week late, my fears were confirmed. We still went out together over the coming weeks, though not as frequently; we still slept together, but without that warm post-coital glow that used to embalm us as we lay in each other's arms; and now we only spent the occasional weekend together. As the term meandered towards summer, he always seemed to have an excuse for not being available. Either there was an important event he couldn't get out of, or there was an unexpected gig he had to play at, or his car was at the garage ... You were convinced he'd met someone else, and I myself began to wonder. But I didn't dare ask him. So we continued this luke-warm relationship, with neither of us ever mentioning any plans for the looming summer holiday.

By the middle of June, with just over a week to go before the end of term, I felt that I simply had to say something. And so one Friday evening we arranged to go out for a drink at a pub neither of us had been to before. I wanted to meet him on neutral ground.

I arrived deliberately late, but Adrian was even later. This was not a good sign. By the time he finally materialised, I'd built myself up into quite a state.

'I hate sitting alone in a pub,' I snapped as soon as he sat down, hanging his jacket over the back of his chair.

'Sorry about that, couldn't help it. There'd been an accident on the –'

'I don't want to hear about the road conditions between Solihull and here. Just get me a drink please, will you? The usual.'

A shadow of a smile passed his lips. For a moment I thought my anger had finally snapped him out of his stupor of the past two months. But no such luck. He made his way over to the bar and returned minutes later with a pint of lager and a large red wine.

Placing my glass in front of me, he glanced at his watch and said, 'I think you'd better get straight to the point, because I've got to be somewhere at nine o'clock. Sorry, but it couldn't be avoided.'

I stared at him. 'You knew I wanted to talk to you this evening, and you've arranged to be somewhere else *at nine?*'

'I said I'm sorry. Couldn't be helped. We've just found out about this last-minute gig, and the pay is too good to miss. You could come as well, but -'

'But you don't want me to.' God, I hated all this.

He frowned at his beer glass. Then he looked at me and said, 'Leah, this isn't working out, is it?'

My mouth went dry. I glanced down at my hands, biting my lower lip.

'Maybe it's just as well,' he went on, oblivious to my pain. 'Better to break up now than later, when things might have got more intense.'

At last I made myself face him. 'But they already *were* intense. You told me that you were falling in love with me ... so what in the world happened? Adrian, I just don't understand –'

'Then might I remind you that when I told you I was beginning to fall in love with you, you chose that very moment to tell me you didn't like getting too close to anyone? How do you think that made me feel?'

'But it was only because of -'

'It doesn't matter,' he said, silencing me with an agitated wave of the hand. 'Maybe it's just as well you said what you did. It gave me the chance to think things through over the Easter holiday, and ... well.'

'Well? Would you mind expanding?'

For the first time since arriving at the pub I noticed that he looked uncomfortable. I dreaded what was coming next.

So he expanded with brutal simplicity, 'Okay, it gave me the chance to re-acquaint myself with an old friend, if you must know.'

I stared at him in disbelief. But all I said was, 'Have you got any cigarettes on you?'

He extracted a pack of *Benson & Hedges* from his jacket pocket and offered me one. I took it with trembling hand, leaning closer to him for a light and getting a whiff of his sexy after-shave.

I leaned back in my chair and blew out a long stream of smoke. 'So let me guess. This old friend you re-acquainted yourself with is an ex-girl-friend?'

He nodded slowly. 'She's someone I went out with before I met you. Someone who I finished with *because* of you. And now -'

'Now the boot's on the other foot.'

'*Because* of you,' he repeated icily. I could hardly bear to look at his eyes. 'You obviously weren't in love with me. Not enough, at any rate.'

'But I *was* – I mean at least I think -'

'Oh, for Christ's sake, Leah. Don't make it worse. You made your feelings perfectly clear to me when you told me that you didn't like getting involved. Anyway, there's no point in talking about it now. I really ought to be going.'

'But Adrian …'

The look he fired at me was almost vicious. Had I really hurt him that much? And was it really too late to turn back the clock? Oh God, how I longed to turn the clock back at that moment!

He downed the rest of his beer in one. Placing his glass back on the table, he looked me square in the eyes and said, 'I'm sorry, but I don't want to talk about this anymore. Things didn't work out between you and me, end of story. It's just the way it is.'

Just the way it is. Was that to be my epitaph?

* * *

Three days later I sat propped up against my pillow at Lyneham-on-Sea, with you sitting on the side of my bed trying in vain to console me.

'It's not fair!' I wailed through hot tears, blowing my nose loudly. 'He said he was falling in love with me … so how could he dump me like that?'

'Because it wasn't true love,' you said, squeezing my hand. 'Oh, I'm sure he tried to convince himself it was the real thing – I'm not saying he's a liar – but obviously it wasn't. Not for either of you.'

'But *I'm* the one who killed it, telling him that stupid thing about not wanting to get too close to anyone –'

'Don't be silly, darling. When all's said and done, if it had really been true love then you wouldn't have needed to say any of that nonsense, would you? And neither would he have dropped you so quickly. Heavens above, just *think* about it, Leah. It can't have been that serious on either of your sides, what with you secretly hankering after Brother Matthew all the time –'

'Well, not *all* the time –'

'And Adrian cheating on you with an old girlfriend as soon as you're out of sight and mind. Anyway, never mind all that now. It's time to move on. You need peace and quiet, beautiful surroundings, and time by yourself to think things through. And you know where the best place to do that is, don't you?'

'Greystones,' I said without hesitation.

'That's my girl.' You leaned forward to kiss my forehead. 'Oh my darling, darling Leah. No matter what happens in life, I'll always love you never-stop-growing. You do know that, don't you?'

'Of course I do,' I said, suddenly overwhelmed by the knowledge of how much you truly did love me. Compared to your love, all the Adrians and Brother Matthews in the world were nothing.

So Greystones is where I went, for the third time, in the summer of 1980. The fated visit. The one I was never honest with you about. But now … now I'm going to tell you everything. And I mean *everything*.

CHAPTER FOURTEEN

1

It's July 1980 and I'm back at Greystones. It's a perfect summer's day, just like it was this time last year when I arrived. The gods are being generous with me.

I've just got off the bus and made my way to the main entrance to the monastery grounds, turning right onto the gravel driveway towards the Gatehouse. After I step inside the entrance hall, I place my bags on the floor and peer at the guest list on the noticeboard. So far everything is like an action replay of last year. Not a soul in sight. There's just me and the silence I'm surrounded by, apart from the distant calling of some bird I can't quite identify. Its plaintive song permeates the walls through a canopy of yew trees, elms, larches and sycamores that cloak the villa in summer mystery.

I find my allocated room number, which turns out to be in the attic. I'm very pleased about this, as the attic room is completely cut off from the main part of the villa. I re-gather my bags and my guitar and trudge up the stairs to the top floor. After unpacking, I breathe a long sigh of contentment. It's a lovely room, with a low-beamed ceiling, homely furniture, a well-stocked bookcase and a double bed tucked into the eaves at the far end. I've been assigned this room because all the others are taken up by the Catholic Association's retreat. Thank God for the Catholic Association retreat, is what I say.

Taking my guitar out of its case, I walk over to the casement window and perch myself on the edge of a mahogany desk that's right in front of it. I start strumming some chords and humming to myself, gazing at the familiar view I so love. Despite my hurt over Adrian, I'm feeling strangely at peace. This is my spiritual haven, I'm telling myself. Brother Matthew is hardly in my thoughts at all, even though I'm within minutes of seeing him again, after a whole year apart. Adrian is the one who is in my thoughts.

But he's not with me right now, because he's dumped me for his ex-girl-friend. I already feel better. Stronger. More able to cope with tomorrow. Not that I want tomorrow to come, because *now* is just perfect, with that divine view of the monastery tucked into the sheep-filled valley and the forested horizon on the periphery of my vision. Who could want more than this?

There's a knock at the door.

'Come in,' I say, expecting to see Father Sebastian. He's still Warden of the Gatehouse and no doubt hell-bent as ever on trying to keep me away from Brother Matthew. Not that Brother Matthew is in my thoughts at this moment.

I turn round to squint at the dark shadow that has appeared in the open doorway, obscured by the glaring sunlight streaming in through the latticed window. It's only when the black form steps inside the room and starts to approach me that I realise who it is.

'Brother Matthew!' I gasp. I mean literally gasp. Oh my God, oh my God oh my God. I feel dizzy …

'Hello,' he says, walking towards the desk where I'm perched. He stops a couple of feet from me.

'Hello,' I say back, smiling with difficulty. 'Sorry – I didn't recognise you for a moment.' *I'd forgotten how utterly gorgeous you are*, is what I meant to say.

He laughs awkwardly, turning his head to the window. This gives me a few seconds to drink in that divine profile I first fell in love with when he showed me my pages in the antiphonal all that time ago.

Returning his eyes to me, he says in a self-conscious voice, 'Did you have a good journey?'

'Yes, thank you.'

'Well, I'm glad you made it here safe and sound.'

'Thanks.'

The atmosphere in the air between us is sizzling. I mean, honestly – it's crackling, sparking, flashing – almost more than I can cope with. More than *he* can cope with. If I were ever sure about anything in life, I'm sure about this moment, right now, on this bright July afternoon in the attic room of the Gatehouse in the summer of 1980. If this were a film, there'd be vibrato violins in the background and soft romantic lighting, and the cameraman would hone in on the faces of the two main characters who are trying not to look at each other and yet doing exactly that, in between catching the occasional forced glance out of the open window for a gasp of much-needed air.

I can't even remember what we talked about. It wasn't much and it didn't last long. But it was enough. Enough to make me realise that this was the moment I'd been waiting for, these last two and a half years since I first met him. The moment of truth.

Our words are stalling, but not our gazes, which keep colliding, lingering on each other in silent communion. Eventually he glances at his watch and makes a move to part. Yes, better to part than remain trapped forever and ever in this low-beamed attic room, with the sun streaming in through the window, locking us in an eternal cry of longing.

Right, I think it's time for a *Reading from the Gospel According to Leah Cavanagh*. In other words, my diaries. I've got them all here on the coffee table. I'm prepared for this to be a very long night. Maybe the longest night of my life.

Remember my diaries, Mother? And that huge row we had, culminating in your usual mantra, *All I want is for you to be happy, darling?*

Bollocks! Let's face it, all you ever wanted was for me to do what *you* wanted me to do.

I need another cigarette. It's not every day of your life that you find yourself about to get married the following morning, and wishing that the clocks would stop ticking. I reckon that a bit of chain smoking tonight is permissible.

* * *

Greystones, 1980

July 22nd Sunday
After Mass this morning I asked Brother Matthew if I could have a word with him. He looked perplexed – not showing any of the warmth from his letters – but at least he agreed. We negotiated a time (12.00), and then I went to the Gatehouse for morning coffee, where I met a posh, garrulous lady from Wigan called Marion Fornby, who uncannily resembles someone straight out of an Enid Blyton story. She asked if I could show her some chords on the guitar, so that kept me occupied for the next couple of hours. Her bubbly, plum-in-the-mouth manner helped blot out the uneasy look that Brother Matthew gave me earlier on. Eventually I made an excuse to leave her, knowing that he'd be coming to the Gatehouse soon.

When he finally materialised we went into Father Sebastian's office, which was empty. The main thing I wanted to ask him was if it would be possible for me to stay on at Greystones a bit longer. I could tell that he felt uneasy about my request and found all sorts of excuses about why it might be difficult. However – perhaps led by the pleading in my eyes – he said he'd see what he could do.

After Midday Office I saw him again. This time he took me to the music room and I practised the piano for a good couple of hours: Bach, Chopin and Tchaikovsky. He didn't stay, though. In fact, I'm sure he's trying to have as little contact with me as he possibly can.

At 6.30 it was Vespers, then supper, and at 9.15 Compline. That's the saddest Office, because it's the last one of the day, meaning I won't see Matthew again until the morning. As the monks were filing down the aisle at the end of the service, I somehow sensed he was going to look at me so I raised my head. Sure enough, his eyes were on me. That troubled look went right through me. I kept thinking about his haunted expression for the rest of the evening.

Later on I phoned Mother to fill her in on everything. The sound of her warm voice made me feel so much better. She thinks the reason Brother Matthew is avoiding me is because he's trying to atone for that visual explosion of desire between us yesterday, when he came up to my room and we couldn't keep our eyes off each other.

Later in the evening I had a solitary walk round the monastery grounds, beneath a crescent moon that seemed to be watching me. In disapproval, no doubt.

Ah, I remember that night-time scene so well. It was just like an illustration from the *Rubaiyat of Omar Khayyam* - that beautiful little book of eleventh-century Arabian quatrains you gave me for my twenty-first birthday. The one I almost gave to Matthew as a parting gift, until I saw

213

the look in his eyes. I never told you that, because by then we might as well have spoken different languages, so huge had the chasm between us grown. So here's July 14th. Oh, what the hell. Let's also have the next few days – right up to July 27th, when the sequence comes to an abrupt end.

July 23rd Monday

Today started off badly for me, because I hardly saw Brother Matthew at all. He didn't come to the Gatehouse for breakfast, and later on, when I was walking down the corridor, I overheard Father Sebastian saying to one of the guests that Brother Matthew had decided to have a 'quiet monastic day'. I went all cold when I heard that, because I'm sure Father Sebastian said it deliberately loudly as I walked past, to make sure I heard.

He didn't come to lunch either, or to supper. Even Joelly commented on that as I helped her with the washing up. But at least I saw him for a handful of minutes in the early afternoon. He came up to the Gatehouse wearing a boiler suit (they were doing some fire training or other), and looking so completely like any other ordinary man, it brought a huge lump to my throat, just imagining what life with him could be like. He asked to see me, joy upon joy! – so once again we went into Father Sebastian's office. He said that he'd managed to jiggle around with some bookings in the Gatehouse, so I can now stay in the attic room until Saturday. That gives me a whole week. I was so overjoyed, it inspired me to ask him if we could go on a walk one afternoon. After the tiniest hesitation he said that we could go to Castle Leeming to pick raspberries, possibly the day after tomorrow. I could have thrown my arms round him!

For the rest of the day I felt much, much happier. I went on a walk to Greystones village, about two miles down the country road. It was hard not to skip all the way, I was SO happy. The weather was perfect, and the tiny village like something out of a fairy tale. I found a tiny, ancient-looking church tucked away just off the village centre, so I went inside to have a look. There was something about the atmosphere inside – as though time had stood still for centuries – that urged me to sit down on one of the pews and spend a few quiet minutes reflecting on the God that Brother Matthew so loves.

So there I was, all alone in this medieval chapel, trying to concentrate at least a little on holy matters, but my thoughts going wildly astray. As I stared at the high altar and the red glow from the ever-burning candle, I imagined myself walking down the aisle in a long white dress and veil that reached the floor, Matthew waiting for me at the front of the chapel in a dark-grey morning suit, looking so unutterably handsome, I'm sure every female present must have been wishing SHE was the one marrying him, not me. I could see it all: there we were, stepping forward to the altar, the priest raising his head to the congregation as he proclaimed, 'Dearly beloved, we are gathered here today in the sight of God to join together Leah and Matthew in holy matrimony…' and then, whizzing forward a bit, asking each of us to repeat the solemn words after him … and of course I said, 'I do', and so did Matthew, and we were pronounced man and wife, and my new husband leaned towards me to push aside my veil and kiss me on the lips, and everyone in the church clapped – or whatever they do at weddings – and we walked back down the aisle as a newly married couple, radiant in our consecrated love.

Yeah, right. Chance would be a fine thing.

July 24ᵗʰ Tuesday

I had a lovely surprise while washing up after lunch today: I turned round from the sink to gather some dishes, and there was Brother Matthew! He only stayed a short while, though. He walked over to me very self-consciously and said that we could have our walk to Castle Leeming tomorrow because he was free in the afternoon. When he left I couldn't help gazing after him for a few moments - and then my eyes happened to fall on Marion, who smiled at me in secret understanding.

The rest of the day whizzed past. I wrote my diary, phoned Mother, practised the piano, and talked with the other guests. In the evening I sat by my wide-open window, gazing out at the dark fields beyond the monastery and unable to believe that tomorrow Brother Matthew and I would at last be together on our walk. There's a special bond between us which has been there ever since I first met him. I guess Mother knew it all the way along.

July 25th Wednesday

Today was both one of the happiest and unhappiest days of my life. When the afternoon at long last came, Brother Matthew and I set off on our walk. The weather was glorious – by far the best day we've had yet. I felt utterly exhilarated as we set out, having him all to myself. He looked completely different in ordinary jeans and a T-shirt. Anyone else would just think we were a normal couple.

The walk from Greystones Abbey to Castle Leeming was exquisite, and Castle Leeming itself just divine. The terraced gardens were awash with brilliant colours – geraniums, herbaceous borders, raspberry bushes - all set against a backdrop of cobalt-blue sky and golden sunshine. When we arrived, Brother Matthew went in search of some receptacles for our fruit-picking, so I waited in a dream-like state amid the raspberries and flowerbeds, gazing at the nearby forest. Eventually he came back carrying a couple of tin containers, so we started picking raspberries. We were chatting away the whole time, as though there had never been any tension between us. He even opened up about some personal things in his life, like the moment he first knew he wanted to become a monk. Apparently it was during a conversation he had with his grandmother when he was sixteen, sitting on the veranda of her house at Derwent Water, which apparently has a long terraced garden that goes right down to the shores of the lake. He said that the gardens of Castle Leeming always remind him of that talk – the decisive one in which his grandmother had given him her blessing. Then he added, 'Derwent Water is an utterly beautiful spot, Leah; I'm sure you'd love it,' which inspired me to ask, 'Are you inviting me there?' But when I saw the expression on his face, I regretted it immediately.

While I was still trying to work out what to say next in order to fill in the awkward silence, a shrill voice called out, 'Cooey!' It was Marion, who was waving at us and approaching like an athlete walker. Brother Matthew greeted her with exaggerated enthusiasm, and within minutes all three of us were picking those bloody raspberries. So much for my intimate afternoon all alone with Matthew.

When we finished with the raspberries, Matthew gave Marion and me a guided tour of the castle. Talk about breath-taking! Every inch of it was like something out of a tale of chivalry: the vast entrance hall with its low-hanging chandelier and coat of arms above the fireplace, the sweeping oak staircase that leads up to the boys' dormitories, the latticed windows that look out over the terraced gardens and forest beyond, the ancient stone kitchen ... everything about the day was so unreal, I kept expecting to wake up at any moment.

As we came out of the castle, Intruder No 2 zoomed into the driveway: Joelly in her spluttering Mini, accompanied by a great whopping Labrador at the back of her car. Skidding to a halt, she wound down the front window and called out, 'Fancy a lift back, lovies?' Honestly, I could have throttled her! But Brother Matthew infuriatingly accepted her offer, so all three of us struggled into the old banger – Marion in front, Matthew and me at the back. Joelly was discreetly trying to suggest having her Labrador positioned between Matthew and me, but I was pleased to note that he completely ignored her. This meant that he had the Labrador sitting on one side of him, and me on the other. It was a small car, so I was fairly squashed up against him! It's lucky we were on our own at the back, because the tension caused by our physical closeness really electrified the air around us. He didn't even bother *moving his leg away from me; he just let it remain pressed tightly against mine. It was the same with our arms and shoulders – neither of us made the least effort to inch away. Brother Matthew hardly said a word the whole time, which meant that I was the one who had to cover up the smouldering atmosphere. I somehow managed to do this by trying to take an interest in the panting Labrador on my right, and giving monosyllabic responses to the constant chatter from Marion and Joelly in front. I wasn't used to Matthew being so silent. I could feel the trembling of his thigh pressed against mine, and could hear his rapid, shallow breathing. As for me …? I hardly dared breathe at all!*

When we arrived back at the Gatehouse he didn't stop for tea, but hurried off straight to the monastery. I felt so bitter, knowing that when I next saw him he'd be in his cassock once again, filled with renewed spiritual strength. I stayed in the kitchen for a while, having a cup of tea with Marion and Joelly, then getting down to the laborious task of washing the raspberries. I was secretly hoping that Brother Matthew would come back, but I didn't see him again for the rest of the day.

July 26th Thursday

Today was Brother Matthew's birthday – something that Marion and I found out quite by chance. We were sitting in the common room after breakfast having a guitar session, when we heard Brother Matthew entering the Gatehouse. The doors to the common room are glass-panelled, so we could see Joelly walking down the corridor towards the entrance. When she spotted Matthew she gave him a big hug and cried out in her broad Yorkshire accent, 'Many happy returns, Brother Matthew!'

Marion and I decided that we had to do something for his birthday, so in the afternoon we caught the bus to Helmsley to look for a card. It poured down with rain all day long, in sharp contrast to the previous few days. Helmsley is a picturesque old town with a medieval church and castle – though everything seems to be medieval round here. After we'd selected our birthday cards, we went to a quaint olde-English cafe for tea and scones. Seeing as it was still throwing it down with rain, we stayed there until the bus came at 6.00. Only once did the conversation turn a bit tricky, when Marion was trying to guess how old Matthew was and I told her that he was 29, proud of my 'insider knowledge'. She looked at me in a troubled sort of way and said, 'You've got a soft spot for him, dear, haven't you?' Taken completely off-guard, I blurted out, 'Not in the least!' But the desperation in my voice must have been a dead giveaway, because she reached out her hand across the table and said in a motherly tone, 'Oh, Leah, do be careful. I'd hate to see either of you get hurt.' I just laughed it off, and the subject wasn't brought up again.

The rest of the evening was bloody frustrating. I only saw Brother Matthew briefly at Vespers when I tried to give him a meaningful smile, but he didn't even look at me. And then, when he neither turned up for supper nor Compline, I became frantic. How could I give him his birthday card? I ended up having to break the Great Silence in the monastery by asking one of the monks if he knew where Brother Matthew was, but he didn't. So in the end I went back to the Gatehouse and put his card on the desk in the Warden's office. I just hope Father Sebastian won't find it first. He'd probably tear it into a thousand pieces and flush it down the toilet.

It was too wet to go on my nightly walk, so I stayed in my room all evening and daydreamed about Brother Matthew and me ending up together one day. And yet I have to admit, at times I find the thought almost too much to bear.

Okay. So here it is at last. July 28th – the day my diary came to a stop. I only recorded the first part of the day, because what happened later was too painful to write about. Too painful even to talk to you about, Mother. But I'm going to come clean now.

Today is my last day at Greystones. Sometimes I try to work out what it is that attracts me to this place. In fact, I talked to Brother Matthew about it this morning after breakfast. He said that most visitors are drawn by the solace, the tranquillity and the spiritual beauty. But I challenged him by saying, 'No, it's not just that. Even with all those things, Greystones would mean nothing to me without your presence.' Then he looked at me with heavy eyes and said, 'I think it's rather the converse, Leah. Without Greystones, I wouldn't hold any significance for you.' But how can he SAY that? As if I could be that shallow!

Anyway, before I had the chance to respond, Marion breezed into the refectory and made her way over to the sink to fill up the kettle. Then the door swung open again and another handful of guests walked in. Obviously it was time for morning coffee. Brother Matthew - looking very self-conscious - asked them if they'd like to go on a tour of the bell tower. I almost cried at that point, because yesterday I myself had asked him about the tower and he said he could show it me, so I thought I'd have him all to myself. Well, that's certainly the last thing I got! More and more people began to hear about this bloody bell tower trip, until about a dozen of us ended up going.

Once we'd all trooped down to the monastery, we made our way into an adjoining building and started climbing up some spiral wooden steps which took us right to the top, getting narrower all the way up. The trek to the top of the tower was like something out of The Hunchback of Notre Dame. It was fascinating seeing the top of the huge dome of the church, and walking past it along a sort of wooden bridge. Next we came to the enormous bell – I forget how many tons Brother Matthew said it weighed. I kept thinking how marvellous it would have been if Matthew and I were alone, as we should have been. Damn it, it was my idea. Why did all the others have to intrude?

Right at the top, the view was spectacular. You could even catch a glimpse of the lakes through the forest. The whole time Brother Matthew kept on with his running commentary, pointing out various buildings and landmarks to all of us, but never once looking at me.

On the way back down I decided I had to make one last attempt to try and have him to myself before I go home tomorrow. So once we were all back on ground level I waited for the others to file past, and then, just as Matthew was about to make his way back to the monks' cloister, I hurried over to him and said, 'Brother Matthew, there's something I need to talk to you about.' Seeing as he didn't ward me off by saying how busy he was, I quickly went on, 'As I'm leaving tomorrow, this is my last chance.' I can remember the words pretty well, because I'd been rehearsing them in my mind all the way down from the bell tower. He agreed – reluctantly, as always – and said that he'd come up to the Gatehouse after supper to find me.

The afternoon sailed past. I went to my attic room to write my diary, but after a while Marion came up and said they were all looking for me – I'd forgotten that we'd arranged to have a singing session and they needed me to play the guitar. So about seven of us went to the common room and ended up having a really enjoyable 'sing-along'. I strummed away until I thought my fingers would drop off. Afterwards we all went to the kitchen to tuck into the rock buns that Joelly had made.

Later on I kept racking my brains to think of what I could talk to Brother Matthew about. I ended up settling on some vaguely spiritual theme that'll oblige him to take me seriously. From there I'll just have to see if I can manoeuvre the conversation towards us. Okay, better stop – it's time for supper. God, I'm so nervous …

That was the last sentence I wrote for several weeks.

CHAPTER FIFTEEN

1

By the time you were twenty-four, both you and Peter Fox had moved up in the world. You'd been promoted to the position of doctor's secretary at the Mass Radiography Unit, and Peter had moved from Manchester to London to work as sub-editor on a national newspaper. He was mixing with more sophisticated people now, and this new circle of associates sometimes included his Irish friend, Dr Dermot Cavanagh, who he'd met while doing research for an article on private medical care.

As Dermot had lots of acquaintances in London, Peter soon became a regular guest at dinner parties hosted by a seemingly endless chain of VIPs. During these lively, boozy events, Dermot often boasted about the holiday apartment he'd recently purchased in the quaint fishing village of Kyrenia in Northern Cyprus, with a view over the turquoise sea and medieval harbour. He explained to Peter that he was considering moving his private GP practice in Lyneham-on-Sea over to Kyrenia, because he'd noticed that the expatriate community in the old British colony was thriving. Diplomats and army bigwigs who tried to keep the Greek-Cypriot terrorists under control were scattered in luxury apartments and villas all over the place, and would certainly benefit from the skills of a home-grown, native English-speaking doctor.

Dermot had invited his journalist friend to come and stay with him in Kyrenia on several occasions, but due to the busy schedule of Peter's work and love life, he hadn't yet taken him up on the generous offer. But no fear – all too soon he will do, am I right, Mother? Once Dermot is fully installed in his sea-view flat in Kyrenia, Peter will be out there in a jiffy, readily abandoning the tooting horns of London for the golden shores of Aphrodite's island. Kismet is fast-tracking forward.

Despite your fears about Peter when he moved to London, he still visited you in Preston as often as he could, though it was never often enough for your liking. He truly loved your parents, even calling them *Mum and Dad*, not having known much happiness in his own upbringing. He was a lost soul forever searching for truth and equality amongst men, forever quoting from the Declaration of Human Rights, yearning to make the world a better place through his journalism. Your mother adored him and always took it for granted that one day he would be her son-in-law. Just why it was taking so long for this event to happen was a conundrum she could never quite fathom. 'You two want your heads knocking together,' she said time and time again, unable to understand why the two of you didn't just get on with the business of getting married, settling in a nice terraced house, having kids and living happily ever after.

Peter visited you and your family every Christmas during the years he lived in London. The celebratory roast dinner that Gran always prepared wouldn't have been the same without Peter gulping it down as though he hadn't eaten in days. He showered your beaming mother with praise about her succulent turkey and home-made stuffing covered in rich gravy that seeped to the brim of the plate, and her brussels sprouts that were cooked to perfection, just as her roast potatoes were – neither too crispy nor too flaky. You truly were a happy little gathering during those times, weren't you? So why did he constantly fail to put that ring on your finger? After all, it's not as if you were a wilting wallflower. Oh no, not *you*, Mother! – the shapely, bubbly, gutsy, much-desired Molly Williams, with her pert smile, her Marilyn Monroe figure and her irresistible charm that never failed to melt the hearts of men. But at times Peter seemed to be impervious to it.

'Haven't you married your boring architect yet?' he'd tease you during your weekly phone calls in the public booth at the end of Talbot Road. But you gave him as good as he got.

'No, not yet. And if you don't mind, his name is Tony Gaston, and he happens to be a very nice, intelligent man.'

'Oh, Molly, chuck the Gastric bugger! He's not worthy of you.'

'So in that case why don't you chuck Latrina?'

'Her name is *Clarina*, and you know she doesn't mean anything to me.'

'All right then, if you chuck Latrina, I'll chuck Tony.'

So eventually you chucked Tony, and Peter chucked Clarina, and he even suggested that you moved into his London flat. To make the rent cheaper.

'You could get a job dead easily,' he said over the phone, 'what with your typing skills and your buckets of charm. So what about it, Chubs? What d'you think? How about joining your man in the big city?'

But it wasn't asked in the proper way. It wasn't a marriage proposal, nor even a repeat proposal, considering his first one had been when you were sweet nineteen. And it sounded too much like a business transaction for your liking. So you didn't join him in the big city of London, and he didn't take the hint about adding marriage into the bargain, and your mother shook her head in tired bewilderment for the thousandth time.

2

Okay. Back to that unfinished diary entry of July 27th 1980.

It's suppertime and I'm in the Gatehouse refectory. Brother Matthew and I are seated opposite each other. Our eyes keep meeting across the table. We're hardly aware of the other guests sitting with us, apart from granting them the occasional smile or enforced fragment of small talk. They keep trying to draw us into the conversation, but we're being deliberately obtuse about this. The time is drawing near for our talk – our last chance to be on our own before I catch the bus to York tomorrow morning, then the train to Lyneham-on-Sea. The very thought of all that travelling, taking me gradually further and further away from him, brings me out in a cold sweat. I can't bear the thought of leaving him, of not seeing him again for another whole year. And somehow, I just know he's feeling the exact same way.

Once everyone has finished eating, I stack together all the plates from our table and carry them over to the sink. After a moment or two he follows me. When I turn round to face him he's standing right behind me with an apprehensive look on his face. My heart goes out to him. This isn't easy for either of us.

'Did you still want that talk?' he asks very quietly.

'Oh – yes, definitely. If it's all right with you?'

'Of course. As soon as you're finished in here, we can find somewhere quiet.'

'Actually, I'm finished now. I did the washing-up after lunch, so now it's someone else's turn.'

'I see. Well then – shall we go?'

We walk out of the Gatehouse together and make our way down the hill, towards the rambling complex of stone buildings near the Abbey that is designated for VIP guests. In the Visitor's Lodge, we climb up the stairs and head for the same room that he took me to on my first trip to Greystones: that lush hideaway with its open fireplace, richly brocaded arm-chairs and gilt-framed portraits of deceased Abbots. We sit down – he on one armchair, me on the other. I cross my legs, rest my hands on my lap, and look at him.

'Well, here we are. My last evening at Greystones.'

'Yes, indeed.' He nods his head solemnly, as though in response to a deeply philosophical comment I'd just made.

We carry on for a few minutes in a similar vein, until gradually our line of conversation becomes more personalised – guided by my skilful han-dling, I have to say.

Once we've become a little more relaxed with each other, I ask him with youthful directness, 'So why did you never become a priest, Brother Mat-thew?' It's a genuine enough question, and one that I've often pondered over. Most of the monks at Greystones Abbey are priests. Only the very young ones – the novices – are still just monks, though I don't know if Brother Matthew would appreciate the inclusion of the word 'just'.

'Because I've always yearned for the contemplative life,' he explains after a contemplative silence. 'I've always longed to be close to God in a simple, meditative way that doesn't require the addition of a higher status. I never wanted any of that. I only ever wanted to be at peace with God. I even considered joining an enclosed order when I was much younger – one where the monks never leave the monastery, never talk to outsiders. But my grandmother persuaded me against it.'

'Well, thank Christ for that!' I say, laughing. 'Sorry.'

He doesn't respond at first. Evidently I've touched on a subject he feels very deeply about. And then he goes straight on: 'I suppose in the long run my grandmother was right to dissuade me from joining a contemplative order. Greystones was a much better choice. It combines the community spirit I grew up with, and a dedication to God that is based upon a balance of prayer, meditation and work.'

'Work,' I echo, 'You mean as in teaching?'

'Well yes, I daresay teaching involves some element of work.' He smiles at me in gentle irony.

'Oh – right, of course.' I flush, but he doesn't appear to notice. He just cups his chin between his fingers and carries on in that calm, eloquent voice I so love.

'There are also my duties at the Gatehouse I have to see to, considering they're planning on making me the next Warden.'

'But you once told me that you'd have to be made a priest if you were ever to become Warden of the Gatehouse.'

'Yes, that's true, and it's something that makes me think I'd be better sticking to teaching. But to be perfectly honest, my heart isn't in teaching Latin or Scripture. I far prefer my duties at the Gatehouse – mixing in with different people throughout the year, giving talks, leading Retreats …'

'So in that case, I guess you probably *will* be made a priest one day, right?'

'Yes, probably. I just keep hoping it won't happen too soon.'

'Me too.'

'Might I ask why?'

'Isn't it obvious?'

He draws his eyebrows together. 'Not being a mind reader, I'm afraid you'll have to spell it out for me.'

So I spell it out. 'If you're made a priest, then that'll take you even further away from me than you already are.'

After an excruciating pause, he says, 'Oh, Leah.'

I don't like the sound of his tone. I don't like it at all.

Glancing at him somewhat edgily, I ask, 'What is it? What've I said?'

He smiles a sad smile, rather like a disappointed father who knows he's about to deliver a lecture to his child but doesn't really want to. 'You haven't done anything, Leah. But maybe – maybe you've *thought* too much. Or felt too much.'

'What do you mean?'

'I mean you shouldn't miss me. By all means miss someone else – this Adrian chap you told me about, for instance. Or your mother, who you say you're so close to. But not me.'

'Are you telling me I can't be honest with myself? Or with you?'

'On the contrary, I want you to be completely honest with both of us. Not in a fantasy way, but in a real way.'

'This *is* real, Brother Matthew. I *am* going to miss you. And I think – I mean, I hope – that you're also going to miss me? At least a little bit?'

Suddenly he leans forward in his armchair and faces me with a look I have never before seen on him. This is it, I think to myself, inwardly shuddering. The moment of truth.

'Leah,' he says in a hoarse voice that is almost a whisper. 'I'm afraid I'm not going to miss you in the way you're hoping for.'

I stare at him, confused. 'What do you mean?'

So he clarifies: 'I suppose what I'm trying to say – very ineptly, I'm afraid – is that you should try to steer your feelings away from the direction they seem to be taking you. You should try *not* to miss me, *not* to hope that I won't be made into a priest. You should try instead to forge real relationships with real people, try to get on with your life and make something of it.'

'But *you're* a real part of my life.'

He shakes his head. 'Just a fantasy part. One which you need to break free from before you can move on.'

'Fantasy? What do you mean?'

'The fantasy of falling for a monk.'

'You think it's a *fantasy?*'

He nods, slowly, solemnly, weighing me up with … could it be *pity?*

I sit forward in my chair, staring at him directly. 'But you also feel … I mean … '

'No, Leah. I don't.'

The look on his face puts an instant halt to everything I wanted to say. I close my mouth and try to control the sudden throbbing in my throat.

'I feel a great fondness towards you,' he goes on with cruel precision. 'You're a lovely, talented, very special person – and yes, of course you're attractive as well. Even monks aren't immune to such things.'

He attempts a laugh, but I do not follow suit. My heart is racing more wildly than I ever thought it capable of doing.

'But at the end of the day, I'm a monk,' he continues. 'I'm a part of a Benedictine order and I've taken solemn vows which I have no intention of breaking. *Ever*. I'm not free, neither do I want to be free, and I feel it's my duty to say these things to you now, before they grow out of all proportion. In other words, dearest Leah, I'm trying to spare you future disappointment and pain.'

His face has assumed a kindly, omniscient expression; mine no doubt a perplexed and pained one. The very kind of pain that he said he wanted to spare me, the hypocrite!

'You mean – you don't feel *anything* for me?'

He shakes his head. 'Not in the way you want me to. I'm tremendously fond of you, but -'

'But these past two and a half years … all your letters, the way you sometimes look at me …'

'You mean the way I'm looking at you now? As a true friend who cares about you? Of course I feel something for you. But it's only affection, Leah, nothing more.'

'You're saying you don't feel for me *at all* in … in that way?'

'Correct.'

'Then you're lying!'

His eyes widen at the sudden sharpness in my voice, which gives me the confidence to plough straight on. 'I don't believe a word of what you've just said! You sound like a – a bloody *robot!*'

I can see that this has both hurt and angered him. He inches a little away before aiming the full brunt of his monkish gaze at me. 'I'm sorry if you think that. But at the end of the day, it's your choice whether to believe in the truth or not. If you examine your heart closely, I think you'll find that *you're* the one who hasn't been quite truthful with yourself. I think you'll also find that you've misinterpreted any innocent words, gestures or looks that I might have given you or said to you over the past couple of years, either in person or via letters -'

'For Christ's sake, stop sounding so bloody pompous!' I shout at him against my will, amazed that I'm capable of doing such a thing. Then I leap up from my chair.

A spark of something akin to panic flashes across his eyes. He follows suit and also stands up. So we are now both standing, facing each other: two bitter opponents at war. My entire body is trembling, my heart thudding against the frame of my ribcage. But I'm determined not to show him any of this. I will never ever again raise my voice to him in uncontrolled emotion. In fact, I will never have any more contact with him, full stop. *Never.* My mind is made up.

'Right then,' I say, clearing my throat as I look at him squarely. 'So that's settled. The feeling isn't mutual between us.'

'I'm sorry ...'

'That's okay. More fool me for having misinterpreted everything all this time.'

'Leah, I'm not blaming you for -'

'No, but *I'm* blaming *you*, Matthew. If what you're saying is true, then you should never have strung me along all this time. You should never have written to me at all, knowing how I felt about you. But you couldn't do that, could you? You couldn't bear to deprive yourself of the flattery of being fancied by a naïve sixth-former. In fact, you've probably accumulated a whole medley of these adoring girls. Every time yet another school retreat comes along you probably add another admirer to your collection, isn't that right? It must be fun, having all these young females pining away for you, writing you letters -'

'Leah, I think you've completely misunderstood every -'

'No I haven't. It's perfectly obvious what you've just said. So now I hope what I'm about to say will be equally obvious. I don't want to write to you anymore. I don't want to come back to Greystones ever again. In short, I don't want to have anything more to do with you. Goodbye, Brother Matthew. Have a nice life.'

And with that, I march towards the door and swish out of the room – a true daughter of Molly Williams-Cavanagh!

3

I couldn't bear the thought of going to the monastery for Compline that evening. I couldn't bear the thought of seeing him – or *anyone*. I didn't know which was worse – my humiliation, my hurt, or my deep, aching sense of loss. Was I really going to break off our relationship? The simple answer was yes. There was no putting the clock back now. I'd said the words and I couldn't take them back. There was nowhere to go from here, except up to my secluded attic room at the Gatehouse, where no one and nothing could disturb me during my final night at Greystones. There, I would be completely alone to nurse my aching heart before facing the morning and catching the first available bus to York. I never wanted to see him again. He had made a mockery of the past two and half years of loving him; a love that I'd dared to hope had been mutual.

After abandoning the Visitor's Lodge I ran all the way up the driveway back to the Gatehouse, then charged up the stairs two at a time and shut myself in my room. No one could get to me now.

Breathing easier, I walked over to the desk, perched myself on the edge of it, and opened the window wide. The bell from the monastery was tolling for Compline, which is where he'd probably be heading now. Hopefully he'd notice I wasn't there.

For the next half-hour I sat perfectly still, staring at the gradually darkening sky. It was a clear evening, not at all reflective of my own tortured thoughts that kept colliding into one another from all corners. The moon was out in full. To help me calm down, I found myself whispering the words of Omar Khayyam that I'd heard so often in the years of my upbringing:

> Ah, moon of my delight who know'st no wane,
> The moon of heav'n is rising once again.
> How oft hereafter rising shall she look
> Through this same garden after me in vain?

In vain; yes, that's what it all was. In bloody vain. A pointless love that I'd wasted two and a half years over. I wanted to stay in my attic room forever, never to be found again by the moon or anyone or anything else.

At that despairing thought, the tear gates at last opened. I poured out my anguish to the indifferent night sky and the faint summer stars. I didn't even bother to stifle my sobs because I knew that everyone would be at Compline and therefore not a soul could hear me. I cried for every letter I had ever written him, every word or look or gesture of his I had ever misinterpreted; but above all, I cried because I had lost him. I had lost the man who had come to mean so much to me, whose voice and eyes and smile I would never forget, even if he very soon forgot me. I cried until I could cry no more. And then, leaving the window wide open to let the moon and stars cast their silvery haze upon the shadowed beams and alcoves, I shuffled over to the bed and lay down on its soft feathery quilt. Then I shut my eyes and willed myself to sleep. Sleep, the only sanctuary.

* * *

I was awoken by someone knocking at the door. Jumping bolt upright, I called out, 'Who is it?'

The door creaked open. It took my eyes several moments to adjust to the semi-dark, through which a shadowed form emerged.

'Leah?'

My hand shot up to my mouth. It was *him*. 'What are you doing here?'

'Can I put the light on?'

'No.'

He hesitated, then slowly started walking towards me, stopping a few feet away from the bed. I was sitting in a crouched position on top of the quilt, still fully dressed, arms hugging my knees, head raised towards him defiantly.

He looked down at me and said, 'You weren't at Compline.'

'Like you'd care.'

Ignoring my bitter tone, he went on, 'I was worried about you after our talk. Are you all right?'

'I'm fine, thanks. You can go now.'

'Oh, Leah, please.'

'Please what?'

'Please can we talk?'

'We've already talked.'

'But *properly* this time. You never gave me the chance to say everything I wanted to say. You jumped to all sorts of conclusions before I'd finished trying to explain how I felt.'

'But you did explain. Perfectly well.' My eyes had by now adjusted to the dark. I could see that the expression in his eyes was sombre, uneasy.

'Then I'm afraid I didn't explain well enough.'

'Okay, so explain again.'

Sighing, he sat down on the edge of the bed. Then he looked straight at me. 'When I said that I didn't feel anything for you, what I meant to say was that I didn't *want* to feel anything for you. I didn't want to let myself get involved.'

'Fine. So then don't.'

For a few moments he didn't reply.

At last he said: 'It would have been so easy to get carried away with your fantasy, but I was determined not to let that happen.'

'It wasn't a fantasy.'

'Yes it was, Leah.' His pupils were gleaming in the semi-dark. 'It's perfectly obvious from all your letters over the past couple of years that it was a fantasy. Whenever you were going through a good time in your life – dating boys and so on – your letters became much less frequent. Then when you were in need of me because someone had broken off with you, you started writing again, wanting to come back to Greystones.'

I was about to defend myself, but decided against it. What was the point?

When he next spoke, his voice didn't sound quite so self-assured. 'What I'm trying to say, Leah, is that regardless of the hurt and misunderstanding I've caused you, there's no need for it to end like this.'

'Oh yes there is,' I snapped, reclaiming my voice. 'There's no sense whatsoever in us continuing. We're at complete loggerheads. I've had enough, Matthew, honestly I have.'

'But *why?*' Was that a tremor I detected in his voice?

I shrugged. 'I've just had enough. This is the end of the road. Tomorrow I go back home and that's that. The End of Greystones. The End of You.'

He looked away. For several moments he sat at the foot of the bed in silence. Then he muttered, half to himself, 'If only I'd never been involved in that retreat.'

I frowned in puzzlement. 'What do you mean?'

After another long pause, he said in a strangely altered voice, 'I'd been asked to put more hours in at the Gatehouse that week, to help Father Sebastian out.'

'That week?'

'The week you first came to Greystones. With the Lark Mount retreat.'

'So – ' I swallowed. 'Are you saying you wish you'd never met me?'

He nodded, but this time didn't offer any further explanation.

Holding my breath, I moved a couple of inches forward, finding myself in a stream of moonlight that must have cast my whole face aglow. I could feel it. So could he, apparently, because he turned his head to look at me.

Our eyes met.

We looked at each other in silence. Then he said just one word, one name, uttering it in a way that sounded like a plea: '*Leah* ...'

I moved closer to him still. Touched his shoulder.

Immediately he took hold of my hand and brought it to his lips. My heart stopped beating. No, honestly, it really did. I'm sure a part of me died there and then. With the feel of his kiss upon the palm of my hand, I no longer required a heart to pump blood through my veins.

I could feel his hot breath. He let go of my hand and turned fully towards me, gripping my face on either side as he kissed my forehead, my nose, my lips – tentatively at first, just brushing them with his own, but swiftly gaining in confidence as our mouths probed urgently. I wrapped my arms round his neck, bringing him closer to me. He shuddered, pushing me back onto the quilt and heaving himself on top of me, interrupting our kiss only long enough to murmur, '*God forgive me …*' before claiming my mouth once again.

My arms tightened round his neck. I moaned as his lips travelled down to my throat, then my breasts, still concealed beneath the thin fabric of my blouse. I moaned harder as he struggled to undo the buttons, his own hardness pulsing and vibrating against me.

I can barely remember the next few moments. I wish to God I could. I wish I could constantly press the re-play button of those perfect moments. How long did they last? Fifteen seconds? Twenty? A condensed lifetime?

The distant sound of footsteps echoed from below.

Immediately I felt his limbs stiffen upon my own. He removed his mouth from my breast, hardly breathing. As the footsteps grew louder, he sat bolt upright. In that moment, I knew it was over.

'Matthew – ' I began, but my whisper was lost in the exchange of voices that floated up the stairs. Father Sebastian's and the cook's.

'*Joelly, have you seen Brother Matthew?*'

'*No, I haven't. Sorry, Father. I was just about to leave.*'

'*That's strange, I'm sure I saw him walking up the hill towards the Gatehouse after Compline.*'

'*Happen he's gone on a walk. You know how he likes his night-time strolls.*'

'*Hmm, maybe. Well, sorry to have bothered you. I bid you goodnight.*'

'*Night night, Father. See you tomorrow.*'

At last the voices ceased and the footsteps faded into oblivion. The final sound that reached our attic enclosure was the opening and closing of the main doors in the entrance hall, two floors below us. Then silence.

Still he didn't say anything. He didn't even look at me.

'Matthew – they've gone,' I whispered, trying to pull him back towards me.

As though shaken out of his stupor, he jolted his body forwards, clutching his head between his hands. I was barely able to hear the words he mumbled through clenched fists. His knuckles were white, the taut skin stretched upon bone.

'Oh God – Oh God, I'm sorry. I'm so sorry ... that should *never* have happened ...'

'No, don't say that!' I edged closer to his back and tried to wrap my arms round his waist from behind. But he stiffened at my touch, flinging me away and standing up with a violent jerk. He looked down at me in a fusion of distress and panic. I'll never forget the expression on his face.

'Leah, please forgive me. Please try and forget that this ever happened.'

'*Forget* it? Are you mad? Can *you* forget it?'

'I - we have to.'

He turned round and started walking towards the door.

'No, *wait*!' I leapt up from the bed and ran after him, pushing myself in front of the door and blocking his exit. 'You can't leave – not just like that! I love you, Matthew, you *must* know that by now – and I know that you also love me, no matter what you say -'

'No, I don't love you.' He tried to push me away, but I didn't budge.

'Then why did – why did that just happen between us?'

He winced. 'It was human frailty. *My* frailty. It never should have happened, and I apologise. But now we have to put it behind us. We have to. There's no other way.'

'Of *course* there is!'

He placed a finger on my lips to still my impassioned outpouring. 'Leah, listen to me. This is the life I've chosen, and it doesn't include you – or any woman. You must do as you promised when we spoke in the Visitors' Lodge.'

'What – what did I promise?' I half-whimpered, knowing it was over, that I had lost, that any moment now he'd be gone.

'To stop writing to me, stop coming to Greystones. To put me out of your life forever.'

'But I *can't* …'

'It's what you yourself decided, before I messed it all up by …'

I hung onto his unfinished sentence, tried to peer at his face as he struggled for words, but the build-up of tears in my eyes blurred my vision.

'But that's behind us now,' he said, apparently having given up on the missing words. 'All I can say, a thousand times over, is how very, very sorry I am that I let it come to this. I can never forgive myself.'

And with that, he grabbed hold of my shoulders – not to embrace me, as I thought for one electrified moment – but just to manoeuvre me out of the way so that he could open the door and leave the room.

He left me standing there all alone, open-mouthed, a broken woman.

4

God knows how I got through the night. I can barely remember what I did after he left me standing by the door, tears streaming down my face. I couldn't give a damn who the hell heard me. Part of me *wanted* someone to hear me, to come hurrying up the stairs to the attic, ask me what was wrong, what was the matter, could they do anything to help ... because even though the answer would have been 'no', at least I wouldn't have been left alone in my urgent need for oblivion.

But of course no one came up to my room. And I wasn't granted oblivion. I can't remember how long I continued to stand there, leaning against the door sobbing my heart out.

Eventually I made my way back over to the bed – the very same bed that he and I had lain on just minutes earlier, his body pressed upon mine, trembling with love and passion and heat, now frozen by his cowardice. His God had made him a man, and all he could do was turn tail and run away in panic. I think at that moment I hated him. Or his God. Or both.

* * *

I didn't wake up till after nine the following morning, with the sun streaming into the room, hurting my head and making a mockery of my despair.

I jumped out of bed, realising that I'd missed Matins, Lauds and breakfast, and that he'd probably think I was avoiding him. But in the next breath I also realised that he would probably be avoiding *me*, so it didn't matter anyway. All I knew was that I had to see him again. Never mind my bitterness from the previous night; I just *had* to see him again, before it was too late.

I scrambled around trying to get dressed, trying to brush the tangled knots out of my hair but giving up half-way through, trying to ignore the migraine I could feel coming on, trying to calm the growing fear that it already was too late.

Running out of my room, I tumbled down the stairs two at a time. Where was he likely to be at half past nine in the morning? I hurried along the corridor to the refectory, hoping he might still be there, possibly chatting to some lingering guests. But as soon as I opened the door I could see that all the tables had been cleared away and re-set for lunch. The only person still there, pottering about in the open-plan kitchen area, was Joelly.

'Hello, Joelly,' I said, forcing normality into my voice.

She was kneeling down by a cupboard near the sink, putting away a stack of plates. Upon hearing my voice she looked up and threw me a warm smile. 'Oh, hello, lovey. We missed you at breakfast this morning. Everything all right?'

'Yes, everything's fine. Have you seen Brother Matthew?'

'No, I'm afraid I haven't. Do you want -'

But I didn't bother hanging around. Her answer of 'no' was all I needed. For once in my life I didn't bother about manners; I just turned on my heel and fled the room, rushing back down the corridor towards Father Sebastian's office. *Please God, let Matthew be there, please let him be there, please let him be there ...*

I knocked at the door.

'*Come in,*' was the unwanted voice I heard from within the office. Not Mathew's.

I was about to turn away, but in the next moment the door opened and there stood Father Sebastian.

'Ah, Leah,' he said, smiling at me with small piercing eyes that uncannily resembled those of a bird of prey.

In spite of the hostility of his stare, I managed to ask, 'Have you seen Brother Matthew?'

'I'm afraid he's gone.'

'Gone?'

'Yes, he's been called away on urgent business.'

'Urgent business?' I was beginning to sound like a parrot.

'Family matters, I gather. He's likely to be away for quite some time.'

'Where's he gone?'

The eagle eyes creased at me in the meanest smile I had ever seen. 'I'm afraid I'm not at liberty to disclose such information.'

'But I'm a close friend of his – I'm sure he'd want me to know.'

'Well, that's where you're wrong, my dear. What he really wants is to be left alone. If you truly are a close friend, then you'll respect his wishes.'

Not giving a damn about anything anymore, I stammered, 'But – but he'd want me to know, I'm sure he would … please, Father, please could you give me his address so that I can write to him?'

'No.' The word said so categorically, so maliciously, my entire body shivered under its impact. But what came next was even worse. 'My dear, might I make a suggestion. I think it would be best for everyone concerned if you didn't come here again.'

By now the tears in my eyes must have been showing. I couldn't speak.

'I also think it would be best all round if you left Brother Matthew alone. I'm sorry to sound hard, but that's the truth of the matter. It's what he wants.' He rubbed his hands together. 'Now then, if you'd like a bus timetable, I'm sure I can dig one out for you, if you give me a minute. From what I can remember, I believe the next bus to York is at twelve o'clock.'

Never before had I felt so wretched. This really was it. This was the moment my life changed. Last night a part of me had died; this morning the process of annihilation continued a step further. I was about to embark on my next journey: a semi-posthumous one. I was now deprived of my life's blood.

Was this how you felt when Peter Fox flew to Kyrenia to stay with his friend Dermot, and you realised he might never come back? That the Mediterranean sun and azure sea and dark-eyed Cypriot girls, as well as the offer to work on *The Times of Cyprus,* might lure him to stay out there forever,

241

never returning to your pining, aching arms? And that the interim boy-friends you'd dabbled with – even getting engaged to one of them, merely to show him you didn't care – would never hold a candle to the sheer power of desire and fascination and deep, everlasting love that you would only ever feel for him, your Peter, and no other man?

Was this to be my fate too?

CHAPTER SIXTEEN

1

The ship is sailing towards Yugoslavia, slicing its way through the deep-blue waters of the Adriatic. Seagulls are flying overhead, their shrill chatter accompanying the low drone of the boat and the steady hum of passengers, all of them sprawled out in various carefree positions upon the sun-drenched deck.

She is one of those passengers, enjoying a holiday cruise of the Balkans with her newly acquired fiancé: a cruise made possible by the impressive architect's salary he is paid. But as luck would have it, he does not happen to be anywhere in sight at this auspicious moment.

Her deep brown eyes are opened wide, because they cannot prevent their gaze returning at regular intervals to the rich red, juicy, dripping water melon that a certain tanned young male passenger is eating his way through as he leans nonchalantly upon the edge of the deck, slurping away and occasionally wiping his strong brown chin.

She stares and stares at that delicious, succulent, mouth-watering melon. She can feel its sweet moisture wetting her lips, cooling her mouth and throat, combatting the gruelling heat that she is not used to, hailing as she does from the chilly Northern climes of Preston. She is hardly aware of the owner of that desired piece of fruit, the eater of its scarlet watery flesh, the swallower of its dripping juices.

And then the bearer of the watermelon, the tanned young specimen of masculinity in its prime, turns his head in her direction, as though sensing her parched, longing gaze.

Their eyes meet. There is a moment of hesitation, self-consciousness, uncertainty … until, with charming foreign frankness, the tanned male holds up the remains of his melon and points to it, then to her, and raises his thick black eyebrows. *You want some?* his expression conveys, and in reply she blushes. Her hand darts up to her pretty mouth in an attempt to cover the embarrassed giggle that is dying to splutter out.

But he does not leave it there. No, he is apparently a true-blue, gallant, foreign male. Straightening his posture, he abandons his reclining position by the edge of the deck and starts walking in her direction.

Her giggle finally bursts out. Despite being the grand mature age of twenty-four by now, as opposed to nineteen when she first met Peter, she is still a girl at heart. An incurable romantic to boot. And that will never change.

The tall foreigner stops directly in front of her, looks down into her widened eyes, holds out his luscious fruit offering. But this time he does something more. He speaks.

'You want?' is what he speaks.

Calling upon all the powers that be, she takes control of her nervousness. She straightens her shoulders, raises her chin, and looks him directly in the eye as she enunciates in her charming English voice, 'Oh, I couldn't possibly! But thank you all the same. It's most generous of you to offer.'

He looks at her blankly. During the course of her sweet young life, which has to date been lived exclusively upon the damp soils of Lancashire, she has not yet chanced upon an encounter with a non-English-speaking foreigner.

He widens his dark brown eyes at her and says, 'You no want?'

'Oh, I couldn't, really.'

'What your name?'

'Molly. And yours?'

'And yours?' he echoes uncomprehendingly.

'What – is – your – name?' she repeats, getting the hang of this foreigner talk.

He beams a brilliant, white-toothed smile at her and proudly proclaims, 'Mustafa Babić,' as though it were the most wonderful thing in the world to be possessed of the name of Mustafa Babić.

'Well hello, Mustafa,' she says, a little coyly.

'Hello, Mol-ly.' He pronounces her name in a way that does peculiar things to her insides.

Suddenly another voice intervenes, causing her to jump out of her sandals. Almost. 'Everything all right, Molly?'

It's the voice of Tony Gaston, her interim fiancé. The one she got engaged to just to spite her *true* fiancé, so as to get her own back on him for having slept with that Latrina floozy, all the way back in the boring grime of Manchester.

'Yes, fine,' she says, darting a meaningful look at the earnest Mustafa before being shepherded away by the uneasy Tony Gaston. A meaningful look that translates: *I'll try and find you later on and then we can exchange addresses, all right?*

And that's exactly what the two of them did.

The following summer, by which time she and Peter had got back together again and then split up again, she made a return visit to Jugoslavia to stay with Mustafa's family in a small mountain village not far from Sarajevo. The handsome hulk of a man had been learning English all the previous year. This was evident in the postcards he sent her, overflowing in complex sentence structures such as: *If you will coming this summer to Yugoslavia, you can bringing the English sherry for my mama? Please more writing to me, Molly. Only your, Mustafa Babić.*

She was intrigued by the writer of the sexy English and his sexy name. It all sounded so exciting and romantic that her daughter, many years later, could never understand why her mother hadn't stayed out there forever, converting to the Moslem faith, learning the local language, marrying the gorgeous water-melon bearer, and having lots and lots of cute, tanned,

Anglo-Yugoslav Babić babies. The daughter often used to ask this, when she was a teenager.

'Don't you regret that you never married him?' she'd pester, totally baffled by the bizarre choices her mother had made during the course of her life.

'But then you would never have been born, darling,' the mother replied with misty eyes. 'And remember, your arrival into the world is what made my life whole again, after Peter died.'

The daughter was never allowed to forget that.

2

'It's now or never, Leah.'

Those were the words Michael Williams said to me in the first lesson of my final year at the Birmingham College of Music. He was of course referring to the piano competition, which had thus far eluded me. Or rather, I had thus far eluded *it*.

'Erm –' I dropped my gaze, examined my fingernails, and suddenly realised they were way too long. I'd neglected them all summer, not having had Maestro Williams breathing down my neck to constantly remind me of the importance of such things.

Too late.

'Leah, just *look* at those fingernails!' the Maestro said with a scolding smile.

I clenched both my hands into fists, hiding the guilty talons from view.

'Well, *that's* not going to help, is it? Pretending they don't exist? For God's sake, Leah, you'll be graduating next June! It's about time you finally had a good dose of ADS injected into you.' No, that was not some disease he wished upon me. ADS was his well-known acronym for *Ambition, Determination and Study*. 'Now *please* get those nails cut before your next lesson. If there's one thing I can't stand, it's the sound of nails clicking on keys.'

'Sorry.'

'Apology accepted. Right then, so what about it?'

I looked at him. He was a little too quick for my slow brain, especially after an even slower summer of pining, weeping and pouring out my broken heart into the piano.

'The Tchaikovsky concerto, for God's sake! What about it? Will it be good enough by the preliminary trials in February? Are you determined to go through with this madness?'

'You mean the competition?'

He rolled his eyes. '*Obviously*. Wake up, Leah! You do realise, I take it, the enormous amount of work that's involved in getting a giant of a work like that up to scratch? Do you honestly think you're up to it?'

'I think so.' Over the course of the endless summer holiday I'd decided to swap the innocuous Mozart concerto for the fiendishly difficult Tchaikovsky B-flat minor. The toughest summer holiday of my life, to match the toughest piano work I'd ever attempted. I had to have *something* to get my teeth into, that awful summer. So I chose Tchaikovksy.

'Well, you'll have to work bloody hard, is that understood? You'd have been much safer with the Mozart.'

'But I've had it up to my eyeballs with Mozart.' This bold statement surprised Michael almost as much as it did me. Inspired by his shocked silence, I pressed, 'I've always loved Tchaikovsky's first piano concerto, and it was always my dream to play it one day. That's why I *know* I'll practise it as hard as I can. Hours and hours a day, I promise.'

He nodded. 'Well, Leah, at the end of the day it's all down to you, so don't make any promises to me. Make them to yourself. This is your last chance. Next year you'll be gone, off into the real world of professional music. Unless, of course, you fail all your exams and have to repeat the year. If you continue as you did last year, that might be a real possibility. So what do you think?'

'No, I – I won't do that,' I said, balking at the very thought of spending yet another year in this huge, sprawling city and this ugly concrete building, cooped up for hours a day in the soulless practice rooms of the fourth floor, punished with Rudiments & Form, Harmony & Counterpoint and all the rest, every week of the year. Not to mention the vile coffee of the college canteen and the enforced company of new students. Tessa Llewelin and Emily Green would be gone by next year, and Adrian had already gone – probably transferred to another college to avoid seeing me. Or perhaps he just gave up classical music altogether and returned to his former world of Medicine and jazz piano. Quite frankly, I couldn't have given a shit.

'Right, so just to be absolutely certain before I put your name down on the list of candidates, are you *positive* you want to enter this competition?'

Suddenly I was engulfed by a terrifying vision: me sitting in a long fancy dress at the nine-foot grand piano in the recital hall on the night of the competition, pounding out all those cascading octaves as my hands leaped about the keyboard in great acrobatic swings. Oh my God. *Was* I truly capable of it?

'Leah, wake up! Are you going for the competition? Yes or no? No or yes? To be or not to be?'

'Yes!' I said, almost adding *sir!* At that moment I was determined to prove him wrong. Oh, ye of little faith!

He laughed at me, and I was amazed to see that it was in actual relief. For the first time ever, his eyes twinkled in genuine pleasure.

There was no other way. I had to do it. You'd have been devastated if I didn't enter the competition, Mother. It was my final year, my last chance to enter, having chickened out both previous years. I could hardly deprive you of the chance to see your beloved daughter in the limelight. You were convinced I stood a good chance of winning the competition, then graduating with distinction, becoming a famous concert pianist, writing a best-selling novel about you and Peter Fox, marrying Brother Matthew, having his children … It was amazing, the faith you had in my future.

Michael Williams stole a glance at his watch. 'Right, we've wasted enough time already. So, what movement do you want to start with? I take it you've been practising all three movements this summer?'

'Of course,' I lied. I'd only practised the first movement. *Only.* That in itself had taken up practically the entire summer, barring the occasional day trip with you. And my two-week stint in Cork. And all that hopeless gazing out of my bedroom window. But never once did I mention to you what had happened on my last night at Greystones. I couldn't bear to talk about it. Not even to you, Mother. My greatest achievement that summer, even more than the Tchaikovsky, was my newly discovered ability to lie. The hoodwinking of reality became my speciality.

'Fine. I'm all ears.' Michael leaned back in his chair, folded his arms across his stomach, and waited.

I flexed my hands. Returned them to my lap. Tucked my hair behind my ears. Coughed. And then, raising my hands once again, I at last brought them down upon the waiting keys with the full force of Tchaikovsky's triumphant opening chords.

He stopped me after just a few bars, as I'd expected. He was back to full, demanding concentration now. But at least he wasn't smiling. He was frowning, which was a good sign. He asked me to start again, this time telling me to put a bit more emphasis in the left hand. I actually think he was impressed.

One hour later, when my wrists and forearms were practically dropping out of their sockets, he looked across at me in the closest expression to earnestness I had ever seen on him.

'Well, Leah, it just goes to show that where there's a will there's a way. You hold the key to success, but no one can tell you which way to turn it, or what will be on the other side of the door.'

Only that's where he was wrong. I now know this with absolute certainty, as I sit here tonight in my solitary cottage. The truth is that none of us can see what's on the other side of the door, and none of us has the key to it. All of this will soon be gone – me, you, Brother Matthew, my diaries, my music. One day there'll just be dust and silence, once the final, triumphant chord has been played.

3

It's November 5th. My friends have persuaded me to go with them to a Bonfire party. It's being held in a stretch of common land in the leafy district of Sutton Coldfield. I've reluctantly agreed to go, but all I really want to do is stay in my solitary bedsit, huddled up by the gas fire as I re-live my last encounter with Brother Matthew for the thousandth time and pour my heart into my diary. I'm not doing a very good job of trying to forget him. But I've agreed to tag along to this bonfire party, and so here I am, standing in silence by the flames.

My friends consist of Tessa Llewellin and Emily Green, as usual. Oh – and also Danny Brewster, the short-term boyfriend who I told to go fuck his double bass. There aren't any hard feelings between Danny and me; all that saga is well and truly behind us. As it happens, Danny rents a room in an old vicarage in Sutton Coldfield, and it is precisely here, in the stretch of common land next to the vicarage, where the bonfire party is being held.

But my thoughts are not on the party. The only thoughts on my mind this chilly November evening, as I stand by the Guy Fawkes pyre, are those of Brother Matthew and the future with him that I have lost. I think of that lost future as a lost world, an entire life that has already happened and been snatched from us. I see it in the inferno, burning to a cinder every last dream we could have realised. The home we could have made together. The love we could have shared. The children we could have had. The old age we could have gently grown into, not afraid of death as we sat by the open hearth of our hillside home, listening to the wind rattling against the windows and seeing the passion of our younger years reflected in the dancing flames. And as I watch the flames before me now, I think of how we can never have any of this. All because of the God he has dedicated his life to. It's a God who I could grow to hate, if I believed strongly enough in Him to warrant such powerful emotions. Only I don't.

There is something about the flames as they flicker and flare and spit at me, at random moments soaring into the opaque sky - so close, their incandescence almost hurts - that makes me think of all the suffering in the world. Although I have no rights to be up there in the high echelons of survivors of horrific trauma, and although I am not living in abject poverty or starvation and do not have any terminal disease, at this very moment I almost wish all those things upon myself, instead of the mere pain of un-requited love. Then at least my own personal suffering could be justified. But that isn't the case. Who else, other than me, can discern this awful, aching longing – a tragedy in its own right – of not being able to have the man you love?

I have reached a point of realisation that no one can help me with. I don't want help, anyway. If I can't have Brother Matthew, I don't want any-one or anything. I just want to be left alone. There is no omniscient God who'll take me by the hand and guide me on the road to happiness. There's no special plan for Brother Matthew and me. There's no special plan for any of us. No Kismet. Only indifference.

And then, when I'm least expecting it, I hear my name called out.

For a moment I think it's Danny. I turn round to look; but no, he's cracking jokes with Tessa and Emily. All three of them laughing, oblivious to my mood.

And then I hear the voice again, a little louder.

'*Leah!*'

I turn to my other side, and there he is, pushing his way towards me through the crowds. For a moment I can't quite place him. And at last his face clicks. It's that annoying guy I met last December at Pebble Mill, when I accompanied the Polish youth choir.

'Oh, hello,' I say, trying to recall his name. At the sound of my voice all three of my friends look round, most annoyingly. I'm going to have to make introductions now.

'You've forgotten who I am, haven't you?' he asks with a twinkle in his eye. Or it might just be the reflection of the bonfire on the lenses of his glasses.

'No, of course not. You're from Pebble Mill Studios.'

'Really?' Danny says a little too eagerly, images of future TV fame no doubt whizzing around his head.

'Well, not exactly,' I correct myself, still trying to dig the man's name out of the thickening torpor of my memory. 'We met last December when I accompanied the Polish youth choir for a programme on local TV.'

'She was a star,' he says, winking at me. Then he turns to my friends. 'Marek Topolski. Pleased to meet you.'

Everyone introduces themselves in a hurried babble of voices, after which Marek astounds us all by changing identity. All at once he becomes a Slavonic cavalier, taking Tessa's hand and raising it to his lips, then doing the same with Emily, and finally, shaking a vigorous hand with Danny. These are the kind of manners that exist only in bygone tales of chivalry for us Anglo-Saxon heathens. Something deep within me stirs.

After a brief question-and-answer exchange, Marek glances at his watch and says, 'Right, better get back to my mates. Nice meeting you all. Hope to see you again sometime, darling.' He adds this last bit to me, sounding more like the brusque guy I first met at the Polish club almost a year ago.

'Yes, that would be nice,' I say a little awkwardly. I'm not all that bothered about seeing him again, in actual fact. There's something decidedly obnoxious about his attitude, whether or not he has enchanting manners.

And yet see him again I did.

4

The day after the bonfire party I woke up feeling a tiny bit uplifted, though I couldn't specify why. By the time I got to college I stopped wondering about it and just got on with the day, until a couple of hours later, when the curious conundrum of my improved spirits hit me all over again.

I'd just come out of my piano sight-reading tutorial and was heading for the fourth floor, hoping some practice rooms would be available so that I could get my stint of Tchaikovsky-bashing out of the way. I reached the lift and pressed the button. Ten seconds later the doors pinged open, and out came Tessa.

'Leah, I've been looking all over for you!' she cried, casting her wide green eyes upon me.

'Why, what's wrong?'

'Nothing's wrong, silly. It's just that man we met yesterday – you know, the Polish one – what's his name ..?'

'Marek Topolski?'

'That's the one. Well, he's looking for you.'

'What?'

'He's in the canteen. I told him you were somewhere around the college but I didn't know where, so he asked if I could find you. He's got a bit of a nerve, hasn't he, expecting me to go all round the building hunting you down.'

'But you agreed to his request, I see.'

'Yes, well apparently he's got an important proposal he wants to make to you.' She grinned at me and added, 'You dark horse, Leah Cavanagh. How long have you secretly been dating him, then?'

'I'm not dating him. There must be some misunderstanding.' And then the penny dropped. 'Oh God. He probably wants me to accompany that chaotic Polish choir again.' I pulled a face. 'Honestly, Tess, it was utter *mayhem* last December. Look, couldn't you go back to him and tell him you've found out that I'm sick?'

'No I could not. Now go on downstairs and see what he wants. Who knows, he might even have a ring in a box.'

Two minutes later I pushed open the door to the college canteen. I spotted him straight away, sitting at a table near the front. He looked up as I approached, put down his coffee cup, and stood up.

'So *there* you are,' he said, as though I'd messed up some arrangements that we'd never made.

I glanced to my left and right, trying to be witty. 'Well – yes, here I am. Where I was supposed to be?'

Not reacting in the slightest, he pulled out a chair for me and sat down again, indicating for me to follow suit. 'Can I get you a coffee?' No kissing of hands this time. Perhaps they didn't do it at every greeting.

I shook my head. 'No, thanks, I really can't stay long. I've got stacks of piano practice to do.'

'Actually, that's what I wanted to see you about.' He took off his glasses, rubbed them with his shirt sleeve, held them up for squinty inspection, then tucked them back onto the bridge of his nose. 'You know that piece you played to me last year when you came for your interview?'

'Chopin's Heroic polonaise?'

'How does it go? Hum it to me.'

I hummed it to him as well as I could, and within seconds his face broke into a smile. Actually, quite an attractive smile, I was surprised to note.

'Yeah, that's the one. Could you play it at a concert next Sunday?'

'Next *Sunday?*'

'It's our Independence Day celebration,' he clarified. 'The guy who normally plays solos at concerts – y'know, the one who had a heart attack last year when you stepped in for him at Pebble Mill? – well, he's getting feebler by the day, so I think you'd be doing him a favour if you let him off the hook. Besides, we could do with some young blood from outside the Polish conclave for a change.'

'Oh – but I don't want to put anyone out.'

'As I said, you'd be doing him a favour.'

A reluctant part of me was tempted. The Heroic polonaise was one of my party pieces. I knew I played it well. Proof of that was the commendation I got for it in my end of second-year diploma exam. It wouldn't need all that much work to polish it up by Sunday, which was only five days away. But they'd have to make it worth my while.

As though reading my mind he said, 'The pay isn't much, but it'll be good experience. You'll be able to put on your CV the fact that you've played at the prestigious Polish club in Birmingham.'

'And the prestigious Pebble Mill Studio.'

'Pebble Mill, of course!' He smacked his hand against his head. 'That's another thing – thanks for reminding me.'

'Don't tell me you want me to accompany the Polish youth choir again?'

'Bang on! As I said, Henryk's almost pushing up the daisies now, so I'm sure he wouldn't mind if -'

'But shouldn't you ask him first?'

'Tell you what, darling, *you* ask him when you meet him next Sunday after the concert. He won't take umbrage from a pretty young thing like you. Henryk's always been a bit of a ladies' man.'

'I haven't agreed to play yet. At either event.'

'Yeah, yeah, I know. But you will, right?'

I paused, trying to look as though I was considering whether or not I could squeeze these two amateur events into the over-filled schedule of my professional musician's diary.

'Tell you what,' he said, leaning a fraction closer and looking me straight in the eye. 'If you agree, I'll take you out to dinner afterwards. On both days. How's that, then?'

I laughed. 'So that's supposed to swing it for me, is it?'

'Of course. I'm from very good Polish stock, I'll have you know. My father fought with General Anders in the Battle of Monte Cassino.'

In spite of his cocky manner, I found myself smiling.

'So you agree?' he pushed. 'To all four things?'

'Four? But I thought you said it was just two concerts.'

'Two concerts and two dinners. That makes four events. Agreed?'

I had nothing to lose, did I? It was hardly worth waiting for Brother Matthew to ask me out to dinner. 'Okay,' I said, looking away. I found the intense gleam in his eyes just a bit hard to cope with.

And then it dawned on me, the reason why I'd woken up that morning feeling strangely uplifted. It was him, Marek Topolski. I must have had a sixth sense that I'd see him again. There was something about his determined manner and grating confidence, and the ironic way he looked at me, that got under my skin.

5

So I played at the Independence Day concert on November 11th, and afterwards, tingling in euphoria, everyone congratulated me on my virtuoso performance. The elderly pianist, Henryk, kissed my hand and said, 'Miss Leah, you play Chopin like I play him much years ago!' When it was all over, Marek took me out to dinner in a cosy Indian restaurant not far from the Polish club. We got on surprisingly well together, laughed a lot, tucked into our spicy food and wine, and three hours later he gave me a lift back to Washwood Heath. I didn't ask him in for a coffee, because I was worn out from the evening's success, and – well, I didn't want him to intrude on my solitary evening routine of sitting in front of the gas fire, reminiscing, and writing my diary.

I didn't invite him in for a coffee after the next event, either – the recording at Pebble Mill Studios. Marek was more on top of things this time round, keeping all choir members under control and preventing them from wandering in and out of the room at all times. I was most impressed with his easy authority. Afterwards we went for dinner at a chic French restaurant, which reminded me briefly of the one that Adrian Midwinter had taken me to in Henley-in-Arden. But the reminder was only fleeting. By the second course I was so caught up with Marek's recounting of his parents' experiences in the Second World War – how they'd survived the Warsaw Uprising and ended up as refugees in England in 1945 – that I no longer had room for thoughts of previous boyfriends or monks. I just wanted to hear more about this fascinating Polish family of which Marek Topolski was a proud member. But still I didn't invite him in for coffee at the end of the evening, because I knew what that was likely to entail, and I wasn't sure if I was ready for it yet. Or ever would be.

Marek was growing on me, there was no doubt about that. All the aspects of his character that I'd originally found irritating were now being transformed before my very eyes. He was over-confident and brusque, true, but he was also extremely knowledgeable about a large variety of subjects –

history, politics, current affairs and chemistry being his specialities. When talking about atoms, molecules, isotopes, chemical reactions and the old alchemists of Dr Faustus' days, he could be positively riveting. His eyes would glint at me from behind his glasses, and every time he cracked a joke – which he did all the time – his mouth would stretch into a taut smile that gave him the aura of a worldly-wise man with a touch of cynicism, yet not enough to rub away the finer tuning of his upbringing.

I learned that he was twenty-eight, he had a PhD, and he worked at a chemist's shop round the corner from his semi-detached house in Sutton Coldfield. His ambition was one day to put all his pharmaceutical knowledge to practical use and set up his own chemist's business. Whenever he talked about this, his whole face lit up and he got me totally caught up in his fantasy. But whereas my fantasies encompassed sitting with a defrocked monk in front of a roaring fire in a hillside manor house overlooking Derwent Water, Marek's leaned more on the scientific side – expanding on potions from his alchemist forefathers that would heal mankind of all its horrible afflictions. I soon realised that he had a knack for making any subject under the sun sound fascinating, whether it was pharmaceutics, local politics, or the Second World War. Or his family, who he kept urging me to meet.

I finally agreed to this familial event about a week before the Christmas holiday. I knew I'd be going home soon and wouldn't be seeing Marek again for a whole three weeks, so I decided that the least I could do was accept his invitation to dinner with his parents.

Talk about stepping into a different world! In fact, on that mid-December afternoon in 1980, when Marek led me through the front door of his parents' house in Sutton Coldfield, not far from his own smaller house, and we entered the dining room where everyone was squashed round an enormous table, I think I fell in love with the whole lot of them. Honestly, what a household! It was all so different, so exotic, noisy, vibrant, cluttered, chaotic – so very unlike the cloistered upbringing I myself had known in Lyneham-on-Sea.

There was his mother, who spoke very bad English but made up for it by lots of hand-clasping, hugging, Cheshire cat smiling, and constantly offering more hunter's stew, more home-made wine, more cherry vodka, more tea, more poppy seed cake … There was his father, who thoroughly approved of me and told me so on my very first visit, emphasised by a raunchy wink and longer than usual hand-kiss. There was his younger brother, who admitted to me just minutes after our introduction that he played the accordion, then promptly disappeared from the dining table to return with said instrument, upon which he launched into a medley of Polish folk songs that the whole family heartily sang along to in foreign words which meant nothing to me but sounded wonderful, and which took up the next hour of the evening. And there was his older brother and sister-in-law and their three small children, who ensured that the bilingual decibel level of the conversation never, ever ebbed. And finally, his grandfather, who nodded sadly at any comment anyone ever made, then turned his old watery eyes on me and said, 'On my days was different, Miss Leah. I never know nothing. I never know if the tomorrow was day that would never come or no. You want more vodka?'

And there was Marek himself, of course. Marek the all-rounder - attentive yet argumentative, listening yet interrupting, smiling yet ridiculing; but somehow, at the end of the day, always the respectful son, grandson, brother, uncle, and boyfriend. Yes, I suppose by this stage he *was* my boyfriend. Even though we hadn't even kissed yet.

When I went home to Lyneham for Christmas, I actually missed him. But whether it was Marek himself I missed or his vibrant family, I couldn't tell. Or perhaps I didn't want to ask myself.

* * *

'He's really nice,' I tried to explain to you one evening as we sat in front of the TV, sipping our coffees and half-watching *Casablanca*. 'Much nicer than I first thought, actually. So is his whole family.'

'So are you or aren't you dating him?' you asked with a hint of disapproval in your voice.

'I guess I must be, considering we've been out for two candle-lit dinners and a third dinner at his parents' house.'

'But you don't sound all that enamoured to me, darling. Calling someone *very nice* is hardly grounds to date them.'

'Okay, so he's more than very nice. He's funny, confident, interesting, and he's got these impeccable Polish manners – you know, hand-kissing and all that - which are completely at odds with his brusque ways. I mean, I don't like the slangy way he keeps calling me *darling* – but apart from that, I really think I'm beginning to warm to him.'

'As a friend?'

'Oh Mother, I honestly don't know.'

And then you asked the inevitable question. 'So what about Brother Matthew?'

I shrugged, trying to convey to you just how far removed I'd become from that faraway Benedictine. I didn't even know if he was still at Greystones; whereas Marek *was* still in Birmingham, and so was I. More to the point, I was looking forward to the beginning of term, when I could see him again.

I saw him again sooner than I thought.

I'd just arrived at my digs in Washwood Heath, straight from the railway station, lumbered with all my luggage and feeling more than a tad depressed. Christmas was over and another gruelling term loomed ahead, as did the piano competition in just over a month's time. The burden of the long, dreary winter days in front of me was almost more than I could bear. Worse still, Tchaikovsky's B-flat minor concerto hadn't yet reached the level that I knew Michael Williams would be expecting.

As I stepped inside Mrs Zoldak's house, I heard voices coming from the dining room at the far end of the hallway. It appeared that my Polish landlady was entertaining friends. Not wanting to intrude, I tiptoed towards the stairs and was just about to go up them when the door to the dining room flung open. Out came Mrs Zoldak, larger than life and beaming her broad Slavonic smile at me.

'Miss Leah, you come back! Happy New Year!'

I smiled resignedly, plonking my cases on the floor. 'Hello, Mrs Zoldak. Happy New Year to you too. Did you have a nice Christmas?'

'Yes, yes, very nice!' Lowering her voice, she hissed at me, 'You have guest!'

I blinked at her. '*I* have guest? Who?'

'Very nice man. Polish. I know him from church.'

Next thing I knew, Marek burst into the hallway bearing a huge bouquet of roses. Grinning at me like a mischievous schoolboy, he said, 'Hiya, Leah, thought I'd surprise you. Welcome home, sweetheart!' This was his latest endearment, which he now interchanged with 'darling'. He strode towards me and thrust the bouquet in my arms.

'Oh, Marek – ' I had to push a couple of rose buds out of my face, 'they're beautiful. Thank you so much.'

He leaned closer and kissed me on the cheek. 'Hey, kiddo. I've missed you.'

'Later, later!' Mrs Zoldak cried. 'You want beetroot soup?'

'Oh – that's very kind of you, but actually I'm quite tired -'

'Of course she want beetroot soup,' Marek said, taking my hand firmly in his and leading me into the dining room. He pulled out a chair and prodded me into it. 'So how was Christmas up north? Any snow?'

'No, afraid not. What about Birmingham?'

But my beaming landlady was not to be ignored. 'Miss Leah, you come to carnival ball on Polish club next Saturday, yes?'

'Carnival ball?' I glanced at Marek.

'It's the beginning of the carnival season,' he explained, 'so I reckoned it would be a nice idea for you to come along. Don't worry – no solo piano playing, no accompanying the choir, just a good old-fashioned ball, with long dresses for the ladies and smart suits for the men, and plenty of good old-fashioned Polish dancing. So how about it, darling?'

'But I – well, for a start, I don't know how to dance.'

'No sweat. I'll teach you. It's a cinch.'

'Oh, I don't know, Marek. I'm not sure if –'

'Good, then it's settled.'

He turned his head to Mrs Zoldak and came out with a long string of incomprehensible Polish babble, which was interrupted every few seconds by her own incomprehensible babble. When they both paused to take a breath, the beaming matriarch clapped her hands together in evident delight at whatever he had said. Then she looked at me.

'Miss Leah, Polish ball is magnific! Like before war – we dance tango, polka, waltza – you love!'

'Yes, you'll love it,' Marek said. 'And don't worry about the tangos and all that. I can show you a few steps beforehand. You're a musician, so you'll pick them up dead easy.'

'But Marek, honestly, I don't –'

'No arguments,' he said, leaning back in his chair as Mrs Zoldak placed a steaming bowl of beetroot soup in front of him. 'You're going to the ball whether you like it or not, okay? So just accept it. Oh, and no running away before midnight. And if anyone asks you to dance with them, I have full permission to tell them to sod off.'

I didn't know whether to thrill at the gallantry of his words, or recoil from them. That was the trouble. I still didn't know exactly what it was that I felt for Marek Topolski.

* * *

During the Polish ball that Marek took me to – picking me up in his car, looking dashing in his tuxedo, emitting a sexy tang of Brut aftershave – I began to get a better idea of how I felt. Especially when I told him that I'd entered a piano competition and was playing Tchaikovsky's First.

'Oh my God, Leah, that's my favourite piece of all time!' he said loudly, competing with the live band as we swayed and swooped to the rhythms of a pre-war Polish tango, together with dozens of other swaying and swooping couples. Marek had taught me the basic steps beforehand, and I was loving every minute of the evening. 'And you can actually *play* it?' he said. 'A piece like *that*?'

I tried to tone down his admiration, pointing out that I wasn't all that brilliant, that I probably wouldn't even get beyond the first round of the competition, and so on. But the very next day he appeared at music college, hunting me down in my practice room and insisting that I played the whole first movement to him.

It transpired that the brusque Marek Topolski wasn't at all the music philistine I'd first thought him to be. He knew the Tchaikovsky concerto very well, as he did Grieg's A minor, Rachmaninov's 2nd, and Beethoven's *Emperor*. In fact, he loved classical piano music full stop. He also adored Chopin, and loved my rendering of the Ballade in A-flat major, amongst countless other pieces that I played to him whenever he appeared at the college over the coming weeks. There's no doubt about it, his animated presence and musical encouragement became an inspiration to me. By the week before the preliminary trials for the competition, he was a daily visitor to the fourth floor. Come six o'clock, there he'd be - straight from work, smelling of hastily applied aftershave, sitting down on the spare stool and proving to be a very useful trial audience. He had a good ear, despite not playing any instrument, and his comments were always spot-on.

And so I got through the preliminary trials in February. That meant I was now an official contestant of the finals in two weeks' time. I couldn't believe it. But when I nipped out to the telephone box on Washwood Heath Road to call you, Mother, and announce this wonderful piece of news, your reaction astounded me.

'That's wonderful, darling. But please don't tell me that it's all because of Marek.'

You'd obviously read my thoughts. 'Well, he certainly has inspired me with all his praise and encouragement over the last few weeks.'

'Ye Gods, Leah! Anyone would think you were talking about your piano teacher, not a chemist who doesn't have any formal musical training. Whatever's happened to you? Has he brainwashed you with some home-grown chemical potion that he slipped into your tea when you weren't looking?'

'Mother, that's not funny. He might not be a trained musician, but he knows his stuff. And he really *did* inspire me.'

This was followed by a deathly pause. And then, as though someone had whispered an admonitory word in your ear, you said in a calmer voice, 'Whatever the case, I'm very proud of you, darling. Well done.'

'Thank you.'

'So when are you next coming home? I was thinking you might want to be here for the third anniversary of your first trip to Greystones. It'll be next week, did you realise that?'

I held my breath. 'Actually – I'm not sure if I want to be reminded of that. Not now of all times, when I'm feeling so good about things for the first time in ages, thanks to Marek.'

Another pause followed. 'So what about your twenty-first birthday? You will be home for that, won't you? I thought of having a little family get-together. After all, it's not every day of your life you celebrate a twenty-first.'

I screwed my eyes tightly. 'Well, now that you mention it …' How could I tell you this? But you'd already guessed. You and your dratted sixth sense.

'You're going to spend your birthday with Marek.'

At that moment I could have cried at the sound of your voice. I knew you couldn't help it. You didn't mean to be nasty, you honestly didn't. You loved me to bits. I was your only child; you'd brought me up practically single-handedly and you wanted to spend that very special day with me, just the two of us. And here I was about to hurt you, yet again.

'Well, he did mention something …'

Your sigh interrupted me. A long, pronounced sigh that was clearly audible all the way down the telephone line between Lyneham-on-Sea and Birmingham. 'Oh, Leah,' you said in that theatrical voice of yours. 'Do be careful that you don't let that man change you.'

'Change me? What do you mean?'

'You know what I mean, my darling. Anyway, I'm afraid I can't chat now - I've got a million things I need to be getting on with. All I ask is that you think very carefully about everything I've said. Don't let yourself be changed by someone who's trying to pull the wool over your eyes with his showy manners and top-surface interest in music. There's so much more to life than that, as you well know.'

'Oh, for God's sake –'

'Sorry, darling, I really must go. Now do promise me you'll get plenty of rest and eat well, and also take plenty of liquids. You have to build up your energy for the finals. When did you say they were?'

'A week on Tuesday.'

'Well, you know I'll be there right with you. Every step of the way.'

'Yes, I know,' I said. And for the first time ever, I hung up on you.

CHAPTER SEVENTEEN

1

It's the day of the piano concerto competition. My hard work and determination, inspired by Marek, has paid off. The audience is packed out with students, lecturers, friends, family … and of course you're there, Mother, and so is Marek, although you haven't met each other yet. That will come soon.

I'm waiting behind the stage of the concert hall, together with all the other finalists. We haven't got a live orchestra at our disposal, just our own accompanist who will play the transcribed version of the orchestral score on the piano. And that's a pretty impressive feat in its own right. As for the rest of us, all dressed up in our long black dresses and suits, we're biting our short fingernails, closing our eyes in meditation, flexing our fingers, pacing up and down the limited floor space behind the curtain, like caged panthers at a zoo. Doing whatever it takes to calm our nerves before our big moment. My accompanist is Michael Williams. He's standing by my side, very calm, not saying a word. I'm wearing a long slinky dress with plunging neckline and narrow waistband. Marek bought it especially for the occasion. It has the translucent texture of a starlit night, and I know I look bloody good in it.

And then I hear my name announced, as though someone's voice is calling me out of a dream.

'Miss Leah Cavanagh, contestant number five, will play Tchaikovsky's first piano concerto in B-flat minor.'

A muted ripple of applause fills the concert hall from beyond the curtain-barrier.

I can't move.

'It's down to you now,' Michael Williams whispers, and I turn my eyes to him. He isn't smiling. He's looking at me with such a deep frown that I know without a doubt, at long, long last, that he believes in me. This is my moment – the one he has prepared me for over the last two and a half years of grinding tuition that at times has reached the point of despair. It's the moment Marek has also cajoled me into, with his impassioned conviction that I'm brilliant. And it's the moment that you, Mother, have been waiting for all your life. Or at least since the day of my first piano lesson, when my teacher told you that I had talent.

As for me? What can I say? It's my moment now. Mine alone. Whether it was you who got me here through your devoted faith in my ability, or Michael Williams through his hard task-master teaching skills, or Marek through his stalwart encouragement … or whether it was the look on Brother Matthew's face as he stood by the door of the practice room at Greystones on my very first visit, when I hadn't even realised he'd been listening … it doesn't really matter. All that matters is that I'm here now, in the recital hall of the Birmingham College of Music, about to play in the finals of the long-awaited competition. I'm going to walk onto the stage any moment now and step into my very own parallel world of music, shared just by the piano and me, and no one else.

So I step into it.

* * *

I don't need to go into the details of my performance, because I know you'll never forget that day. Even now I can bet that every phrase of Tchaikovsky's First is etched on your memory. Just thinking of it still sends the proverbial shudders down my spine: those victorious opening chords in D-flat major, recognised even by music heathens; the breath-stopping feats of the cadenza near the end of the first movement; the perambulating chords of the slow movement and the exhilarating climax of the third movement, with a cavalcade of octaves that thunders from one end of the keyboard to the other within the space of five seconds flat – an ending to end all endings! Any pianist who has ever played that concerto and got through till the end unscathed deserves a prize. As for my own interpretation? I played like there was no tomorrow, pardon the cliché, because there really *was* no tomorrow, as there never is when you're performing to your full potential. And later on, when the results were announced after an excruciating half-hour's wait, I honestly thought I was dreaming when I heard my name called out. I stood like a zombie behind the curtains, until Michael Williams elbowed me in the side and hissed, '*Leah, it's you! You've done it! You've got first prize!*' But still I couldn't move, and neither could I believe it. This just could not be happening. It was almost as wild as my dreams in which Brother Matthew and I walked down the aisle as bride and groom, to the loud pealing of church bells. But this was no dream, I was fast beginning to realise, as everyone to my left and right started congratulating me, hugging me, crying out, *Well done!*

But *how* had I done it? I didn't deserve to do so well. I'd never been one of the top students; I'd kept chickening out of the competition in previous years; I'd only started practising seriously after Marek came on the scene.

Marek. He was the crux of the matter. And suddenly, I wanted to see him.

Pushing the curtains aside, I walked onto the stage to the loud pealing of applause and cheers. Not quite the same as church bells, but suddenly it didn't matter anymore.

* * *

Afterwards, when everyone was filing out of the auditorium, Marek came rushing up to my side even before you did. 'Leah, you were absolutely and totally *amazing!*' He swept me in his arms and held me so tightly, I could hear the thudding of his heart.

'She wasn't bad, was she?' Michael Williams joined in, hovering nearby and smiling at me for the first time in normal, uncontrived pleasure. 'Well done, Leah. You thoroughly deserve that prize.' He took my hand and squeezed it, then hurried off in search of the second-and third-place prize-winners.

Marek drew me closer to him. 'This calls for a mega-celebration, sweetheart. I'm going to take you out to the best restaurant in Birmingham tonight. And afterwards -'

'Oh – but we can't. My mother's here, remember?' I extracted myself from his arms just in time before you materialised out of thin air.

'*Darling* ...' Your voice tripped on a hiccup of uncontained emotion. I stepped forward to hug you, then turned round to my boyfriend.

'Mother, this is Marek Topolski.'

You aimed your all-encompassing smile at him. 'Ah yes, Marek. I've heard so much about you. Pleased to meet you at last.'

'The pleasure is all mine. Mrs Cavanagh, I take it?'

You nodded, still smiling, and held out your hand to him. No doubt you expected him to shake it in the usual manner of greeting. So when he raised it to his lips, I'm sure you must have been at least a *little* impressed. Not that you showed it. No, I could immediately tell that it was going to take more than a kiss of the hand to do the trick.

'I can certainly see the resemblance,' Marek said with a glint in his eye. 'Would you care to join Leah and me for a celebration dinner?'

Thankfully, you weren't in the least fazed. 'Oh, that's so kind of you, Marek, but I'm afraid my daughter and I have already made arrangements for tonight. Isn't that so, Leah?'

I nodded impotently.

'Okay, no sweat. Maybe some other time. You've got an amazing daughter, Mrs Cavanagh. She's one hell of a lady, and now I can see exactly where she gets her genes from.'

You laughed a little too effusively. 'Oh, you Poles and your charm!'

'Charm? What charm?' He grinned, again taking hold of your hand and drawing it to his lips. Then he did the same with mine, but before releasing my fingers, he looked at me in sudden earnestness and said, 'Once again, well done, sweetheart. I'm so proud of you.'

'I couldn't have done it without you, Marek. Thank you *so* much. For everything.'

Of course that was the wrong thing to say, with you standing right by my side. But it was too late. The stiffness in your posture forced me to look away. I'm sorry, I know it was insensitive of me. Although it's true that Marek inspired me, it was you who started me on the piano in the first place, you who encouraged me throughout my childhood and teens, urged me to apply to music college, who never gave up on my musical dreams, even when I myself did.

Marek's voice jolted me out of my stupor. Smiling at me more tenderly than I thought he was capable of, he returned his eyes to you and said, 'Right then, I'll leave you two lovely ladies to enjoy the rest of your evening.'

With an elegant little bow, he turned round and made his way across the buzzing concert hall towards the exit.

2

Half an hour later you and I were sitting opposite one another in a cosy restaurant that I'd selected for our celebration dinner, just off Broad Street.

'This is for you, darling,' you said, placing a carefully wrapped gift in the middle of our table. 'It's for your twenty-first birthday – yes, I know it's a little early, but I wanted to give it to you tonight, as a memento of your success.'

'Oh, Mother …' I put my knife and fork on the side of my plate. 'What is it?'

'Open it and you'll see.'

So I opened it. And there it was. My beautifully bound, miniature edition of the *Rubaiyat of Omar Khayyam*. The one I kept in my bag right until the day I intended to give it to Brother Matthew, but couldn't because of what he was saying, the way he looked at me.

After I'd thanked you again, and leaned across the table to kiss you on the cheek, we moved on to other, more pressing matters.

'He seems like a nice young man,' you said as we tucked into our respective steak and chips that had just been served.

'So is the rest of his family,' I said with full mouth, then paused to swallow. 'Honestly, you should see them – it's like they're straight out of a comedy film! They're all larger than life in an Italianesque kind of way. The mother speaks really bad English …'

'Well, I can see they've certainly made an impression on you. But what about you yourself, darling?'

'Me? What do you mean?'

'I mean what are *your* feelings for him? You've never been very clear about that in any of your phone calls, so I'm glad we can have a chat about it now.'

'I like him a lot,' I said, suddenly on red alert. 'At first I wasn't so sure, but recently – I mean these last few weeks – he's really been growing on me.'

'Yes, I can see that. I can also see that he's completely smitten with you. But do be careful, darling.'

'Why?'

'I'd hate to see him get hurt. You can't play with people's feelings just because you want to prove a point. Oh, come on, Leah, you know what I'm getting at.'

'No, I don't think I do. Could you expand on that?'

'Now don't you get cocky with me. I'm just trying to protect Marek. You do realise that you're going to finish with him sooner or later, don't you? No matter how delightful his family is, he's just not your type.'

'Oh, for God's -'

'You're a chip off the old block, my darling. At times I think I know you better than you know yourself. Remember what I did with poor Tony Gaston – getting engaged to him and all that silly business, just to make Peter jealous? It's exactly what I can see you doing with Marek.'

'But I'm not engaged to Marek.'

'You know what I mean. Marek will end up getting hurt, just like poor Tony did. And all because you want to show someone else that you don't care about him anymore.'

'Someone else? And who might that be?'

'Leah, that brittle tone of voice doesn't fool me one bit. The only person you're fooling is yourself.'

I tried to steady my breathing. 'Mother, can I remind you that Brother Matthew hasn't written to me since last July? And it's now half-way through February? You should be *glad* I've found someone else.'

'If it's what you truly want, then of course I'm glad. But *is* it what you truly want?'

My mistake was in not being able to reply immediately. In fact, I didn't reply at all. So you ploughed straight on: 'Marek *is* a bit on the brusque side, wouldn't you say? Despite his Polish manners that so impress you?'

'So you don't like him. I knew it. It's not that you're worried about him getting hurt. You just don't like him.'

'Don't be ridiculous. Anyway, I can see that you're not in the mood to talk about these things tonight, and I can't say I blame you. After all, you *have* just come first place in a prestigious piano competition.'

'Oh for God's sake, the Birmingham College of Music competition is hardly the international Chopin competition. I doubt that Deutsche Gramophone is going to be knocking at my door first thing tomorrow morning.'

'There you go again.'

'Sorry, but where exactly is that?'

This resulted in a long drawn-out sigh. 'Leah, I must say I don't like some of the changes I've noticed in you ever since you started dating Marek.'

A sobering wave of guilt crashed over me. Before you had the chance to plunge into your imminent lecture, I quickly said, 'Oh, please let's not talk about men anymore, just for once? It's *our* night tonight.' I tried to smile, and you tried to smile back. All was forgiven. Almost.

We reached our hands across the table and touched fingertips, holding onto that special mother-daughter moment, that special bond, that special something which no man, no circumstance, no power on earth, can ever break. After all, isn't it true that *the hand that rocks the cradle is the hand that rules the world?*

So why did our bond have to break?

3

On the morning of my twenty-first birthday, three days later, I woke up from a dream about Brother Matthew. It was as if Kismet was being spiteful to me.

As soon as I opened my eyes, I stared at the cracked ceiling of my cold, lonely bedsit in Washwood Heath and felt like dying. Okay, that's a bit hyperbolic, but back then, on that February morning of 1981, it's how I felt. I felt like dying because the Benedictine monk who'd been looking into my eyes with an expression of utmost devotion was no longer there. He was gone in a puff of smoke, back to the intangible world of dreams; and I was still here, devoid of his loving arms, back in the malicious world of reality.

I heaved myself into a sitting position, blinking away the hard winter sunshine that filtered into my room in cruel needles of light. My eyes smarted with the horrid disillusionment of wakefulness. Why do we ever have to wake up?

Before the tears had chance to take hold, I was jolted out of my self-pitying state by a sharp knocking at the door.

'Come in,' I called out guardedly.

Mrs Zoldak's faceless body burst into the room. The reason she had no face is because she was carrying an enormous bouquet of flowers that entirely covered her broad Slavonic features.

'Miss Leah, they for you!' she cried from behind the multitude of carnations and tulips. 'Twenty-one flower! I count!'

'Oh my God!' I cried right back in spite of myself. 'Who're they from?'

But that was a silly question, because of course I knew who they were from. His brusque, ironic smile was already dancing before my eyes, chasing away all remnants of foolish dreams.

And suddenly, I wanted to live again.

* * *

When Marek dropped me off home shortly after midnight on my first day of being the grand age of twenty-one, I finally decided it was about time I invited him in.

'Fancy a coffee?' I asked in as casual voice as I could muster as he pulled his car up onto the pavement by Mrs Zoldak's Victorian abode.

'You sure?'

'What's there to be sure about? You've just bought me an extravagant dinner and sent me an even more extravagant bouquet of flowers.'

'Actually you're wrong there, darling. The dinner was far more extravagant than the flowers. It set me back half a month's salary.'

I laughed. 'Okay, so the least I can do is offer you a Nescafe served up with a slice of Lancashire Parkin, courtesy of my mother.'

'Oh.' He pulled a face. 'I'm not sure if your mother would approve of you sharing your Lancashire Parkin with a man of bad intentions.'

'Really? But surely someone whose father fought in the battle of Monte Cassino can't be *that* bad?' Oh, I was learning fast! Becoming twenty-one overnight had suddenly grown me up. I felt like Marlene Dietrich.

'I didn't say *I* was bad, darling. Just my intentions.' As always, he had the upper hand.

So that was that. He switched off the ignition and I dug out my keys from my Pandora's handbag, pushing aside my newly acquired *Rubaiyat of Omar Khayyam* in the process. Climbing out of the car, we trudged across the badly lit driveway towards the house. I opened the front door cautiously so as not to wake the hopeful Mrs Zoldak, who totally loved the idea of an Anglo-Polish husband for me. We tiptoed across the tiled hallway, but when we were just three steps up the staircase, the door to the old woman's room creaked open.

'*Miss Leah?*'

We froze on the spot, like two burglars caught out in the night.

'It's only me,' I quickly said. 'Erm - and Marek.'

'Ach!' she cried, stepping forward and breaking into a long, garbled string of Polish words directed at Marek, who responded with an equally voluminous reply, delaying our escape by a good two or three minutes. At last the old dear called out to me, 'Goodnight, Miss Leah! You have good Polish boyfriend, he make good Polish husband!' I laughed awkwardly; Marek somewhat more freely.

Once inside my bedsit, I made my way across the mangy carpet to the kitchenette part of the room. Marek followed close behind, no longer laughing. Neither was I.

'Make yourself at home,' I said over my shoulder, trying to sound perfectly at ease as I filled up the kettle and stooped to the mini-fridge to take out the milk. Just as I was straightening up, he placed his hands on my hips and turned me round to face him.

'God – you made me jump!' I cried out, suddenly as nervous as a schoolgirl.

'The tea can wait,' he said in a voice that for once did not contain the slightest hint of irony. Transferring his hand to my face, he raised my chin and kissed me full on the lips. Before I had the chance to respond, his other hand started working its way over my breasts towards the buttons on my blouse.

'Marek, wait – ' I said in an urgent whisper. But this wasn't a game, and neither was he a man to be messed with.

He shut me up by re-claiming my mouth, and then expertly proceeded to undo my buttons, one by one, until there wasn't a single one left open, nor a single shred of doubt left in my dizzied, swirling head.

4

There's a phone call I remember clearly. Yes, I know it's late now – quarter past two in the morning, to be precise - and I should be thinking of bed. But sleep is the very last thing on my mind at the moment. My wedding is less than twelve hours away, and with all these memories that keep crowding my mind, how can I possibly think of sleep?

The phone call in question is a few months after my twenty-first birthday. It goes something like this.

'Mother, you've *got* to stop worrying.' I'm clutching the receiver for dear life. 'I'm happier than I've been in a long time, honestly. Marek is just so … *wonderful.*'

'Oh, I'm sure he is,' you say in a tone of voice which I choose to ignore.

'No, I mean it. Sometimes I can't believe he's that same guy I first met at the Polish club a year and a half ago. He's attentive, caring, generous … and his family have completely taken me under their wing. I'm almost beginning to feel Polish myself.'

'But Leah, how much of this is the real *you* and how much of it is just Marek taking you over?'

That is such a typical thing for you to ask. 'How can any of us know who the real person is that we present to the world?' I reply, trying not to sound snappy. 'I only know that Marek is someone I enjoy being with; someone who admires and respects me, who has made me happier than I thought was possible since … ' I stop myself short. But it's too late.

'Since Brother Matthew. Come on, Leah, be honest with yourself.'

'Okay, since Brother Matthew. But what exactly did Brother Matthew ever do for me? What did he ever give me? Certainly not happiness, that's for sure.'

'My darling, love isn't just about giving each other happiness. It's about understanding each other, valuing each other …'

'As Marek and I do! He *completely* understands my love of music. That's why he's got me involved in so many Polish concerts, encouraging me to play to packed-out audiences who really adore me ...'

'Polish concerts, good heavens! Not quite the same as recitals in the Birmingham Philharmonic.'

'But at least I'm *playing*. And *enjoying* it. Not all that long ago I was actually considering giving up music altogether.'

'Oh? You never told me that.'

'You never asked. You just assumed all the time.'

'Assumed what?'

'That I can never be happy unless I'm a concert pianist. Unless I'm married to Brother Matthew. Unless I'm living the exact life that you've carved out for me.'

This is followed by an excruciating silence. And then: 'Oh, Leah. How can you say such cruel things? I only want what's best for you.'

I wince. 'No, Mother. You only want *your* idea of what's best for me. You're not interested in what I myself really want.'

'Ye gods, Leah, just listen to yourself! So all right then, tell me what the dickens it is you really want.'

That bit isn't hard. At this very moment I know exactly what I really want. I want to be part of Marek's world. Part of his vibrant family, his rich Polish culture, part of his ambition to have his own chemist's shop just down the road from the future house he plans on buying on a leafy cul-de-sac opposite that lovely park in Sutton Coldfield. I can take the vision further by imagining myself to be at home waiting for him each evening with a hot roast in the oven, our pretty future-daughter rushing towards the front door and throwing her arms round her father's neck as the two of them exchange a rush of Anglo-Polish greetings. And then all three of us sitting down to dinner, chatting animatedly about our busy day – mine filled with piano teaching and practice for my next recital, our daughter's with the ups and downs of school life, my husband's with the pressures and rewards of running his own business. I can take it still further by imagining the nights, when our daughter is tucked up in bed and Marek and I have finished our wine and retired to our bedroom with its lush view of the park, and at last the X-rated part of our day takes over. His skilled, probing hands exploring my body, and my urgent desire expelling the other, far more dangerous yearning that could never come to anything.

Of course I don't say any of that to you over the phone. All I say is, 'Look, Mother. I like Marek a lot, and you have to accept that.' I don't bother mentioning that I'm now spending practically every weekend with his family, and playing the guitar at Polish Mass every Sunday, and enrolling on a Polish-beginner course. And I certainly don't mention that I feel myself close to falling in love with Marek. Because the trouble is, whenever I try speaking to you about anything like that, I suddenly find myself doubting everything. Absolutely everything.

Is it just escapism? Is it a rebound reaction from a greater love who let me down? Were you right all the way along? Do you know me better than I know myself? I only know that the safest way forward is to shut Brother Matthew out of my mind completely and pretend that he never existed.

Things came to a head one drizzly Sunday in June, shortly before the end of my final year in Birmingham.

It was after Mass, when we'd all trooped along to the Polish club just down the road for a drink. All of us being Marek, me, and a handful of Anglo-Polish friends I'd acquired over the last few months. And it was one of these friends who mentioned something that brought me out in a cold sweat.

Her name was Ania Kowalska and she was sitting right beside me, telling me about a retreat that she and a few others from the Polish youth club were going on at the weekend.

'Father Ignatius has managed to arrange it for us,' she explained to me in her broad Brummy accent, despite being born of Polish parents. 'He's got connections with a priest over there who's got Polish roots. I've seen the brochure. The monastery looks bloody amazing.'

At the mention of the word 'monastery', distant warning bells tolled in my head. Reaching for my wine glass, I asked, 'Where is it?'

'North Yorkshire,' she said. 'Greystones Abbey.'

My hand froze in mid-air. The bells weren't tolling now; they were booming.

'It's supposed to be a real beauty spot,' she blithely went on. 'We'll be staying in a guest house near the monastery, and we can even take part in the Offices that the monks do. Those are all the psalms they chant every day. I'm really looking forward to it. It'll certainly make a change from the boring prayer groups that Father Ignatius keeps trying to organise every year. Hey – maybe you'd like to come as well?' She looked at me questioningly. 'Leah?'

But I wasn't listening. My head was still reverberating under the impact of the words *Greystones Abbey*. I barely heard Marek's concerned voice, right beside me.

'You all right, sweetheart?'

At last I found my own voice. 'Yes, I'm fine.'

'You sure?'

'I'm *fine,*' I said, my entire being consumed by guilt and shame. Because the fact of the matter was that for the first time in months, I wished that it wasn't Marek who was sitting by my side. I wished it was ...

You *know* who I wished it was.

6

The next week dragged by in an agonised blur. I lived for no other purpose than to await the return of the Polish group that had gone to Greystones Abbey. I waited for the first Sunday after their return, when we all trooped along to the club after Mass. Then at last I could made my way over to Ania to ask her how the retreat had gone, and whether she had met a certain monk by the name of …

'Brother Matthew?' She broke into a wide grin. 'Why, d'you know him?'

Glancing away, I said, 'Kind of. I went on a retreat to Greystones myself, a few years ago. I didn't think he'd still be there.'

'He's a bit of all right, don't you think?'

'Hey, what's all this, then, eh?' Marek tucked his arm round my waist before turning back to Ania with a mock-frown. 'You're not supposed to think of monks in that way, you naughty girl.'

They both laughed, and somehow I managed to join in. But my heart was already floundering, sinking, gasping for its life's blood, knowing that I'd drown from sheer despair if I never saw him again, now that he was back in my awareness. And also knowing, in one of those prophetic moments that life very occasionally throws at you, that Marek was not my life's blood, and never could be.

* * *

So I finished with Marek. I just couldn't go on, knowing that the very mention of Brother Matthew had been enough to send me into a dizzying whirlwind of longing from which I knew I would never recover. I couldn't live a lie anymore. I *had* to finish with Marek. I think it must have been one of the hardest things I ever did in my life.

'For Christ's sake, Leah!' he shouted, oblivious to the stares of fellow-drinkers in the *Copper Kettle* pub in Perry bar, where I'd arranged to meet him. 'What's got into you? I just don't understand.'

I looked away. 'I'm sorry, Marek. I don't fully understand myself.'

'So that's supposed to get you off the hook, is it?'

'No, I didn't say -'

'Then why are you doing this?'

'It's hard to explain.'

'Well you'd better fucking try.'

I winced. He never swore, not like that. He was really hurting. But before I had the chance to attempt any explanation, he went on, hell for leather, 'It's ever since Ania mentioned that retreat she went on, and that bloody monk. What was his name?'

'Brother Matthew.'

'Jesus!' He grabbed his beer glass, took several long swigs, and slammed it back down on the table. One or two people near us cast wary glances in our direction. 'So what is it with this Brother Matthew prat? Is something going on between the two of you?'

'No, of course not.'

'Stop pissing me about! And will you please *look* at me, for fuck's sake.'

So I looked at him.

'I'm waiting,' he demanded with cold, chemical precision.

'Okay.' I took a long draught of my wine before continuing. 'I had a crush on him once, when I was a teenager. That's all.'

'So you're finishing with me because of a crush you once had for a god-damn *monk*?'

'No, it's not that ...'

'Then *what*?'

I scanned my brain for all the possible excuses that could come to mind, which weren't many. 'I've just been feeling a bit – well, kind of overwhelmed these past few weeks. I'm sorry. It's just been a bit too much. I think I need a fresh start – or at least a break. And Dorrington Hall is an ideal opportunity for that.'

Ah yes, Dorrington Hall, near Leeds, where I'd been accepted at a teacher-training college for the coming academic year. Michael Williams had advised me to get a teaching qualification to be on the safe side, seeing as making a living as a concert pianist is nigh impossible unless you're a world-class virtuoso.

Marek fixed his eyes on his beer glass. Both of us fell silent. And then, almost imperceptibly, his shoulders started trembling. I swallowed, dreading the prospect of having to witness his tears. But thankfully, he spared me that.

Pushing his beer glass away, he looked at me with a frozen expression that sought neither explanation nor comfort. 'So this really is it, then. You've fallen out of love with me.'

I didn't reply. How could I tell him that I'd never truly been in love with him in the first place?

The thing is, Mother, you were right, as always. Just as there was only ever one man for you, there was also only one man for me. And the man sitting opposite me now, with the slumped shoulders and wounded eyes, was most definitely not him.

CHAPTER EIGHTEEN

1

'Oh, come *on*, Chubs, you can't be serious about going to Yugoslavia again?'

Peter was sitting opposite her in the kitchen of 48 Talbot Road. Her parents and sister were out, so the two of them had the house all to themselves, though not for long. All too soon, Peter would be heading for Preston Railway Station to catch the train back to London.

'And why not?' she asked, stirring her teacup a touch too vehemently.

'I mean, going all that way – to *Yugoslavia* – to be with someone you just casually happened to meet on a cruise? While you were still engaged to your puppet-fiancé? How is he, by the way? Your Gastric architect?'

'I'll thank you not to talk about him like that. Tony Gaston is a very nice man, as a matter of fact. Far, far nicer than you could ever hope to be.'

'Well thank Christ for that! I don't want to be *nice*. Sometimes *not* being nice is a far better way of making people sit up and listen.'

'How very dramatic of you.'

'And how very dramatic of *you* to get engaged to someone else while you're still with me, and then to meet yet another bloke while you're still with your puppet-fiancé who you don't even love.'

'Oh, stop calling him that! As a matter of fact, I'm not engaged to Tony anymore.'

'Ooooh …' He leaned back in his chair and placed his hands on his chest. 'I see. Well, do please accept my deepest condolences. What happened? Did one of the buildings he designed collapse on your head? Or maybe Mustafa proposed to you even before the bricks began to fall?'

'No, he did not. And I'll have you know that sarcasm is the lowest form of wit.'

Suddenly he sat forward with manic eyes. 'Molly, what's got into you? What the hell are you playing at?'

'And what are *you* playing at? The name Latrina doesn't ring a bell?'

'No it bloody well does not, because her name is *Clarina*, for crying out loud!'

'Or Delilah?'

'*Delia.*'

She turned her head away.

'So that's what it's all about, is it? Getting your own back on me for a couple of idiotic flings I had which meant absolutely nothing?'

'Then why have them in the first place? Why waste time on something which means absolutely nothing?'

'Aha! So then Tony Gastric and Mustafa Babble *did* mean something to you.'

'Tony *Gaston,* if you please. And it's Mustafa *Babić.* With a soft *ch* sound at the end.'

'Ooh ...' he pulled down that sexy corner of his mouth. 'We mustn't tussle with the Professor of Linguistics from Preston University, now must we?'

'Oh, for heaven's *sake.*'

His face slackened. Leaning back again, he said, 'Chubs – this is getting us nowhere.'

'No, it certainly isn't.'

And then he sat forward again. His forwards and backwards dance on that rickety old dining chair could have amused her, if she hadn't been so upset about his imminent departure: back to London and his journalistic friends. His other life.

Grabbing both her hands, he said in a strained voice, 'Molly, I beg you – please don't go to Yugoslavia. Don't you realise how dangerous it is out there? I won't let you go!'

She smiled. It was a rare event indeed when she succeeded in evoking such intense emotions in her incorrigible, loveable, ultimately doomed boyfriend. Or rather, fiancé. They had split up and got back together again so many times by now, in this their sixth year together, she was no longer sure whether he actually *was* still her fiancé, technically speaking. But whatever the case, here he was now, staring at her with those eyes, clutching both her hands in his. She could see that he truly did not want her to go to Yugoslavia. Whether or not it was dangerous, he didn't want her to sail into the arms of the hunky Mustafa, whose dark foreign gaze might sweep her off her naïve English feet and encourage her to stay out there forever, amongst the olive groves and white-washed villages and dazzling cliffs that spilled head-on into the glittering Adriatic Sea. And yet there he was, planning his own daring trip. No amount of arguing on her part had thus far succeeded in changing his mind.

'So what about your own trip?' she asked, easing her hands out of his grip.

'That's different.'

'No it isn't, it's completely the same.'

'Ah, but the difference is, I'm not travelling a thousand miles to see some non-English-speaking Casanova who has secret designs to keep me out there forever.'

'I've already told you, Mustafa isn't the reason I'm going to Yugoslavia. He might have been last year, it's true – but you and I weren't together back then, so I had every right to go and stay with him. This time it's different. I'm travelling with my friend Marge, and we're going to book ourselves into a hotel and do lots of sight-seeing. I have no intention whatsoever of seeing Mustafa. That's all over now.'

Peter leaned back in his chair and lit up a cigarette. 'Even if what you're say is true,' he began, shaking out the match, 'I'm still extremely worried about your whole hair-brained scheme. Yugoslavia is a dangerous place for two young women travelling alone.'

'Not alone. With each other.'

'It's still dangerous.'

'So *your* hair-brained scheme of travelling round Europe and the Middle East on a flimsy moped isn't dangerous?'

'No, it isn't. And I'm sorry, Chubs, but nothing you can say will convince me otherwise. I've been saving up for this trip for the past twelve months, and I'm not going to give it up now. It's the biggest chance I've had yet to make a name for myself as a freelance journalist.' She tried to interrupt, but he was on a roll now. 'Don't you see it's the only way I can really make a difference? Make people aware that they can't just go on living their cocooned lives as if nothing mattered anywhere else, as long as they're safe? Try to make them think about all the intolerance and prejudices we spread across the planet?'

'But Peter – travelling all that way on that silly moped of yours – you don't think that's just a *little* bit reckless?'

'It won't all be in one go. Obviously I'll have the occasional break for a few days - even a few weeks. My first one will be in Cyprus – y'know, where that Irish doctor-friend of mine lives. I can report on the Suez crisis from there.'

She rolled her eyes. 'You and that blasted Dermot Cavanagh. I wish you'd never met him.'

2

When I was offered the post of part-time music teacher in the quaint cathedral town of Lichfield, your reaction surprised me. I'd just graduated from my one-year teacher-training course at Dorrington College, and the following day I was due to return home to Lyneham-on-Sea. But first I wanted to phone you to tell you my good news.

'Lichfield?' you echoed into the telephone receiver. 'Isn't that near Birmingham?'

'Yes, why do you ask?'

'Oh, it's nothing. I just thought you said you'd had enough of Birmingham. And yet here you are, barely a year after leaving it, going straight back there.'

'I said it was *near* Birmingham, not *in* Birmingham. Besides, does it matter one way or another where I end up getting a job?'

'Darling, you're welcome to work wherever you like. It just seems a bit strange that out of all the vacancies in schools all around the country, you should pick one that's on the doorstep of the place you spent three years studying, and never even liked all that much.'

'Well, so what? And besides, I didn't *pick* that job, I was *offered* it – only after having been rejected by three others, remember?' I couldn't help but wonder if it was the fact that I'd only be a twenty-minute train journey away from Marek that worried you most of all. The realisation of our accidental close proximity had occurred to me as well. And it wasn't all that unpleasant a thought.

'There's no need to get all uppity with me,' you said. 'I was just pointing out an obvious fact, that's all.'

'Well, I'm sorry, but actually it isn't obvious to me. What difference does it make where I work? At least it's a job.'

'Only part-time.'

'Yes, but I'll be able to fill up the rest of my hours giving private piano lessons. Apparently there's a big demand for them within the school.'

'Good heavens! Part-time work, private piano lessons, and living in Birmingham.'

'No, in *Lichfield*. And I'm sorry if I can't earn my living giving concert tours round the world. I'm sorry if I've disappointed you.'

All traces of ill-humour immediately vanished from your voice. 'Oh, Leah, how can you even think that? You could *never* disappoint me, darling. I'm just not sure if a part-time job teaching music at some primary school in Lichfield is going to be all that fulfilling for you. At the end of the day, all I want is for you to be happy.'

'Well, you have a funny way of showing it.'

I'm sorry, Mother. I really don't know exactly when it was I started developing that brittle tone of voice with you. We still had our lovely moments together, but by now quite a lot of them were marred by edginess and antagonism. It was as though I was having a delayed adolescent rebellion. Or maybe I was just trying to learn how to let go of you.

3

The summer holidays of 1981 passed by mercifully quickly. I was beginning to get restless by this stage. More to the point, I was keen to start my new life as a working woman. And so, after my usual two-week stint in Cork with Dad's family, I made several day trips to Lichfield to try and sort out accommodation before the start of term in September. I eventually found an end-terrace cottage in a semi-rural location, with a beech wood directly opposite and a quiet, leafy park at the end of the road. There were six cottages altogether, all of them picturesque from the outside, but riddled with damp on the inside. This is no doubt why the rent was so cheap. But damp or not, I loved it, and so did you, when you eventually came to visit.

In the meantime, life at Belle Vue continued, busy as ever. Apart from all the usual cooking and cleaning and changing of beds, we also threw ourselves into the task of converting Gran's old room into a second lounge for guests. The re-decorating of the room was the easy part; by far the hardest was trying to persuade you to get rid of all her things which had been lying untouched since her death three years ago. As it happened, most of Gran's knick-knacks ended up joining the general clutter of your various display cabinets and shelves; a collection I will one day inherit from you, which will be equally hard to part with.

And then there was poor old Mr Tomlinson, your loyal admirer. He stayed at Belle Vue for a longer spell than usual that summer - about a fortnight, I think it was. His constant advances practically drove us both round the twist! The fact that they were always disguised in a bad-tempered tone of voice didn't help. 'Where's that mother of yours?' he'd ask me whenever I happened to be passing by. 'Doesn't she realise the bloomin' pipes are banging again?' Another time it would be: 'You'd better tell your mother to get up to my room fast! The shower's on the blink again.' But breakfasts were by far his favourite line of attack, because it was then that he was guaranteed to get hold of you – though not physically, poor man.

'You take that toast rack straight back to the kitchen, young lady, and tell your mother to bring me a fresh batch which hasn't gone stone cold. What *is* this, a respectable Bed & Breakfast establishment or a cheapskate hostel?' And I'd humbly reply, 'Sorry, Mr Tomlinson. The toast is always the hardest part to get right. I'll tell my mother.' To which he'd snap, 'No you won't blinkin' tell her; she can come here herself and I'LL tell her!' Although he drove you mad, at the end of the day I think you actually felt quite sorry for him. In fact, I'm pretty sure that you were the unrequited love of poor old Mr Tomlinson's life.

As for my own unrequited love? I increasingly felt I couldn't talk to you about Brother Matthew anymore. I just knew that you'd carry on filling me with unrealistic hopes, thereby deepening my heartache and making me more irritable than ever.

* * *

One blustery evening in late July I went out for a drink with Jenny to the *Nag's Head,* just off the old town square in Lyneham. By this stage I was feeling the increasing need to escape your intense company. Sorry, Mother, but that's the truth. Of course I still adored you, and I still cherished our evenings when we had a laugh over Mr Tomlinson, or reminisced about your youth, or looked at old letters and photos of Peter Fox, or had a bit of a weep over a particularly heart-breaking film ... but at some deeper level I could sense that things were changing. I don't know whether it was you who was becoming more cloying than ever, or me who was growing up and needing more space. It was probably both.

Jenny leaned back in her chair and twiddled the stem of her wineglass between her fingers. 'God, it seems like *ages* since we last had the chance for a good old chin wag.'

'I know what you mean,' I sighed. 'Oh, Jenny, don't our Lark Mount days seem so far away? Here we are – me a qualified music teacher, you on your way to being a lawyer -'

'*On the way* being the operative phrase. Anyway, never mind all that. What is that's bothering you? C'mon, out with it.'

Again I sighed. A long, helpless plea from the heart.

'Bloody hell, that sounds ominous.'

'No it isn't. It's just that … as I said, I need to talk.'

'Well, that's what Auntie Jenny's here for, love,' she teased, and instantly I found myself relaxing.

'Okay, do you want to hear the good news or the bad news first?'

'I think we'd better get the bad out of the way, don't you?'

I nodded. 'Right. Okay. Well, the worst of it is that I'm afraid I still haven't got over him and I'm honestly beginning to wonder if I ever will.'

'Hang on a minute, who is it you're talking about now? Not the silent hunk at Dorrington College who turned you on by stroking the erogenous zone behind your knees?'

I shook my head. 'And before you ask – no, it isn't the Ukrainian poet, either.'

She looked at me with what I can best describe as a disappointed-parent expression. 'Oh, Leah. Then I guess it's the one I was really, really hoping it wouldn't be.'

I nodded. 'It's now two years since I last saw him, and I still can't forget him. I've tried, Jenny – really I have – but it's not so simple, trying to forget someone you're still totally and utterly … well …'

'In love with.'

'Right.' I lowered my eyes. 'Nights are the worst. I can go for quite a long spell hardly thinking about him at all, and then totally out of the blue, I have a dream about him. A dream that seems so real, I want to curl into a ball and die when I wake up.'

'Leah, you *know* he's never going to leave the monastery for you. If he was, he'd have done it by now. So why waste your life pining over him?'

'Because I just know that there'll never be anyone else for me.'

'Sorry love, but you're beginning to sound like a Mills & Boon romance. D'you think we could get back down to earth? Anything else to get off your chest, before we move on to the good news?'

'My mother.' I reached for my wineglass. 'I'm starting to worry about her more and more. It's as though she's in love with Brother Matthew herself, even though she's never met him. Or maybe he reminds her of Peter Fox. I mean, she's seen a couple of photos of Matthew, and she did mention once that there was some resemblance – but I'm not sure it's that, either. It's more like she's trying to force my destiny, wanting me to be romantically fulfilled in a way that she herself never was. Then I become her, Brother Matthew becomes Peter Fox, and bingo, she's found the perfect solution to both our unrequited loves.'

'Bloody hell, you'd make a good psychoanalyst!'

'No seriously, Jenny, I can't think of any other reason why she's so desperate for me not to give up on Brother Matthew. I honestly think she's convinced that I'll end up with him one day. And that makes it all the harder for me to bear, because I *know* I won't. I just know it. I don't even think we'll even see each other again, let alone end up together. I mean, the last time I was at Greystones … ' Jenny waited without prodding, bless her. 'The last time was different. Before that, it had just been a kind of girlish fantasy. Brother Matthew himself was convinced that's all it was. But then … well, things changed. After that last visit I knew – I know – without any doubt - that it wasn't a fantasy anymore.'

'Jesus, Leah – you didn't shag him, did you? Oh my God, *did* you?'

'No, of course not.' I looked away, trying not to remember that night in the attic, but remembering it all too well.

Jenny reached out her hand to give my shoulder a squeeze. 'All right, let's leave that alone,' she said in a softer voice. 'So how about the good news at last?'

'What? Oh, right. Well, the good news is kind of divided in two.'

'Do tell more!'

'Well, to begin with, I've got a job in Lichfield teaching music in a private school.'

'Oh Leah, that's brilliant! Well done, you.'

'But that's not the main part.'

'It isn't?'

'No. The main part is that Lichfield happens to be near Birmingham.'

'O-*kay* ... and where exactly is this leading?'

'Well, Birmingham happens to remind me of a certain ex-boyfriend. And I don't mean Adrian Midwinter.'

Her face lit up. 'You mean you've been in touch with Marek again?'

'No, not exactly ... but I have been considering it. The thing is, I've found myself missing him quite a lot lately. And wondering why we ever split up.'

'Sorry to be brutal, love, but you *dumped* him, remember?'

'Yes, I know.' I found myself smiling. 'I think I must have been mad. Marek was such an all-round nice person. Not boring nice, but *fun* nice. And an *amazingly* good lover.'

'Okay, so this is what you do.' Straightening her back, Jenny faced me with no-nonsense lawyer precision. 'Once you've started your job in Lichfield, you go along to the Polish club one weekend. Maybe to a Mass, like you used to.'

I shook my head. 'No, I couldn't do that. He's bound to have met someone else by now. It's a whole year since I last saw him – and we didn't exactly part on the best of terms.'

'Okay, so then why don't you go incognito at first, to see if you can find out anything about his status?'

'And how, pray, am I supposed to do that? Put a mask on?'

'Oh, I don't know, there must be some way. The most important thing is that you've got to get in touch with him again. You've *got* to, Leah. This sounds like your best chance yet of ridding your system of that bloody Benedictine once and for all.'

I laughed, but deep down I knew she was right.

I went back home later that night feeling far more uplifted than I would have done if I'd spoken to you about the same matter. Sorry to say it, Mother, but I actually think that by this stage I was beginning to realise that you were just a little bit mad.

CHAPTER NINETEEN

1

At the beginning of September I moved into my end-terrace cottage in Lichfield. You managed to snatch a couple of days away from Belle Vue to go with me and help me set up home. It was an exciting time for us both: sorting out and arranging a proper house for me, rather than just a bedsit. We trawled the bric-a-brac stalls on the market and the local second-hand shops, and in no time at all managed to enhance the spartan furnishing of my new abode. Thanks to your keen eye and experience in bartering, we bought a wealth of home-making artillery: a wobbly lamp with a tasselled shade, a frayed Oriental rug, a pair of brass candlesticks for the mantelpiece, a wooden plant stand to tuck in a mouldy alcove, a smattering of satin cushions to cover the stains on the sofa, a Haywain print to brighten the cracked plaster walls … by the time we'd finished our mad round of interior design, we'd transformed the place into the kind of cottage that Goldilocks might have lived in.

After I'd waved goodbye to you at Lichfield railway station, I stood alone on the platform for several minutes. I already missed your warm voice, your smile, the brightness of your company, and was filled with unease at the thought of starting a new job in a new town and not knowing a single soul. And when I returned to my cottage, it occurred to me that the semi-rural street it was on was actually a bit creepy at night – a fact that was accentuated by the sinister beech wood that lurked opposite. But I loved it all the same. It was my first proper home as an independent woman, and the following day I was about to start my new life as a teacher. Things *had* to be looking up.

My first few weeks at St Alban's Primary School consumed all my wakeful hours. Although I was only employed as a part-time teacher, I earned additional income by giving private piano lessons during lunch breaks and after school. So to all intents and purposes I was working full-time, which was just what I needed to stop myself from falling into the *if only* daydreams that were in danger of taking over my life.

I spent most evenings preparing my music lessons for the following day. These consisted of singing, arranging pieces for glockenspiels, recorders and keyboards, selecting popular pieces from the classics, and inventing simple aural tests in the form of games. The pupils enjoyed my lessons, and very soon I was being praised by all the other teachers for raising the profile of music in the school. By half-term I felt like a fully established member of staff, despite being the youngest and the least experienced. I didn't play at any recitals, of course, and just occasionally I did wonder about my long-term future. What had been the point in all those hours of practice, all those dreams of being a concert pianist, even getting as far as winning that competition, if all I ended up doing was teaching music to children? But at the end of the day I liked my job and home, and I was beginning to feel more content with life than I had done in a long time.

One murky Saturday in November I made a shopping trip to the Bull Ring Centre in Birmingham, just twenty minutes from Lichfield by local train. It was there that I spotted a poster advertising the annual Polish Independence Day concert. Immediately I found myself flooded by a torrent of nostalgia and regret. Recalling Jenny's advice about paying the Polish club a visit, I decided that I had nothing to lose by going along to the concert and … well, seeing if Marek would be there. And if he was, then seeing what might happen next.

So I went.

* * *

The auditorium was packed out, as it always was at these big Polish events. I managed to find a seat near the back of the concert hall, half hoping no one would notice me and half hoping they would. I was pleased to note that the programme didn't include a solo piano performance, which hopefully meant that my presence over the last year would have been missed. Still, it was a good concert on the whole – especially the dancing troupe and the accordionist, who performed a touching medley of pre-war favourites. But when it came to the closing speech, my heart leapt into my mouth. It was Marek who gave it. I didn't understand a word of what he said, but seeing him again after more than a year – as he stood at the front of the stage, holding the microphone to his mouth and teasing the audience in that cocky manner of his – brought me out in tingles. I hadn't even been in love with him, and yet here I was, hiding away in the back row, thrilling at the sound of his voice and the sight of his face. The same face that had glared at me accusingly last time we met, with raw pain etched on every contour of his square jaw and wounded eyes.

When he finished delivering his speech, the room filled with a hearty applause that lasted a good couple of minutes. At last a tide of bodies rippled across the rows of seats. This was the moment I'd been dreading. What now?

And then I spotted him. He was walking down the aisle in my direction, chatting away to an attractive young woman by his side. His hand was touching her elbow as he guided her through the crowds, his face turned towards her in animated affection. The two of them looked very much like an established couple. I stared at them for a disbelieving moment, though I don't know why I should have disbelieved – after all, what did I expect? Had I thought he would have remained celibate after I'd dumped him?

Quickly turning away, I scooped up my coat and bag and made my way over to the end of the row, hoping upon hope that I could make a speedy getaway without being seen by anyone.

And then I heard a young female voice calling out my name.

'*Leah,* is it you?'

I turned round. It was Ania. The Ania who'd gone to Greystones on that retreat with the Polish club.

'Oh – hello,' I said reluctantly, hoisting my bag higher up my shoulder.

'Hey, it's *wonderful* to see you again. You're looking great.'

'Thanks. So are you.' I wished she'd keep her voice down. But it was too late.

The very next moment Marek turned his head to us, as I did to him. He hesitated only two seconds before mumbling something to the girl by his side, giving her a valedictory peck on the cheek, and heading towards me through the dispersing crowds. There was no getting away now.

He stopped directly in front of me. 'Well, well, this *is* a surprise. Leah Cavanagh, I do believe? To what do we owe the honour?'

I cleared my throat. 'Hello, Marek.'

Before he had the chance to continue with his repartee, Ania jolted me out of my semi-stupor. 'So come on, Leah, tell us what you've been doing with yourself all this time.'

'Oh, this and that,' I said distractedly. 'Teacher-training in Yorkshire last year, working in Lichfield this year ...'

'Lichfield?' Marek echoed. 'What're you doing there?'

I still couldn't quite read the expression in his eyes as he looked at me. The lenses in his glasses provided a convenient barrier.

'Sorry, I've gotta go now,' Ania said in a hurried voice. 'Luke's waiting for me – but promise you'll come and join us for a drink, okay? It's wonderful to see you again!' And off she went.

The moment I'd both dreaded and longed for was upon us. We were on our own.

Unlike me, Marek did not appear to be in the least bit fazed. 'So what are you doing in Lichfield?'

'Oh, I've – it's just a part-time job at a primary school. Teaching music.'

'Wow, a real working woman? Congratulations.'

'Well – it's not exactly what I dreamed of, but at least it pays my keep.'

He was looking at me the whole time, neither smiling nor frowning, just staring in that direct, glinting way of his. 'So where are you living?'

'In a dilapidated cottage just out of the centre of Lichfield. It's a lovely place, but riddled with damp. If I stay there much longer I'll probably develop rheumatic fever and die.'

'Well, I bloody well hope not. At least not before we've had a drink.' He didn't sound in the least bit strained with me. Not a fraction of any bad feelings seemed to be left – or at least he didn't show any. I admired him tremendously for that. 'How're you fixed right now? Fancy getting away from here and finding somewhere quieter?'

I glanced to my left and right. Where was that attractive girl he'd been with? Failing to spot her, I looked back at him. 'But aren't you busy? I mean – don't you have commitments here?'

He shook his head. 'Nah, I've made my speech, so I'm done. How about the *Spotted Dog* just down the road? Unless you've get someone you're hurrying back to?'

'No … but haven't you? That girl you were with just now …'

'What, Iza?' For a moment he looked confused, and then, suddenly, he laughed. 'She's my cousin from Poland. We've known each other since we were knee-high. She's staying with my parents at the moment.'

'Oh. Right.'

'So then, are you up for it?'

'Up for what?'

'A drink at the *Spotted Dog*, of course. You naughty girl, what did you think I meant?' He winked at me.

I burst into an embarrassed giggle. In an instant all the tension of the past few moments dissipated before our very eyes. 'Yes, why not?' I said.

* * *

302

A couple of hours into our drinks at the *Spotted Dog*, Marek and I had caught up on our respective news from the past year. Both of us avoided any reference to our break-up. By the time the bell rang for last orders, I was overwhelmed by a great sense of loss – knowing it had been a nice evening, that Marek didn't bear any grudges, that he was astounded I'd remembered the Independence Day concert, but that we were now on the fast track to slipping back into our separate lives. The thought made me miserable, yet I couldn't explain why. I didn't want to say goodbye to this man sitting by my side, with his glinting way of looking at me and his frisky way with words that made everything seem ironic. I didn't want to remember all the times I'd spent at his family home, or the dreams I'd allowed myself of a happy future in an extended Anglo-Polish family, sharing their celebrations, making a name for myself as an upcoming pianist within the Polish community, bringing up bilingual children …

I glanced at my watch. 'Right. Better be getting home. My last train leaves in twenty minutes.'

Marek guffawed at this. 'You're not expecting me to let you take a train back home all on your own in the middle of the night?'

'Well, it's hardly the middle of the night – and I am a big girl -'

'Yes it is, and no you're not. It's half-way between sunset and dawn, which makes it precisely the middle of the night. And you're a very light-weight girl, which hardly constitutes *big*. So come on then, let's go. You're getting a chauffeur service tonight. In payment you can play me some Chopin. I take it you do have a piano in this damp-riddled cottage of yours?'

'Of course I have a piano. Do you honestly think I could survive without one?' I grinned at him, and this time he grinned back without any parody in those eyes of his I had grown so fond of, even if they were covered by thick spectacles.

We looked at each other for a long, unblinking moment. And then, inspired by the final ringing of that bloody bell – this time accompanied by the barman calling out to the few remaining customers, *'Come on, folks, ain't you got no homes to go to?'* I said, 'The neighbours would complain if I played the piano at this time of night.'

In response to this he gave me his most twinkling grin yet. 'Then you'll have to play for me in the morning, won't you? After you've made me a slap-up breakfast.'

So that was it. The beginning of my reconvened relationship with Marek Topolski.

In the run-up to Christmas, Marek and I became closer than we'd ever been before. After our year's break there was a new intimacy between us – not just sexual, but something *special,* to coin a phrase. Was it that I was falling in love? Could that be it, I kept asking myself, holding my breath. *Oh please say yes!* I implored the God of Greystones, the God of Brother Matthew. But not you, Mother.

Once again I became a regular visitor to the Topolski family, who didn't appear to hold any grudges against me. On the contrary, they welcomed me back with open arms – the mother and father, the grandfather and two brothers and sister-in-law and three nieces and nephews. Once again I was part of that lively, noisy, chaotic, aromatic den in the leafy suburbs of Sutton Coldfield. Only this time there was a difference. Last time I had been charmed by the newness of it all; this time I felt like I truly belonged, even though I hardly spoke a word of Polish. I felt accepted, loved, admired – especially when asked to play Chopin on their old upright piano, which was tucked away in their back sitting room.

'Miss Leah, you play piano with Polish heart!' the mother enthused many a time.

'It remind me like before war,' the grandfather added, teary-eyed. 'Many place have music before Germans take away. You give back again!' Then he'd turn to his daughter-in-law and come out with a long swoosh of Polish garble, out of which all I'd recognise would be the word 'vodka'. So the mother would promptly disappear into the kitchen and re-emerge two minutes later carrying a tray filled with tea glasses, cakes and the much-cherished Slavonic tipple. Whenever in the Topolski's house I always had the feeling that I was stepping into a Woody Allen film that was a bit weird to fathom, but would probably have a happy ending. Oh God, how I wanted that! I'd had my fill of pain and longing and unrequited love. Now, at last, it was my turn for happiness.

As the Season of Goodwill drew near, and Marek tried to persuade me to join his family for a traditional *Wigilia* Christmas Eve, I felt tempted to accept. The only thing that held me back was the thought of you, Mother. You being all alone at Belle Vue. If I accepted Marek's invitation, it would have meant leaving you on your own. I just couldn't do it.

'Then invite your mum as well,' Marek said to me one evening as we sat snuggled up on the sofa in front of the gas fire in my damp Lichfield cottage.

'Oh God. I couldn't possibly do that.'

'Why not? Christmas is a family time, isn't it? And my family would love to meet your family, even if that does just constitute your mum.'

I floundered. How could I even begin to explain to him the complexities of the relationship you and I shared? 'I just can't,' I said. 'I'm sorry, but it's too soon.'

I felt his entire body stiffen. Pulling his arm away from my shoulder, he said, 'It's that bloody monk, isn't it? You still haven't got over him.'

'No, of course not! That was just a girlish crush.'

The remainder of the evening was tainted. When we went to bed I couldn't get the visage of *that bloody monk* out of my head. I have to admit that it was Brother Matthew I made love to that night. '*Oh Matthew ... I'll never love anyone but you,*' I murmured into his throat as his body moved in immaculate timing with mine. '*Nor me you,*' he moaned back, his muscles hardening, his breath quickening. But thankfully, not being a mind-reader, Marek didn't appear to notice my infidelity as he huffed and puffed away. And when he whispered to me in the aftermath of our passion, 'I love you,' I just gave him a reassuring squeeze, which seemed to do the trick.

* * *

Both you and Marek came to Lichfield for the end-of-term Christmas concert at St Alban's. It was my big moment as a newly qualified music teacher and I wanted you both to enjoy my special night.

The concert itself was fine – how could it be anything else in a primary school full of adorable children dressed as angels and shepherds and Wise Men and Joseph and Mary? After the nativity play, the older children performed carols in my ensemble for glockenspiels, recorders, keyboards and guitars, and at the end of the concert I conducted the staff choir with a gutsy rendering of Elvis Presley's *Blue Christmas,* which went down a treat.

You and Marek sat in the front row of the audience. I must say I felt proud of myself. Not only was the programme of a high standard, I also felt confident on stage in my black velvet dress, high-heeled shoes and hair tied back in a French plait. I knew I looked good and I was glad that Matthew was sitting right at the front, together with you. I mean Marek, of course, not Matthew. For a moment I honestly thought it *was* Matthew sitting there in the front row, smiling at me encouragingly while I introduced the next carol to the audience. I smiled back; but then I caught Marek's eye. He winked at me and broke the spell.

'You do know what it means when I wink, don't you?' he said to me after the performance, amid the whirlwind of congratulations, thanks, goodbyes and Happy Christmases that engulfed us. At this point you'd nipped to the toilets, most conveniently.

'What?'

Leaning closer, he whispered, 'It means I can't wait to carry you to bed.'

Laughing, I pushed him away. 'That's going to be just a little difficult, with my mother staying the night.'

'Oh, shit, I forgot she was staying. *Sod* it.'

'Afraid so. Which means back to Sutton Coldfield for you tonight. Oh come on, Marek, don't look at me like that. I could hardly have *both* of you stay, could I, in my tiny two-bedroomed cottage?'

'I don't see why not. Your mum could sleep on the couch.'

As always, I only realised he was joking when his face broke out into one of his devilish grins. 'Oh, *Marek,*' I said, giving him a whack with my handbag.

307

Next thing I knew, you appeared right beside us. 'My word, Leah, that isn't very ladylike.'

Trying to straighten my face, I said, 'It's all right, Mother, he deserves it. Anyway, come on, let's get out of here. All that singing has made me famished.'

So the three of us went to dinner in a small restaurant that I'd booked near the central square of Lichfield. I knew it was just your type. We sat at a table near the window, with a view of the floodlit cathedral spire peeking out above a dark silhouette of ecclesiastic rooftops. But despite the lovely view and warm ambience, I didn't fully relax for one moment. Even though Marek was on best behaviour, I could still tell that he irritated you. No matter how sparkling and witty his conversation, he just couldn't quite camouflage that certain impatience of manner and mocking turn of phrase that made anyone in his presence feel he was making fun of them. It was just the way he was. When I first met him it had irritated me as well; now I took it in my stride. But not you. Neither did you like the way he called me 'darling', which I must admit was nothing like the way *you* called me 'darling'. But you needn't have worried, because with Marek the word was always said in a light-hearted way, as was 'sweetheart.' If he was in a genuinely tender mood, he just called me Leah.

There was also his family, who he was forever bringing into the conversation. I could see that the constant mention of his parents, brothers, nephews, nieces, grandfather, aunts, uncles and cousins made you edgy. Even jealous. After all, you were from the exact opposite type of family – just you, your parents and your sister. Oh – and Peter Fox, I suppose. Peter was practically family, wasn't he? But it was nothing like the Topolski household. I think part of you already realised the threat we were all under – you, me, Belle Vue Mansions, our whole way of life at Lyneham-on-Sea. I think you intuitively knew that everything was going to change from now on. That nothing would ever be the same again.

By ten o'clock we'd finished eating and the atmosphere was flagging. We were all tired from the strain of the past few hours, and I knew you were eager to go back to my cottage and unwind over a hot drink in front of the TV. Dissect how the evening had gone.

When the waitress emerged from the kitchen, Marek raised his hand to her and called out, 'Can we have the bill now, darling?'

I think I cringed even more than you did. But you were an expert at covering up your emotions. You merely smiled at the waitress as she approached our table, and said to her, 'Let me have that, please.'

'Don't be ridiculous; tonight's on me,' Marek said, snatching the bill out of your hand and knocking over his wine glass in the process – though it was empty, thankfully. I could see your eyelids quiver.

'Bloody hell, that was a close shave!' he cried out, and I laughed with him, though more out of embarrassment than humour. 'Anyway, that'll teach you not to try and pay in future, won't it, Mrs Cavanagh?' Looking back at me, he added with a wink, 'Isn't that right, sweetheart?'

'Heavens, it's a good job that glass was empty!' you said, raising a disapproving eyebrow.

Later that night, as you and I sat in our dressing gowns on the sofa back at my cottage, watching *Waterloo Bridge* with Vivien Leigh and sipping hot Ovaltine, I could tell you were dying to talk about Marek. During the first set of adverts you looked across at me and smiled. 'Happy, darling?'

'Of course I am,' I said, having more than a hunch where this was leading.

'But are you *truly* happy? With Marek?'

'I wouldn't be going out with him if I wasn't, would I?'

'Despite his … well, his rather common ways?'

I felt my hackles rising. 'There isn't a single common thing about Marek.'

'There's no need to get uppity with me, Leah. Really and truly, listening to that unpleasant tone of voice of yours, anyone would think I was your worst enemy! All I'm trying to do is give you a realistic perspective on things – because if I don't, then I can't think of anyone else who'll put you back in the land of the living. Quite frankly, my darling, you seem to have lost all sense of reality at the moment, and it saddens me to the bottom of my heart.'

'What exactly are you trying to say?'

Taking a sip of your Ovaltine, you faced me full on. 'If you honestly want to know, it's just about everything to do with the man that worries me.'

'I'm afraid you'll have to expand on that.'

'You know what I'm talking about. His brusque turns of phrase, the crude way he looks at you, the way he calls you *darling* as though you were both part of a *Carry On* film ... In fact, that's exactly what comes to mind whenever I think of Marek. A rather crude sort of comedy.'

'Well, I can't help the way you think about him,' I said, trying to keep my nerves intact. The last thing I wanted was a bad atmosphere building up between us, with it being the end of term and so near Christmas. So I added in a gentler voice, 'Oh Mother, I wish you could see through that brash façade he puts on. There really is a lot more to him than that. You'll understand what I mean when you get to know him better.'

'Heavens above, you *do* sound serious! So you're not planning on finishing with him this time round, then?'

'No, of course not.'

'Well, let's hope Brother Matthew doesn't suddenly crop up in your life again. Because if he did, then mark my words, Leah, you'd drop Marek like a hot cake, just like you did last time.'

'But I've no intention of dropping him, so you don't have to worry.'

'But I *do* worry, because you're my daughter and I care about your happiness more than anything in the world. Can't you understand that?'

I almost cried out, *No, I can't!* but manged to slam the brakes on.

'Darling,' you began with admirable restraint, 'my only concern is that if Brother Matthew does come on the scene again, then the shallowness of your feelings for Marek will be exposed. Honestly and truly, I'm not trying to insult the man – he seems like a pleasant enough sort of person; he's intelligent, he obviously cares about you, and he certainly has good prospects as a chemist. I also admire the way he wants to start his own business – and judging by his determined character, I've no doubts that he will one day. But when all's said and done, there's a whole *world* of difference between show-love and true love.'

I was just about to cross-examine you on your definition of the term 'show love', but at that very moment the adverts came to an end and we were plunged straight back into the late-night film. By the time Vivien Leigh had thrown herself under the truck that whizzed across Waterloo Bridge, you had nodded off to sleep, leaving me alone with my thoughts. After ten minutes or so I couldn't stand my thoughts any longer, so I stood up, walked over to your side, and gently shook your shoulder.

Yawning, you said, 'Goodness, is that the time?' You heaved yourself up from the sofa, shook out the cushions, kissed me goodnight, and trod up the stairs to your bedroom while I took our empty mugs into the kitchen.

Five minutes later I myself was in bed, exhausted from the strain of the evening. I fell asleep with the comforting knowledge that the train would be taking you back to Lyneham-on-Sea the following morning.

4

I managed to get out of spending Christmas with Marek, but New Year's Eve was a different matter. I couldn't reject him twice in a row without creating a scene. For all Marek's newborn tenderness, when pushed to the limits he could still revert to the harsh man I had first met. And so when he phoned me in Lyneham to invite me to a New Year's party that he was throwing at his house, I gave in without a struggle. By that time I hadn't seen him in over a week and I was missing him.

I caught the train back to Birmingham on the afternoon of December 31st, trying to ignore the martyred look on your face as we parted with a strained hug on the platform at Lyneham Railway Station. Two hours later Marek picked me up at New Street Station and drove me to his house, where I spent the rest of the afternoon helping him prepare for the party. Guests started arriving around eight and by eleven the place was heaving. Half the Polish community must have been there, as well as all Marek's family, plus some new additions I hadn't met before. I could barely keep up with the continual ringing of the front doorbell. More often than not the job of answering it was down to me, because whenever I went in search of Marek he was either in the garden getting the fireworks ready, or in the kitchen preparing yet another tray-load of drinks, or locked so deeply in combative dialogue with a fellow warrior that his ears were oblivious to the regular *ding dong* which merged into the cacophonous score of the household.

But just before midnight he was suddenly by my side again, his eyes re-charged with that dynamic gleam I found so sexy. Leaning closer to me, he shouted above the din of *Bon Jovi*, 'Let's go outside!'

So he led me outside, grabbing a bottle of champagne and two empty glasses on the way. Most of the party guests were by now squashed into the long back garden. Just on midnight he popped open the champagne cork, and even before we had the chance to toast in the New Year, he drew me towards him and whispered hotly into my ear, '*Marry me.*'

* * *

Later that night I lay in Marek's arms, staring out of the window at a silvery moon that was half-obscured by a thin skein of clouds. The moon always reminded me of that last evening with Brother Matthew. That's why there were tears on my face right now, as I lay in Marek's arms staring at the moon and thinking of another man. Would it always be like this? Would every relationship I ever had always lead to a dead end? Would I baulk at the insurmountable barrier of true commitment, always pulling away at the last moment, just before it was too late? But too late to do *what*, exactly? You never quite managed to clarify that, Mother. All you ever did was continually urge me to win the heart of a man who wasn't in a position to give his heart away.

So was this, then, all the world had to offer? Was that really your master plan: to stop me marrying anyone who wasn't quite *the one*? Even someone I was very fond of, who I found sexy and enjoyed making love to; someone I felt completely relaxed with, who made my fears about the future fade away in the comfort of his strong embrace and confident laugh, and … Actually, when I looked at it like that, it wasn't such a bad prospect, after all. Hardly something that warranted the self-pitying rhetoric of *was this all the world had to offer?*

Marek stirred.

'Leah?' he whispered, turning his head towards me. He lifted himself up and squinted through the darkness at my face. 'What's the matter? Have you been crying?'

'No, of course not.'

'Don't lie to me. What is it?'

'Nothing.'

'Nothing? So those tears aren't real?' He stroked my cheek, wiping away the wet streaks. 'Come on, tell me. What's so upsetting about knowing you're going to spend the rest of your life with me?'

'I haven't said yes yet.' I tried to laugh, but my voice got caught in a hiccup of restrained emotion. Wiping my eyes, I mumbled, 'Sorry, must be all that champagne I drank. I feel so tired … and yet I can't sleep.'

'Well, maybe I can help with that.'

Placing his hand on my bare stomach, he started stroking my warm flesh, gradually working his fingers lower and lower until they were doing their magic tricks. I closed my eyes and forgot all about my confused longings. And then, just as I was beginning to get into the mood, he stopped. Opening my eyes again, I looked at him.

'Marry me, Leah.'

I sighed. 'We've already been through all this before. I need -'

Again he touched me, this time with a tickling motion. I gasped.

'Say yes, or I'll turn my back on you and go right back to sleep.'

'Oh, Marek, come on …'

His fingers intensified their skilled manoeuvres. 'Say yes,' he whispered, lowering his head over my face and kissing my lips, my throat, each breast in turn, my belly … and each time he moved an inch lower, he paused to raise his head and repeat the words, '*Say yes*,' before moving lower still.

I moaned louder.

'*Say yes*,' he murmured a final time before levering his body on top of mine. Oh, God, I blush even now to think of the tactics he used – and the state he got me in! By this stage I was so totally off the planet, how could I possibly have said anything other than a loud, resounding: 'YES, oh *YES*!'

It was only when I woke up several hours later, to the dull light of New Year's Day, that I fully realised the impact of what I'd agreed to. But I didn't regret it in the least. I'd said yes! I'd agreed to marry Marek Topolski. He loved me and would always love me and look after me and make me feel cherished and protected till the day I died. I was an engaged woman. I already looked forward to choosing the ring and couldn't wait till the shops opened again. Like the following morning.

There was only one short circuit to my happiness that day, and it wasn't the thought of Brother Matthew, just for a change. No, Mother, it was the thought of *you*. How in the name of God was I going to tell you that I'd just got engaged to be married, but not to the man of your dreams?

CHAPTER TWENTY

1

I can't believe it's almost three in the morning. I should go to bed, but I don't feel in the least tired. I suppose that's because I know that if I drift off to sleep, when I next wake up it'll be the morning of my wedding day. How much time do you think we have left, before this night is out?

Certainly a lot longer than you and Peter Fox had, that's for sure. I remember the last time you ever spoke to him. Or rather, *you* remember it, and through your vivid stories that filled my growing-up years, I remember it too.

Would you have let Peter go to Cyprus if you had known what the future held? Would you have let him go if you had known that as a result of his death you'd end up giving birth to a baby girl who you would love more than life itself? Or would you have relinquished the chance of having that future little girl, if it meant that you could have been with Peter for the rest of your life? What would you have chosen?

Actually, I can't bear to think of it.

* * *

She's hurrying down the empty street with a cardigan tossed round her shoulders.

'*You'll catch your death, Molly!*' her anxious mother calls after her dwindling form. But it's no use.

It's a dark, damp November night and, unbeknownst to her, the last one in which she will ever hear her beloved's voice. The two of them have arranged to wait in a public telephone box at a given time, so they can speak to each other before he departs for Aphrodite's golden shores.

She reaches the phone booth at the end of Talbot Road. She steps inside, picks up the receiver, dials the number he's given her: the number of a phone box somewhere near his flat in London.

After just three rings, he picks up. 'Chubs, is that you?' His voice sounds nervous, she notes. A bit panicky.

'No, it's Greta Garbo. So come on, then, why all the urgency? What are you playing at?'

'I'm not playing at anything. I just wanted to speak to you before I board that plane to Nicosia. You haven't forgotten that I'm going tomorrow, have you?'

'No, I haven't forgotten.' The very thought of it robs her of the last vestiges of her forced humour.

'You know I don't have to go if you don't want me to. You do know that, don't you, Chubs? I mean – come on, what's a wasted plane ticket compared to a lifetime of happiness?'

This time it's her turn to pause. For once in her life, she doesn't know what to say.

So Peter goes on: 'Look, Molly, I've been doing a lot of thinking. I know I've hurt you, but you've got to believe that I never, ever intended to. I've just been a prime idiot, searching for the moon when I've already got the stars.'

She sighs with a wearied impatience beyond her twenty-six years. She's always been an incurable romantic; but tonight she's become the one whose feet are firmly planted on the ground. 'Peter, now isn't the time for flights of fancy. What is it you're getting at?'

'That we're being prime idiots! That your mum's been right all the way along. We want our heads knocking together. Why do I need to go to Cyprus? Why do you need to go to Yugoslavia? Why can't we go to both places together one day instead?'

'I still don't understand what it is you're trying to say. You'd better be quick, because I haven't got any more coins on me and we're going to get cut off soon.'

317

'For God's sake, Molly, I'm trying to say *let's get married!* Let's set a date at last and forget about our idiotic travel plans. Just for once let's concentrate on what *really* matters. I mean it. I'm prepared to forget about Cyprus if –'

'What about this Irish friend of yours? Wouldn't it be rather rude to let him down at such short notice?'

'What, Dermot Cavanagh? No, he'll understand – no worries there. Any road, look – I'm willing to come up to Preston and start making wedding plans, if you're willing to drop your mad Yugoslav scheme. Chubs, you *know* there's never going to be any other woman for me. You do know that, don't you? So let's not waste any more time. Let's get married, for Christ's sake!'

She pauses a good three or four seconds, despite the risk of the phone line cutting out. But then her voice box clicks back into gear. 'No, Peter. You know how much this trip means to you, how long you've planned for it, not to mention how much it's cost. When all's said and done, let's face it – you're just not the marrying type.'

'That's not true!'

'It *is* true. Just stop to think for once, will you? How many times over the last seven years have you been keen for us to get married, only to change your mind as soon as another pretty face distracts you? No. This last-minute cancellation of your trip would be more foolish than anything you've done so far.'

'But *Chubs* -'

'No, Peter, I mean it. You must do your thing and I must do mine. And when we come back together after our separate travels, if you still feel as convinced as you do now, only *then* should we talk about getting married. Not now.'

There's another long silence. One in which she hopes he'll fight for her – for their marriage, their love, their united lives – and she knows that if he does, she'll give in. But her incipient wish is cut short by the operator, who crisply announces the number of seconds left.

When Peter next speaks, his voice is resigned. 'All right, if that's what you really want. I can see I'm not going to change your mind. But when I come back you'll see that I feel exactly the same way I do now. You *will* see, I promise. Oh, Chubs, you've *got* to believe how much I lo -'

But at that moment the phone cuts off, and so she never hears him utter that most beautiful of all words in any language under the sun. Neither does she ever hear his voice again. Only the echo of it in dreams.

Peter boarded the plane to Cyprus the next day, and shook hands with Kismet.

2

I spent the next three days in a kind of stupor. I wasn't sure if I was in seventh heaven or merely resigned to my fate. But I didn't care. I was beyond caring now.

On the first day, January 1st 1983, Marek and I stayed in bed till late afternoon, making love again and again and again. After each session we lay in each other's arms talking about our future. Well – Marek did most of the talking, and I the listening. But I didn't mind. When we finally dragged ourselves out of his bedroom and went downstairs to face the chaos from the previous night's party, it was already getting dark. Ignoring the mess that reigned in every room, I cleared enough space in the kitchen to make a big fry-up, which was one of my specialities, thanks to all those years of cooking full English breakfasts at Belle Vue. We ate my culinary feast on our laps in the sitting room with the television on for background company. When we finished, I carried our trays back to the kitchen and added them to the enormous mountain of crockery that hadn't yet been washed up. As soon as I returned to the sitting room, Marek stood up from his armchair and drew me towards him, pulling me over to the billowy folds of the sofa. The evening continued in this manner until we became hungry again around ten o'clock, so I made a snack of left-overs from the party, which we also had on our laps, this time in candlelight. Then we made love again and talked some more while lying in post-coital contentment amid piles of silky cushions. Eventually, in the early hours of the morning, we trudged up the stairs and collapsed into bed, this time falling straight to sleep. I was so exhausted, I didn't even think about phoning you to wish you a Happy New Year. It was Marek who thought of that, on the second day.

* * *

'Hadn't you better give your mum a ring?' he asked as we sat at the kitchen table over breakfast. We'd finally cleared away the mountains of dirty crockery still remaining from the party.

'I suppose I ought to,' I said haltingly, 'but then I'd also have to tell her about our engagement, and I'm not sure if I'm ready for that.'

'Then wish her a Happy New Year and don't mention the engagement yet.'

'But that would be tantamount to lying. I'd feel awful, talking to her over the phone and not mentioning the most important thing in my life.'

'Is it?'

'Well, yes – isn't it for you?'

'You don't need to ask that, Leah. Ever.'

Standing up, he took our empty plates over to the sink, then returned to my side of the table and tugged my hand, pulling me into a standing position. 'C'mon, up them stairs with you, Miss Cavanagh!' he ordered, pushing me in front of him and tapping my bottom.

So I allowed myself to be dragged out of the kitchen, laughing, up the stairs and back to that well-used double bed which we never bothered making. What was the point?

In the afternoon we walked to the High Street to select an engagement ring. When we found the right one – a small emerald which Marek said brought out the green hues in my eyes – he placed it on my finger with such tenderness, a totally unexpected lump came to my throat. I looked at him, my fiancé, and realised that this was it. There was no turning back now. We were going to get married.

On the third day we went to the Topolskis' house, just a fifteen-minute walk from Marek's. We'd been invited for lunch, which seemed like the ideal occasion to inform the family of our engagement. The entire clan was there, seated at their long, cluttered dining table, laughing and bickering and stuffing their mouths with food and their throats with drink, chastising and kissing the raucous medley of children that varied in age from toddler to teen. About halfway through the gargantuan feast, Marek clinked his spoon against his tea glass and stood up, as though he were on the stage.

He started his announcement in English, no doubt for my benefit. 'Mum, Dad, dear aunts and uncles, cousins, children, grandfather … Leah and I have an announcement we would like to make.'

That's as far as he got. '*You getting married!*' Mrs Topolska cried out, clapping her hands together and rising from her chair as though she'd become a helium balloon.

Next thing I knew, there were cheers and whoops and banging of forks on the table, and a toddler crying somewhere amid all that dissonance, and Mrs Topolki hurrying over to my side, hugging me so violently I had to gasp for air.

'Now you my really *córeczka!*'

'*Daughter,*' Marek corrected with an affectionate smile at his mother, before breaking off into a jumbled stream of Polish words which he later translated as: *Don't you think it's about time you learned English now, if only for the sake of your future daughter-in-law?* To which she apparently replied, *No, I'll teach her how to speak Polish instead.*

The grandfather was particularly emotional about the news of our engagement. 'Miss Leah,' he said in a wobbly voice, 'you remind me of very beautiful girl who die in Warsaw bombs. My girl. My fiancée, before I meet Marek grandmamma.'

'Oh, I'm so sorry,' I said. 'How -'

But Marek hissed into my ear, 'Don't get him started! Change the subject, quick!'

So I said, 'Erm –' but luckily at that very moment Mr Topoplski emerged from the kitchen carrying a bottle of Bison Vodka in one hand and a cluster of small tumblers in the other. Following closely behind was Mrs Topolska, bearing another tray crammed to the hilt with cakes: cheesecake and apple cake and honey cake and poppy seed cake, which was my favourite.

Amid all the commotion, I hadn't even noticed the parents disappearing from the table.

Once the glasses had been placed in front of each adult and filled, the father raised his tumbler high in the air and announced in surprisingly good English, 'To the future Mrs Topolska!'

'The future Mrs Topolska!' echoed the entire table-full. And then everyone – except the children, who'd been given cola instead – downed their vodka in one gulp, just like something out of *Fiddler on the Roof.*

'Welcome to the family, darling,' Marek said, squeezing me round the waist.

* * *

Later that night, as we lay in bed in each other's arms, Marek looked at me with an expression that for once was deadly serious.

'What is it?' I asked.

Stroking my shoulder, he replied, 'Your mum. It'll be January 4th tomorrow and you still haven't phoned her.'

I stared at the ceiling.

'Come on, Leah, don't you think she deserves to know? She *is* your mum.'

'Exactly. And you don't know her like I do. She's brought me up single-handedly since my father walked out on us, and that's made us extremely close to each other.'

'Well, there's nothing wrong in that. I'm close to my mum as well.'

'It's not the same,' I snapped, but instantly regretted my harsh tone. I turned my face towards the man lying beside me, and suddenly caught my breath. It was Brother Matthew lying beside me! But of course it wasn't; it was just my imagination playing up. I swallowed. It wasn't the first time that trick of vision had happened, and somehow I knew it wouldn't be the last. I just had to be patient, that's all. I mean, didn't Time heal all?

I looked at the ceiling again, trying to expunge the lingering image of those blue, sparkling eyes. Not that they were sparkling much when I last saw him. 'I'm sorry, Marek, I really can't explain any of this.'

'It's all right, you don't have to. Just phone her.'

'Oh, God.' I closed my eyes.

'Come on, you daft beggar, it won't be *that* bad. Not when it comes down to the nitty-gritty. Just think of all those deliriously exciting wedding plans you and your mum will be able to share.'

'For God sake, Marek!' I clamped my hands to my head to emphasise my disbelief. 'You don't know the first thing about my mother! She will *not* rejoice in making deliriously exciting wedding plans, because she does not want me to marry anyone who doesn't meet with her approval.'

'You mean I don't?' he said, tickling my chin. I didn't respond. 'All right then, you can meditate on it tonight, but tomorrow you phone her. No arguments.'

So that was that. Our three-day parole was over. And on the fourth day I at last phoned you.

3

'Hello, Mother, happy New Year!'

Pause. 'Well, this *is* a surprise, I must say.'

'Look, I'm sorry – I know I should have phoned before, but I've come down with a stomach bug these past few days and I've been practically bed-ridden.'

'Well, then you *still* should be in bed, darling. What on earth are you doing up? Do you have any hot water bottles in your house? And honey?'

'Don't worry, I'm on the mend now – which is just as well, seeing as school starts again on Monday.'

'But Leah, you must make sure you're completely well before you go back. Promise me.' Worries about my health always did the trick.

'Okay, I promise. Anyway, there was something I wanted to tell you.'

'You've got a piano recital coming up?'

I counted silently to five. 'I've told you before, I don't have time for recitals at the moment. This is something even bigger. Can you guess?'

'Even bigger than the possibility of having your first recital since you won the piano competition all of a year and a half ago? No, I'm afraid I can't guess.'

I closed my eyes. Opened them again. Took a deep breath. 'Marek and I have got engaged.'

And at last, the reaction I'd been fearing ever since New Year's Day. A huge, gaping, thunderous pause.

And then: 'Well, my darling, I can't say I'm surprised.' With a tone of voice like that, you might as well have said: *Please accept my deepest condolences for your sad loss.*

'Right. So you did guess.'

'Oh, yes. Marek is very transparent, I'm afraid. It's obvious that he's wanted this from the very beginning.'

'What, you mean I'm such a big catch? You mean he can now get his hands on all those millions that we've got stashed away at Belle Vue?'

'Sarcasm is the lowest form of wit,' you said in a voice that had turned to ice in one second flat. 'My word, I can see how that man has changed you.'

'I haven't changed in the least. *You're* the one that's changed.'

'*I'm* the one that's changed? Just listen to yourself! Leah, what on earth's got into you?'

'Nothing. I just don't want us to argue.'

'And neither do I! All I want is for you to be happy, don't you understand? That's all I've ever wanted. I want you to be *fulfilled* - in a deep, lasting sense. I'm sorry, my darling, but when all's said and done, I can't see that ever happening with Marek.'

'But don't you see how he's –'

'No, now hear me out. Even though I don't like having to say these things to you – and I know you certainly don't want to hear them – I feel I *have* to say them, as your mother. If I don't, then no one else will. I'm just so afraid that you're losing sight of your original dreams and ambitions, and one day when you're much older, you'll regret it all.'

'How could I ever regret being happy? Because that's what I am right now, Mother. I'm *happy* with Marek. Honestly, you've *got* to believe me.'

'Oh, I believe you. Right now I don't doubt that you're happy. But committing yourself to marriage at the age of twenty-two, and teaching music at a primary school … that isn't exactly what you had in mind when you were doing hours and hours of practice every day for all those years, is it?'

'But I love my job! And I'm almost twenty-three. And with Marek's high-up connections in Polish clubs throughout the country, he'll be able to get me fixed up with all sorts of concerts.'

'*Polish club* concerts. And before you bite my head off, I'm not saying anything against them – I'm sure they're wonderful experiences in their own right, just as your job as a music teacher is. I'm also sure that you're a marvellous teacher. I could see for myself what amazing things you achieved at that Christmas concert and how all the children adored you. But darling, no matter how satisfying all of this is for you now, it isn't part of the bigger scheme of things. It isn't part of your life's plan.'

'Oh, so I have a life's plan now, do I? And who wrote it, might I ask?'

'Ye Gods, there you again! Will you just *listen* to yourself! That man has changed you beyond recognition. This isn't the old Leah I'm hearing. You're even beginning to sound like him now.'

'So I take it he's not part of my life's plan, either?'

'He's a trespasser in your life, that's what he is.' As though regretting this venom, you added, 'Of course I can see that he's very fond of you – what man in his right mind wouldn't be? But he isn't the sort of man you dreamed of spending the rest of your days with. Come on, now, be honest with yourself. He isn't a bad person – I know that. He just isn't for you.'

'How can you be so sure of that? You're not me.'

'No, I'm your *mother*. I know you even better than you know yourself, believe me. Oh Leah, can't you see how you're giving up too easily on all your dreams? You can tell me till you're blue in the face that you're happy with Marek; only time will reveal if you're just kidding yourself. Honestly and truly, darling, wouldn't it have been better to have waited at least a little longer? What's the rush?'

'But -'

'Now listen to me,' you said, your voice adopting a tone of urgency. A dangerous tone. I could visualise you sitting on the bottom step in the hallway at Belle Vue, the telephone upon your lap, your mouth pressed conspiratorially against the receiver.

'I'm listening,' I said in resignation.

'I know you're not going to like what I'm about to suggest, but I have to say it, all the same. I have no choice.'

'Okay then, so say it.'

'Why don't you get in touch with Brother Matthew again?'

'*What?* Are you *mad?* For God's sake –'

'No, hear me out. Why don't you write to him and see if he can book you in at Greystones for a weekend? You haven't seen him in well over two and a half years, so maybe if you go back there, you'll find that your feelings for him have changed. You might find that you don't feel the same way about him anymore. Then you'll be able to relax, knowing that you won't be spending the rest of your days regretting what might have been, simply because you threw your life away on the wrong man.'

'But that's just it,' I mumbled, close to tears. 'If I gave up Marek for Brother Matthew, I really *would* be throwing my life away on the wrong man.'

After another of your meaningful silences, you said, 'Oh, my darling.'

4

From the moment of that phone call, things changed.

When Marek suggested having the wedding in Birmingham, I point-blank refused. No matter how difficult you were being about the whole thing, I knew that I couldn't cut you out of my Big Day. So Marek and I decided to risk a weekend trip to Lyneham in order to check out possible venues for the wedding. We tried our hardest to include you in all our plans. We insisted that you came with us as we drove around Lyneham and the nearby vicinity to trawl potential venues for the reception, but you found a problem with each and every place that we considered. When looking at the beautiful Bartle Hall hidden away in the leafy outskirts of Lyneham, you said to Marek, 'Goodness me, I'm afraid my budget doesn't stretch quite as far as you seem to think. Belle Vue isn't the London Savoy, you know.' And when he reassured you that he was capable of covering the cost, you said, 'But I thought you were hoping to set up your own chemist's business one day. Don't you think that such expenditure is rather extravagant?' So then we succeeded in hunting down The Duck and Partridge – a much cheaper, somewhat seedier pub, but at least it had a large dining room upstairs that was available for bookings. As soon as we stepped inside the spartan room, you raised your eyebrow and said, 'Heavens above, you Poles certainly have strange taste.'

Even the question of which church to get married in became problematic. Marek was insistent on having a Catholic wedding ceremony for his family's sake, whereas you displayed a bizarre loyalty to the Church of England which you had never before shown the slightest inclination towards. For the time being we decided to leave open the matter of Catholic or Protestant.

Eventually we settled on a venue that was a compromise – better than The Duck and Partridge but less extravagant than Bartle Hall. You allowed Marek to put a deposit on it, which astounded me, knowing your famous generosity. I knew it was just a ploy to make things so difficult for Marek and me that sooner or later we'd have to cave in and call the whole thing off. Then I'd come running back home to you, having realised *marry in haste, repent at leisure.* Come on, let's face it. Isn't that what you wanted all the way along?

By the time Marek and I returned to Birmingham, I was desperate to be away from your negative, cloying presence. I was also desperate to sleep with Marek after our weekend's abstinence, not having been allowed to share a bedroom when we were under your roof. But I was prepared to let that go. It was yet another ploy: you pretending to be all fuddy-duddy about pre-marital sex, while in reality you and Peter were at it like rabbits after your 21st birthday.

Over the coming weeks Marek and I browsed through a wide selection of wedding catalogues. When on my own in the city centre, I gazed at bridal displays in shop windows and eventually bought a dress. Exquisite satin, long veil, tiny pearls beaded at the V-neck collar and sleeve cuffs … when I looked at myself in the mirror, a haunted apparition stared back at me. I desperately wanted you to be there when I nodded my approval at the shop assistant, who was probably wondering why I was all on my own. But I couldn't bear the thought of you being there. Or you not being there. I couldn't bear it when Marek came to collect me and said, 'What's up?' and I brushed it off with a casual, 'Oh, just pre-wedding nerves.' I couldn't bear it when we got back to my cottage and I hurried upstairs to stash my new bridal gown in my wardrobe, shielded from the world as *I* wanted to be shielded.

I still phoned you every Sunday, despite the fact that our conversations had now become nothing less than a herculean ordeal. Each time I put the receiver down after yet another tortuous forty-five minutes of listening to your objections, which were becoming more vituperative by the week, I felt the urgent need for a glass of wine and a cigarette.

For the first time ever I didn't go home for my birthday in February. I know it hurt you, but how could I have done, with you being so critical of Marek all the time? If I'd spent the entire weekend listening to your re-criminations, I'd be in danger of returning to Birmingham and looking at Marek in a different light. *Your* light. Seeing him through *your* eyes.

Instead, I spent my twenty-third birthday at the Topolskis' house. Marek's parents threw a celebratory dinner in my honour, with all the usual family members present. There was plenty of vodka - I was getting used to the fiery drink by now, though I still couldn't down it in one go like they could – and an enormous chocolate gateau preened itself on a crystal cake stand in the centre of the table. After the meal everyone sang *Sto Lat*, which is sung at all Polish celebrations, and I was expected to blow out all twenty-three candles in one go. I only managed it with Marek's help.

'Did you make a wish?' he whispered to me as the smoke from the extinguished candlewicks swirled around the table.

I nodded, turning my face towards him, and then …

My muscles froze. It was Matthew who was there, smiling at me, reaching out his hand to stroke my cheek as he asked in that beautiful voice of his, *Are you all right, Leah?* I smiled back at him, overjoyed, confused – but then his visage faded, and once again it was Marek's concerned face that was looking at me.

'Are you all right, Leah?'

I wanted to cry out *No!* to him, to his family, to you, to the whole world. *No, I'm NOT bloody all right!* But I only managed a gulp, suddenly wanting Matthew so much, it actually hurt – I mean with a real, searing pain. It was as if a demon from hell had thrust its claws deep into my chest, ripping away at ribs, muscles, ligaments, heart tissue, tearing it all to shreds. But the pain wasn't only for Matthew … it was also for you, Mother. Yes *you,* in spite of everything. My God, when, exactly, had you metamorphosed into this censorious, judgemental Valkyrie whose harshness was under the cunning guise of *darling* this and *darling* that, and *all I want is your happiness?*

'Leah sweetheart, what's the matter?'

331

I shook my head, blinking away tears, swallowing back nausea. 'I think I'm going to be sick,' I spluttered, covering my mouth with my hand, shoving my chair from the table and lurching out of the room.

The mother put it down to too much vodka, Marek later told me, and the father to too much cake.

The second half of term hurled past. St Alban's in the daytime, private piano lessons in the evenings, and a barrage of wildly indecent emotions from morning till night that pinged right off the Richter scale. I didn't have the time or energy to *think*, let alone organise any recitals. Sometimes I mulled over your words from the difficult phone call we had just after New Year's Day. Was it true that I'd given up my dreams too easily?

I spent the February half-term holiday at Marek's house, even though he was out at work most of the time. I didn't want to be on my own all day long in my damp cottage, which was becoming increasingly dreary as my mood plummeted. And I didn't want to go to Lyneham, where you'd no doubt remind me at least ten times a day that it was the fifth anniversary of when I first met Brother Matthew. As if I wasn't aware of that.

As the snows of February melted into the showers of spring, things went from bad to worse. During one particularly harrowing phone call you announced to me, in this low, theatrical voice, that there was no way your conscience would allow you to attend the wedding, and so you advised Marek and me to make our own plans. Which meant cancelling everything we'd booked in Lyneham. That stung like a thousand hornets. My God, how could you not come to your own daughter's *wedding*, for fuck's sake? How could *any* mother do that? But before the smarting even had time to ease off, you surprised me yet again, this time by coercing me into going on a week's holiday with you to Scotland. *The last chance for us to be truly together*, as you put it. An utterly disastrous holiday that only succeeded in turning me more against you than ever.

* * *

It's a wet, miserable day in June. We've just returned to Lyneham from our Oban holiday. There's a train to Birmingham at seven in the evening that I'm desperate to catch. If I don't catch it, I'm going to have a nervous breakdown. This train has been sent straight from heaven. Without it, I'll be destined to spend even more time with you, on top of the gruelling eight days I've already spent with you, and I just can't do it. I have to get away from you, Mother. I'm sorry, but I really have to get away.

All week long in Oban I've tried my hardest to appreciate our beautiful surroundings, but it's been bloody horrendous. I've done my bit for you; now it's time to get back to my own life - and to Marek, who I have increasingly ambiguous feelings about.

We're in the dining room having a cup of tea, both of us sitting at the same table that has been witness to so many deep, heart-to-heart talks between us over the years.

'Did you enjoy the holiday, darling?' you ask, evidently in one of your *pretend that everything is all right* moods.

I nod, but without looking at you. I'm looking at my teacup instead, fingering the bone china handle. You have so many lovely things in your house. Sometimes I wish I could be one of them – nurtured and cherished by you, day in day out, without any chastisement or recriminations. Just to be loved by you once again, as in days of old.

'Well, you certainly haven't got much to say for yourself.'

'Sorry, I'm just tired.'

'You're *tired?*'

I wriggle my shoulders uncomfortably.

I can see that your mood is changing. I can feel it happening. And it's all my fault, yet again. When you next speak, the transition is final.

'Do you realise you haven't even thanked me for the holiday?'

'Sorry. Thank you.' I force a smile. 'No seriously, I mean it.'

'*Thank you,*' you echo in a harsh, mocking tone.

I take a sip of tea and glance at my watch, my heart thumping wildly. 'The thing is, Mother, I've been away a whole week, and I … well, I really do need to get back to Lichfield now. So I've – if you don't mind, when I've finished this tea I'll nip upstairs to get my things together. There's a train at seven.'

You stare at me with a face that has turned to alabaster. 'You're catching a train *tonight*?'

I nod, averting my eyes.

'We've just come back from a week's holiday which has cost me five hundred pounds, and this is the thanks I get?'

'Look, I don't want to argue ...'

'You think I do? Ye gods, Leah, just listen to yourself! A *whole week*, you say. You've been away *a whole week*, as if it's been such an ordeal for you! Never mind that you spend practically every day of your life with Marek when you're in Birmingham ... you can't even bear to spend one more night with me ... not even *one more night?*' Your voice catches on a smothered sob.

'Mother, please ... '

'No, Leah, don't start with any of your excuses.' You straighten your shoulders and clear your throat, preparing to launch into one of your bitter diatribes. 'I'm going to be straight with you. Don't think for one moment that I like having to point out these unpleasant things, but I'm your mother, and if I don't do it, then who will?'

'So what sin have I committed now?'

'See what I mean? I can't say anything to you without you biting my head off.'

So I don't say anything.

You take a long sip of tea. I can see that your hand is trembling. So is mine.

You re-aim your eyes at me and launch straight into fourth gear. 'This holiday I've seen a side to you that quite frankly scares me, Leah. And I don't like it. You've barely made any effort all week long. You know how much this holiday meant to me, and all you've been bothered about is rushing back to Birmingham as soon as you can. To *him*. No, Leah, I

335

don't like it at all. From being a loving, gentle person, you've become hard, selfish and callous. You haven't shown the slightest consideration of how I might be feeling, how much you've hurt me, time and again ...' Your voice begins to wobble. 'Honest to God, I don't know how much more of this I can take ...'

And then – so suddenly that it scares me – I snap. Yes, I snap. Just like that.

Shoving my chair back from the table with a violent grate, I leap up and face you like a tigress, trembling from head to toe. '*You* don't know how much more you can take? *You* don't know? Well, then join the bloody club! I can't take another single moment of your sanctimonious, self-righteous company! *You're* the one who's selfish, not me! *You,* Mother! I've done everything to try and make you happy – *everything*! And I've had enough! I mean it! *I – have – had – ENOUGH!*'

I start sobbing, choking, losing control. I run out into the hallway, sprint all the way upstairs to my room. Slamming the door behind me, I collapse on my bed face down, wailing into the pillow, kicking my feet, thumping my fists against the wall ... oh God, it's horrible, it's truly *horrible*. I've never experienced anything like it before. I have completely lost control. I've gone temporarily insane. And you must know it too, because you don't even come up to my room to try and calm me down. You remain downstairs, well out of my way. And it's a good job you do that, Mother, because right at this moment I hate you so much, I don't know what I would've done if you'd come into my room and tried to talk to me. If there had been a knife by my bedside, I'm sure I would have used it.

In less than an hour it's all over with. I lie utterly still on my bed for some minutes, staring at the ceiling, hardly blinking, just waiting for my breathing to return to normal. When it does, I get off the bed and walk over to the sink in the corner of my room. I turn on the tap and splash cold water over my face, then lean closer to the mirror to inspect the watery battleground of my eyes. After all that crying, I don't want Marek to see me looking like some grotesque, black-and-red-eyed clown when he meets me at New Street Station in three hours' time.

Marek. The man I'm marrying in three weeks. Oh, God.

After wiping my face and re-applying a touch of mascara, I abandon the sink and pack my things as quickly as I can. Then I go back downstairs, my case thudding on each step as I lug it behind me.

You must have been waiting for me, because as soon as I reach the bottom step you emerge from the kitchen, jacket and shoes already on.

I completely ignore you as I hitch my bag over my shoulder, grab my keys from the hall table and open the front door.

'Wait,' you say in a hollow voice. 'I'm coming with you to the station.'

I shrug. I'm beyond caring now.

We leave the house together in silence. I walk in front of you all the way to the bus stop, not saying a word. We wait for the next five minutes, also in silence, and when the bus finally arrives we clamber on it, in silence.

It's only when we're standing on the lone platform of Lyneham-on-Sea railway station that you at last speak.

Looking at me with eyes that seem to bear all the grief of the world since time immemorial, you say, 'One day, Leah, one day when you have children of your own, you'll understand.'

I stare straight ahead, my eyes fixed to the rail track that stretches out into the darkening evening. 'No I won't,' I say. 'I'll never understand.'

I returned to Lichfield an emotional wreck. Worse still, I started to view Marek differently. I wanted to love him, I wanted to marry him, but I also found myself needing distance from him. Most dangerously of all, my need to see Brother Matthew again was returning with a vengeance that terrified me. It was as though that gruelling eight-day holiday, followed by my mini-breakdown in Lyneham, had released some dark forces within me, like a drug addiction that was coming back full-force.

I couldn't stop thinking about Matthew, couldn't stop seeing him, everywhere – in the kitchen, on the sofa in the sitting room, in my bedroom, in Marek's house, even at school. Once, when I'd just finished a lesson and let the kids out, I saw a shadow by the door so I looked round. Lo and behold, there was Matthew, arms folded, smiling at me as he leaned against the door post, just as he had done on my first trip to Greystones when he'd secretly been listening to my piano playing. 'Matthew!' I cried out, and he laughed, stepping towards me and taking me in his arms. 'You have a wonderful way with the children,' he murmured into my ear, pushing away my hair … but then the invasive grate of giggling broke the spell, and I reopened my eyes just in time to see a gaggle of pupils scurrying away down the corridor, ranting, '*Miss Crazy Cavanagh!*' I didn't care. I was beyond caring.

I knew I had to see him once more. Just once more, before I got married. Just to exorcise him. Convince myself I was over him. After all, marriage was a huge step. Once I was a married woman I certainly wouldn't be able to see him again, would I? This was my last chance to indulge in a little nostalgic dreaming at the very least.

And so, over the coming week my secret plan to go back to Greystones materialised. You were the only other person who knew about it. Marek certainly didn't know, and neither did Brother Matthew, because I booked myself into the Gatehouse under the pseudonym of *Mrs Cope*. That was your idea. You'd randomly selected the name of one of your guests at Belle Vue. It meant that neither Father Sebastian nor Brother Matthew would realise who I was when they saw my booking, or what my ulterior motives were – not that I myself was sure what they were. But in a way, it didn't matter. The very act of sharing my furtive plans with you meant that the two of us could at last grow closer again. I could obliterate that awful falling-out we'd had, put Marek out of my mind, and start, tentatively, to rebuild our mother-daughter relationship.

We discussed what you should say to Marek in case he phoned over the weekend – which he almost certainly would do – and we also arranged for me to stop overnight at Lyneham on my way to and from Greystones. It would meaning missing school, but we'd planned that, too. My migraines would be to blame. Our mutual secret made the guilt worthwhile. But most worthwhile of all was the prospect of seeing Brother Matthew again, after three years of unrequited dreams.

And so it was that one Friday afternoon in July, just two weeks before my wedding to Marek, I caught the train to York and from there the bus to Greystones Abbey. I was going to see Matthew again.

It was really happening.

VESPERS

For some we loved, the loveliest and the best
That from his Vintage rolling Time has prest.
Have drunk their Cup a Round or two before,
And one by one crept silently to rest.

Rubaiyat of Omar Khayyam, v. 22

CHAPTER TWENTY-ONE

1

So here I am, on the bus to Greystones. The sheep-scattered hills and picture-book villages are gliding past the window on this mild summer evening, as are my troubled thoughts. Bitter-sweet memories gate-crash the pastoral views, making it difficult to focus on the task at hand. I'm hoping that Marek's loving visage in my mind's eye will throw a bucket of cold water over all leftover romantic fantasies, once I arrive at the Gatehouse. But the trouble is, Marek's visage is now blurred and confused, and my mind's eye insists on honing in on just one face, which most definitely is not my fiancé's.

The bus pulls to a halt. I climb down the steps onto the rough pavement. I'm not lumbered with my guitar, because this is only going to be a short visit. I don't intend to sit by the window in my room strumming chords and gazing out at the horizon; neither do I intend to accompany any folk hymn sessions. There isn't time for that. I have just one purpose in mind on this visit: to see him again and, hopefully, to be cured once and for all. He'll be thirty-two now. The whole thing should have been nipped in the bud all of five years ago, when I first met him. *You* should have nipped it in the bud, Mother. I couldn't be blamed for dreaming, back then. But you could.

I make my way through the early evening stillness towards the entrance to the monastery grounds. The Gatehouse swings into view as I turn off the country road and head up the driveway. Reaching the villa, I push open the front door and step inside. A sepulchral hush immediately greets me. Placing my bags on the floor, I walk over to the noticeboard and check the guest list to find which room I've been placed in. I have mixed feelings when I see that it's the attic room. They probably squeezed me in there because it was a late booking. Or is it an omen?

Unwilling to dwell on such thoughts, I scoop up my bags and head towards the stairs.

* * *

One hour later, showered and changed, I go back downstairs. It's 7.30, suppertime, which means that any moment now I'm likely to see him again.

Taking a deep breath, I push open the door to the refectory.

The room is full, buzzing with the hum of small talk and the clinking of cutlery upon plates. I spot a free place at the nearest table and walk over to it. As soon as I sit down, all four diners greet me warmly. Within seconds I've been introduced to people whose names I know I will never remember. I smile and make appropriate replies. They explain where they're from and ask me where I'm from. After a while we all start talking about Greystones, and soon it's revealed that the spare seat beside me is where the Warden of the Gatehouse normally sits.

When I ask if the Warden is still Father Sebastian, the middle-aged lady opposite me says in a plummy accent, 'No, Father Sebastian retired last year. He's been transferred to another Abbey. Somewhere down south, I believe.'

'So who's the Warden now?' I ask, forcing composure into my voice.

'Father Matthew,' the bespectacled man sitting to my right says. 'As a matter of fact, he should be here any minute now.'

As though on cue, the door to the refectory opens, and …

Oh God. I wasn't prepared for this. Oh God oh God oh God …

I quickly look down at my soup dish. But it's too late. It's him. Brother Matthew. Or rather, *Father* Matthew. He's a priest now. So they got him in the end.

'Ah, Father Matthew!' the middle-aged lady calls to him with a jolly smile. 'We have a newcomer tonight –' she looks at me, 'Sorry, what did you say your name was?'

'Leah.'

At last I raise my eyes to him. We look at each other. Not a word comes out of either of our mouths. Dare I say *time stands still*? He hasn't changed at all. No, that's a lie. He's even more devastating than I remember. There I go again. Oh, the clichés of love!

And then, finally, he speaks. To me. With an ill-concealed frown on his face. 'So – you're Mrs Cope?'

I nod. But still don't say a word. I'm sure the other guests must notice.

'Do sit down, Father Matthew,' an elderly lady at our table says, beaming up at him. Evidently he's just as popular as ever.

His hesitation is palpable. 'Er – no, I'm afraid I've been called away. There's something ... someone at the monastery I need to see.'

He's bullshitting. It might not be immediately apparent to anyone else, but it sure as hell is to me. I look down at my soup again.

My table companions try to detain him a bit longer; but without further ado he bids his farewell, turns his back on us, and leaves the room.

For the next few moments conversation is consumed by the topic of Father Matthew: why he appeared to be so distracted, why he didn't join us for supper, what could have been so urgent as to have called him away ... I can't bear it anymore. I just can't bear it.

Pushing my chair back with an unintentional screech, I stand up, mumble some excuse about a migraine coming on, and make my exit from the room.

As soon as I'm out of earshot I run all the way down the corridor towards the entrance, fling open the door and rush out into the cool evening. It's barely been a minute since he left, so hopefully he hasn't got too far. Squinting into the twilight, I spot him in the distance. He's nearing the bottom of the hill, approaching the monks' entrance to the monastery.

I start racing down the path. '*Matthew!*' I call out breathlessly, still running until I finally reach his side. Then I stop. So does he. We face each other in a fusion of fear and hostility.

'What are you doing here, Leah?'

'Matthew, *please* don't look at me like that! I don't want to – I mean -'

'So what do you want? What could you possibly hope to achieve by coming back here, after –' Now it's his turn to falter. At least he's facing me the whole time, not avoiding eye contact.

'Look, you've no need to worry,' I say, determined to keep a steady voice. 'I'm engaged to be married. I made up the name Mrs Cope, to distract you. The wedding's very soon, so I – I just needed to come here one last time, to have a complete break from all the pre-wedding nerves. And to have a spiritual boost.'

After a marked pause, he says a hollow, 'Congratulations.'

'What for?'

'Getting married. I'm very happy for you. Truly I am.'

'Well, my mother sure as hell isn't. That's one reason I came back to Greystones. I needed to … for God's sake, Matthew …'

'It's *Father* Matthew now, as a matter of fact.'

This is not going well. 'Yes, I noticed. So you finally gave in.'

He looks away.

'Matthew, please – don't shut me out.'

He winces at this, then turns his head back to me and views me in unveiled dismay. 'What did you expect, Leah? I'm not too proud about the way we parted last time you were here.'

'And neither am I! But that's not why I'm here now, you *have* to believe me. I just need to talk to you … I'm so confused about everything – the wedding, my future - please, Matthew, can't we talk later on? After Compline? Couldn't you come to my room -'

'*No.*'

I shudder at the determination in his voice.

'I'm sorry, Leah, I just don't see how I can help. If you need to talk to someone, I can put you in touch with another priest.'

'I don't want another priest. You know that.'

344

'Then you'll have to make do with praying. We've got plenty of space for that here.'

I'm beginning to realise that I've very likely wasted a whole lot of time, effort and emotion on a totally fruitless journey. I should never have come. And suddenly, my mind is made up. I am not going to stand here and beg. I have not stooped that low yet. I hope I never will.

I nod at him, turn round, and start walking away.

After a mere handful of seconds he calls out, 'Leah – wait!'

I stop walking, and face him once again.

He's looking at me with an expression I can't decipher for all the tea in China. 'Okay then, we can talk. But not in your room.'

'Where then?'

'Wait for me in the common room. I'll come up after Compline. Just for half an hour, no more.'

'Thank you,' I say, then head back up the hill.

2

I'm in the Gatehouse common room, sitting on a leather sofa that faces the window. It's quarter to ten at night and he still hasn't arrived. All the guests must have gone to bed, I presume, because I can't hear a thing. Evidently they're not into partying into the small hours. Through a gap in the partially drawn curtains I can see the moon. The moon was also out in full on that other, fated night.

The sound of footsteps upon gravel interrupts my reverie. Someone is approaching the Gatehouse, stepping inside the entrance. Catching my breath, I turn my head from the window and look at the door. There's a moment's silence, then the footsteps move across the hallway towards the common room. The door opens, and at last his form looms into view.

'Leah.'

He says my name, just like that. I try to smile but can't. My face is locked in a paralysis of anticipation. We continue to look at each other, neither of us able to utter a word.

At last I snap out of my paralysis. Standing up, I say to him in rushed words, 'Matthew – I'm sorry, but I lied to you earlier on.'

'What?'

'I lied to you.'

'Yes, I heard. But what do you mean, you lied to me?'

'It isn't pre-wedding nerves. It's pre-wedding *doubts*. Oh, God, Matthew, I've missed you *so* much …' Both my hands shoot up to my mouth in a futile attempt to stop the huge, gulping sob that I can feel rising from deep within my throat. I screw my eyes tight. But it's no use. Now my shoulders are shaking, and out gushes the sob. Having lost the battle, I start crying uncontrollably; crying for the years of longing and frustration and hopes that have been dashed again and again. But most of all, I'm crying because I know without the shadow of a doubt that I still love him, and always will.

Through the sounds of my grief I hear him walk over to me, feel him take me in his arms. He pushes my hair away from my damp face, whispers to me, 'Leah, don't cry – I've missed you too, you've no idea how much ...'

Raising my chin, he kisses me, tentatively at first, but growing in confidence as my own lips part and my arms coil themselves round his neck. I push my body closer to his and he immediately responds with a violent shudder, drawing me closer still, squeezing me so hard I can hardly breathe. I don't want to breathe; I want to stay trapped in his embrace forever, no longer having to worry about our volatile future. *Now* is all that matters, here, in the arms of the man I love. It's as though we've stepped into one of the countless dreams that have visited me ever since I first met him. Only this isn't a dream – how could a dream possibly cope with this level of passion?

But we can't stay here forever. We can't even stay here a moment longer. What if someone comes into the common room?

Pulling myself out of his arms, I grab his hand and lead him towards the door. We step out into the corridor and tiptoe up the stairs, me in front, still clutching his hand behind me. There is no way I am letting him go now!

At last we reach the attic. Before going inside, he turns me round to face him. We kiss again, my back jammed against the door, my thighs and stomach pressed against his trembling body. I free one hand just long enough to flick open the door handle that's jabbing into the small of my back. As soon as it opens we stumble into the room and somehow, amid our frenzied kissing and groping, we manage to stagger through the darkness over to the double bed under the eaves.

Thrusting me down onto the quilt, he murmurs, '*Leah* ...'

I moan as he pushes up my T-shirt and bra so that he can kiss each nipple in turn, lingering over my exposed flesh, lowering his head to kiss my stomach, struggling with the zip on my jeans ...

I'm sorry, but this is where I have to stop. All the details – *all* of them – are in safe-keeping in my diary, exactly where they belong, just for me alone.

3

I awake to the dull light of early morning. It takes a while for me to draw myself out of a dream in which I'm lying in Brother Matthew's arms after a night of urgent love-making. By the time my consciousness is fully reactivated, I suffer that horrid moment of knowing that reality will never, ever match that kind of wonder, that beauty, that fulfilment.

And suddenly, I'm hit by a second awakening. I reach out my hand to touch his body. The warmth of his flesh beside mine reassures me that this is no dream. He's right here, next to me, his eyes closed, his breathing light and regular. He was there when we fell asleep just a few hours ago in the aftermath of our sexual heat, and he's still here now, in the fragile light of dawn.

I smile to myself in a moment of pure happiness. 'Matthew,' I say, gently shaking his shoulder.

He stirs.

'*Matthew,*' I say again, a little louder, pulling myself into a sitting position.

Turning his head, he opens his eyes.

'I think you ought to get up,' I whisper, though I don't know why. Who's going to disturb us all the way up here in this secluded room?

And then he sits up with a jolt. For a moment I fear he's going to kick away the quilt, spring out of bed, yank on his scattered clothes and flee the room, leaving me to cope with my heart-ache all over again.

But he doesn't. He just looks at me, fully awake now. Glancing at his watch, he says, 'I have to go. It'll be Matins in ten minutes.'

'I know.' I lean closer to him and rest my head on his shoulder. *Sod Matins* is what I'm thinking.

'Leah, I can't miss Matins. They'd notice if I did. I really do have to go.'

'I'm not stopping you.'

'Good.' He pulls himself away and climbs out of the bed.

Some deeply ingrained sense of modesty urges me to look away as he reaches for his discarded cassock: the garment that converts him into a monk once again. By the time I turn my eyes back to him, the transition is complete. He's fully dressed, all in black save the white priest's collar round his neck. He's looking at me with an unfathomable expression in his deep-blue eyes.

'Well then … I expect I'll see you later.' There's a new edge to his voice. The cassock has apparently transformed more than his outward appearance.

The hairs on my skin bristle in panic. I can't lose him again, I just can't. 'Matthew – you will come back, won't you?'

'Yes, I'll come back. But I don't know when. You have to be patient.'

'How patient?'

'I don't know. I need time to think.' He turns round and heads for the door. But before opening it he glances over his shoulder and throws me a look that is already not quite the same as it was minutes earlier, when he just woke up. 'I'll find you later.'

'Do you promise?'

'Yes, I promise. Please don't come looking for me.'

He opens the door and steps out onto the landing. The soft watercolour of dawn filters through the skylight and encircles his head in a halo.

I listen to the sound of his footsteps fading away down the stairs. *Please let him come back, please let him come back …*

The remainder of that morning was nothing short of torture.

I stayed in my attic room during Matins and Lauds. I couldn't bring myself to go down to the monastery and face the wrath of the elusive God who I didn't fully believe in, yet who nonetheless had the power to reduce me to a quaking bag of guilt. But I did go to the refectory for breakfast, hoping to see Matthew. He wasn't there. Neither did I see him at lunch. By this time I was at my wits' end, knowing that this was my last day, that tomorrow I'd be heading back for Lyneham and, more to the point, to Marek, who at this moment seemed as far away from me as the other side of the world.

As the chilly morning metamorphosed into a warm, summer-scented afternoon, I knew with growing certainty that I did not love Marek and would never marry him. There was only one man I had ever loved, and would ever love. You were right, Mother, as always. I'd rather remain single for the rest of my life, nourished by memories and dreams, than be forced into a second-best marriage that would barely keep my soul alive.

After lunch, while I was drying up the dishes that Joelly handed to me one by one, I found myself filled with a sharp rush of envy. It wasn't fair that she should be allowed to live here, so close to Matthew, while I was trapped far away in the real world of events that had nothing to do with my own choice. The supposed free will that God grants us all. *What* bloody free will?

'You look a bit peeked, love,' she said to me with a glance that was a cross between pity and curiosity. 'Are you all right?'

'I'm fine,' I said too quickly, then made it worse by adding, 'I don't suppose you've seen Father Matthew, have you?'

She switched off the tap and turned to me. 'Oh, lovey. You're still sweet on him, aren't you?'

Instantly I froze. 'Of course not. As a matter of fact, I'm engaged to be married.'

'Really?' For a moment she looked floored. 'Well ... how lovely. Congratulations.' As I didn't reply, she went on in forced joviality, 'So what are your plans for the afternoon?'

'I thought I might go on a walk to the lakes.'

'Ah yes, it's the perfect day for that. Just mind you don't get lost now.'

I hadn't even thought about what I'd do all afternoon, but now that I'd mentioned the lakes, I realised it was a good idea. What else was I going to do? Hang around the Gatehouse in the hope that he'd turn up? Sit by my attic window, waiting until I spotted his distant form heading up the hill from the monastery? And then what? Wait for his next move? What if there *was* no next move?

No, there wasn't any point in wasting a single moment more. I'd had enough waiting to last me a lifetime.

5

The walk to the lakes gave my thoughts time to calm down. Since waking up in the early morning and facing the unbelievable reality of Brother Matthew lying beside me in bed, I hadn't had the chance to stop and think. Now, as I strolled down the country road that led away from the Abbey, my mood changed yet again. Now I was feeling calm. Rational. Despite the uncertain future that loomed ahead, I was contented. And who wouldn't be, on a warm summer's afternoon such as this? The birds filled the air with their virtuosic arias, accompanied by the occasional discordant moo from a nearby cow; the po-faced sheep ba'ad at me as they safely grazed, the intermittent butterfly fluttered past in a rainbow splash of colour, and the wooded hills stretched out far and wide, obscuring those tranquil, elusive lakes. Somehow, the thought of their still shores, so well-shielded from the public eye, acted like a sedative.

After about forty minutes I reached the first lake, which is the one where Matthew and I had walked to when I was just nineteen. Now I was twenty-three, older but hardly any wiser. Still in love with the same man. But now there was a difference. Now I was convinced that he must love me too. Why else would he have broken his vows? He once explained to me how long it took a new entrant to become an official part of the Community. First you were a postulant for six months, then a novice for a year, then a junior for a further two years, then you took your first set of vows for three years, and finally, you took your solemn vows for life. Brother Matthew had been a fully-fledged part of the Benedictine community for fourteen years, and here I was, turning his world upside down. I could almost feel sorry for him, when I looked at it like that. He'd never asked me to disrupt his life; I just kept ploughing straight back into it, whether he liked it or not. But this time it was different. This time there was no running away from what had happened, unless he was a total and utter coward. This time he would have to face things one way or another, whether he wanted to or not. He had to choose between his God and me. One of us was going to have to be let down.

I veered off the country lane to the left, taking a narrower path that led into the forest. Here I was in another world entirely. Where just a few moments ago there'd been warmth, birdsong and pastel skies, now everything was in shade. A jungle of undergrowth and soaring treetops surrounded me, only occasionally punctuated by thin shafts of sunlight that flitted in and out of the tangled canopy.

I made my way through the thicket of brambles and twigs towards the bench that was just a few feet away from the lakeside. The same bench that Matthew and I had sat on once before. I remembered it so clearly: how Father Sebastian had passed us on the road shortly after we'd set off from the Abbey, and how self-conscious Matthew had been for the rest of our walk. But now Father Sebastian was out of the picture, Matthew had taken his place as Warden of the Gatehouse, and there was no one to advise him against going on walks with wicked sirens. The thought brought a smile to my face as I watched a ripple of sunlight dance upon the water.

After I'd been sitting on the bench for about ten minutes, I heard the rustling of leaves.

'Leah?'

I spun round, but already I knew it was him. He was standing uncertainly amongst the trees and brambles, wearing ordinary jeans, T-shirt and trainers, and looking at me with an indecipherable expression. Was it anticipation? Regret? Guilt?

'You knew where to find me, then,' I said, clutching onto the arm of the bench.

'I came looking for you after lunch. Joelly told me where you'd gone.' His frown deepened. 'Did you say anything to her?'

'No, of course not.'

'It's okay, don't worry. I just thought she seemed …'

'What?'

'I don't know, maybe I'm imagining things.'

He walked over to the bench and sat down beside me, staring straight ahead. For some moments neither of us spoke. I stole a glance at his profile. The emotional turmoil he was going through was clearly etched on his puckered forehead.

At last he broke the silence, his voice heavy with more things in heaven and earth than I could ever have dreamed of.

'Oh, Leah, what have we done? Where in the world do we go from here?'

So he too was thinking of the future, using the word 'we'. Not avoiding it altogether, like last time. Here he was, right now, right by my side, referring to a future which might include *us*.

I looked straight at him. 'My heart's an open book, Matthew. It's time you showed me yours.'

I had to wait a good few seconds for his reply. 'All I've only ever known is this,' he said. 'My life amongst the Benedictines. Castle Leeming at eight, Greystones at thirteen. How could I live any other way? How could I?'

'I don't know,' I said, trying to fight this sinking feeling in my gut. 'Unless -'

A sudden stillness hung over us.

'Unless what?'

I braced myself. 'Unless you love someone so much, you just know there's no other way. That life will never be complete if you can't be with that person.'

A ray of sunshine broke through the latticed pattern of trees. Feeling I had nothing to lose, I leaned closer to him and kissed him on the cheek. Placing my hand on the side of his head, I turned him towards me so that I could transfer my kiss to his mouth, cautiously at first, but steadily gaining in confidence as his lips responded to mine. I wrapped my leg over his thigh, moving closer still, so close that I knew, within moments, there'd be no turning back.

There wasn't.

* * *

The walk back to Greystones wasn't easy. I wanted to hold his hand, put my arm round his waist – anything to reaffirm what had just taken place between us. Last night could have been a one-off outburst of desire; today was different. He had come looking for me – I hadn't asked him to accompany me to the lakes – and although he hadn't pledged to love me till the end of his days, at least he hadn't claimed that he *didn't* love me. As we made our way back towards the Abbey, every now and then he turned to look at me, as I did at him, and we half-smiled at each other. We couldn't hold hands or walk arm in arm, but there was a silent communion between us. Something in the air had changed.

Half an hour later we were back in the monastery grounds, standing on the driveway at the point where our paths separated: mine to go up the hill to the Gatehouse, Matthew's to escape to the sanctity of the cloister.

He looked directly at me before we parted. 'Leah, I need time to digest all this.'

I nodded, biting my lip.

'But I want you to know I'm not running away from it; I just have to think things through. I suggest you do the same. We both need a bit of space between us before we decide what's the best course of action to take.'

'You sound like a bloody counsellor.'

He winced at this. 'I'm sorry, but I can't say any more now. I promise I'll be in touch as soon as I can.'

'Do you *really* promise that?'

'Of course I do. I'm a man of my word. You have to trust me. I'll write to you as soon as – as soon as I can collect my thoughts.'

'Have I really had such a devastating effect on you?'

He didn't reply to this; just frowned at some invisible point in the distance.

'Sorry, I didn't mean to be flippant,' I said.

'It's okay.' When he turned his eyes back to me, I was alarmed to see the amount of pain in them. 'Leah, I *do* care for you,' he said in a quieter voice, 'But this isn't easy. Please be patient. In the meantime, I promise to keep you in my heart and prayers.'

'Oh God, this is beginning to sound like a goodbye.'

'I'm afraid it is. At least for now.'

'But I'm not going back home yet. I still have all this evening – and then there's supper, and tonight we could …'

'*No.* We need time apart to reflect. Please don't try and persuade me otherwise.'

'Okay, okay, I won't! Jesus, what do you think I am?'

'Sorry. I didn't mean -'

'It's all right. Neither did I.'

Before parting we stood opposite one another for a few moments more, looking into each other's eyes as though it might be the last time we'd ever meet.

But of course it wasn't.

6

When I went back to Lichfield I knew that my life would never be the same again. I knew that I couldn't be with Marek anymore; that he had been a passing episode in my life, whereas now I was waiting for my *real* life to begin. I knew that I had to go on a different journey from the one I'd taken thus far. There could be no more lies, no more self-delusion, only truth.

For almost two weeks I struggled to maintain a semblance of normality in my life, while waiting each day for the postman to bring a letter from Matthew. And when each day came and went and there was still no letter, I felt like curling up into a ball and dying. My phone calls to you were a great help to me at that time. You had far more optimism than me, being the incurable romantic that you are. You felt convinced that everything would work out in the end, that Matthew and I would come to our senses in a way that you and Peter Fox never did, and that we'd end up living happily ever after. You urged me to keep on hoping and believing, and that's exactly what I did. Thank you for your faith, Mother.

And then one fragrant July morning, just a handful of days before the wedding, the postman finally delivered a letter from Matthew. I was in the kitchen clearing away my breakfast things when I heard the clank of the letter box. Immediately I hurried into the hallway. When I saw the familiar handwriting on the white envelope lying on the floor, I could hardly breathe. My hands trembled as I stooped to pick it up and tore it open.

Dearest Leah,

I've had the chance to do some thinking over the past couple of weeks, as I hope you yourself have. Would you be able to meet me in York next Saturday? I've checked the train times from Birmingham New Street, and there's one that arrives in York at 12.30. I could meet you at the station by the main entrance. Please let me know if this is convenient for you.

Yours, Matthew

7

I'm at York Railway Station.

I've just got off the train from Birmingham and made my way to the main entrance, where we agreed to meet. My train arrived twenty minutes late and I'm panicking that he won't have waited for me. But he's a monk – an honourable, reliable, ethical person – surely he's hardly likely to dump me without even turning up to tell me so? No, he *will* be there, I know it. But what I don't know is how he'll be with me, what he'll say, what the expression in his eyes will be like as we greet each other. Another, less rational part of me is thinking, if he really is so honourable, reliable and ethical, then surely he wouldn't have broken his vows in the first place by making love to me? By doing that, he's let down his God. He's been unfaithful. So who's to say he won't be unfaithful again? – by not turning up, for instance, and afterwards just sending me a cowardly note saying, *Sorry, but I've had second thoughts.* But what were his *first* thoughts? Did he have any at all, or was our outbreak of passion nothing more than that – just a brief sexual explosion that he had no control over? And since that time, what if he's regained control? What if he now wants to meet me merely in order to apologise, beg forgiveness, explain that what happened between us was an aberration and could never happen again?

As soon as I step outside the station into the light drizzle, I spot him. He's standing a few feet away from the main entrance, holding a large black umbrella, wearing an anorak and jeans and looking like any ordinary guy. Except that this is no ordinary guy.

Tucking my hair behind my ears, I walk straight up to him. 'Hello.'

He smiles at me. I wish he wouldn't. I wish he'd throw me a tortured, haunted look. 'Hello, Leah. How are you?'

'Fine, thanks.'

Neither of us says anything for the next few moments. Not in words, anyway. Our eyes are trapped in a gaze that neither of us is prepared to relinquish. We've tripped into a time bubble where words are redundant.

But time resumes its tick, and eventually he says, 'Shall we find a café? Are you hungry?'

'No, but a coffee would be nice.'

'Okay, splendid. Well then, there's a nice little place near the Minster we could try.'

'Sounds fine by me.'

'Good. So then ... shall we go?'

We start walking away from the station. I haven't brought an umbrella, as it was perfectly dry this morning. So we walk together, both of us huddled under his big black umbrella but somehow managing not to touch each other. Not even the faintest brushing of shoulders. He's being careful. Very careful. Polite, dutiful, and careful. For the thousandth time since first meeting him, my heart sinks.

Five minutes later we're sitting opposite each other in an old, low-beamed café on a narrow medieval street within spitting distance of York Minster. I think it's called *The Pot & Kettle,* or something like that. The room is filling up with people trying to escape the rain, shaking out umbrellas as they step inside and glance around for a free table. We were lucky to get one by the window. Our steaming coffees are in front of us, but neither of us has yet taken a sip. All the time we keep glancing at each other, on the brink of saying something that could change our lives forever, but not having the courage to say it.

Until, at long, long last, he does say it. 'Leah – I have something to tell you.'

I daren't reply. This is worse than awaiting the results of a piano competition. Far, far worse. It's the most excruciating waiting I shall ever have to experience in my life.

'Your mother wrote to me.'

My eyes widen at him. 'My mother *wrote* to you?'

He nods. 'But don't be alarmed. She meant well. In fact, I'm glad she wrote to me. Very glad.'

'But *why*? What on earth did she say?'

'It's not so much what she said, but rather, what she did.'

'Sorry ... what exactly are you getting at?'

'She sent me a copy of some extracts from your diaries.'

My mouth drops open. 'She did *what*?'

My God, Mother, what in the world have you done? That's what I'm thinking, right at this moment, in *ye olde* medieval café that's sheltering us from the rain.

He leans forward. 'Leah, I swear I never would have known how deeply you felt for me. I always thought that your feelings were nothing more than a schoolgirl fantasy which you hadn't yet managed to outgrow. I was always convinced you were just caught up with the *idea* of being in love with a monk, rather than the reality of loving the real me. That's what I always thought. Even after we'd ...'

'Made love.'

He nods. 'Yes. But your diaries – they paint a completely different picture. They've enabled me to see – to understand – the real *you*. And your feelings for me.'

I'm still reeling under the shock of what he's telling me. I still can't believe that you've stoop so low as to actually copy out extracts from my diaries and *send* them to him! I'm also madly regretting that I ever left the bloody things in my bedroom at Lyneham rather than took them with me to my cottage in Lichfield. But as he continues to look at me, I begin to calm down. Slowly, I begin to realise that your outrageous actions might well prove to be the best thing you ever did. Because now he's looking at me in a way he's never looked at me before. Not with desire, not with fear or guilt or regret, not with tortured longing, but with ... how can I describe it? With understanding? With relief? With a new-born confidence?

And I realise, in a warm rush of replenished love for you, that once again your sixth sense has proved right.

'Leah,' he continues, taking my hands in his, 'Do you think we could possibly – just *possibly* – make this work?'

I don't even hesitate in my answer. 'No, I don't think so,' I say, enjoying the fleeting spark of anguish in his eyes. 'I don't think we could make it work.' Then I lean across the table towards him and add in a voice that is trembling with joy, 'I *know* we could make it work.'

CHAPTER TWENTY-TWO

1

I'm no longer in my damp Lichfield cottage. It's no longer the night before my wedding to Marek. I'm with Matthew now. In Cumbria, at Derwent Lodge.

So was this when my life began? Was it when Matthew and I decided to follow the path of our hearts rather than our obligations? Was I wrong in calling off the wedding to Marek at the last minute? Almost as last-minute as it gets? But at least I didn't run away from the altar, as they so often do in films. At least I phoned Marek early in the morning, and offered to pay my share of all our cancelled bookings - reception, church service, invitations, Order of Services and God knows what else. He thought I was joking at first. When he realised I wasn't, he tried to persuade me with every trick of the trade to come back to my senses. And when, finally, he could see that there was no turning back, he spat out a machine-gun battery of swear-words into the receiver, made a choking kind of sound, said an agonising *'Leah, what have you DONE?'* and hung up.

I phoned you next, Mother. I can't even begin to tell you the relief I felt in hearing the joy in your voice. The two of us at last reconnected.

Of course I felt terrible about Marek. Of *course* I did. But hey, who doesn't get their turn to suffer sooner or later in life? And anyway, what about Matthew? He must have suffered as well. Unless you've been a priest, I don't suppose it's possible to understand the psychological turmoil that goes on in your heart when you fall in love with a woman and want to marry her, yet at the same time still feel committed to the God you dedicated your life to many years earlier.

We had to wait two years before getting married. That was the hardest bit. All we managed to scrounge for ourselves was a handful of hours during the occasional day-trip to York, and lots and lots of letters. That's how we kept our feelings alive. No sex, just love and faith in each other, and plenty of enforced patience. Of course Matthew could just have left the monastery and married me regardless, but he wasn't that kind of person. He had to seek dispensation from the Church, and when he finally received it through all the formal processes, he explained to me that as he'd been ordained a priest he would always remain a priest, even though he'd broken his vow of celibacy in order to lead the life of a married man. I tried to understand, but it was hard. So was I married to a priest, then? In a way that suited me fine, because it meant there'd always be that special, forbidden part of him that had been so compelling since I first met him. It's who he was; the man I fell in love with and was now married to, and I would always cherish that part of him.

Our wedding was a modest affair, certainly not the kind of wedding most girls dream of. Of course you were there, your eyes brimming with happiness throughout the day. A couple of Matthew's old brethren from Greystones also appeared, determined to stand by him even though the whole affair in their eyes was very sad, rather like a divorce from the Benedictine Community.

The wedding service was held in a small church in Lyneham. I wore a white satin dress with a high neck and low waist and a veil that reached the floor, creating rather a medieval effect. I knew that I made a beautiful bride. The photographs we have from that day reflect my radiance. Matthew was drop-dead gorgeous in his grey morning suit and tails, which were provided by his doting grandmother. As we uttered the solemn words to one another by the altar, I was reminded of my former dreams in the summer of 1980, when I had imagined this very same scene in the small Catholic church in Greystones village. It was too good to be true, and yet it *was* true. When the priest pronounced us man and wife and Matthew lifted the front of my veil to kiss me, and then we walked down the aisle as Mr and Mrs Haddon, I felt that my life was now complete.

We spent our honeymoon at the lake-view manor house where Matthew's grandmother had lived all her life: that hilltop haven deep in Cumbria, with rambling roses and clematis climbing up the white-washed walls, and drooping willow trees at the front that hid us from the narrow road. The wooden veranda at the back of the house overlooked the terraced garden that meandered its way down to the shores of Derwent Water, and was every bit as divine as Matthew had described it to me. I couldn't believe I was now sitting on the very same wicker chairs that he had told me about; the same spot where he and his grandmother had sat during that life-changing conversation he'd had with her when he was sixteen and told her he wanted to become a monk.

On the first morning of our married life we woke up together in the master bedroom at the back of the house. As we lay in each other's arms, gazing out of the bay window with its panoramic views of the Cumbrian hills, we found ourselves musing over the uncanny course of events that had consumed our lives ever since we met.

'So when did you first realise you loved me?' I asked, almost shyly.

He squeezed my arm. 'I've often wondered about that myself. Maybe it was the first time I heard you playing the piano in the music room at Greystones, when you didn't know I was there? Maybe that was the moment I realised there was more to this lovely girl than a pretty face.' He squeezed me again and kissed the top of my head. 'What about you? When did you realise that your feelings for me were more than a schoolgirl fantasy?'

I smiled longingly – no, not longingly. I was his wife, Mrs Haddon, and we would be together for the rest of our lives. No need to long for anything anymore. 'Probably on my first night at Greystones,' I murmured contentedly. 'I had a migraine and was sitting by the open window in my room when you walked past. You looked up at me and smiled, and at that moment, I think I somehow knew.'

He laughed. 'But it was dark – you could hardly have seen me properly. And you didn't have a clue who I was.'

'All the same, I knew that something special had happened. I never had that same feeling with any other boyfriend, ever.'

And it was true, Mother. You were right all the way along. We had conspired with love and fate, and moulded them both to our heart's desire.

2

Matthew and I started married life in a small flat in York. By this time I'd given up my post at St Alban's in Lichfield, and Matthew had secured a job at a private Catholic boys' school in central York, teaching Latin and RE. Very quickly I managed to build up a private piano teaching practice – a meagre income which was supplemented by giving the occasional recital.

Matthew settled relatively well into his new job, but he'd been accustomed to the silence of the countryside from an early age and found it difficult to adjust to the noise of urban life. Although our city-centre flat had a view of York Minster, with its medieval towers dominating a cluster of ecclesiastic buildings, there was no garden, no greenery, no distant wooded horizon to gaze at, and soon I realised that it must have resembled a prison to him. My priest-husband needed his hills, to which he could lift up his eyes and gain his strength.

The death of Matthew's grandmother came like a gift from God. Despite his grief over her loss – something I dared not tread upon – it soon became apparent that new possibilities were in the air. And so, late one evening as we sat cuddled up on the sofa, I decided to broach my burgeoning idea with him.

'Matthew,' I said, resting my head on his shoulder.

'Hmm?'

'I've been thinking.'

He laughed softly. 'Okay, I can see that you're dying to tell me something. I'm all ears.'

I snuggled up closer. 'Well, you know your grandmother's house that she left you in her will?'

'I should hope so. We spent our honeymoon there, I seem to remember – unless that was a dream?'

Ignoring him, I pushed straight on: 'Didn't you say she sometimes rented rooms to help with the upkeep of the house?'

He paused, then said a touch cagily, 'What exactly are you getting at?'

'Well … couldn't we do that? You and me?'

'Do what?'

'Couldn't we rent it out? Make it into a Bed & Breakfast place?' I pulled myself out of his arms and sat up straight. 'No, don't look at me like that. Just think about it for a minute. It's got six bedrooms, right?'

He nodded.

'And it's got a spectacular view of Derwent Water from the back, also right?'

'You know it has.'

'And at the front it's got a gorgeous mature garden, well hidden from the road. Don't you see? – it could be the *ideal* beauty spot for tourists who love rambling in the countryside, or who just want to get away from it all. I've been brought up in this kind of business, so I know what I'm talking about. In fact, I've had the perfect training. I can cook a pretty impressive full English breakfast.'

'You can indeed.'

'And you'd make a *totally* charismatic landlord – I mean, just look at you!' He laughed, but I went straight on. Maybe you could even give the occasional retreat, like you did at Greystones. We could market it as a Catholic Retreat House in the wilds of Cumbria – you know, for sixth form groups and all that sort of thing. If two guests slept in each bedroom and we kept one bedroom for ourselves, we could have groups of up to ten. So what do you think?'

At first all he said was, 'Phew!' But later on, as we began to discuss my plan in more detail, it soon became apparent that he liked the idea.

And that was that. Within twelve months we'd resigned from our respective teaching jobs in York, and moved to Derwent Water to set up our own guest house. And as if that wasn't enough happiness to last a lifetime, I now found myself pregnant.

Derwent Lodge. That's what we called the old manor house that Matthew had inherited. We put our hearts and souls into converting it into a B&B, something that was made possible thanks to Matthew's grandmother leaving all her worldly goods to her beloved grandson. Had he not left the monastery, everything would have gone to Greystones – a fact I'm sure can't have made him too popular with his former Abbot.

We worked hard to make a success of the business. It was a true labour of love. Even after our baby daughter was born – Grace, named after Matthew's grandmother – I continued to change beds, cook breakfasts and clean the entire house on a regular basis, leaving Matthew to take turns in seeing to Grace and dealing with the administrative side of things. He made a totally impressive front man. His telephone manner never failed to lure guests to our country retreat from far and wide, and they were never disappointed when they arrived. I didn't mind in the least doing all the manual chores myself. I was so, so happy. Even if I'd had to sweep the chimneys I still would have whistled while I worked.

At first we planned on changing one of the downstairs guest bedrooms into a second nursery when the time came, but as it happened, the time never did come. I had a miscarriage after Grace's birth, followed by severe complications, and was told that I wouldn't be able to have any more children. But the strange thing is, I didn't mind. I honestly didn't mind. With one beautiful daughter already, and a husband who loved me more with each passing year, and a modest but successful B&B business, and you coming to visit us whenever you could spare yourself from Belle Vue, what more could I have wanted? Life was perfect. I could hardly ask for heaven as well.

* * *

Okay, life wasn't *completely* perfect, but near as damn it. There were Matthew's occasional lapses into depression, which were hardly surprising if you think about it. He'd been a fully-fledged Benedictine priest not all that long ago, and here he was, lumped with the role of husband, father and businessman. Whenever these low moods descended upon him, he would withdraw from the secular world and plunge himself right back into the spiritual existence that had been his elixir, his life support, as far back as he could remember. At such times he'd be consumed by the need to return to Greystones, where his former brethren always gladly welcomed him back. I didn't like it, but I could hardly put my foot down and order him not to go, could I?

The first time it happened I felt hurt, confused and overwhelmed by the fear that he was regretting his decision to leave the monastery. Luckily, you were able to come over from Belle Vue and stay with me during his absence.

'You have to remember, darling,' you said as we sat by the oak kitchen table sipping our tea, 'he was a monk for many years before he married you.'

'But it was *his* choice to leave the monastery! I didn't make him do it, so why is he regretting it now?'

'He isn't *regretting* it, Leah, don't be silly. He's just working his way through the long, difficult process of shaking off all remnants of his former life. When all's said and done, you can't expect him to switch from priest to husband and father without at least *some* side effects, can you?'

'No, I guess not.' Already I was feeling calmer.

'You mark my words, darling. As the years pass by, his need to go back to Greystones will gradually subside. You'll see.'

And you were right, of course. I just had to be patient, that's all. I had to accept the fact that there would always be a little corner of Matthew's heart that was reserved for God, and for God alone.

That's probably why our Derwent Lodge retreats became such a success. By about the third year, word had spread about them. Matthew soon learned to capitalise on the fact that he'd been a priest, rather than be ashamed of it. The retreats brought out the true charm of the man I was now married to. I felt a rush of pride whenever our guests addressed Matthew in that reverent, slightly awe-stricken way – especially on the nuns' or Catholic Association Retreats, which were almost like Matthew Haddon fan clubs. What I didn't like so much was the occasional sixth-form retreat we housed, including girls from Lark Mount. When lumbered with a group of sixth formers for an entire weekend, at times I prickled in unease and – well, okay, let's be honest. And jealousy. I hated the way they looked at my husband, and how he responded to their adoration. Did he really have to be *quite* so generous with his twinkly-eyed smiles? Whether he realised it or not, he was an immense turn-on for those girls, and I loathed having to witness their doe-eyes and their giggles as I served up breakfast and tried to pretend that nothing was the matter. I knew exactly what sparks were flying around in their heads when in the presence of a handsome male who had the added kudos of being an ex-priest. Oh yes, I knew! Although I was now twenty-seven, with a thirty-six-year-old husband and one-year-old baby, I still remembered it well. I knew how they felt, because I still felt it now. I was still one of them. And Matthew was still the Benedictine monk I had first fallen in love with.

'Honestly, Matthew, do you have to be *quite* so gushing with them?' I once asked him as we sat at the kitchen table, our toddler-daughter plonked in her highchair between us.

He looked at me in confusion. The spoonful of baby food he was about to deliver to Grace's open mouth remained suspended mid-air. 'What do you mean, *gushing*?'

'I mean – well, flirty. Enjoying their adoration and making the most of every single minute of it.'

He put the spoon in Grace's mouth before returning his eyes to me. 'Leah, do you honestly think I'm playing games?'

I shrugged, resenting the sulky feeling I felt coming upon me, yet unable to fight it.

Shaking his head in disbelief, he went on, 'You think I'm flirting with girls who mean nothing at all to me? Who are young enough to be my daughter? What's got *into* you? Don't you have any idea how much I love you? How devoted I am to you, still now, after all these years?' He reached his hand across the table and squeezed mine reassuringly. 'You're my girl, Leah, and always will be. You and Grace are the two most important people in my life.'

And that was good enough for me.

4

As Grace changed from baby to toddler to small child, our life took on a new dimension. By her third year we were at last able to hire a receptionist and cook, which freed me to get back to some decent piano practice, as well as give the occasional recital. These were rather like soirees, with me seated at our Beckstein grand in the bay window of our sitting room, and our audience positioned wherever they could carve a place for themselves – on the sofa, the armchairs, or cushions tossed upon the parquet floor. At first we organised these small musical gatherings exclusively for our B&B guests, but soon word of my pianistic skills spread, as did the idea of such a charmingly Victorian style of entertainment, and so people from further afield started to come. In no time at all I found myself being hired out to play at other local venues for the occasional evening of Chopin, Schubert and Beethoven.

I was blossoming at this stage. Without meaning to sound vain, I felt beautiful. Our male concert-goers must also have thought this, judging by their reaction. Whenever I finished playing at one of our soirees, I'd mingle with our modest audience, sipping a glass of wine that was included in the price of an entrance ticket, and feeling like Audrey Hepburn in my slim-fitting black dress with its plunging neckline, my hair tied back in a large velvet bow. As I navigated my way through the milling bodies, thanking the guests as they congratulated me on my playing, I'd thrill under that familiar look of male desire that was so often directed at me. Sometimes, as Matthew passed nearby with a tray-load of wine glasses, looking damn impressive himself with his dark wavy hair, crystal-blue eyes and naturally sophisticated poise, he'd whisper into my ear, 'I know you can't help being beautiful, but maybe you could tone down the sex appeal just a *little* bit?'

So we had an even score.

Life really was too good to be true.

5

One crisp February afternoon on the day before my thirtieth birthday, I felt the miracle of my happiness so acutely, it almost hurt.

Everything was perfect that day. There was a thin layer of virgin snow on the ground from the previous night's fall. Matthew and Grace were out on a lower terrace of the back garden, building a snowman. You and I were sitting on wicker chairs out on the veranda, rugs tossed over our laps, mugs of steaming coffee in our hands to keep them warm while we watched my husband and daughter laughing and throwing snowballs at each other. It was one of those afternoons when the sky hung overhead in seamless perfection, with the low winter's sunrays teasing the distant lake water at the bottom of the white-coated hill.

'Just look at all this,' I said, inhaling the bracing air. 'What more could anyone want?'

As you didn't reply, I stole a glance at you. It wasn't like you to remain quiet. 'Are you all right, Mother?'

You shivered. 'I'm fine, darling – just a bit chilly.'

'Yes, I suppose we ought to go in soon. Oh, but just *look* at it!' I returned my eyes to the panorama of hills, forest and lake beyond the fenced enclosure of our garden. 'To think I'll be thirty tomorrow, and I'm still every bit as much in love as when I first met him.' I smiled coyly. 'Except he was a forbidden monk back then, and I never believed that we'd end up together. But we did. We really did. Isn't it like that old film – *All this and Heaven too?*'

You smiled back at me. 'I'm so glad you're happy, darling.'

'Oh God, I'm *more* than happy – I'm in seventh heaven! Honestly, I just don't know how I got to be so lucky.'

At that moment Matthew suddenly approached us, out of breath from trekking up the steep garden. Blowing steam into the air, he said, 'I'm afraid you didn't.'

'Sorry?' I felt a prickle of alarm. 'What do you mean?'

'You didn't get to be so lucky, is what I mean. Come on, Leah, get a grip on yourself.'

His face had grown blurred. Or was it my vision that was blurred? I looked at the picturesque lakeside panorama once again. To my alarm, it had become one vast, amorphous sea of grey-white clouds. Or was it concrete? I shuddered.

Turning my eyes back to you, I said in a constricted whisper, 'Mother … where am I?'

'In your home,' Matthew replied instead. His voice had grown faint. 'In Lichfield.'

'Lichfield? But -'

'You need to go back, Leah.'

'What do you mean?'

'*Go back.*'

'But where?'

Panic seized my throat, my hands, my entire body. I dropped my coffee mug, but nothing spilled out of it, because nothing was there. Neither you, nor Matthew, nor Grace, nor the perfect winter's scene, nor me. None of it was there. It all paled before my eyes, just as your face did, vanishing into the snowy wonderland of my mind's eye.

So I had no choice but to go back.

COMPLINE

Dreaming when Dawn's Left Hand was in the Sky
I heard a Voice within the Tavern cry,
"Awake, my Little ones, and fill the Cup
"Before Life's Liquor in its Cup be dry."

Rubaiyat of Omar Khayyam, v. 2

CHAPTER TWENTY-THREE

1

Sometimes I think I've spent more of my life dreaming than living. That's the trouble with us diary-keepers and nostalgia-addicts.

Isn't that how it's always been with you, Mother? At the end of the day, aren't we just two hopeless dreamers, lost together in a world that has no place for the likes of us? Aren't we just waiting for something better? Hoping we'll be able to meet again – you, me, Peter Fox, Brother Matthew – with all the anger, pain and hurt gone? If that's what's going to happen one day, then it would make everything worthwhile. But if not, then what's the point of it all?

But I don't want to be negative. And I don't want to believe that you and I will never be reconciled. It's still dark outside, here in Lichfield. You're not even aware that I'm sitting here thinking of you, wanting to say how sorry I am, even though I'm not sure what for.

I can't bear to think that this night is a kind of farewell for us. Just like it was for you and Peter on that drizzly day in December, all of twenty-seven years ago.

* * *

December 9th 1956. The date you'll never forget.

You were upstairs in the bedroom that you shared with Doreen. She was out with Paul, the boyfriend she'd end up marrying. It was late afternoon and they'd gone to the cinema to see *Seven Brides for Seven Brothers*. They'd invited you as well, as though sensing your growing listlessness since Peter had gone to Cyprus. But you'd politely declined their offer.

Peter had written to you several times since leaving England, with his usual mishmash of humour and affection. He said he was missing you desperately, and when you read that bit your heart went bumpity-bump-

bump. He also said that he'd probably come back sooner than he'd planned, to prevent you from going on your hair-brained trip to Yugoslavia to reconnect with a hunky foreigner who had probably married his neighbour's nubile daughter by now in exchange for a herd of goats. You didn't find that bit funny. But the last letter he wrote was addressed to your mother, strangely enough. In fact, I've got it right here with me, on the coffee table. Hang on a minute – it's somewhere amid all this chaos … ah, here it is.

Dear Mum,

Molly says you're worried about her – but doesn't tell me why you should be. I can only assume it's because of the silly Yugoslav experiment. If you could let me know what her plans are without breaking any confidences, I'd appreciate it. If Molly is still determined to go out there, do all you can to prevent it for her sake.

All right, enough of Molly. My biggest news here is that I've got a job on a British newspaper, the Times of Cyprus. Their office is in Nicosia, and it's quite a haul to get out there each day. You wouldn't believe the rickety, goat-filled buses that traverse the perilous mountain road from Kyrenia every morning at 8.00. I've filled the vacancy made by their last reporter, Angus McDonald, who was shot dead by Eoka terrorists just 2 weeks ago, so I'd better watch my back now, eh? I wouldn't be in the least surprised if Molly's forgotten to tell you all this, what with her mind being so full of Yugoslavia and hirsute foreign men who are only after one thing where English girls are concerned.

Must stop – I'm meeting my friend Dermott Cavanagh at the Harbour Club in half an hour. Hope you're all keeping yourselves well. Tell Doreen she can be Maid of Honour at her big sister's wedding.

With love, as always,

Peter

That prophetic letter was your last contact with Peter. But let's get back to December 9th. To the story I've heard so many times, I could recite it as though from a *Cautionary Tale for Young Lovers*.

* * *

Your father was at work on Preston Docks; your mother in the kitchen preparing the tea. Doreen was out with Paul, and you were upstairs in the bedroom, dancing to the song *Always*. It was on a record that Peter had given you the previous Christmas, and it was your favourite. *I'll be loving you always, with a love that's true always …*

There wasn't that much room to dance in the squashy bedroom, but somehow you'd managed to carve a space in front of the sash window that overlooked the grimy back yards of Talbot Road. So away you danced – eyes closed, lips upturned. You were halfway through the second verse when you heard the doorbell ring. You didn't think anything of it at first. You left chores like answering doors to your mother, who was always pottering about in the kitchen downstairs.

You were still dancing when your mother came upstairs, opened the bedroom door and asked you to turn the gramophone down because she couldn't hear herself think. So at last you stopped.

'What is it?'

Your mother held out the brown envelope and said in a small voice, 'I think you'd better open it, love. It's a telegram from Cyprus.'

'A telegram? What the dickens has Peter been up to *now*?' You stepped forward to take the envelope. 'Landed himself in prison, I expect.' You rolled your eyes. 'He's probably been taking snapshots of some anti-British riot or something of the sort, as material for one of his articles. And now the daft beggar's gone and got himself arrested and he needs our help.' You laughed, but your mother didn't.

Opening the post office telegram, you extracted the piece of paper and unfolded it. And then you read the words from the Under Secretary of

State from the Colonial Office of Cyprus. Those terrible words that you would never, ever forget.

DEEPLY REGRET TO INFORM YOU THAT GOVERNOR CYPRUS HAS REPORTED PETER DONALD FOX SHOT AND FATALLY WOUNDED BY TERRORIST IN KYRENIA AT 1725 HOURS LOCAL TIME YESTERDAY STOP HE DIED ON WAY TO HOSPITAL
UNDER SECRETARY OF STATE COLONIAL OFFICE

You read the words again, unable to believe them. Then you looked at your mother. With a shaking hand you held out the telegram to her, hoping upon hope that there'd been some mistake. But when your ashen-faced mother read aloud the very same words that you herself had read just a moment earlier, you knew there hadn't been any mistake.

There was a frozen moment in time when neither of you said or did anything. But then the whistling of the kettle downstairs brought you back to your senses. As its hissing rose into a scream, you screwed your eyes tight and with a long, inconsolable wail you cried out his name – *'PETER!'* – before sinking to your knees and terminating the most beautiful journey of your life.

2

It's 1983 and I'm at Greystones. I've gone back, just as Matthew told me to. In my story, I mean. The one I wrote as an extension to my diary while I was in Lyneham last week, mentally preparing myself for my last journey to Greystones. The one you called my *make or break* journey. I suppose my diary-story was a case of gross negligence in a way. Or perhaps gross hyperbole: as a writer, dreamer, daughter and lover. But I wrote it all the same, then closed my diary, put it in the top drawer of my desk, and set off for Greystones. I didn't want to take it with me. It seemed like tempting fate.

And now here I am with Brother Matthew in the attic room. He's sitting with stooped shoulders on the edge of the bed in which we've just spent a wonderful, unforgettable night, and he's holding his head in his hands.

Sorry, telling fibs again. That didn't happen, either. Well, it did, but not in this world. All sorts of things can happen in the *other* world, where our deepest desires live, isn't that so? The trouble is that those desires are unwelcome guests in the real world, which has a cruel way of slamming the door on them, making them homeless, condemning them to live in some land of displaced dreams. We can dream till we're blue in the face; we can spend hours and hours on bus or train journeys where we enter our other-world; we can spend even more hours at night star-gazing and crying for the moon, but at the end of the day we have to wake up, unless we go mad.

I wish I had gone mad. But unfortunately, cold-hearted Truth shook me by the shoulders and slapped me hard in the face, jolting me out of all those pages and pages I wrote in my diary, where I had created a future for the three of us. Yes, Mother, it was a future for you as well. I never would have abandoned you. Not in the world I created for us. But I'm not in that world any more. Not in York or Derwent Lodge. Not with my priest-husband or imaginary daughter. Not sipping coffee with you on the veranda.

So it's June 1983 and I'm back at Greystones. I'm with Brother Matthew, but not in the attic room. We never got that far. He never let me.

We're at the lakes, where I succeeded in persuading him to go on a walk with me. At least I managed that much. We're sitting on a bench near the jetty, staring straight ahead at the glassy water, neither of us speaking. But I don't mind that we're not speaking – at least not yet – because right now I'm just grateful to be with him, knowing that he's back in my life again, even if he feels like a stranger to me. And then it occurs to me, in one of those defining moments that life occasionally throws at you, that for all our contact over the years, for all our letters and meetings, our walks in the valley, and that one near-miss in the attic room, I don't really know Matthew at all. He's like a stranger to me, and always will be. My infinite stranger. Wasn't that also the case with you and Peter Fox, Mother? For all your heartbreak and passion and misunderstood love, wasn't Peter ultimately a stranger to you, at rock bottom?

But enough talk about strangers! I've come here in a last-ditch effort to see if there's any point in fighting for our united future. Of course you're convinced there is. But so far nothing is going quite according to plan.

At last Matthew decides to break the Great Silence.

'Leah, there's something I think I ought to tell you.'

I steal a sideways glance at him. His profile is immobile, unreadable. At last the moment of truth, I'm thinking.

But still he isn't looking at me. He's staring straight ahead at the lake. Deciding to help him along, I reach into my jacket pocket and pull out a miniature book – the beautifully bound *Rubaiyat of Omar Khayyam* that you gave me for my twenty-first. I've been mentally preparing for this moment for ever: to let him have a token of my love. Whatever today's outcome, let him at least have that. And hopefully, much, much more.

I hold it out for him and say, 'I want you to have this.'

He glances at the book, then at me. 'What is it?'

'A present my mother gave me for my twenty-first birthday. Poems about the beauty of life, and why we should make the most of it while we're here. It's yours.'

'I – I can't take it,' he says, frowning at me. But it isn't a proper frown. His brow is puckered; and now, suddenly, I realise there are tears in his eyes. Yes, *tears*. The sight of them is so shocking, I momentarily forget the hammering of my heart.

He swallows, looks away almost angrily. And repeats in a stronger voice, 'I can't take it.' No explanation offered. Nothing. There's something about his expression that is so utterly non-negotiable, I find my hand withdrawing itself of its own accord. I tuck the book back into my pocket. And wait.

Pausing again, he continues in a slow, guarded voice, as though measuring the currency of each word: 'I've received a letter from your mother.'

I gulp. '*What?*'

'Yes, that was my reaction.'

'A *letter?*' I still can't quite take it in. 'But she never mentioned – I mean – did she tell you I was coming to Greystones?'

'No, she just said that she was extremely concerned about you. About your wedding plans. Congratulations, by the way.'

It's now my turn to look away. My mind is reeling under the impact of hearing that you've written to him. What were you *thinking*? But that was nothing yet, was it? Compared to what was still to come, any moment now.

He breaks the taut silence. 'She obviously doesn't want this wedding to go ahead.'

'No, she most certainly does not.'

'So who's the lucky man?'

'I'd appreciate it if you didn't resort to clichés.'

Instantly I regret the harshness of my words, but it's too late to take them back.

'I can see I've touched a sore point,' he says, adding, 'though I don't see why it should be. Getting married should be a joy.'

'I'm sorry. I'm just angry with my mother, that's all. I know she doesn't want me to marry the man I'm engaged to, but that's *our* business – my mother's and mine – not yours.'

'So who is your fiancé?'

'Someone I met at the Polish club.'

'Well, if you're marrying him, then you must love him.'

'Why bother asking, if you already know?'

'Because I wanted to hear it from your own lips.'

I shudder at the sound of the word *lips*. 'Why, do you doubt that I love him?'

'No, of course not.'

'Then why ask any of this?'

'Oh, Leah.'

'I hate it when you do that.'

'Do what?'

'Say *Oh Leah* in that patronising tone of voice. As if you were my father.'

'Well, to a certain extent I am your father. I'm everyone's father.'

I groan. 'For God's sake, please spare me the bullshit!'

I can't understand it, but suddenly I'm so angry, my entire body is trembling. There is something about his reserve, his impenetrable passivity, that makes me want to give up right there and then and go straight back to Marek, who loves me unreservedly. If you thought you were succeeding in pushing me away from Marek, the result was the exact opposite. Irony of ironies, it was *Matthew* you turned me away from, when I found out what you did. And what you did, let's get this straight, was to put a nail in the coffin of the loving relationship that you and I once shared.

He returns his eyes to the lake, his frown deepening. Immediately I hear warning bells ringing loud and clear in the summer air. Something's up. There's a part of the equation that hasn't yet been filled in. He's hiding something from me.

'What is it?' I press. 'Is it something else my mother said?'

'No, not *said*, exactly, just … quoted.'

'Quoted? Would you mind elaborating, please?'

Sitting forward, he rests his elbows on his knees and scowls at a sparrow that's hopping about on the jetty. And at last he elaborates.

'Your mother sent me some extracts from your diaries.'

'*What?*' My hand shoots up to my mouth.

'Rather a lot, actually.'

Neither of us speaks for a good five or six seconds, possibly more. Then he adds, almost apologetically, 'I think she was trying to prove to me that you shouldn't be marrying this man you're engaged to, when you're still in love with … well …'

'With you? Come on, *say* it.'

'Yes, with me.'

My mind is reeling under the shock waves of this latest piece of news. I couldn't have felt more devastated if I'd been told I had cancer. It was horrible, Mother, just *horrible*. How could you have done such a thing? Isn't that maternal love gone mad? Within a kaleidoscopic whirl in time, all the entries I have ever made in my diaries over the past five years flash through my mind's eye, each one making my agony of shame and humiliation all the more excruciating. And - oh my God - all those pages and pages about our fictitious lives together, the imaginary sizzling sex we had … he must have read them as well.

Through my mounting agony, I gradually realise he's talking to me.

'I could so easily have got caught up in your fantasy,' he's saying; words I'm hardly listening to, yet I *am* listening to them; words that sound far away, as though they were coming out of one of those echoing seashells. 'So very easily, with someone like you …' He glances at me, swallows, looks away again. I can see his Adam's apple. Didn't even realise he had one. 'But I didn't allow myself to get involved. And that's why I can't accept your – your gift. Because you're giving it me in the wrong – for the wrong reasons.'

'You don't even know the bloody reasons,' I snap, and I see his shoulders stiffen.

Ignoring my challenge, his frown deepens at the lake as he goes straight on: 'I'd already chosen my life's journey a long time ago. And although I came near to losing my way with ...' another pause, another swallow. Guilt rather than regret? 'With you, I found it again. I have no further doubts about what I want. *This* is what I want – the monastery, my community, a life dedicated to God. As for you, Leah ...' At last he turns his head to me. He attempts a smile, but his eyes are red-rimmed. 'It should be marriage, a home, children ... but not with me. You have to accept that it will never be with me.'

I find myself nodding mutely, staring at my hands.

'So my advice to you is not what your mother wants to hear, not what you yourself want to hear, but it's the only advice I can give. Marry this man. Even if you still harbour confused feelings for me, marry him, and then forget me once and for all.'

Still I don't say anything. He sits forward on the bench. I can feel his eyes on me, probing, worrying. 'Are you all right?'

Shuddering, I at last face him. 'Yes, I'm all right. I'm not about to go and jump in the lake, in case that's what you were thinking.'

'Oh, Leah.'

'There you go again.'

He smiles at me – a sad, weary smile - and for the tiniest fragment in time I think I detect something in his expression as he looks at me, some intangible longing that will never be stilled as long as I keep barging into his life, no matter what he tries to tell me, no matter how he tries to con himself. And so it is at this very moment that I decide enough is enough. I will do exactly as he advises me. I have no choice.

'Come on, let's get back,' I say, standing up and heading towards the forest path.

And that's it. We hardly speak a word all the way back to the Abbey.

The following morning I caught the bus back to York and from there a train to Lyneham, where you were waiting for me, no doubt anxious to hear how my weekend had gone.

As a matter of fact, I couldn't wait to tell you how it had gone.

3

'How could you do it, Mother? How COULD you? I hate you!'

That's me, less than twenty-four hours later. Just two weeks ago. We're in the dining room at Belle Vue, standing at opposite ends of the table like contestants in a ring just before battle. I'm wild-eyed and trembling, you cold and self-righteous.

You say nothing, just survey me with large, hurt eyes. Where has all their sun-kissed warmth and sparkle gone?

'He'll think I'm a total nutcase! He'll think I'm from a family of nutters! My diaries are *personal*, they're meant to be read by me, and me alone. I can't *bear* to think of him reading all that romantic bilge – oh my God, I can never go back to Greystones now, never! You've fucked everything up well and truly this time!'

You wince, but I plough straight on, relentless in my fury, 'And you know what? Even if Marek finished with me tomorrow, I'd *still* never go back to Greystones! You've ruined everything, *everything!*' I'm practically screaming. I can't remember if any guests are at Belle Vue that weekend, but quite frankly, I couldn't give a shit.

All you say, in a stony voice, is, 'No, my darling. *Marek* is the one who's ruined everything. You've just become too wilful and blind to see it. Ever since meeting Marek, you've become a different person. A much *less nice* person, I have to say. Before that man came along, everything was fine between us.'

'Well it sure as hell isn't fine now! And don't you dare blame it on *that man*. He loves me – *really* loves me, and I'm going to marry him, whether you like it or not.'

'But Leah ...' Suddenly, you're struggling to hold back tears. I absolutely hate seeing you cry. It always makes me want to cry too. Already I can feel my anger dissolving into muted frustration and pity. 'What about Brother Matthew?' you continue in a shaking voice. 'What about your love for *him?* Oh my darling, all I want is for you to be happy – for *both* of you to be happy.'

'Well now, that's a spurious point.'

'Will you *stop* talking to me in that tone of voice!' Your own voice changes drastically within seconds, its quivering tone receding as self-righteous anger takes over. 'Ye gods, you've changed beyond recognition ever since that man walked into your life!'

'*That man,*' I echo bitterly. 'You can't even bear to say his name.'

'No, you're damn right I can't! And is it any wonder? Do you really and truly think you're going to be happy married to someone like – like *that?*'

'Someone like what, exactly?'

'You know what I mean, Leah. And being rude isn't going to pull the wool over my eyes for one minute. I mean someone who will never be able to fully understand the inner you, with your artistic soul and all your dreams and yearnings …' You lift your hands in frustration. '*Hells bells,* Leah, Marek doesn't understand the first thing about that side of you! And no wonder. How *can* he understand you? He's a chemist – a practical man without one iota of finesse in his body.'

'Let he who is without sin,' I say contemptuously.

'There's no need to get shirty. My goodness, how you've changed.'

'Yes, so you keep saying. But I think you're losing the plot.'

You swallow hard. I can almost hear you counting the seconds, willing yourself to calm down. 'Look, darling,' you begin in a new tone of voice – one that sounds like it's been straight-jacketed, 'even if by some miracle you learned to put up with all Marek's crassness, which I know you never will do, don't you see how a life with him will only drag you down more and more, year by year?'

I fold my arms, but say nothing. What's the point?

'My God, Leah, how on earth can you marry Marek, knowing that you're still in love with another man? Do you think that will make him happy? Whatever my thoughts about Marek, I certainly don't wish misery on him. And he *will* be miserable, Leah, mark my word. Sooner or later he'll tire of being with a woman whose heart is elsewhere. Eventually he'll meet someone else and leave you, and by the time you're middle-aged and no longer as attractive as you are now, you'll suddenly find yourself all alone, without any man.'

'Well, you managed to live like that.'

'Only because of *you*! Don't forget, there were many, many lonely years I had to put up with, after Peter's death and in the early years with your father. Oh darling, I couldn't bear the thought of you going through the same mockery of love that I had to go through. Ever since Peter's death -'

'Yes, I know, and yes, I'm sorry about what happened to Peter, but honestly Mother, it happened almost *thirty years* ago. It's time to put it behind you and move on – and also let *me* move on. Brother Matthew isn't ever going to leave the monastery, any more than you'll ever be able to resurrect Peter Fox. That's final. And I *do* love Marek – in a completely different sort of way. If I didn't love him, I wouldn't be marrying him.'

'So you're settling for second best.'

'No, that's not -'

'Marek has poisoned your idea of love, that's the problem, my girl. And you're right about Peter. I may have had the love of my life stolen from me, but at least I still know what love is. In the hands of that common clown, you've obviously forgotten.'

I should defend Marek. Make you take back your ugly words. But already my rage has worn itself out. I just feel weary. And sad. So very, very sad. For all of us.

Just before leaving Belle Vue the following morning, a letter from Matthew arrived in the post. You were in the kitchen at the time, sullenly preparing packed sandwiches and flapjack and a thermos for me. I wished you wouldn't bother. I couldn't wait to get away from you. More to the point, I hated it when you did a so-called 'good deed' for me in defiant silence, sulking like a child and willing me to feel your pain.

As I was putting on my jacket in the hallway, wishing you'd hurry up so that we could get this horrible business of parting over with, I heard the clunk of the letterbox. Straight away I recognised the handwriting on the white envelope that lay on the carpet. *His* handwriting. Stooping to pick up the letter, I glanced over my shoulder to make sure you were still in the kitchen. You were. I slipped the envelope into my jacket pocket, not wanting you to see it. I couldn't bear the thought of any further mention of Brother Matthew.

It was only when I was on the train back to Birmingham that I realised my mistake. The letter wasn't in fact addressed to me; it was addressed to you. Brother Matthew had written a letter to *you*, not me. It was as though the prophecy of your past was being fulfilled. Peter Fox had also written to your mother, just before he died.

I tore open the envelope. And no, I don't have any guilty conscience about reading it, because what you did in sending him my diary extracts was a thousand times worse.

So anyway, here it is.

February 7th 1983

Dear Mrs Cavanagh,

I have now had some time to reflect on what you had to say in your letter to me, and although this will not be a comprehensive reply, I hope it may enlighten you a little as to my own position and feelings in all this.

I agree that I may need a one-to-one relationship to reach my full potential, as most people do. Where, perhaps, we disagree is that a) this should necessarily be with Leah, and b) that it is not possible within the monastic life and setting.

I believe two things very strongly. The first concerns a relationship of love, which must in my opinion be mutual and desired by both parties before it can be realised. The second thing I believe is that a person can choose, despite their inclination and nature, to become a monk, and place their inclinations and nature in God's hands to be used as He wishes. I realise that this factor makes the monastic life incomprehensible to most people, but that has been the lot of monks for a very long time. It is with these two beliefs in mind that I dare not even suggest to you or to Leah that I love her. I use the word 'dare', not because of any fear I have that I may in fact love her – but fear that she in particular will hope for more than those words convey.

I have read some of her 'diary' and it confirms for me that I am in fact nothing to do with it. I fear - and this may sound very brutal - that it is a fictional love affair, and that Leah has wilfully, even shamelessly, misinterpreted any kindness, attention or look from me to fuel her own fantasy. And from your letter I have to infer that in all of this you were a more than willing accomplice.

As for Leah herself – I naturally care that she should keep on growing, that she should learn to make a real relationship, that she should be loved and learn to love in return. I am certain that her marriage to Marek is the best opportunity she has yet had to discover these things and to break completely with the fantasy of loving a monk.

I have debated for a while as to what I should do with Leah's diary extracts. As I said above, they have nothing to do with me in reality, and therefore they are not 'mine' to keep. I have decided to burn them, and I suggest you do the same with any copy you may have made. I do not of course 'forbid' or rule out any further communication with either yourself or Leah. But it might be wiser if she tried to forget me entirely, and I, for my part, will not write again unless there is some very serious reason.

I remain yours sincerely,

Matthew Haddon OSB

After forcing myself to read the whole thing six times through, the pain inside me was so intense, I thought I would die from a heart attack there and then. I *wanted* to die from a heart attack there and then. I wanted to cease upon the midnight with no pain, to be done with this horrible, wasted, unbearable thing called love. It had never made you happy, and now here I was, headed down the very same road. But whereas your heartbreak was through the tragic loss of death, mine was merely through rejection. God knows what you said to Matthew in your own letter. Would he have gleaned the full extent of your madness? Did you make him run a mile? *'But what about the madness of your OWN fantasy, Leah?'* I can almost hear you asking me. But Mother - you're the adult, the parent; you should have protected me! My own madness was a mere detour: a different road taken, through the private escape route of my diaries. There was no excuse for your insane intrusion into the private core of my being.

Anyway, his letter certainly proved one thing to me. I was not going to waste another moment on a man who was out of my reach, whether from a true calling, from martyrly self-denial, or just being an emotional wimp. Something that Marek was the diametrical opposite of.

To be honest, I didn't care anymore. I was going to marry Marek Topolski whether you liked it or not, and at last say a final *adieu* to Brother Matthew Haddon, *Order of St Benedict*.

CHAPTER TWENTY-FOUR

1

Her first thoughts, when she arrived at Nicosia airport on June 6th 1957, could be summarised in one short sentence: *Oh God, what have I done?*

As she stepped out of the doorway of the plane, she was immediately assailed by a harsh, alien glare. *Hot* was scarcely the word. It was as though the earth had moved several million miles closer to the sun. She paused on the top step, letting other passengers go in front of her as she opened her bag and rummaged through the concealed chaos for the new pair of sunglasses she had bought shortly before leaving England. Once she found them she placed them on her head, wiped the back of her neck, and paused a further moment to take in her new surroundings. Dry, arid, the middle of nowhere, the din of cicadas everywhere. *Where the dickens am I?* And again, *oh God, what have I done?* And an immense desire, if she was perfectly honest with herself, to turn round, get back inside the plane and beg the pilot to take her home.

Instead, she pushed her chin up and, with her usual Molly Williams gumption, started the clanging descent of the aircraft steps, forcing her mind to concentrate on placing one foot in front of the other, holding her face in a ladylike manner, and hiding the express-load of darker emotions that were tearing about inside her at a hundred miles per hour. She was in Cyprus, the place where her adored fiancé had died; she was about to meet his Irish doctor-friend; she was barely on speaking terms with her mother, who had pleaded with her not to go; she was jobless, having given up her very fulfilling work as doctor's secretary on the Mass Radiography Unit, and she had no idea what the future – immediate or otherwise – held in store for her.

As she took the last step and found herself on firm ground, she barely had the chance to register a panorama of distant mountains etched against a heat-hazed sky, before hearing her name called out.

'Miss Williams?'

At first she thought it was Dermot Cavanagh, because he'd written to say that he'd collect her from the airport. But as soon as she saw the uniformed officer step forward to greet her, and then another three men close behind, also in uniform, she was hit by a second wave of irrational fear. These were British army men. Her naive, youthful brain had no way of assessing the situation. What were they going to do? Arrest her? Send her back to England? (And suddenly, in true fighting spirit, she no longer wanted to beg the pilot to take her home.) Link her with the murder of her former fiancé? – the man whose grave she had come to visit; the man for whom her grief was utterly fathomless, even six months on?

'Would you mind stepping this way, madam?'

'Certainly,' she replied with forced smile. 'Is anything wrong?'

'Just a formality. We'd like to ask you a few questions, that's all. Please. Follow me.' He spoke with a clipped British accent; the very type she had so often mimicked to Peter back in her Amateur Dramatic days, causing him to keel over in laughter.

With a light touch of her elbow, the officer who appeared to be in charge led her across the rough gravel to a barracks building. He held the door open for her and as soon as they stepped inside, her mind registered the angry whirring of a ventilator. As though guided by a conjuror's hand, she presently found herself seated at a desk, with the British officer sitting opposite her. The other three men merged into the background, and after this point she had no further recollection of them.

'I'd be grateful if you could answer a few questions, if you don't mind. I'll be as quick as I can.'

'You can take as long as you like, officer. I'm in no rush.'

'Are you Miss Molly Williams of 48 Talbot Road, Preston?'

'Yes, officer, I do believe that's me.'

'Former fiancé of Mr Peter Donald Fox?'

'Yes.'

'Who was fatally shot by an EOKA terrorist on December 8th of last year?'

'Yes.'

Apparently satisfied with her answers thus far, he leaned further back in his chair, entwined his long-fingered hands together and rested them upon his chest.

'So would you mind telling me, Miss Williams, what brings you to Cyprus?'

'Oh, so that's it,' she said. 'You've been reading the papers. *Preston girl goes to Cyprus to seek former fiancé's killer.*'

'Is that why you're here?'

'Of course not. You shouldn't believe everything you read, officer.'

'And you, Miss Williams, shouldn't play with fire. This is a very dangerous place to be, especially for a young British lady on her own. So why *are* you here?'

At last she allowed herself a sigh, and said in as controlled a voice as she could muster, 'I'm here to visit my fiancé's grave, that's all.'

As this was met with no more than the raising of a doubtful eyebrow, she elaborated: 'That's what I told the reporters who pestered me back in Preston, and that's what I'm telling you now. I want to talk to people who knew Peter, in particular his Irish friend who he was staying with in Kyrenia. I want to visit his grave, perhaps see the place he worked. Above all, I want peace of mind.'

The officer nodded in polite acquiescence, and so she continued with increased conviction, 'Call it sentimental if you wish, but anyone who has lost someone close would naturally want to see the surroundings in which they died. I'm certainly not looking for a killer. Peter would have been awfully cross to find that I came here on some mission. Nothing I or anyone else can do will ever bring him back.'

'And you don't feel any anger towards the terrorist who did this? You don't harbour any secret wish for justice?'

'Justice?' She smiled. 'Oh, yes, officer, we all have a secret wish for that. Or at least we *should* have. Peter certainly did. It was one of the main reasons why he became a journalist. He saw it as a way of standing up to man's inhumanity to man – all the poverty, intolerance, wars and countless other evils that we spread across the planet. He even knew the Declaration of Human Rights by heart. He thought it sounded like poetry. Do you know it?

'Well –'

Her smile deepened. 'You don't need to apologise. Before meeting Peter I hadn't even heard of it. But it's worth learning, you know. We all should learn it. That's what Peter believed. He believed that it should be taught to every child in school as soon as they're old enough to understand words such as *whereas* and *inherent*.' For the briefest of moments her grief was gone; the airport ceased to exist, and she was with the Amateur Dramatic Society in Preston once again, on that stage where reality was ousted by dreams; where she was holding the hand of her very own dream, her leading man by the name of Peter Donald Fox. She closed her eyes and began: '*Whereas recognition of the inherent dignity and of the equal and inalienable rights of all members of the human family is the foundation of freedom, justice and peace in the world ...*'

An embarrassed cough brought her back to her senses. Opening her eyes, she quickly re-adjusted to her present circumstances. 'Well, anyway,' she said with a touch less defiance.

The officer nodded in awkward empathy. 'So what do you intend to do while you're here?'

She gave a little shrug. 'As I said, visit Peter's grave, talk to people, and then ... try to get on with life, I suppose. Look for a job. Earn some money to support my stay in Cyprus. It might even be that I start a new life here, the place where Peter ended his. All I know is that it's a journey I have to make. I owe it to the memory of ... of my fiancé.' She wanted to hold on to the tenuous right to that title as long as she possibly could.

And at last she won a smile from her antagonist – or so he seemed to her at the time.

'Well, Miss Williams, I think that will be all. Thank you for your time. And do please accept my sincerest condolences over your sad loss.'

'Thank you,' she said, retrieving her bag from the floor as she stood up and tried discreetly to pluck her moist dress away from her hot, sticky thighs.

'Do you need a lift anywhere?'

'No thank you. Someone is meeting me at the airport.'

Suddenly overwhelmed by a rush of emotion, she offered a valedictory smile at the officer and hurried out of the room. She had to get out, to be by herself, at least for a few minutes. In spite of her rising curiosity about the man who was at this very moment waiting for her in the tiny Arrivals hall of the ramshackle airport, and whose flat she was going to stay in while she sorted herself out, she now wished more than ever that she could turn the clock back. *Backward, turn backward, oh Time in your flight…*

The truth of the matter was that there was only one man who should have been waiting for her, and it most certainly was not this Irish doctor, who had stumbled into her life thanks to a terrorist's bullet.

2

So, Mother. There you are. Peter died and your life ended. Or might as well have done, because I just became a medium for you to re-live your broken dream through me. Brother Matthew became Peter, I was you. We both lost our loves, and quite frankly, probably neither of them would have worked out anyway. Can't we leave it at that, and move on now? Because honestly, that's what this pre-wedding night has taught me. There's no Kismet, no grand plan, and there should be no trying to remould things to our heart's desire. At least you had Peter Fox's unequivocal love. At least you had that much. What have I got?

But what am I saying? I have Marek, don't I? The love of a *real* man. Is that so terrible?

In fact, I think I'll give him a ring. It's seven in the morning now, so he's bound to be up. As for me, I haven't slept a wink all night. Neither have you, I daresay.

Oh Mother, how I wish everything could go back to how it used to be between us. Do you think, in time, it will do? If you learn to accept Marek, even like him, and if a grandchild comes along – maybe not Grace, I mean *definitely* not Grace - but a real, flesh-and-blood grandchild for you to adore, as you once adored me, maybe you could adore us both, in time? And I could accept you the way you are – charming, infuriating, charismatic, head-strong, more than a little crazy, but above all, a dreamer like me.

* * *

'Hi Marek, it's me.'

'Leah?' He sounds tired. Sleepy.

'Did I wake you up?'

'No, of course not, you daft thing. You think I'd still be sleeping at seven in in the morning of our *wedding day*? The day you're going to make me the happiest man in the world? What're you like?'

There's laughter in his voice, and it makes me smile. 'I'm an idiot,' I say.

'A gorgeous idiot who's going to turn every male's head as she walks down the aisle, and make me the proudest man on Earth.'

I laugh. 'I doubt it. I didn't get a wink of sleep last night. I'm going to look *awful*.'

'Leah Cavanagh, you couldn't look awful if you tried.'

'Soon to be Leah Topolski,' I say, and my smile wavers.

'Actually, that'll be Leah Topolsk*a*, if you want to do things the Polish way. Feminine names always end in an 'a', remember?'

'Right.'

Neither of us speaks for a few moments. And then Marek asks, in a slightly less cocky voice, 'Hey gorgeous, no last-minute regrets?'

I try to hang onto my wavering smile.

I glance into the living room adjacent to the kitchen; at the coffee table that's cluttered with letters, diaries, photos, my GOD IS HOPE box ...

'Hang on a minute,' I say, placing the receiver on its side as I go into the living room and search through all the scattered memorabilia for a photo that I suddenly need to see. It's the one where Peter is looking through a telescope, with you by his side, peering through a pair of binoculars. Searching for the future the two of you should have had.

I find the photo. You look beautiful in it, Mother. You have such a lovely profile. Peter looks pretty bloody good himself. Tall, lean, high forehead. You make a striking couple.

But the thing is, you never did find that future, did you? So *now* is the time to find it. Now, with me and Marek, and Marek's family, and the future grandchildren who you will one day spoil and adore.

Still clutching the black and white photo, I go back to the kitchen and pick up the suspended receiver. Marek's voice sounds a tad edgy when he next speaks.

'Leah, what were you doing?'

'Oh, just something for my mother and me.'

Pause. And then: 'Hey, you never answered my question. You don't have any last-minute regrets, do you?'

I close my eyes. Force myself to take a deep breath.

'Leah?'

They say that at the moment of death your whole life swims before your eyes. I'm not dying, and yet, as though this were a terminal moment, my whole life really does swim before my eyes. Belle View, Lark Mount, Greystones, you, Peter Fox, Matthew …

'Leah, you still there?'

I open my eyes again. 'Yes, I'm still here. And no. No regrets.'

'Well, that's a bloody relief! You had me worried then.'

'Don't be silly.'

'Right then, gorgeous. Fancy meeting me at the church at twelve?'

'Sounds good.'

'Don't you dare be late, unless you're prepared to face the severe consequences.' I laugh, and Marek says, 'You think I'm joking?'

We bid each other goodbye, then I put the phone back on the hook and go upstairs to my bedroom, where my wedding dress is lying in wait, together with the rest of my life.

END

ACKNOWLEDGEMENTS

Infinite Stranger has undergone many metamorphoses since the story's earliest inception, way back in 2014. Throughout the changes, edits and rewrites that it has passed through, I have felt indebted to a number of special people for their ongoing support and advice.

I am hugely grateful to my trusted reader-friends, Vivian Hill and Mairead Murphy, who gave invaluable feedback upon my novel's first draft and later introduced it to their respective book clubs. A big thank you also to Karen Majors, Andy Harris and Jennifer Tobey for their enthusiasm and encouraging comments; and a special thank you to Maria Klimko for the inspirational message she sent me in the middle of the night, when she finished the last page and told me she just *had* to email me straight away.

Particular thanks go to my former husband, Tim Murphy, for his unflagging faith in my writing and his assistance in editing and proofreading the final draft. A huge thank you also to my three amazing children, Vivienne, James and Ellie, for putting up with all my fluctuations in joy and despair during the novel's various stages of development, as well as for their highly perceptive insights. And congratulations to my enormously talented graphic designer, Jamie Harris, on creating a beautiful book cover that is perfectly suited to the infinite yearnings of my protagonist.

I couldn't finish this list without expressing my keen thanks to Curtis Brown Creative for all the support they provided during my novel's penultimate stage of development, especially to Anna Freeman, Jack Hadley, Aby Parsons, and my wonderful cohort of fellow-writers.

Finally, I will forever be grateful to the memory of my unique but not always easy mother, Molly Williams; and to Peter Donald Fox, who now sadly lies in an unmarked grave in the British Cemetery of Nicosia, Cyprus. His remembered zest for life and turbulent love for my mother provided me with enormous inspiration throughout the writing of this book.

About the Author

Wendy Skorupski had an international upbringing in Cyprus and Vienna and graduated from the Royal Birmingham Conservatoire in England. She lives in the beautiful historic city of Krakow in Southern Poland and works in the field of international education. Her first dream was to be a concert pianist, just like Leah Cavanagh in her novel, therefore she writes about this little-known world from first-hand experience. Wendy's late mother's fiancé, Peter Fox, was murdered by a Cypriot terrorist - a tragic event that changed the course of her life and provided the backdrop to *Infinite Stranger*.

Wendy is the mother of three wonderful children and the owner of a stubborn but loveable Belgian Malinois. During her daily brisk walks with this high-energy dog, ideas for her writing abound. Wendy is also the author of the novel, *Once Upon a Thousand Hills*, available on Amazon. She is currently working on her next novel.

Wendy's blog can be found on: wendyskorupski.com.

ONCE UPON A THOUSAND HILLS

In the shadow of secrets, lies and shame

Bridget Jones' Diary meets A Thousand Splendid Suns – a punchy love story that tears down the barriers between race and religion, showing how even the greatest traumas of genocide can be overcome.

Naomi Lieberman is young, feisty, and addicted to guilty secrets. Despite having a degree in forensic science, she works as a sales assistant at a sex shop in Soho, pretending to others that it's a posh little boutique. Her Orthodox Jewish family in Liverpool are eager for her to marry her long-time sweetheart, Ephraim, but Naomi is not ready for a wedding under the chuppah and producing six babies in a row.

John Paul Chambers is arrogant, aloof, and trying to free himself from the emotional curse of the genocide in Rwanda that orphaned him twenty years earlier. Despite his inauspicious beginnings, he has moved up in the world and now juggles the positions of Head of English at a private college, and Volunteer Manager of a London refugee centre - which happens to be in need of another volunteer.

When Naomi sees an advert for the position, she is convinced that this is just what she needs to redeem herself. She applies for the job immediately. But when John Paul interviews his flighty and irritating applicant, neither he nor Naomi has the slightest idea that their lives are about to change forever.

PROLOGUE

Kigali, Rwanda, April 1994

The boy couldn't breathe. At first he thought it was a feverish dream. One of those dreams where you want to run but your legs have become lead, or you want to gasp for air but your lungs have turned liquid. And then he understood why he couldn't breathe. Something was pressed against his mouth, preventing the passage of air. He tried to move the obstruction, but to do so he had to free his hands from other obstructions. Warm, slippery-soft obstructions that smelt peculiar. Salty.

It was an arm that was pressed against his mouth. His mother's arm. And next to it, lots of other tangled bodies and parts of bodies and torn clothes and hair and sweat … and blood. So much blood, he wanted to retch.

It all came back to him. Better not to come back, but memory is a cruel automaton. So it came back to him, without mercy, just like *them*. And with the return of memory, an urgent desire to escape his bloodied, tangled hell, and breathe oxygen rather than blood.

He freed himself from his mother's arm and several other still-warm limbs from school friends and relatives and neighbours who had been running and screaming and wailing in a helter-skelter of frenzied panic not so long ago. But now all was silence. All was death.

Except him. He wasn't dreaming, and he wasn't dead. He had to get out. He had to hold his breath, close his eyes, heave himself out of the pile of bodies and run for his life before they came back. Because they would come back. He knew that. They came back to check if there were any survivors and dispose of them.

He screwed up his eyes, raised his legs, and gave an almighty push forwards, freeing himself from the mound of death.

He was the only survivor. He could see that now, as he crouched on the floor beside the pile of corpses. His mother's body was at the top, next to where he himself had lain. The gingham dress that his father had bought for her last birthday was pushed up to her waist, revealing shreds of bloodied underwear. There would no longer be any innocence.

He looked away, and then saw his father's body. And his sister's, and his two brothers.

He stood alone on the floor, next to the corpses, amid the grand, hallowed space of the school hall where they had thought themselves safe. Here they were, all dead, and here he was, the only survivor. He felt nothing. Just the blood on his face and head. He had been cut. That's when he must have lost consciousness, and they thought him dead.

And then he heard them. Again. The distant voices, gaining in volume; the laughter, the shouting, the bursts into patriotic Hutu songs, and the whistle.

It was the whistle that did it. The whistle meant for them *get to work*, and for him, death by machete. Unless he acted fast. No time for fear, despair, panic … he had to act now, play the most skilful role of his life, far better than any childhood make-believe game he had ever taken part in. He had to climb back onto the pile of bodies, wrap his mother's arm round his face once again, close his eyes, play dead.

His eyes darted from the door to the corpses as he heard the killers storm the school building, their leader still blowing his whistle.

NAOMI

Kigali, Rwanda, April 2014

Tweets

naomi lieberman *@NaomiLieberman … 2s*

@PaulKagame I urgently need to contact John Paul Chambers. I know he's somewhere in Rwanda. Please, Your Excellency, help me find him!

CHAPTER ONE

Soho, London, one year earlier

It all began in a sex shop.

At six o'clock in the evening of Friday, 22nd February, I was just about to leave Sugar Lace and head back to Finchley to join the Blumenbergs for Shabbat dinner. And then Mr Hossein walked into the shop.

He strode across the dimly lit room and slapped one of our Ready-Made Massage Kits onto the counter. It's a brilliant deal, this kit; a boxed set that includes lubes, gels, a mini-vibrator thrown in for fun, and a special candle that turns into scented oil as it melts, so that it can be poured straight onto one's skin ready for the massage – and all for the unbeatable price of £19.99. He certainly wouldn't find a better deal anywhere else in Soho!

'How can I help you, sir?' I asked cheerily, but he averted his eyes. He often does that, as though wrestling with the shameful prospect of making optical contact with a sex shop worker.

He stood still for a good five, maybe six seconds. The wall clock above the serving counter ticked away. For want of something to do while waiting for him to enlighten me, I started flicking through the pages of *The Liverpool Jewish Chronicle* that lay on the counter in front of me. Mum keeps sending me the damn thing, month after month. I haven't got the heart to tell her that I'm simply not into all that Judaistic stuff anymore. Not since I swapped the home hearth of Liverpool for the bedazzling lights of London six and a half years ago. But there you are. There's a soft heart for you. Always gets you in a pickle, prodding you to do dutiful things you don't want to do, and *not* do naughty things you do want to do. But I do them anyway. The naughty things, I mean.

At last my reticent customer scratched his ear and announced, 'I have a problem.'

'Oh?' I looked up at him, with a smile, as always. 'Perhaps I can help?'

'I sincerely hope so.'

'Well, that's what I'm here for, sir.' *No matter what they say, keep smiling!* That's Fred's motto.

'Good.' I should add that Mr Hossein is one of our regular customers. He comes in roughly once a month and stocks up on a large number of latex items which I assume can't all be for his own use, so my guess is that he transports them to various corners of the earth where they are not readily available.

As he still did not deign to elaborate on his problem, I flicked some more through the Jewish rag. And then widened my eyes in alarm.

The sweet, heart-shaped face of Dinah Bloch gazed up at me from the glossy middle page.

I stared at her. I mean at the picture. What was *she* doing in a magazine? As in Dinah of the gooey brown eyes that made her look like butter wouldn't melt in her mouth. (A phrase I've inherited from Mum.) I hadn't thought about Dinah Bloch in years and years, and here she was, radiating that same, do-goody aura of unconditional obedience. The teachers at King David's were always falling for her obsequious charm. They never fell for *my* charm, possibly on account of it never being obsequious. I just came out with whatever entered my head. And still do.

The rasp of Mr Hossein's cough snapped me back to attention.

Drawing his oily-black brows together, he looked at me as though I were a naughty schoolgirl who ought to be chastised. (We offer a large selection of implements at Sugar Lace for such activities.)

'I bought ten sets of these Massage Kits last month,' he began, 'and I have received a number of complaints. There is a problem with the … mini-vibrator.' At this point he lowered his angle of vision, thereby continuing his discourse with the counter that separated his world from mine. 'The batteries do not last long enough.'

Well then maybe your users take too long! I wanted to shout at him, but merely said, 'Oh, I see.' And then, unable to stop myself, I glanced back down at the article.

Dinah Bloch, former pupil of King David School, has kept herself busy since graduating in Theology from Manchester University. Unable to find a suitable job after receiving her MA two years ago, she decided to fill her time doing 'things that make a difference'.

'So, unless this can be fixed, I should like a full refund.'

'Of course, sir.'

"When you graduate from university, you just assume that the next step in your life's journey will be securing a job," Dinah explained from the elegant living room of her newly built apartment overlooking Liverpool Docks. "No one prepares you for how hard it'll be."

'It just isn't good enough. When you buy something from a shop, you don't expect to have to deal with such irritating malfunctions.'

I nodded at him. 'Absolutely. I couldn't agree more.'

Soft-spoken Dinah went on to elaborate how she decided to try her hand at volunteer work rather than sitting at home trawling the job vacancies and getting more frustrated by the day. "It was the best thing I ever did," she added with a modest smile. "Not just for the disadvantaged people I was helping, but also for myself. I've never looked back since."

'*Excuse* me, madam, but are you listening to anything I'm saying?'

I jumped back to my senses and slapped the offending pages closed. 'Oh – yes, of course. Sorry. You said you have a problem.'

'I said unless the problem can be fixed, I'd like an immediate refund.'

'Right. Well, I shall have to speak to the manager about that. I'm afraid I can't make such decisions by myself.'

Before he had the chance to respond, his mobile phone juddered from some invisible location upon his person. Frowning, he dug the sleek black contraption out of his pocket and mumbled, 'Excuse me.'

While he proceeded to jabber away in cryptic vowels and syllables, I re-opened the magazine and skimmed forward to the last couple of paragraphs of the article.

Miss Bloch spent the next eighteen months working as a volunteer in nursing homes, orphanages and crisis centres across the North West of England. Her untiring efforts led to her winning the distinguished title of "Volunteer of the Year". She was subsequently headhunted by the 'Adelstein Centre for Challenge to Youth', and now acts in an ambassadorial role which involves travelling across the country, giving speeches to people of all ages who feel the need to help others. To reiterate the remarkable young woman's own words, she 'has never looked back since.'

For several moments I stood in rigor mortis, stiff as a prick. (I thought that one up during a particularly boring English lesson with Mr Goldstein, way back in the halcyon days of school.)

Dinah Bloch … how could it be? How could she have deserved such success? I mean, come on, working as an *ambassador*? And here am I, working for Fred at the kind of place Dinah and her cronies would never *dream* of setting foot. It wasn't fair! I did better than her in my exams – a fact which apparently still shocks the King David school community to this day. And yet there she is, working in … in whatever poncey place it is, having her two-page spread in the *Liverpool Jewish Chronicle*, winning *Volunteer of the Year*, when all she did was boring things like go to school pageants instead of discos, and swot instead of dance, and hand in essays instead of smuggle rude limericks under the desks …

Dinah Bloody Bloch.

As a matter of interest, the name Dinah means 'judgement' in old Hebrew. As in: *Thou shalt be judged!* The name Naomi, on the other hand, means 'goodness on all levels'. So surely *I* should have been the one to reach such altruistic heights, not her?

With an explosive valediction, Mr Hossein stuffed his mobile back into his pocket and returned his intense gaze upon me. 'So. When can you speak to him?'

'Sorry?'

'The manager. When can you speak to him?'

'Oh. Now, hopefully.' I glanced over my shoulder in the direction of Fred's office, tucked into the murky nether-regions of the shop. Was he still there? Or had he nipped out via the back door to buy me a snack for my journey home, even though I keep telling him there's barely room to breathe in the tube at six o'clock on a Friday evening, let alone eat?

'One moment, please.' I turned round and headed for the thick velvet curtain that hid the door to Fred's hideaway.

'Please be quick. I assume this request will not be too mentally exhausting for you?'

I stopped. And turned back round. No longer smiling. How dare he stand there belittling me! Did he honestly think it was my childhood dream to endure eight hours a day within four walls that are crammed to belching point with vibrators, lubricants, rabbits, handcuffs, Tuxedo Bunny outfits, Bedside Nurses and lascivious lingerie?

'Sir,' I said tightly. 'It might surprise you to know that I have a Master's degree from University College London. The reason I happen to be in my current line of employment is because I spent half a year looking for a job in my field, to no avail. Not all sex shop assistants are brainless Barbie dolls, you know.'

He stared at me in horror.

And suddenly, Gran's dear old face loomed in my mind's eye. It was a face that had been etched by overlapping years of brutality, survival, release, a new world and, at last, love, when she met Grandad in the local Jewish community just after the Second World War. She had been a refugee, arriving in Merseyside at the age of fifteen without a word of English. I never asked her what that was like, being a stranger in a strange land. I'd always been more interested in the gory details of how she'd survived wartime Poland, rather than her arrival in England.

And now … thinking of all that Gran had gone through back then, and the bigoted attitude of this customer, and Dinah Bloch's mega-sensational achievements – I mean, *I've* also helped people in need – there were times in my sixth form days when I'd give all my pocket money to that poor old homeless man who used to sit on the pavement outside Tesco's, but I didn't get any *Caring for the Homeless* award, did I, because no one even knew about it – yet now, thinking of how unfair life can be, I just sort of … I don't know. I just *crumpled* deep inside.

And that was it.

That was the moment it occurred to me that my life was meaningless. That all my years of training as a forensic anthropologist – all my ambitions to work on a UN mission in some war-torn part of the world, helping to piece together and identify the bones of victims dug out of mass graves – had come to this: dealing with a dissatisfied customer in a Soho sex shop, and being overtaken by a former school rival in Liverpool. What about all that promise, right from birth? All those genes, all those clusters of chromosomes, those coils of DNA, all that pre-programmed intelligence and talent, when at the end of the day it amounted to nothing?

Without another word, I turned my back on my speechless customer and headed for Fred's office.

My life had turned into a meaningless bowl of gruel, and unless I did something about it pretty quick, there wouldn't be much point in continuing.

So I resolved to do something about it pretty quick.

Printed in Great Britain
by Amazon